R.V. BOWMAN

JABBERWOCK'S CROWN

BOOK 3
LOOKING GLASS CHRONICLES

KINGDOM
OF
WONDERLAND
OBSIDIAN MOUNTAIN
THE GREENING
UNDERHILL
BOGLANDS

FAELANDS

To Katherine "Kitty" Allevato
June 13, 1927 ~ April 25, 2024
I will always regret I didn't get this done in time so you could read it.
Even though you never got to see how Alice's story ended, I'll always remember you were one of my biggest fans.

Prologue

NETTLE HUDDLED INTO THE farthest corner of her cage as the footsteps came closer. She knew it didn't do any good, but she couldn't keep herself from trying to hide.

"Now, now, I only need a tiny bit more of your wing." The woman smiled, but her dark eyes were cold. She unlatched the cage and reached towards the bumble faery, who mewled and tried to evade the small hand.

The woman frowned as she chased Nettle around the cage, finally blocking her into a corner and grasping her small body. Nettle wiggled but didn't bite. She'd learned that wasn't a good idea the first time she'd tried it and almost died.

The woman flipped her over, and Nettle felt a tugging as the woman clipped off another section of wing. Nettle couldn't help whimpering, and the woman clucked her tongue. "You Fae have more magic in your smallest finger than we do in our entire bodies. It's only right you should share a little. I'm not even taking any of your essence this time."

She tossed Nettle back into the cage and shut the door before turning back to the table where she worked on her formulas. Nettle curled up in the corner. She wasn't the only captive here, but she didn't want to know who the others were. Not anymore. Despite what the woman kept saying, Nettle knew she was never leaving this place, at least not while she was still alive.

She sniffed back a tear. It didn't help and only made her head ache. Instead, she closed her eyes and escaped into sleep.

Nettle wasn't sure how long she had slept when a cry startled her awake. She froze in her corner, her gaze sweeping around the room. The woman stood at the table, holding up a small gold ring, admiring it. A ruby set in the thin band winked in the sun slanting in from the window. From where the light hit the table, Nettle guessed it was probably afternoon. Not that it mattered.

The woman whirled towards Nettle's cage, her long white-blonde braid swinging off her shoulder. She lifted the ring towards the bars of Nettle's cage. "I should thank you, little one. Without your wing dust, this wouldn't have been possible."

She reached into her pocket and pulled out a handful of colored sugar crystals and tossed them onto the bottom of Nettle's cage and smiled. "That's a small thank-you for your donation." She gave a trill of laughter, her eyes shining, before she almost skipped from the room. A few moments later, Nettle heard the front door open and close.

Nettle crept over to where the crystals lay and gathered them up into her ragged skirt. She wouldn't eat them all at once. She put one in her mouth and let its sugared sweetness melt on her tongue. A sigh slipped from her lips, and she closed her eyes. For a moment, she could forget she was locked in a cage in a cottage deep in the forest with no hope of escape. She could imagine she was back in the meadow with her sisters and aunts.

A rustling made her eyes pop open. She jerked backwards, spilling her crystals. A pair of bright eyes and a button nose were just visible outside Nettle's cage. It was the young coinin faery, the latest of the woman's victims. The girl stood on tiptoe, her long, furred ears sticking straight up and twitching with any small noise. She was trying to reach the latch on Nettle's cage. "We have to hurry," she whispered. "I don't know how long that woman will be gone."

Not quite able to reach, the girl dragged over a chair and climbed on it.

Fine tremors shook Nettle's body. "But what if she catches us?"

The girl paused in her work on the latch, and her mouth thinned. "It can't be worse than what she's doing to us here."

Nettle wasn't so sure about that, but she wasn't about to turn down freedom. As soon as the door swung open, she tried to buzz out, but she faltered and lost altitude. Only a burst of wing-flapping kept her from crashing to the floor. She twisted to look back at her wings. One of them was half the size of the other.

The girl nodded at the window, even as she moved to the half dozen other cages. "Go out that way."

Nettle flew up to the table in fits and starts and landed on the sill. Reaching up, she undid the latch and pushed the window open, almost falling out. She glanced over her shoulder. "Aren't you coming?"

The girl nodded. "As soon as I open the rest of these."

A loud creak made them both freeze. It was the front door. She was back. The girl waved a hand at Nettle and shimmered out of view. Her voice floated in the empty air. "Go. Hurry."

The latch of another cage twisted open, seemingly on its own. Nettle hesitated, wondering if she should try to help, but she could hear footsteps moving around the front room. At any moment, that woman could open the door and Nettle had no doubt she'd kill them both.

"Come on," Nettle whispered, her eyes darting to the door.

There was no response. There were two more cages, but their occupants were lying unmoving on the cage floors. Nettle wasn't even sure they were still alive, but even if they were, they wouldn't be for long.

Nettle waited until she saw each cage door open and heard the patter of the girl's footsteps coming towards her before she flew out the window. Behind her, there was a shout. She hoped the girl had gotten out, but she didn't look back. Nettle flew as fast as her mangled wings could take her away from the cottage and the woman who looked like a doll but was really a witch.

Chapter 1

ALICE REALIZED SOMETHING HAD gone terribly wrong with the Looking Glass.

The trees and plants around her glowed an intense, pulsing green, and each bud and flower almost blinded her with their vivid hues—a far cry from the muted colors back home.

However, the biggest clue that this was not Somerset, England, was the tall, blue-skinned man standing a few yards away. He had asked her something, but she had missed it.

"I beg your pardon?" she said.

The man's lips quirked into a smile. "Have you done something you need to beg pardon for?"

"Of course not," Alice retorted, and then wanted to bite her tongue. Despite his smile, she didn't like the gleam in his silver, cat-like eyes. She slid her hand in the pocket of her dress, and her fingers closed over the smooth stone Chess had given her. Its cool weight anchored her racing heart.

The man raised an eyebrow. "There's no need to be rude. I was merely trying to be friendly." Amusement lurked in his voice.

"Is that what you call it around here?"

His mouth turned down in an exaggerated frown. "You don't sound like you believe me. I'm hurt." He walked closer, and Alice resisted the urge to back up.

Instead, she crossed her arms. "I doubt that. Now, I'd be much obliged if you would tell me where I am because I'm quite sure this isn't where I meant to go."

His eyes widened. "You truly have no idea?"

"I think that's rather obvious." Alice lifted her gaze to the tree canopy, using the excuse to take several steps away from the man. He had done nothing threatening yet, but she thought it wise to stay out of grabbing distance.

He gave a fancy flourish of his arm. "You, my lovely flower, are in the Faelands, and this is the Greening." He said it as if it should mean something to her.

"The Greening? I'm afraid that doesn't help me much."

His eyes narrowed. "You're telling me that you never heard of the Greening?"

Alice felt something brush across her senses, and the hair on the back of her neck stood up. Instinctively, she pushed the feeling away, and a frown flitted across the man's face.

"Willful," he muttered under his breath.

She wasn't sure what he meant by that, but she used his moment of distraction to step further away, his sudden suspicion making her nervous. Her heel caught, and she stumbled, catching her balance on a nearby tree, the bark fuzzy under her fingers.

A faint gasp and squeak near the tree's exposed root pulled her eyes away from the blue man and down to a small, golden-skinned creature. It lay sprawled on its back, half of one of its round wings missing, its tiny face shriveled. The creature shivered, its ragged dress hardly any protection from the mossy, leaf-littered ground. It drew in a shuddering breath and whimpered.

Its obvious pain tugged at Alice, and she turned to examine it more closely. The man behind her made a strangled noise.

She glanced at him over her shoulder. He backed up, and his amused expression had turned into a frown.

"What?" she asked, unable to keep the impatience from her voice.

He swallowed. "Were you aware you have a snark on your skirt?"

Alice straightened, twisting to see, which made her twirl in a rather ridiculous circle. "Wickle?"

"You've named it?" His face turned a paler shade of blue.

Alice ignored him as the small bundle of fluff scampered up her back and onto her shoulder. Alice held out her hand and Wickle hopped into her palm. Some of the tension leaked from Alice's shoulders even as she frowned down at her little friend. She didn't want to admit how relieved she was to have at least one ally in this place.

"What in the world are you doing here, Wickle? I saw you go into the labyrinth myself."

No leave my Alice.

Alice's mouth twitched into a smile. She glanced over at the Fae man who was staring at her as if she had two heads. "Well, my friend, I *am* glad to see you, even if you shouldn't be here." Alice tipped her head in the man's direction. "Keep an eye on that one, would you? I need to help this little creature."

Wickle peeked over the edge of her palm. He twittered and let out a loud sigh that blew his blue fringe of bangs upward. *Too late for faery. Almost gone.*

So, that's what it was. "I have to at least try." She knelt next to the little faery and set Wickle on the ground.

Alice leaned closer to inspect the suffering creature and frowned. She wasn't sure what was wrong with it, but it was clearly badly injured and looked malnourished, its skin sallow and loose.

She laid one hand on its shoulder and put a finger gently on its forehead.

"I don't think I should let you do that." The man's voice buzzed over Alice's skin. "For all I know, you caused this."

She shot the man a glare. "Don't be daft! I'm trying to help her, if you'll shut your yap long enough to let me concentrate." She bit her lip. It never failed. Whenever she was nervous or upset, she reverted to the familiar words of her childhood on the streets.

Well, it couldn't be helped now. She turned back to the little Fae, letting her eyes close as she tried to trace the problem.

Leaves crunched behind her, and Wickle let out a loud hiss, breaking her concentration. Again.

"Do you think it's possible for you to call off your snark, my sweet?"

She didn't open her eyes. "No."

Once again, she focused on the small creature and almost jerked her hands away as the pain flowed into her mind. There was a deep hollow at its very center, but it was mostly empty. A few glowing strands clung in that hollow, but she had an intuitive sense that it should be much fuller. The small body's life force was flickering, but no matter how much she focused on fanning it, it only got weaker. Whimpers escaped from the creature. The man said something again, but Alice was too busy trying to soothe the Fae's pain to pay him any attention.

The pain receded. A tiny smile curved the Cupid's-bow mouth, and the golden eyes slid shut. The creature let out a soft sigh.

And then the flame shimmered and snuffed out.

Alice sat back on her heels, letting her hands fall into her lap. The tiny face, despite its obvious suffering, wore a peaceful smile. At least she'd done that much. Alice's eyes prickled and the back of her nose burned. She blinked rapidly to clear her vision.

"You're not what I was expecting." She looked up to find the man watching her from a safe distance.

Wickle trundled over and clambered up Alice's arm. She waited until he settled on her shoulder before she answered the Fae man.

"I don't see how you could expect anything since I'm not supposed to be here. Which I've told you several times already."

Again, that buzz over her skin, stronger this time. "I'm afraid I don't believe you, my flower."

Alice got to her feet. "I don't mean to be rude, but frankly, I don't care what you believe. I only need you to tell me if I can get to the Red Palace from here."

Both his eyebrows rose. "So that's where you're from—but you should know you can't walk to the Red Palace from the Faelands." The full lips, a deeper shade of his purple-blue skin, quirked into a half smile. "Unless, of course, you really aren't from the Red Palace at all and are just trying to throw me off the trail."

"Look, I'm very sorry about your friend." She gestured at the little Fae crumpled on the ground. "Whatever happened to her, she was too far gone to heal, at least by me. I haven't been doing this very long, so maybe someone more skillful would have been able to help her. It's quite sad, but I need to go home, and the only way I can do that is if I go back to the Red Palace." Alice pressed her lips together to stop her babbling.

The silver eyes gleamed with curiosity. "You keep saying *home*. Just where is this home if it's not the palace?"

"Somerset," she said. At his blank expression, she added, "The Mirror World?"

"And what was someone from the Mirror World doing at the Red Palace?" He circled around her. Alice spun with him so she could keep her eyes on him. Wickle hissed again. "Your story is making less and less sense, my sweet. You can't merely take a wrong turn from the Red Palace and end up here. This is an island, after all."

No like. Make go away.

"I'm trying," she muttered.

Alice's mind churned as she absently patted the snark. How *had* she ended up here, in the Faelands? The name sounded familiar. The man knew about the Red Palace, so it had to be part of Wonderland, but he also said it was an island. She sighed. Zander had said the Looking Glass could be finicky. It was too bad it had chosen her trip home to malfunction and send her here, of all places. Now, this man seemed to be her only way back to anyone who could actually help her, and she didn't trust him an inch.

"It's almost painful to watch."

Alice glanced up to find the man uncomfortably close again, even though Wickle had puffed up on her shoulder to almost twice his normal size. She narrowed her eyes. "What is?"

"Your mind working so hard to come up with a plausible story." He smirked. "That is what you're doing, isn't it? Trying to decide what to tell me?"

"No, I'm trying to figure out how to get back home." She crossed her arms. "If you were a gentleman, you'd help me."

His smile sharpened. "I don't recall saying I was a gentleman." He tilted his head, his silvery hair sliding over one shoulder. Alice's skin buzzed again, and she swayed towards him. "And I hardly think a lady would go around killing innocent Fae. Bumble faeries can be annoying creatures, but hardly a threat to anyone. So, let's start again, shall we? Why are you truly here?"

His accusation should alarm her, but the deep timbre of his voice mesmerized her. She couldn't look away from the sharply sculpted planes of his face. The silver cat's eyes twinkled, warmth radiating from their depths. She'd been wrong. She could trust him. The words spilled from her lips. "Because they sent me through the Looking Glass."

The man smiled. "Who sent you, my sweet?"

Wickle wheeked loudly in her ear, and Alice jerked her eyes away from his chest, her face flushing as her thoughts came back into focus. "Were you trying to charm me, just now?"

He chuckled, the sound a deep rumble. "I am quite charming. How kind of you to notice."

Alice narrowed her eyes. "That's not what I meant, and you know it."

The man shrugged, as if he didn't care that she'd found him out. "It's a much easier way to get answers, but I must ask—how does someone from the Mirror World have any knowledge of Fae charms?"

Alice ignored his question, focusing instead on his earlier words. "You don't have to manipulate answers out of me. I didn't kill anyone. As I've told you at least half a dozen times now, I was supposed to be going home—to the Mirror World—but something happened with the Looking Glass and I ended up here instead."

He tilted his head. "Are you so sure it was an accident? You said someone sent you."

Alice blew out a breath. "Yes, because someone did, but not here. I was supposed to go home, to Somerset. How many times do I have to tell you that something went wrong before you'll believe me?"

He studied her for a long moment. "It does seem odd that you would work to heal the bumble, but you could have merely been doing that to throw off suspicion from being caught red-handed."

Alice resisted the urge to roll her eyes. "What reason would I possibly have to kill a faery?" She clasped her hands together, trying to gather her thoughts. "Look, I know you don't have any reason to believe me... erm, sir, but—."

"Indigo. My name is Indigo, and it's only fair you tell me yours now."

"I'm Alice. Prince Zander and his father the Red King are the ones who took me to the Looking Glass." She figured it wouldn't hurt to drop a few names.

"So sincere." Indigo shook his head. "I would almost believe you if I didn't know that the he died over a year ago and his son has been missing for almost as long."

Alice's stomach sank at his words. The Faelands must be in a very isolated part of Wonderland if he hadn't at least heard about the Great Ballroom Battle. "I'm afraid you're behind on events, but there's an easy way to find out if I'm telling the truth. Send a raven to the Red Palace. They'll confirm what I'm telling you."

He considered her words for a long moment, and then he bent and scooped up the dead Fae, cradling it in his large hands. "Well, we won't settle anything out here." He nodded towards the faint path that wound through the forest. "Come along, then."

Before Alice could ask where they were going, a voice spoke from behind her, nearly startling her out of her skin. She whirled to find a woman standing several yards away.

The woman jabbed her finger in Alice's direction. "Indigo? Who is this and what has happened here?"

"This is Alice." He grinned. "I found her."

The woman glided closer, her feet skimming soundlessly over the forest floor. She was clearly related to Indigo. She had the same sculpted features, but her skin was a paler blue, without the purple tinge. Her hair, a darker silver shade, was in rows of tight braids interwoven with feathers the same color. She wore stretchy armor that looked as if it were made of leaves, and two feathery wings rose above her shoulders. Alice briefly wondered what the woman's animal form was. Citrine had told her all Fae had the ability to shift.

The woman's eyes, the same silver as Indigo's, narrowed with suspicion. She glanced from the dead Fae Indigo held to Alice and back again before her hand moved to her waist. In one smooth movement, she pulled a sword out. The point stopped about an inch from Alice's chin.

"I am arresting you for the death of this Fae."

She'd barely gotten the words out when Wickle let out a vicious snarl, and before Alice could stop him, he launched himself from her shoulder.

Everything seemed to happen in slow motion. Wickle's tiny body flew towards the woman, his fangs extended. The woman's blade made a graceful arc through the air.

At the last second, Wickle twisted in the air so the flat of the blade smacked into him rather than the sharp edge. Alice watched in horror as he sailed through the air and thudded into a nearby tree trunk, bouncing off before hitting the ground with a sickening slap.

Alice darted towards him, but the sword whipped in front of her, and she skidded to a halt.

"Please, he's hurt. Let me help him."

The woman's face remained impassive. "Check the snark, Indigo."

"Me? You're the one that injured it, Azalea."

The woman made a noise in the back of her throat. "Stop being a child. It's probably dead, anyway."

Alice blinked back tears. "If you'll only let me…"

The woman's sword flicked up almost to Alice's chin. "You will stay where you are." Neither her sword nor her gaze wavered from Alice when she spoke again. "Indigo?"

Alice bit her lip as the man walked over to the blue ball and gingerly poked at it with his foot. Wickle was disturbingly limp. He pushed harder. The small body flopped over, and Alice swallowed down a sob.

"You're right. I think it's dead." A grin spread across the man's face. "You have always had more than your share of luck, sister."

"Skill is not luck." She jerked her chin at Alice. "We will go now."

Alice repressed the instinct to shake her head, afraid she'd accidentally slit her throat on the sharp blade. Instead, she scowled at the woman. "At least I tried to heal your bumble faery. You killed Wickle." Her voice cracked, and she blinked rapidly, not wanting to cry in front of either of them.

The woman lifted an eyebrow. "One less snark is a blessing. It is unnatural for you to care about those creatures."

Anger bubbled up in Alice. "The only reason he attacked you is because you threatened me. He shouldn't have to die just because he was loyal." She narrowed her eyes. "The only person who killed anything here is you, and the only thing I'm guilty of is trying to heal someone and failing."

"Of course, you would try to cover your actions by appearing to help. Nobody announces their evil intentions. I am not so easily fooled by a lovely countenance as my brother." She waved the sword towards a distant point in the forest. "You will come with me to see King Thorne. Tell your story to him." She nodded at Indigo. "Bring her."

Indigo rolled his eyes. "That's where we were going anyway, if you hadn't interrupted things." He turned to Alice. "If you are telling the truth, you'll need Father's help to return to the mainland, anyway."

Alice digested the news that these two were some kind of royalty. Her gaze slid back to the woman, and she swallowed. The other woman fairly bristled with weapons. She had another sword on her hip that matched the one in her hand, and she had strapped a dagger to each arm. Between her wings, the top of a bow poked up. Alice scanned the forest, a sense of inevitability weighing her down.

Indigo slid next to Alice and grasped her upper arm, starting up the path. Azalea fell into step behind them. Because he was so tall, Alice had to trot to keep up, but she was afraid to slow down, sure she'd feel the sharp blade of Azalea's sword if she did.

She only hoped the King was more sensible than these two.

Chapter 2

CHESS WIPED HIS FACE with the hem of his sweat-soaked shirt, the salty tang stinging his eyes. The soldier he'd been sparring with moved off to get a drink, his boots crunching on the dusty ground.

Suddenly, the soldiers milling around the practice area straightened, the clank and jingle of their armor filling the air. The Commander came into view and Chess set down the sword he'd been using and trotted over to his father.

"I didn't expect you back so soon," he said as he got closer.

The question he really wanted to ask remained stuck in his throat.

"Alice got off safely," the Commander said.

Chess gave a rueful smile. Apparently, he didn't have as much of a poker face as he thought. He gave a sharp nod of his head. "Good." He wanted to say more, to ask if she seemed happy or if she hesitated, even a little, but he kept his lips clamped shut, knowing it would only give his father further fuel to criticize him.

The Commander tipped his head towards the row of practice swords. "Do you want to go a round?"

Emotions buzzed under Chess's skin. He understood it had been the right choice to send Alice back home, but from the moment he'd said goodbye to her, he couldn't stay still. Now, the idea of working some of those feelings out on the Commander was oddly appealing.

He nodded. "Yeah, all right."

The Commander ducked under the fence and strode over to grab a sword, and Chess picked up the sword he'd just been using, the metal cool against his skin as he adjusted the grip in his hand.

He moved to the center of the ring, his boots kicking up dust with each step, and the Commander squared up across from him. Out of the corner of his eye, Chess noticed more soldiers gathering to watch.

They ringed the fence, and their anticipation weighted the air. Chess was sure there were more than a few bets being placed—probably in his father's favor. He smirked. Well, he was good at exceeding everyone's very low expectations of him. It was part of his charm, after all.

Instead of taking his own stance, the Commander twisted his sword, seemingly absorbed with its plain handle. "You did the right thing, letting the girl go. I know you cared for her, but it's for the best." He took up his ready stance and finally met Chess's eyes, blue clashing with blue. "Shall we?"

The words threw Chess off-balance, and he almost didn't block his father's first strike, the clang of the blades jarring his bones. Trying to make up for his distraction, his feet danced over the hard packed earth as he blocked a flurry of blows.

They separated and circled each other, the snap in the air cooling the sweat on Chess's back.

"You'd understand all about that, wouldn't you?" Chess couldn't keep the bitterness out of his voice.

"Yes, I do." The Commander lunged forward and drove Chess towards the fence. Chess's back hit the wood as their swords clashed and held, the rough boards digging into his spine through his shirt.

His father's eyes bore into his. "You're from two different worlds. Trust me—it wouldn't have worked."

Chess's muscles strained as their swords pushed against each other. "Maybe not for you." His anger gave him fresh energy, hot and bright, and he shoved his father back, making the older man stumble.

Taking advantage of the Commander being off-balance, Chess' sword became a blur of movement, singing as it sliced the air. To give the Commander his due, the man still managed to block all his strikes, grunting with the effort. Once the Commander found his feet again, he struck Chess's sword, the impact juddering up Chess's arm, almost knocking it from his grasp.

"No, not just for me." The Commander backed up a few steps, wiping a hand across his brow. "I don't want to see things more difficult for you than they already are."

Chess's eyes narrowed. "What's that supposed to mean?"

His father ran a hand through his hair before he lifted his sword into a ready stance again. "Why must you twist everything I say?"

"Why must you always assume the worst about me?" Chess lunged forward, his sword clanging against the Commander's.

The Commander's face twisted as he blocked another of Chess's strikes. "I'm trying to tell you I'm proud of you." He blocked another strike. "For not being ruled by your emotions. There's too much of that lately."

Chess's gut twisted, and Alice's face flashed into his mind. Her big eyes, the purple hue of twilight, looked up at him full of questions. His distraction cost him. The Commander's sword smacked his arm with a dull thud, making it throb, but he managed to keep his hold on his own sword.

A tiny mocking smile hovered on the Commander's face. "She's gone. Stop letting her distract you." His words hung in the sharp air.

Sweat dripped into Chess's eyes, and he lunged forward, the metallic sound of swords colliding ringing in his ears. The Commander's eyes widened at the fury of Chess's attack.

Chess pushed himself, driving his father across the practice ring with a series of blows until he pressed the Commander up against the fence, the weathered wood creaking and groaning, their swords once again straining against each other.

"I sent Alice back because she needed to go. Not because it was best for me." Even if it had almost killed him to do it—but he kept that thought to himself.

His savage sword work earned several whoops and whistles from the watching soldiers, and his chest swelled with an unfamiliar sense of pride.

He stared into his father's eyes. "Unlike you, I want what's best for the woman I care about."

Something like hurt flickered over the Commander's features before he shoved hard, pushing Chess back and freeing his own sword, with a grating rasp of metal on metal.

The Commander slashed his sword towards Chess, but Chess blocked him, knocking the blade aside. He brought his own sword up under the Commander's chin. The older man let his weapon fall to his side and held up his other hand.

"I give. You're the winner this time around." The Commander wiped a hand across his brow, breathing hard. His blond hair was dark with sweat.

Chess stepped back, his own chest heaving with his exertion. Despite his irritation, Chess couldn't help the grin that spread across his face. "Never thought you'd live to see the day, did you, Commander?"

The Commander pushed off the fence and clapped a hand on Chess's shoulder. "You're capable—when you make the effort." He lifted an eyebrow. "The men would follow you if you exerted yourself."

Chess shrugged off his father's hand and smirked. "I'll leave that to Zander. It's not my style."

The Commander frowned, the lines around his mouth deepening. He lowered his voice to a rumbled whisper that Chess had to strain to hear over the clang of swords and grunts of exertion from practicing soldiers. "I don't believe the men trust him anymore."

"What does that mean?"

But before his father could answer, the mood among soldiers shifted. The air seemed to thicken with unease.

Several drew back, boots scuffing nervously in the dirt. Others stiffened, knuckles whitening on sword hilts.

It was then that Chess saw Zander striding towards them, sunlight glinting off his practice armor.

The Commander nodded towards the uneasy soldiers. "That's what I mean."

Chapter 3

ALICE'S WHIRRING THOUGHTS SLOWED to a halt as they stepped out from the forest into a small clearing dominated by a large hill. A breeze stirred the carpet of candy-colored wildflowers, and a symphony of sweet scents tickled Alice's nose.

Instead of going around, they stopped in front of the hill. As she tried to puzzle out why, Indigo let go of her arm and drew shapes in the air with his finger. Each stroke left a shimmering line in its wake. The sunlight glinted off each one as they hung in the air before slowly fading.

With a deep sigh, the earth in front of them split open, revealing a tunnel wrapped in flowers and vines. Even as she watched, several buds swelled and burst into flower, each one a different color, their petals lacy and delicate.

Curiosity and caution warred inside Alice. If she entered that hill, would she ever come out again? She glanced at Indigo to find him watching her lazily.

He swept out his arm. "After you, my sweet."

Alice hesitated.

Something sharp poked her back. "Do not consider the possibility of fleeing." Azalea's voice held none of Indigo's mesmerizing timbre. Instead, it scraped over Alice's ears.

Alice turned towards the other woman. "I'm not sure..."

The sword came up again, and Alice swallowed as the tip hovered above her collarbone.

Azalea's eyes flashed, her voice harsh. "I *am* sure. You will see the King and explain yourself." Azalea jabbed her sword towards the tunnel. "Go."

Indigo pushed the tip of his sister's sword down with one fingertip. "You are giving our guest an entirely wrong impression of us. How will I convince her to stay if you are threatening her?"

Azalea's face darkened. "She is not our guest and her opinion of us is of no concern to me. Do not let a pretty face make you a fool, brother."

Indigo laughed. "Just because I don't like to play with pointy objects doesn't make me a fool, sister. Beauty is its own reward."

Alice's gaze bounced between the two and then back to the forest. She took a small step sideways, but Indigo grasped her arm.

"Don't let my sister's opinion of me sway you." He leaned down so his lips hovered by her ear. "For instance, I know it would be a mistake to underestimate you despite that beautiful face." He straightened and smiled down at her.

Alice shivered, suddenly more afraid of Indigo than his sister's sword. She tried to pull away, but his fingers tightened around her arm like a band of iron. He tugged her forward. "Come along, my flower. We wouldn't want my sister to get fidgety."

Alice let him lead her into the tunnel. After all, what choice did she have? Azalea stepped in after them, and the entrance sealed back up. Alice swallowed, and she couldn't help wondering if she'd ever see the outside again.

She wished Wickle was with her. The memory of his small body crumpled on the ground made her breath catch, and she blinked back the tears that welled in her eyes. She couldn't think about that now. She needed her wits about her. Grief would have to wait.

Indigo's hold on her arm loosened, and she glanced up at him. "You know you don't have to hold on to me. It's not as if I can run away."

"No, but Underhill is rather confusing to the uninitiated. Besides, my sister will balk if you aren't *secured*." He rolled his eyes, making it clear what he thought about that idea. "Let's do this instead." He took her hand and threaded it through his elbow. "Is that better, my sweet?"

"Maybe if your sister removed her sword from my back," Alice said, glancing over her shoulder.

Behind them, Azalea snorted. "I will put it away when I am satisfied you are not a threat."

Alice didn't waste her breath trying to argue with the woman. It was obvious she wasn't changing her mind. Instead, Alice lifted her chin and tried to ignore the fact that there was a sharp blade pointed between her shoulder blades.

The tunnel twisted and turned and seemed to wind in all directions. Although they were supposedly underground, it wasn't dark. A sunny glow lit the passageways that were alive with plant life. There were the flowering vines, but also branches that grew from the walls to arch over them, and several times, Indigo had to part sheets of moss in hues of green and blue that hung from the ceiling.

Periodically, tiny creatures flitted through the tunnels. At first, Alice assumed they were overly large butterflies or dragonflies, but closer inspection revealed that they were tiny people. The further they walked, the more Fae they saw. She couldn't help her fascination of the variety represented. They seemed to come in all shapes and sizes, some with delicate wings like insects and others with wings that were covered in feathers or leathery like bats. Quite a few, like Indigo, didn't have any wings at all, at least none that were visible.

Just when Alice wondered if they were going to walk forever, the passageway stopped, and they entered a spacious, circular room. It was bustling with Fae of all kinds, all walking, scurrying, or flying somewhere.

High above her head, a blue sky arched, wispy clouds floating lazily. Since they were underneath a hill, she wasn't sure how that was even possible, but she didn't have time to consider it.

There was so much color and activity, Alice's eyes could hardly take it all in. Eventually, her attention caught on a woman, her features beautiful but sharp. The woman paused and bowed to Azalea and Indigo. Her deep auburn hair flowed to her waist, and two furry triangular ears poked out on the top of her head. Her golden eyes darted to Alice, and when she caught Alice staring, she gave a low growl. Alice hastily dropped her gaze to the ground.

"Almost there, my flower." Indigo patted her hand and headed towards a passage that opened off the main room like spokes on a wheel.

Alice walked into another passageway similar to the one they had recently come through. Thankfully, this one was much shorter, and it didn't take long before they reached another room.

Instead of walls, the room was ringed by thick tree trunks, their canopy forming a living green ceiling. Swaths of flowers hung from the branches here and there. As in the tunnels, tiny Fae people flitted here and there, their wings flashing like jewels through the air as they tended the trees and plants. The heady scents of rose and violet mixed with something earthier and wilder.

A large basket chair swayed, making the overhead branch creak. It was only then that Alice realized there was a man lounging on it. As he unwound himself, Alice lowered her eyes. Even without the woven crown on his head, she would have known this was the King. His presence was overwhelming, and Alice had the almost irresistible urge to drop to the ground and bow to this man. Instead, she dipped into a deep curtsey and lowered her head. She stayed in that position until the man spoke.

"Rise, my child." His voice had the same rich timbre as Indigo's, but there was a comforting warmth to it. "I am King Thorne, and I welcome you to my court."

Alice had a moment to take in the King's dark-brown skin, silver hair, and the two antlers that curled out of the top of his head before Azalea jumped in. "We found this human next to a dead bumble faery." She nodded at the creature still cradled in Indigo's hand.

A frown wrinkled the man's face, and his dark eyes drilled into Alice. It was all she could do to keep herself upright under the weight of his stare. A sensation like a thousand ants crawled inside her skull. Instinctively, she pushed against it, and the feeling receded.

The man's shaggy eyebrows rose. "Hmmm." He studied her for another long moment before he spoke again. "Tell me how you came to be in the Faelands."

It wasn't a question, and again Alice had the impression she wouldn't be able to resist answering even if she tried. "It was a mistake, Your Majesty."

"How so, child?"

"The Red King"—at the mention of the name, the frown on the King's face deepened— "he and Prince Zander escorted me to the Looking Glass. It was supposed to take me to my home in the Mirror World, but something happened." Alice spread out her hands. "I have no idea why I ended up here, but all I'd truly like to do is go home, sir."

The King's gaze flicked to a shadowed corner of the room before returning to Alice. "As the Red King has been dead for over a year, I find your story difficult to accept."

"Your Majesty, I'm afraid you are not aware of the most recent events. He's not dead at all." In her enthusiasm, Alice stepped closer to the King, and Azalea's sword shot out, blocking her way. Alice looked down at the razor-sharp blade and slid back before continuing. "He was cursed and hidden in the middle of the Wonderland labyrinth."

The shaggy eyebrows drew down. "Cursed?"

Alice hesitated. She didn't know how many details she should tell this man. It would be best to keep it simple. "Yes, but we freed him from it, and he is doing well now."

"I see I *am* behind the times. And what of his son? The last I had heard, he was missing, and the kingdom was under the rule of the King's young widow."

Alice hesitated again, her mind whirring. Were the Faelands really that cut off from news from Wonderland, or were they being kept in the dark for some reason? Again, she kept to the basic facts. The less she said, the less chance she had of putting her foot in it.

"He has been found and is doing well. The Red King and his son are overjoyed to reunite again."

"And what of the young queen? Is she equally happy to be reunited with her husband and stepson?"

Drat! Alice had hoped to gloss over the Queen and her part in recent events. She had no idea what the relationship was between the Red King and the Fae King. How much of the royal family's private business should she share with this man?

She hesitated too long, and the King leaned forward. "Did you not understand the question?"

Again, his overwhelming presence bore down on her, and the urge to drop to her knees and tell him everything she knew was almost unbearable. Clenching her hands into fists, she resisted, her gut telling her to tread carefully with this man, no matter his warm demeanor.

"She is gone at the moment. I believe she's visiting her home in the Northern Estates."

The King stared at her, his eyes boring into her soul. She smiled, hoping it showed she was sincere, even if she was fudging the truth a bit.

"Your story is easy enough to verify." He lifted a hand and beckoned. Almost immediately, a Fae creature about the size of a cat zipped to hover close to him, bowing in midair. The jet-black feathers that covered the wings on his back extended in a wide stripe over his head. His skin was a shade lighter than his feathers, and his hooked nose reminded Alice of a beak. He wore a tunic and breeches the same color as his wings, but they looked like leather.

The Fae noticed her staring and crossed his arms, scowling. "Paint a picture, why don't you?"

Alice felt her cheeks heat, and she averted her gaze.

The King ignored the exchange. "Go see what you can find out at the Red Palace, Zephyr. Make sure nobody sees you."

Zephyr bowed again and then flew out of the room and down an adjacent tunnel.

The King turned his attention to Azalea and Indigo.

"I'd like to know why you think this human girl has something to do with this most recent death."

Azalea stepped forward, sheathing her sword. "We discovered this bumble faery in the Greening. She appears as the others we've come across, drained of her essence. However, she was still alive when Indigo found her and the human." She tipped her head in Alice's direction.

"As much as I appreciate your enthusiasm, daughter, it is unlikely that this girl from the Mirror World possesses the ability to drain one of us." The glance he gave Alice reminded her of one you'd give a lame dog. "They don't even acknowledge or demonstrate Gifts in their world."

Azalea's expression tightened. "Perhaps not in the Mirror World, but she possesses the Healer Gift. She tried to use it on the bumble."

The King frowned again and nodded at Indigo, who stepped forward, his languid air gone for the moment.

"Indeed, Father, the human attempted to heal her. But the faery's life force was too weak. I'm uncertain if even a truly skilled Healer could have saved her. I sincerely question whether a Healer is the person who has been draining our people, especially an unskilled one like this. It goes against their nature to harm."

The King regarded Alice thoughtfully and gave a nod. "I must agree." His gaze returned to Azalea. "You made the right decision to bring her here, daughter. Any stranger in the Faelands is troublesome at this moment with these disappearances and deaths."

He shifted his attention back to Alice. "Even though I doubt your involvement in our current crisis, I won't be easy until someone at the palace verifies your story. You'll stay as our guest until we can do that."

Alice wanted to ask how long that would be, but she closed her mouth tight over the question and instead dipped her head in agreement. "Thank you, Your Majesty."

A smile tipped the man's lips. "It's no hardship to have someone as lovely as you grace Underhill."

He shared a look with Indigo before he waved a hand in her direction. Apparently, she was dismissed. A wave of relief swept through Alice. Even though she'd need to wait, at least she would go home—eventually.

After taking only a few steps, a voice spoke out of the shadows, sending a shiver over Alice's skin. "Is that wise, Your Majesty?"

A whip-thin man stepped away from among the trees. Alice wasn't sure how he'd not been visible. His bright auburn hair and dark-gold tunic didn't lend to blending in with the surrounding foliage. His smile, though filled with warmth and hospitality, failed to reach his golden eyes as he turned towards her. She couldn't help the way her shoulders curled inward under his gaze.

"I'm sure you're dying to tell me why you think otherwise, Advisor Solus." The King lifted a silvery brow.

"As much as I agree with you that the girl is probably harmless, do we want to take any chances? If the Red King is alive"—he glanced at Alice— "not that I doubt you, my dear"—and then turned back to the King—"it doesn't bode well that we weren't told about this turn of events."

"What do you suggest, then? I am loath to punish her for something we don't know that she has done." The King's eyes flickered over Alice, who stiffened in response. "As a Healer, it would be odd indeed if she were our killer."

Solus lifted his shoulders almost apologetically. "I propose, Your Majesty, that we test her and the deceased Fae for a magical signature. It should be easy enough to tell if there is a match. Then we can know what part she's played."

Alice knew she should stay quiet, but she couldn't keep the words from bursting out. "But I tried to heal her. Of course, you're going to find my magical-whatever on her."

Irritation flickered over Solus's face, but he smoothed his expression back into a smile. "Yes, but if you are innocent, this will undoubtedly prove it. There isn't any reason you wouldn't want that, is there?"

"No, of course not," she stammered, somehow feeling wrong-footed, as if she were guilty.

The King looked at her for a long moment before he made up his mind. "Send for the tester then, Solus. We'll need to wait for Zephyr to return, anyway. We might as well gather as much information as possible before then. She can be our guest until that time. She might even be here for the Luna Feast."

"Again, not that I want to question your Majesty..."

"Yet you always do," Indigo muttered loud enough for everyone to hear him.

Solus ignored the interruption. "It might be best to keep her contained for her own protection. Until we have the proof of her innocence, our people might be... less than friendly once they find out she was found with a dead Fae." He waved towards the bumble's body. "Of course, I'd be happy to take charge of her and see to her safety."

His eyes slid to Alice, and she shrunk back towards Indigo.

The King sighed. "I don't believe that would serve our interests, Advisor Solus. However, it might be advisable to lock her up in one of the cages and send a message to the Tester." He turned his attention back to Alice. "You have nothing to fear—if you are telling the truth."

As Azalea led her out of the King's room, Alice wasn't so sure about that. She had a feeling that this Solus character, with his smiles and shrugs, wouldn't be satisfied until she took the blame for whatever was killing the Fae here. And she'd never get home if that happened.

Chapter 4

THE CLANK OF ARMOR and the clash of metal on metal filled the practice arena, but all Chess could hear was the echo of the Commander's words about Zander and the soldiers. There wasn't time to press his father about what he meant by all that, because Zander had almost reached them. The soldiers nearby hastily straightened and bowed in Zander's direction.

Zander smiled in greeting and nodded at them, but a good number of the men wouldn't meet their Prince's eyes. A cloud passed over Zander's expression, but his smile didn't waver as he ducked into the arena.

The Commander dipped his head. "Your Highness."

Zander smiled at the older man. "Did I miss a good match?" He gestured between Chess and the Commander. "Do I have to ask who won?"

A faint smile curved the Commander's lips, and he put a hand on Chess's shoulder. "I'm afraid he bested me this time around."

Zander's smile widened into a grin. "Do you mind if I take your place, or perhaps you want another chance?"

The Commander bowed his head again and presented the sword to the Prince. "I'm afraid that will have to wait for another day." He glanced between Chess and Zander. "Don't forget that the King is expecting you both in about an hour. We have things to discuss before the Council meeting tomorrow."

Chess waited until his father was out of earshot. "That reminder was for me, you know."

Zander pushed his hair off his eyes before he crouched, his sword at the ready. "You always think the worst of him, Chess. I'm sure he was reminding both of us, not only you."

Chess rolled his eyes. "He's always expecting that I'll mess up, even if I'm not at the moment."

Zander paused before touching his sword to Chess's. "Well, you beat him today. That has to count for something." He grinned. "Maybe I don't want to practice with you."

Chess smirked. "Don't worry, cousin. I'll take it easy on you."

They circled each other before coming together in a flurry of strikes and parries. While the mock fight wasn't nearly as intense as it had been with the Commander, Chess still didn't relax too much. Unlike him, Zander had beaten the Commander—more than once. Of course, Zander also practiced regularly.

They danced around the ring, their swords clashing and clanging. The soldiers drifted away, and Chess could tell Zander noticed by the way his gaze kept skittering back to where the men had been standing. Ever since the Prince had shifted into his Jabberwock form in front of the Council, protecting Alice and the Red King from the Queen's attack at the labyrinth, word had spread—in the palace, at least. While everyone was still respectful, some of the staff and many of the soldiers acted ill at ease around the Prince. Chess knew it bothered Zander, although he never mentioned it.

Chess blocked a low blow, and before Zander could recover, he hooked his sword underneath Zander's blade and knocked it out of his hand.

Zander grinned as he stepped back and picked up his sword from the dirt. "Have you been practicing on the sly? It's not that you weren't good before, but you seem..." He trailed off when Chess laughed.

"You don't have to say it. You usually win." Chess shrugged. "I guess my father's right. I probably do need to exert myself more often."

Zander squinted at him. "Should I ask what—or who—made the difference?"

Chess's face heated, and he was glad that his darker skin hid it. Instead of answering, he changed the subject. "Has the King hinted how he wants to handle things with the Council?"

Zander ducked out from under the fence and hung his sword on a wooden rack that held the other practice swords. "Not in any detail. He's... well, but he's still recovering from his ordeal." A frown creased his face. "Sometimes, he seems like he's far away, and I'm afraid he remembers too much of what happened in that place."

Chess placed his sword next to Zander's. He wanted to reassure his friend, but he clearly recalled the King's face when he had seen Leander's remains in the labyrinth. True, the King had been cursed to be turned into a Minotaur at the time, but it didn't change the fact that he'd torn the Queen's brother apart. Chess had also noticed the King wasn't himself, but he imagined you didn't just move on after an ordeal like his.

He clapped Zander on the back. "You have to give him some time. He was in that labyrinth for over a year."

Zander's shoulders slumped. "You're right. I suppose it'll take time."

"I understand it has to be hard, but you basically got your father back from the dead. It can only be up from here, right?"

Zander chuckled. "Always the optimist."

Chess grinned. "What can I say? I'm not much for doom and gloom. It never gets you anywhere, anyway."

As they walked back towards the palace, Zander's expression sobered. "Speaking of doom and gloom, I'm not looking forward to the Council meeting. Lord Beecher, especially, would probably throw me out on my ear if he could."

"Everyone knows he's a big blowhard. Besides, your father supports you, and everyone also knows that."

Zander shoved his hands in his pockets. "Beecher might be the most vocal, but I'm afraid the others feel the same way. They're just too polite or too afraid of Father's reaction to say anything."

"Well, he is the King. That should go a long way for your cause." Chess didn't add he was also worried about the Council's reaction. It wasn't only that Zander had the Drifter Gene, but everyone in the Council had very recent memories of the Great Ballroom Battle. It was almost impossible not to make comparisons with the long-ago prince who was the original cause for banning the Drifter Gene in the first place. Zander acting like he had done something wrong didn't help things.

Zander interrupted his thoughts. "I'm not sure that will be enough if this gets out to the Kingdom." He ran a hand through his shaggy bronze hair. "I might still get run out of Wonderland and be lucky not to be tarred and feathered in the bargain."

Chess rolled his eyes. "You're borrowing trouble, friend. They might not like that you have the Drifter Gene, but the people love you. Besides, tarring and feathering is *so* last season."

Zander didn't even smile at his jest. Instead, he frowned. "It might not be enough." He paused before they reached the steps to the Red Palace. "Perhaps there's still a chance I can keep it from the general population."

Chess rolled his eyes. "You have a better chance of convincing everyone your creature form is a unicorn. Gossip is practically a Gift in this Kingdom."

Zander's shoulders slumped, and he sighed.

Chess stopped at the foot of the palace steps. "Look, Zan, I'm not saying you aren't in a tough spot, but the people will follow your lead on this."

"What does that mean? It's not like I can help that I have the Drifter Gene. If I could get rid of it, I would."

"But would you? Really? Or are you only saying that because you're afraid of how people will react?"

Zander threw up his hands. "I already know how they'll react. I'm not blind. Don't think I didn't notice everyone's reaction at the practice ring, and I've trained beside those men for years. If they're uncomfortable around me, how will the general populace feel?"

"Well, maybe if you confronted them, made them say out loud what exactly they're afraid of, they'd be able to see past it. See that you're still the man they've always known."

Zander crossed his arms. "Sure, as if it's that easy."

"I'm not saying that it'll be easy, but you've been walking around here like you've done something wrong. It only makes people more suspicious."

"I hate to tell you this, but I've already confirmed their suspicions, and it's worse than doing something wrong." He breathed out a short laugh, his mouth tipping into a bitter smile. "I was born wrong." He whirled and jogged up the steps.

Chess rubbed a hand over his face. That had gone well. With a sigh, he ran to catch up to Zander.

He caught up to him in the palace entryway. "Look, Zander, I—"

The sound of raised voices coming from the King's study made him stop. He and Zander exchanged looks. Without saying a word, they both headed towards the noise.

.

Chapter 5

Azalea led Alice back into the passageway using a side tunnel. Before they stepped through, she glanced at her brother.

"You do not have to come with us, Indigo. In fact, it would be better if you flitted off somewhere and amused yourself with something other than the human."

Indigo laughed. "You can't get rid of me that easily. Besides, I'm bored."

Azalea rolled her eyes. "You should be working on the centerpiece with the Feast coming up."

Indigo tugged on one of his sister's braids. "You worry too much about *shoulds*. I have plenty of time to finish the centerpiece." He winked at Alice. "I find this far more entertaining."

His sister stared at him for a long moment and then relented. "Oh, all right. It is more trouble than it is worth to dissuade you, but you can be the one to tell Father if you do not get your work finished."

A lazy smile spread across his face. "Your concern for my welfare is touching, sister, but you needn't worry. I've never let the feastgoers down yet, have I?"

Azalea humphed, but when she turned away a tiny smile hovered on her lips.

Indigo fell into step beside Alice as they followed his sister. Alice couldn't help staring at Azalea's feathered wings, which reached almost to her knees. The light flickered over their various shades of silver and grey, and Alice wondered again what type of animal the Fae woman was able to shift into. The question was on the tip of her tongue, but she bit it back, afraid she'd make Azalea dislike her more than the other woman already seemed to.

Still, her curiosity got the better of her. Trying not to be too obvious, she discreetly examined Indigo's back, but she didn't see any trace of a bulge under his billowy shirt. That seemed odd, since the two siblings otherwise resembled each other.

Alice reined in the questions buzzing through her brain. Hopefully, she wouldn't be here long enough for the answers to matter. She slipped her hand into the pocket of her dress, her fingers running over the smooth edges of the stone Chess had given her.

She hoped both Azalea and Indigo would leave once they locked her up so she could contact Chess. She was reasonably sure King Thorne would let her go—eventually—but that didn't mean she was going to wait around, either.

A touch on her hair interrupted her thoughts. Indigo was examining one of her curls. She stopped, pulling her hair away from him. "Do you mind?"

He grinned. "Not really."

When she glared at him, he held up both hands, but his amusement was still evident. "My apologies, but your hair is such an interesting color—not a true black, but not brown either."

Before she could respond to this, Azalea snapped, "Leave her alone, Indigo. She is a prisoner, not one of your pets."

Indigo's mouth turned down into a playful pout. "Stop being such a spoilsport, Sister." He nudged Alice's shoulder. "Tell Azalea you'd rather be my pet than her prisoner." His eyes danced. "I treat my pets like queens. The same can't be said for prisoners."

Azalea gave him an irritated look. "She does not have that choice, Indigo. She is our prisoner."

"Not if I can convince Father otherwise." Indigo winked at his sister.

She ignored him, and they came to a halt in front of a wooden door. She twisted open the large lock, and with a creaking sigh, it swung inward. Alice's gaze fell to the inside of the door where a keyhole was visible. She swallowed when she realized what that meant: the door locked from the outside. Once she went inside, she'd be stuck—unless she had a key. Azalea walked through, gesturing for Alice to follow. It was too narrow for two people, so Indigo hung back to let Alice go first.

She hesitated, her stomach clenching with nerves. Something silky brushed against her shoulder, and Indigo's warm breath tickled her cheek as he leaned over and spoke into her ear.

"Don't worry, my sweet. I won't let anything happen to you."

"Come along," said Azalea, her tone curt as she shot an annoyed look at her brother.

Alice stepped through the door and found herself at the base of a stone staircase that twisted upwards, only the first few steps visible from where she stood. It was clear the stairs wrapped around a tower or turret of some kind.

How that was possible under a hill made her brain hurt. She decided for her own sanity to accept things the way they were without trying to figure out the *how* of it all.

Azalea reached around Alice and pulled the door shut, and then unclipped a key that hung from the belt around her waist and locked the door. The clank of the lock made Alice's lungs tighten. Azalea brushed by her and started up the stairs, and Alice trailed after her, dread weighing down each step.

The stone walls on either side pressed in on Alice, and her only view was Azalea's back with its array of weapons.

They went up about two dozen steps and came to a landing. Azalea didn't even pause but continued upward. After about the third landing, Alice developed a stitch in her side, but the other woman wasn't even breathing hard.

When she paused to catch her breath, Indigo loomed up behind her.

He winked. "If you're too tired, I can carry you, my pet."

"Not bloody likely!" With renewed energy, Alice hurried after Azalea, Indigo's chuckle following her.

Finally, they stopped. Alice had long since lost track of how many steps they had climbed or which landing this was.

Azalea turned the lock on the outside of the door. Once again, it could only be opened from the inside with a key. When she cracked it open, all Alice saw beyond her was empty air.

The Fae woman pulled the door open wider, and Alice got a clearer view.

Sunlight filtered through a large open-air dome topped with a wooden lattice over which grew an abundance of plants, flowers and vines. The open space was criss-crossed with wooden beams from which vines draped in graceful loops. Attached to the vines by golden chains hung gilded cages at varying heights throughout the space, like so many fancy lanterns. The ground was very far away.

Azalea pulled a hidden lever tucked into the doorframe, and one of the closer cages slid down its vine towards them.

Alice's breath sped up, and her heart thumped.

The cage bumped into the stone ledge outside of the door, swaying slightly. Azalea pulled the cage door open. It fit neatly into the doorway of the tower so that the edge of the cage abutted with the small ledge.

Azalea turned to Alice. "If you will step inside."

"Erm, I'm not sure..."

Alice backed up and bumped into Indigo's broad chest. His hands landed on her shoulders. He squeezed gently, his breath warm on her ear, making her shiver.

"It's all right, my flower. There's nothing to fear." His voice soothed over her nerves, and Alice's heart slowed.

A distant part of her brain wondered why she suddenly felt so calm, but the soothing warmth of his words was too inviting to resist. His hands slid from her shoulders down her arms and back up again.

"That's right, my pet. Everything's fine."

Of course Indigo was right. The cage wasn't that bad. In fact, it looked quite comfortable.

His right hand slid down her arm again and he took her hand, keeping his other hand on her left shoulder.

Azalea moved out of his way as he guided Alice from the landing into the cage. Her first step into the cage made the floor sway, and she paused, trying to find her balance, but again his voice was in her ear. "It's safe. Nothing will happen to you. I promise."

Alice heard his sister make a noise, but it faded into the background. She focused on the comforting timbre of Indigo's voice washing over her. He still held her hand, but she was facing him now.

A pleasant sensation buzzed over her skin as he slipped his hand from hers. "Why don't you sit down and rest, darling girl? You've had a long day. You deserve to relax a bit."

Alice nodded her head and moved over to what looked like a large pillow covered with soft blankets. She sank into the cozy nest.

The floor moved again, and Azalea and Indigo receded. Again, a distant part of her mind tried to get her attention, but the soothing buzz of Indigo's voice washed over her again. "You're all right, my pet. Just rest."

He was right. There was no reason for her to get up. She nestled down into the pillow, pulling one of the soft, feather-light blankets up to her chin.

The gentle swaying made her eyes flutter, and letting it carry her away into sleep was much easier than any of the unpleasant things her mind was trying to bring to her attention.

Chapter 6

ZANDER STOPPED OUTSIDE HIS father's study, his body rigid with nerves. Through the door, two voices rose and fell, but the only one he recognized was his father's.

"Your son is a risk to this Kingdom, and I want to know what you're going to do about it."

Zander exchanged a look with Chess, who shrugged. Apparently, Chess didn't know who the other man was, either.

"The Prince is no more of a risk than he's ever been. You may have just found out about his Drifter Gene, but he's had it all along." The King's voice was calm but held an edge.

"With all due respect, you weren't present at the Great Ballroom Battle. Anyone attending would tell you that the Prince was certainly a danger that night."

"If memory serves me correctly, you weren't there either, Baron Belier." The Commander's voice delivered the jab smoothly. "The only thing you have to go on is hearsay."

Zander's stomach sank. If this was the Baron's opinion, what would he go back and tell the rest of the Northern Estates? The small flame of hope that he could continue to keep his Drifter Gene a secret outside the palace and Council flickered and went out.

Even through the door, the other man's spluttering was audible. "Well... that is... can you deny the Prince destroyed the ballroom and put countless lives at risk?"

There was a pause, and when the Commander finally spoke, he seemed to choose his words carefully. "I don't deny the ballroom sustained damage. It would have been a miracle if it didn't under the circumstances; however, I don't believe the Prince ever purposely put anyone in danger."

"Well, it doesn't matter much to someone if a Jabberwock kills them on purpose or not. They'll still be dead!" The Baron's voice rose until his last word shrilled.

"My son has never willfully killed anyone without cause, nor would he..." The King suddenly stopped speaking.

As the silence stretched on, Zander looked at Chess. "What's going on?" He mouthed the words.

Chess shook his head and leaned closer, putting his eye to the crack in the door. Then he pulled back. "I can't see them from this angle," he whispered.

Zander considered pushing the door open and walking in to check on his father. It might almost be worth it for the Baron's reaction, but the Commander's smooth voice stopped him. "Baron Belier, both the King and I understand your valid concerns about the Prince. Nobody is happy about his Drifter Gene, but we can both assure you, he'll be supervised."

A faint buzz started in Zander's ears as his uncle's words pierced him, and he missed the Baron's response.

Beside him, Chess stiffened. "I can't believe him," he muttered under his breath. "I'll give him *supervised.*" Chess put his hand on the door. "This has gone on long enough."

Zander grabbed his arm and pulled him away. "We can't go in there, not now."

"Why not? That supercilious snot can jolly well look you in the eye while he assassinates your character, and as for the Commander..." Chess turned back towards the door.

"Please, Chess. This isn't the way to handle this." Zander rubbed the spot between his eyebrows where a headache was beginning. "The Northern Estates are important, and with Renard and his heir dead, things could get touchy." He still couldn't believe the Queen had killed her own father, but her brother Leander's death in the labyrinth had left a leadership void in the region.

The voices continued to rise and fall, but they were far enough away now that the words were indistinct. Zander was rather glad. He'd heard enough.

The idea of seeing or speaking to the Baron right now caused a panicky feeling to rise and almost choke him. He paced in a tight circle.

Chess stepped in front of him, forcing him to stop. "Zander, that Baron doesn't speak for everyone, and just because he's a royal idiot doesn't mean all the Northern Estates will look at things the same way."

Zander shook his head. "You don't know that."

"Well, you don't, either." Chess put his hands on his hips. "Like I said before, you have to stop acting like your existence is some kind of crime."

Zander's mouth twitched. "Well, actually, it kind of is."

Chess paused and then snorted. "You know what I mean."

Zander recognized Chess was trying to help, but he didn't understand. He didn't know what it felt like for people to look at him with fear, for maids to skitter away and men he'd counted as friends to avoid him.

The walls closed in on him, the air suddenly heavy. Zander longed more than anything to escape to the wilderness, to release his Jabberwock. He'd give anything to feel the cold rush of air on his face, to forget all of this. He didn't miss the irony that the part of him that complicated his life the most also helped him when anxiety or panic crowded in.

He headed towards the doors, Chess a few steps behind him. He strode past the soldiers, ignoring their salute, and clattered down the front steps.

Chess followed him around the side of the palace and into the gardens before he grabbed Zander's arm, pulling him to a stop. "Hey, nobody's chasing you."

Zander shrugged off his friend's hand. "I... I needed some air..." He closed his eyes and took a deep breath, letting the soft droning of bees and the heady scent of the roses wash over him.

Chess tilted his head. "Look, I realize this isn't easy, but you can't let that idiot Belier get to you like this. It means he wins, and someone as sad and sorry as that should not win anything."

A smile tugged at one corner of Zander's mouth, but it quickly disappeared when he remembered the Commander's words. "It's not only people like Belier, though."

Chess's lip curled. "If you mean my esteemed father, ignore him, too. He's almost as much of an idiot as the baron."

Zander shook his head. "But that's the thing—he's not." He began walking again, aimlessly following the path. Chess fell into step with him.

"When it comes to family over duty, he most certainly is." Chess snapped a rose off a bush and brought the vivid yellow petals to his nose.

"You don't mean that, Chess. I realize you and your father don't quite see eye to eye—"

Chess snorted. "More like we aren't even looking at the same thing." He waved a hand. "But we aren't talking about me right now. The truth is, you're going to have to deal with people like Belier now that your Drifter Gene is out in the open, but their opinion doesn't change who you are."

Zander kicked at the gravel under his feet. "What if I could get rid of it?"

Chess halted on the path. "Rid of what?"

"My Drifter Gene."

Chess's mouth fell open. "Surely, if that was possible, others would have done it before now. I mean, they ban it now, but back at the beginning, they were exterminating people left and right."

"Citrine found something in Sacklepenny's lab." Zander kicked another stone. "She almost died finding it."

"Why are you just telling me this now?" Chess shook the rose in Zander's direction, several of the petals floating to the ground.

"Well, it's not as if I've had loads of free time, what with dealing with my father's return from the dead and sending Alice back through the Looking Glass."

At the mention of Alice's name, Chess's gaze flicked down at the flower he held before returning to Zander. "Citrine actually found a way to get rid of the Drifter Gene?"

Zander shrugged. "Not exactly. She found evidence in Sacklepenny's notes of someone getting rid of their Gift." He blew out a breath. "You know Citrine. She determined that since you could get rid of one Gift, you could get rid of another. She said she was going to investigate more when she got home."

"Have you heard anything yet?"

Zander shook his head. "No, but it hasn't even been a week since we parted ways. And she had Stongorr's death to deal with, too." His chest tightened at the memory of Citrine's grief over one of the Pearl Palace's gargoyles.

They started walking again and rounded a bend in the path, but had to stop. Dugin, the groundskeeper, was bent over something with a shovel, his bulky form blocking the walkway.

As they got nearer, he straightened and pulled his cap off his head. He gave a quick bow. "Your Highness. I'm sorry to be in the way."

Zander waved a hand. "No, it's fine. We're the ones interrupting you." His eyes went to the sack at Dugin's feet and the lumpy pile next to it. When he looked closer, Zander realized the pile was bloody fur.

"What happened here?" he asked.

Dugin twisted the cap in his hands. "It's only a dead hedgepig. If you'll give me a few minutes, I'll get it cleared right up."

Chess edged closer and grimaced. "Whatever killed it really tore it up."

Dugin shrugged. "That's what all of 'em has looked like. 'Twern't hardly anything left of the poor critters. But then, hedgepigs cain't really defend theyselves."

"All of them? How many have there been?" Zander asked.

Dugin stroked his chin. "Well, I'd say this makes about half a dozen this week."

Zander raised his eyebrows. "I don't recall this being a problem before, or was I not aware of it?"

"No, no, this is new." Dugin frowned. "Sure, every once in a while you find a hedgepig. As I said, they cain't defend theyselves, and between you and me, they're none too bright, neither."

Chess pushed the animal with the toe of his boot. "Do you have any idea what did this, Dugin? It doesn't appear like whatever tore this poor creature apart was looking for a meal."

The groundskeeper shrugged. "That's not the oddest thing, though." He looked around and then leaned towards Zander. "Whatever's doing it has sucked the blood right out of it. They's all been that way. I don't know of any creature that hunts like that."

Dugin's words hung in the air. Zander's stomach turned, and he looked away from the mess on the path.

A faint breeze rustled the leaves, and the perfume of the roses overlaid the smell of death, creating the sickly-sweet scent of rot.

Footsteps crunched on gravel, and both he and Chess spun towards the sound, Zander's heart picking up speed.

Anders, the palace steward, came into view, panting. "There you are, Your Highness. The King wishes to meet with you promptly in his study."

Zander shifted so he blocked the steward's view of the dead creature. He inclined his head. "Thank you, Anders. We'll be right there."

"Don't you think—" Chess started to say, but Zander elbowed him into silence.

He waited until Anders turned and trotted back up the path before he turned back to Dugin. "I'd appreciate it if you didn't spread this around. It may... unsettle the rest of the staff, and I'd like to find what's doing this before rumors start running rampant."

Dugin nodded. "You don't need to worry none about me and my boys. We haven't said a word about this and don't plan to. I'll tell 'em to keep an eye out too. I don't fancy some creature running wild in my gardens."

Zander nodded at the man. "Thank you, Dugin. Please inform me if you hear or see anything. I want to be kept updated about this."

The man bobbed his head in agreement.

Zander turned towards the palace, and Chess fell into step beside him. "Well, that definitely puts a damper on midnight strolls in the garden."

Zander frowned at him. "Please don't mention this to anyone, either. We have enough to worry about without any more stories swirling around the palace."

Chess raised his eyebrows. "Are you sure that's a good idea? I mean, the creature might be dangerous to the staff."

"The only thing it's killed are hedgepigs."

Chess stared at him for a long moment before lifting one shoulder in a shrug. "I suppose you're right. I won't say anything."

Zander released a breath as they started up the path to his meeting with the King. He couldn't help the dread that coiled in his gut.

Chapter 7

ALICE SAT IN THE center of the cage, her mind turning over her predicament. When she had first woken up, she hadn't been sure where she was. It didn't help that she had a pressing need to use the facilities, and there didn't seem to be any.

Thankfully, she had found a chamber pot in a curtained-off section. Of course, the floor swaying under her feet had been rather disconcerting. It hadn't taken her long to explore her small prison. It was only about ten to twelve feet across, and besides the chamber pot and nest-like bed, the only thing she'd found was a brush, an empty basin attached to a stand, and a folded towel.

She'd made the mistake of trying to see the floor, which was so far down, it was obscured in shadows. She'd had to close her eyes for a minute to stop her head from spinning. However, once she backed away from the bars, she found if she didn't think about how high she was, she could cope. Besides, she had more important problems—such as the way Indigo had charmed her without her even realizing it.

She shivered and pulled the blanket closer, wishing Wickle was with her. A lump rose in her throat at the last memory of his little body lying on the forest floor. She wiped at her eyes and drew in a shaky breath. She didn't have the luxury of grief right now.

She slid her hand into her pocket to retrieve the stone. Her fingers closed over the smooth edges.

"Halloooo!" A voice echoed and Alice started, yanking her hand out of her pocket as if she had been burned.

"Erm, hello?"

"I must admit, it's refreshing to encounter another human."

The voice came from somewhere on her right, but she didn't see anyone. "I'm sorry, but where are you?" She stood and moved to the edge of the cage, her stomach swooping a bit as the floor slanted in that direction.

"I'm up here!" A skinny arm waved at her from a cage close to the top of the dome. His enclosure tipped alarmingly, and Alice cringed. "I'm Arthur Tweed."

She looked up and saw a man's face pressed against the bars. It was difficult to get a good look at him because a bushy red beard threaded with gray obscured the bottom half of his face.

She waved back. "I'm Alice."

The man slid to his knees, peering down at her, a pair of crooked glasses smashing against the cage. "It's so good to have company. I haven't had anyone to talk to in ages and ages." He stopped, his eyes going wide. "Oh, erm, I don't mean it's good you're in here, of course.

That's obviously quite horrible, I'm sure. It's only..." He trailed off, his body slumping.

Alice shifted so she could get a better view. "It's all right, Mr. Tweed. I know what you meant." She paused, questions crowding behind her lips, but she only let one escape. "How long have you been here?"

"Hmmm..." Arthur counted on his fingers and muttered to himself before he finally refocused on Alice. "Perhaps five years. It's hard to tell. Time passes differently here than in the Mirror World."

This piqued Alice's interest. "You're from the Mirror World too? How did you get here?"

"That's a long story, Miss Alice."

Alice felt a bubble of hysterical laughter rise, but pushed it down. "Well, I don't know about you, but I'm not busy at the moment."

The man chuckled. "Yes, you're right, of course." He settled himself cross-legged, his knees bumping the bars. "It's been so long. It seems like a dream now. I suppose everyone has forgotten all about me, probably given me up for dead."

The wistfulness in his tone made Alice's heart pang with sympathy. "Do you have a family that's missing you?"

The man sniffled and, to Alice's horror, began to cry. "I'm so sorry. I didn't mean to..."

The man waved a hand as he fished out a handkerchief from a pocket. "No, no, it's... it's been a long time since I let myself remember them." He gave a watery smile. "My son would be in his twenties by now." He sniffed again and dabbed at his eyes with the dingy square of cloth. "He might be married with a family, even. I could be a grandfather." At this, the man broke down and sobbed, covering his face with the handkerchief.

"Oh dear, is he having hysterics again?" The tiny voice behind Alice made her whip around, the cage swaying precariously.

Three tiny faeries hovered on the other side of the bars. The one that spoke had reddish-orange hair that was made more vibrant by her grass-green skin.

She gestured at the other two faeries, who were each holding one side of the handle of a large basket. "We brought your dinner."

"Dinner?" Alice repeated.

One faery who held the basket rolled her pale-green eyes and flicked her vibrant pink hair over her shoulder. "You didn't think King Thorne would starve you, did you?" She giggled. "He only does that to prisoners he doesn't like."

The third faery, this one with a nimbus of white corkscrew curls around her head, gave the pink-haired one a reproachful look. "Foxglove, that isn't true. You're being unkind."

Foxglove rolled her eyes. "Don't be such a wet leaf, Thistle. I was only having fun with the human." She looked at Alice. "If you're done staring at us, this is getting rather heavy." She nodded at the basket that was easily three times her size.

Alice wasn't sure what she was supposed to do. "Do you... need help?"

The first faery buzzed up close to Alice. "Oh no, silly. We need your permission to come into the cage." She clasped her hands in front of her. "Even though you are a prisoner, it is rude to wander in and out of your prison without permission, and it could be dangerous. For us. At least, that is what King Thorne says."

"Don't you have a key?" Alice asked, puzzled.

Foxglove snorted. "You're a human. There's no reason to lock these doors." When Alice looked at her, the small faery gave a huff. "You can't fly, and I wouldn't suggest jumping. Unless, of course, you want to go *splat*!"

"Foxglove!" Thistle said, her pale-green face twisted in horror. She turned her large hazel eyes in Alice's direction and lifted her end of the basket. She offered a tentative smile. "May we come in?"

"Oh, yes, of course."

The two faeries flew closer with their burden and stopped. "Poppy—the door," Foxglove snapped. "This basket isn't getting any lighter, and we still need to feed the other one."

"Oh, oh, right!" Poppy flew around to the door and pulled on it. It swung open easily. Alice swallowed. It was a good thing she hadn't leaned on it or she might have—as Foxglove so eloquently put it—gone *splat*.

Poppy buzzed into the cage, followed by the other two. As they set the basket down and unloaded their burden, Poppy came to hover in front of Alice.

"You're pretty. Not all the humans are. The one up there is old. And his skin is all wrinkly like a dried nut shell."

"Erm..."

"What's your name? Where did you come from? Why did the King put you in here? He rarely puts young women in here, especially pretty ones. The Prince usually keeps them as pets. Well, until he gets tired of them.

Which he does. A lot. But I suppose he has to finish the centerpiece for the Feast. So?" She looked up at Alice, her dark-green eyes shining with curiosity.

Alice blinked, a bit bewildered by the flood of words. "I'm Alice, and I'm originally from the Mirror World."

Poppy bounced in the air, fairly vibrating with excitement. "Truly? So is the other human. Do you know him?"

Foxglove fluttered over next to Poppy. "Don't be a julkap. The Mirror World is a big place, and the male has been here for years. How would she know him?"

Poppy's iridescent wings drooped. "I just thought since they were from the same place..."

"Do you know every Fae in the Faelands?"

"Well, no, but..."

"See how dumb you're being? She probably doesn't even want to talk to you. I certainly wouldn't if someone made me a prisoner." She pushed her face close to Poppy's. "In fact, she might grab you and pull off your wings!"

Poppy squeaked, her eyes going wide, and she backpedaled away from Alice.

Alice's mouth twitched, but she sent a stern look at the pink-haired faery. "You're obviously the troublemaker of this trio." She turned to Poppy, who was now hovering by the door. "It's true. I'm not happy to be here, but I won't hurt you. I promise." She smiled. "After all, you brought me this tasty-looking food."

The orange-haired faery glanced between her and Foxglove, looking uncertain. Thistle turned to Foxglove, her face creased with concern. "If you don't stop being so mean, I'm going to tell Bluebell, and you won't be allowed to do deliveries anymore."

Foxglove narrowed her eyes. "Neither of you can take a joke." She jabbed a finger at Poppy. "She believes anything you tell her, and you"—she pointed at Thistle—"are too soft-hearted." She jerked her head at Poppy. "Come on, we need to get the rest of this to the other one."

She waited until Poppy picked up the other end of the handle, and the two flew out of the cage. Poppy kept glancing over her shoulder, a frown on her small face. Alice hoped she'd get another chance to show the little faery she wasn't dangerous.

"I'm sorry for my sister's behavior."

Alice's attention snapped back to the white-haired faery, who now hovered in front of her. "It's fine. I'm sure I'm a novelty to her."

The faery twisted the fabric of her skirt, which resembled a tiny upside-down thistle. "Foxglove is a prankster and she can be unkind, but she doesn't mean any harm. Not really." She glanced up shyly at Alice. "I wanted to tell you, if the food isn't to your liking, we can make changes." Her brow furrowed. "At least some, so if you'd like more of something or less of another, please let us know."

Alice smiled even as she wondered what kind of prison asked about your food preferences. "You're very kind, but I'm sure whatever you brought me will be fine."

"Well, if you change your mind, you only have to tell me." Thistle curtsied, and a smile peeked out before she buzzed away.

Alice watched her go and turned to the food the faeries had brought. A large bowl of what looked like purple whipped cream sat beside a slice of brown bread.

Next to that was a pile of pale-blue cubes. She sat down and poked at the food. Above her head, she heard the chatter of the faeries as they brought Arthur his food.

She absently put a cube into her mouth and let it melt. It had a savory, salty flavor that was quite good. She dipped a finger in the purple whip and put it in her mouth. It tasted like sun-warmed berries.

She waited until the faeries had left and then tucked a hand in her pocket, even as she took a bite of the bread. She ran her finger over the smooth stone and looked around again. Arthur's tale of being here for five years made her more determined to contact Chess. She had no plans to get stuck here, even if the food was delicious. She took another bite of bread and closed her hand over the stone.

"I see our food agrees with you."

Alice froze, her hand still in her pocket, as Indigo shimmered into view on a nearby beam.

Chapter 8

ZANDER AND CHESS REACHED the study door just as Baron Belier was exiting. The Baron bowed smoothly to Zander.

"Good morning, Your Highness." He nodded at Chess. "Sir Chess." He smiled warmly, and if Zander hadn't heard him earlier, he would have been convinced the other man was sincere. "I hope you are both well."

Next to him, Chess muttered, "Hypocrite."

Belier tilted his head. "Pardon?"

Chess straightened. "I said, I hope you are too."

Zander nodded his own head in greeting, trying to hide his awkwardness behind the etiquette his parents had trained into him since he could walk. "Belier. It's good to see you. Will you be enjoying our hospitality for a while longer, or will you be heading back home soon?"

The man's eyes darted back towards the study and then to Zander. "Not yet. I have a few... matters to attend to."

"In that case, we'll likely run into each other again. If you'll excuse us." It was a clear dismissal, and the other man bowed again before escaping down the hallway.

While outwardly calm, inside, Zander's gut churned. He hated the falseness of court. How someone like Belier could smile to your face all while plotting behind your back to get rid of you, he'd never understand. Chess bumped his shoulder.

"What a toady! I wonder if he'd kiss your big toe if you asked him to."

Zander rolled his eyes. "No doubt, and then turn around and try to get me booted from my own kingdom."

Chess lifted one shoulder in a shrug. "He doesn't have that kind of power. He's only a very noisy gnat."

Zander wished that were true, but even if he squashed the Baron, he was only one voice of many. With this gloomy notion swirling around, he pushed open the door and entered his father's study.

The King was standing behind the desk, shuffling a stack of papers. Zander paused, a well of gratitude rising in him. Even if it had caused all kinds of problems, he'd shift in front of the entire Kingdom again if it meant keeping his father alive.

Concern niggled at him, though. Despite the Palace Healers saying his father was fit, the light pouring in the large picture window illuminated the dark circles still under his eyes, and none of the sharp edges of his gauntness had softened yet. Still, he was beyond thankful to have his father back, even if he needed a bit more healing time.

"Son, come in and shut the door. We have much to discuss before we meet with the Council tomorrow."

The King broke into Zander's thoughts and waved a hand at the door.

Zander pulled it shut behind him and walked across the study to drop into a chair. "I noticed the Baron came to visit you," he said while observing his father intently, curious if he would disclose the truth or attempt to shield him.

So he didn't miss the glance the King shared with the Commander. "Yes, well, about that." His father dropped into his own chair and leaned forward, steepling his fingers. "The Baron expressed some... concerns."

"Is that what he called them?" Chess muttered, and Zander shot him a warning look. Chess rolled his eyes but subsided into silence.

"He's upset about my Drifter Gene, isn't he?"

The Commander raised his eyebrows and looked at the King before zeroing back in on Zander. "It's best we don't dodge the issue. The Baron has concerns—justifiable in my opinion—about the safety of a Prince who can shift into a Jabberwock."

"But I..."

The Commander held up a hand to stop Zander. "We are aware you aren't a danger to anyone right now. Even when under the curse, it was obvious you tried your best not to hurt anyone while also defending yourself. But the real danger lies in the fact that an enemy *could* curse you in this way."

Chess leapt up from the window ledge where he'd been perched. "It's not as if that's Zander's fault. The Queen is the one who cursed him. She's the danger to the Kingdom, not Zander."

The Commander frowned. "You're letting your emotions cloud your logic, son. Everyone knows Zander is a young man of character. Nobody doubts that, least of all the people of this Kingdom, but his Drifter Gene is a weakness others can exploit. People like the Baron are worried about that, and you can't blame them."

"The one you should be blaming here is the Queen." Chess glanced at the King. "I mean no offense, Your Majesty, but your wife is a witch."

"Chess!" The Commander's tone was sharp.

The King held up a hand towards the Commander. "No, Zavier, he's only stating the obvious. It was my... weakness that allowed her access to the palace and Zander."

The conversation swirled around Zander as he stared at his clasped hands. He was aware that he should say something, but it was all true. His Drifter Gene was a liability, and it wouldn't be long before everyone in the entire Kingdom found out. He realized that the room had gone silent, and when he looked up, everyone was waiting for him to respond.

"I'm sorry... what?"

The King met Zander's gaze and his mouth tipped up at the corners. "I said we have two issues to deal with here. As young Chess has so rightly pointed out, one of them is the Queen. She needs to be tracked down and... brought to account for her actions." He sighed and looked down at his desk. Zander could see the effort it took for his father to speak about his wife, and his chest tightened with sympathy. His father had truly cared about Lyssandra, and her betrayal had to be hard. "The other issue is the citizens' perceptions of you. As much as we've tried to keep this within the palace walls, the story will get out—if it hasn't already."

"I'm not sure how I can change what anyone thinks." Zander shrugged.

The King's eyebrows drew down. "That's not the type of attitude you need to take," he snapped.

Zander looked up in surprise. "I only meant that I can't change someone's mind. Only time will do that."

The King's frown deepened. "Well, time isn't something we have an excess of, now do we? We have no idea what Lyssandra is up to or where she's gone."

Even the Commander looked surprised by the sudden change in the King's tone. "I can take some men and search for her. My Tracking Gift is strong. I should be able to at least find the area where she's hiding."

A flicker of hope sprang up in Zander's chest, and he turned to the King. "I'll go with him, Father. Perhaps being out of sight for a while will let some of the fear subside."

The King didn't answer. Instead, his eyes had lost their focus, and he seemed to stare at something none of them could see. It wasn't the first time this had happened since his father had come out of the labyrinth.

Zander leaned forward, afraid of startling the King, and spoke a bit louder. "Father?"

"Hmm? Oh, yes, erm, what did you say?" The King straightened a stack of papers that were already perfectly aligned.

"I said I should go with the Commander when he leaves to track the Queen."

"You could visit Citrine. Find out if..." Chess trailed off when Zander frowned at him and gave a quick shake of his head. He didn't want to reveal the possibility of getting rid of his Drifter Gene—in case it was all a waste of time. Better that he be the only person with dashed hopes.

Whatever had stolen the King's focus a moment before was evidently gone now. The King slapped a hand on his desk. "Absolutely not! The last thing you need to do is disappear. You should be front and center so you can assure the people that you are just as you've always been."

"But Father, do you think that's wise?"

The King frowned. "If I didn't, would I have suggested it? You need to get out in front of the people. Don't be a coward."

Zander drew his head back, feeling as if he'd been slapped.

"I'm sure nobody would accuse Zander of that." The Commander's glance bounced between the King and the Prince and landed on Zander. "But in this case, I agree with your father. While I'd love to have you along, it's better that you get out and let the people see you. Quell any rumors."

Zander let out a sigh. They were probably right, but the idea of being the subject of everyone's stares and whispers wasn't something he looked forward to. Maybe he really was a coward. "I don't suppose there's any chance we can keep this quiet? Get the Council to agree to silence?"

Chess snorted. "Have you ever known Lady Perma to be silent on something this juicy? And Beecher will take every opportunity to bluster his opinion to anyone who will listen—or who he can corner, at least. I'm afraid this cat—or Jabberwock—is out of the bag, my friend." Chess gave him a sympathetic look.

Zander's shoulders slumped. Chess was right. "I suppose the only question is, how will we present this to the Council?"

The King's expression darkened. "You only need to follow my lead. I can handle Wilfred Beecher, and once I've put him in his place, the rest will fall into line."

Chess smirked. "I can't wait to witness that, Your Majesty."

The King chuckled, his former irritation dissipating as suddenly as it had appeared. "I have to admit, the man gets on my nerves."

The Commander nodded, a small smile playing at the corners of his mouth, but Zander wasn't so sure. He thought his father was underestimating how upset the old man truly was.

The King stood. "I think we've covered everything. The Commander will leave as soon as possible to find the Queen." He nodded at Chess and Zander. "You may all go." He dropped back into his chair and rubbed at his forehead. "I still have so much to catch up on."

Chess hopped up and bowed to the King before he headed out of the study. The Commander also stood and walked towards the door.

Zander pushed to his feet. His father was staring at his desk. "Will you be joining us for tea?"

The King didn't answer and instead continued gazing downward.

"Zander, are you coming?" Chess called from the hall.

Zander held up a hand and turned back to his father. "Father?"

The King twitched in his chair, his hands clenching on his desktop. Zander took a step closer. "Father, are you all right?"

His father's body jolted as if someone had prodded him. "I'm fine. Stop fussing," he snapped.

"I... I was just wondering about tea..." Zander trailed off when his father jerked his head up.

The sun had come out from behind a cloud, and a patch of light slanted through the window, hitting his father's face, making his eyes glow red. Zander blinked, and then his father shook his head. When he spoke, the irritation was gone. Instead, he merely sounded tired. "I have too much work to do, but thank you."

He smiled at Zander, but it seemed forced. Zander didn't want to push him. It hadn't even been a week since his father had escaped the labyrinth and all its horrors, after all.

Zander returned the smile. "I'll see you later, then."

"Hmm, yes." The King shuffled through the papers on his desk again as Zander turned towards the door.

As he hurried to catch up to Chess, unease slithered up his spine. Surely, his father was fine. The Healers had said so, and they knew what they were about. Didn't they?

Chapter 9

CITRINE SHUT THE BOOK and got up from her chair, her muscles protesting from sitting for so long. Bliss, her steward, had laid a fire in the library hours earlier to take the chill from the morning air. It was the only fireplace in use in the Pearl Palace these days since she tended to spend most of her time here. She worried about the cost, but she had to admit, it lent a cozy atmosphere to the book-lined room. She bent and scratched Seamus's head, and the big dog thumped his tail on the floor. His rough tongue swiped her wrist.

Love you. Seem sad.

She stared into the dog's eyes. "Thank you, Seamus. I love you too, and I'm not sad. I'm... Well, I don't know what I am at the moment." She stood and paced over to a bookshelf on the far side of the room. Her eyes scanned the spines of the books for the thousandth time. "I'm frustrated. That's what I am." She pushed her spectacles up on her nose and tipped her head to look at the shelves above her. "The formula is clear, but there's nothing about any side effects, and any reference to 'a Fae artifact' is vague. Why can't I find anything specific?"

Marmalade, one of the many cats that lived in the library, thumped down on the floor. He padded over to sit at her feet. He licked a paw and ran it over one large, tufted ear. *Perhaps because it's not here to find.*

"But if it's not here, where is it?" Citrine swung her arm in a wide arc. "I've looked on every shelf. I even combed through Mother's old journals, and the only thing I've found were a few hints here and there, but nothing close to a proper answer!"

Marmalade blinked up at her. *Perhaps the answers aren't in here, or there is nothing to find. Perhaps the formula's creator was vague for a reason.*

Seamus thumped his tail on the floor. He obviously had nothing to add to the conversation. He was very loyal, and he'd defend her to the death, but he wasn't what you'd call *academically gifted.*

Citrine rubbed a hand over her forehead. Maybe Marmalade was right. Simply because she'd found a few sentences scribbled in a dead Alchemist's notebook didn't mean anyone had actually used the formula—or used it successfully. She was aware that it was unwise to let her emotions become a part of her research, but she couldn't forget the hope in Zander's eyes.

She squatted down and scratched the big orange tomcat behind his ear. His purr rumbled in the quiet room. "Perhaps it's for the best I've found nothing." She blew a stray curl out of her eye. "I'm not aware of anyone ever removing their Gift. It's unnatural, and I'm not sure there wouldn't be terrible consequences."

Marmalade rose and rubbed his side against her knee, almost unbalancing her. *Humans often do unnatural things. You are strange creatures.*

A laugh bubbled out of Citrine, and she pushed to her feet. "I suppose you're right about that, my friend."

A long, lean black-and-white cat stood and stretched on a shelf high above. She peered down at Citrine, her green eyes bright. *Have you tried your Alchemist friend—the rabbit? It seems to me that if anyone knows, it would be Sir Lapin. After all, you are only a Scholar, my Queen.*

I don't recall inviting you to this conversation, Isla.

I don't need your permission to talk to the Queen, Marmalade. The black cat sniffed and stuck her nose in the air.

Citrine shook her head at the two cats. "Now, now, you two, let's not fight."

A commotion in the hallway made her spin towards the door. Bliss had appeared, his hair a bit mussed. Alarm prickled down Citrine's spine to witness her un-flappable steward decidedly flapped. "What's the matter?"

"Madam has visitors who wish to speak to her." He surreptitiously used his leg to block something behind him. "If Madam is not otherwise occupied, of course."

Citrine bit back a smile even as her curiosity bubbled to the surface. "Of course, Bliss. Show whoever it is in, please."

She'd barely gotten the words out when a small herd of selbys flowed into the room. Bliss's ability to hold them off for so long impressed Citrine. Their mossy green-and-brown-furred bodies tumbled over each other, their high-pitched voices all chattering at once so that it was impossible to understand what they were saying.

At her feet, Marmalade stood and arched his back, letting out a low growl. *Stupid creatures.* Then, with fluid grace, he leapt onto the back of her armchair and then onto a top shelf before sitting down and glaring at the chattering horde.

Citrine waited a moment, but when they continued to chatter over each other, their small gopher-like bodies churning in a giant seething mass, she clapped her hands sharply. "Quiet, now."

The chattering immediately ceased. The herd of selbys all froze, their beady black eyes trained on her. Citrine smoothed a hand down her blouse and pushed up her spectacles. "Now, then, will one"—she held up a finger to underscore her words—"and only one of you, please tell me the reason for your visit?"

There was some jostling and muttering before someone shoved a lone animal forward. The small creature looked back over his shoulder and wrung his paws together.

Citrine smiled and crouched down so she was closer to the small fellow's eye level. "What's your name?"

The creature bobbed his head and peeked up at her. *It's Hegbert, Your Majesty.*

"All right then, Hegbert, please share the reason for your visit, and in such a state of uproar."

Hegbert bobbed his head again, clasping his paws in front of him. *Well, Your Majesty, it's like this, it is. There's trouble up at the Red Palace, there is.*

A chill ran down Citrine's spine, but she quickly hid the dismay she felt. "What kind of trouble?"

He glanced over his shoulder again, and several of the other selbys made shooing gestures. A large female in the front clacked her buck teeth at him. This seemed to encourage him, and he turned back to Citrine. He bobbed his head again and peered up at her. *There's been… deaths, Your Majesty.*

Citrine's eyes widened. "Deaths? That sounds quite serious."

Yes, Your Majesty, lots of 'em. Old Piggle, who lives in the garden at the palace, got word to Hester, who told Fritz. He's the big crow as lives down by the foot of the mountain. He told Alistair, who told Frieda, and she was the one—

Citrine held up her hand. "Hegbert, I don't need to know how the message got here. Please, just tell me what it says."

Hegbert twisted his paws together, hunching his round little body until his face was barely visible anymore. *Somethin's been ripping up animals and stealing their blood.* He peered up at her again, his whiskers twitching. *Leastways, that's what we was told. We realized we'd best get right over here and let you know. That was right, wasn't it?*

Citrine smiled at Hegbert. "You did exactly the right thing. Did, erm, whoever passed on the message tell you anything else? Did Piggle see or hear anything when these deaths happened?"

*Piggle ain't nocturnal. All the killings happened at night. Leastways, nobody was dead before the sun went down, but they was when it came back up again. He said *he thought he heard snorting and huffing, but he's not sure it had anything to do with the deaths.*

Citrine tapped her lip. "I suppose it's too much to hope that anyone saw anything? Perhaps one of the royal griffons? They're housed not too far from the gardens, and they have very keen senses."

Herbert shrugged his furry shoulders. *Piggle was too afraid to ask, Your Majesty. Griffons ain't too friendly with brocks, you know.*

"Quite right." Citrine sighed and pushed to her feet. She looked down at Hegbert. "One more question, my friend." The small selby ducked his head at the word *friend*. "Did Piggle say whether anyone was aware of these animal killings?"

Herbert's ears drooped. *Piggle didn't say.* He scuffed a clawed foot on the floor. *Humans don't generally take no notice of us little creatures.*

"Well, I'm taking notice, Herbert. You have my word. I will look into this."

Chapter 10

ALICE SLID HER DAMP palms out of her pocket, leaving behind the reassuring weight of the stone.

"How long have you been lurking there?" Her voice was tart even as she eyed Indigo warily. She hadn't forgotten how he had lured her into this cage with his charm. She'd be on her guard this time.

Indigo lounged along the length of a wooden beam, legs stretched out, leaning on his elbow. He had a small pad of paper balanced next to him.

He continued drawing with a stick of charcoal and didn't look up when he answered her. "Long enough to hear old Tweed's sob story, and the Wildflower Sisters' inane twittering."

Alice sat up straighter, trying to hide her alarm. "It's not a sob story if it's true, and the sisters were sweet."

Indigo rolled his eyes before he resumed his drawing. "They may seem sweet, but the small Fae can be tricky. You'd do well to be on your guard around them."

"Funny, I find the big Fae to be more of a worry." Alice smiled sweetly.

His mouth twitched, amusement sparking in his eyes. "I never said we weren't, but humans like you are more taken in by the small ones. You mistake *adorable* for *harmless*." He flicked a finger towards Arthur's cage. "I believe that's how Tweed ended up here."

Alice stood up and walked over to the bars. Perhaps Indigo's interest in her would be of help to Arthur, as well as herself. "What *did* he do?"

Indigo gave the paper a last once-over. "Something to do with a book he was writing. I don't know. Solus is the one that threw him in there." He added another stroke with the charcoal and held up the pad, examining it. "Come to think of it, he's probably forgotten the man is even in here."

"Maybe you should remind him. Arthur's been rotting in here forever. Whatever he did couldn't be too bad if everyone's forgotten about it."

Indigo finally looked up from his drawing. "I doubt Tweed would thank me for bringing him back to the Advisor's attention, my sweet. It's the ones that Solus takes an interest in that tend not to survive very long."

He gave her a meaningful look, and a shiver snaked up Alice's spine. Above them, she could see Arthur's face pressed against the bars, listening to the conversation. "Well, that sounds ominous. What does he do to them?"

"Trust me when I say it wouldn't be in either of your best interests to come to the Advisor's attention."

Alice digested this bit of information, a sense of dread coiling in her stomach. "If you think I'm in danger from your Advisor, why don't you let me go? While you're at it, why not let poor Arthur go, too? He's obviously harmless."

Indigo smirked. "Are you saying you're not harmless?"

"Don't twist my words. You know I don't belong in this cage, and now you're telling me I'm not safe either. I'm sure if you spoke to your father, he'd let me go."

Indigo used his thumb to smudge something on the page. "You say that as if it would be easy, but you don't realize the half of it. Solus would squawk and be difficult. Besides, Father won't release you until he's had you tested. He can't, not after he agreed to it in front of the Advisor."

Alice gripped the bars of the cage. "But he'll do that soon, right?"

Indigo lifted one shoulder. "He's busy with the Feast and might not want to be bothered until after it's over."

"Well, when is this feast?" Alice asked, hoping it wasn't a month from now.

Indigo scowled. "Four days and three hours."

Alice blinked. That had been oddly specific. She shook her head. Focus. She didn't want to be in this cage with that Advisor lurking around for another day, never mind four.

"I don't suppose it's possible for you to convince your father to move up the testing, is it?"

At her words, Indigo swung himself upright into a seated position, his legs dangling into the empty air. He tucked the small sketch pad into his shirt pocket, his languid air gone.

"Now why would I do that when you're so entertaining, and I've been so bored lately?" The sudden gleam in his eyes made Alice's nerves jitter.

She backed away from the bars. "Trust me, I'm not. I'm actually very boring."

"Don't be so modest, my sweet. Watching you try to manipulate me into helping you has been vastly amusing."

Alice swallowed. "Is that what you think I'm doing?"

He chuckled. "Why else would you suddenly be so chatty when you were so eager to see the back of me before?"

She crossed her arms. "Well, maybe I'm bored, too. It's not as if Arthur is much of a conversationalist, and I've been alone in this cage for hours now. I'd be willing to talk to almost anyone at this point."

"Just anyone? You have mortally wounded me, my flower." Clutching his chest, Indigo leaned forward, but instead of stopping, his body tipped off the beam.

Alice stifled a scream as he hurtled past her cage. She squeezed her eyes shut, her heart thumping as she waited for the inevitable thud.

A wheezy huffing noise made her eyes pop open. A ferret-like creature hovered outside the bars of her cage, its shimmery wings a blur of movement. Silver fur covered its long, lithe body, but blue tipped its ears and tail, and made a mask on its face and socks on all four legs.

"What—?"

The creature chittered at her before diving at the cage bars and squeezing through. It landed with a faint thud on the bottom of the cage and sat up on its hind legs, its wings spread out behind it like it was posing for a portrait.

Alice studied the creature, noting its coloring and the cheeky grin that wrinkled its muzzle. "Indigo?"

He dropped to all fours and spun in a circle before bounding over to her and rising to put a paw on her knee. *I knew there was a brain in that lovely skull of yours, my sweet.*

"That's hardly a compliment. I mean, you just toppled off that beam, and it would have been rather odd if a ferret suddenly appeared after all that for no reason. Besides, I know all Fae have an animal form."

The ferret started, tilting its head to stare up at her. *You can understand me?*

Alice lifted an eyebrow. "What do you think?"

The ferret chirped at her and butted its small head against her leg. Alice couldn't help melting a bit with that endearing face looking up at her with its blue mask. She reached down and scratched him under his chin.

The button eyes squinted in pleasure and a deep chuckling sound vibrated the fur under her fingers.

Most of my pets find this form tremendously appealing.

Alice laughed. "I can't say that I blame them. I think I prefer you this way myself."

Suddenly, the ferret shimmered and stretched, and then Indigo was standing there. Much too close for comfort. He leaned a hand on the bar above her head and grinned. "Of course, they find me appealing in all my forms, my sweet."

Alice ducked under his arm and put a safer distance between them. "I thought you weren't supposed to come in here without an invitation."

"You were happy enough to see me a minute ago."

"Yes, well, you were an adorable ferret then, not a..." Alice waved vaguely at him.

"It's all right if you're overwhelmed by my presence. Most are. I can be a lot."

"You've got that right," Alice muttered.

"I didn't quite catch that, my pet."

Alice blew out a breath. So far, he hadn't done more than charm her into this cage and flirt outrageously, but his large body swallowed the space, making her feel claustrophobic. "You need to leave. I don't think your sister or father would be pleased to find you here."

"Is that so?" His smile turned sly as he prowled closer. "But what do you think, my flower? Are you pleased to find me here?"

He stopped right in front of her, and Alice crossed her arms. "I don't recall inviting you, so there's your answer."

"I noticed you didn't say no."

Alice rolled her eyes. "What you *should* notice is that I don't want you in here."

He ignored her, bending down until they were eye to eye and then brushing a thumb over her cheekbone. She jerked her head back, almost hitting it on the bar, and batted his hand away.

"Stop that!"

He straightened and stepped back. "Sorry, it's only I didn't realize humans had eyes the color of dusk. I'll need to remember that when I finish your portrait."

Alice skirted around him and moved to the opposite side of the cage, sending it swaying again. "I never said you could draw my portrait."

He spun towards her; his expression baffled. "You should be thanking me. Everyone wants one of my portraits."

"Well, I don't. I just want you to leave me in peace."

"You're not even a tiny bit curious to see it?" He patted the lump in his pocket.

Alice opened her mouth and then hesitated. Taking this as a yes, Indigo pulled out the sketchbook, flipped it open, and then held it towards her.

She blinked. The drawing showed her laughing up at Poppy. Thistle and Foxglove hovered in the background. The drawing captured such exquisite detail and appeared so realistic, even in charcoal, that she expected all of them to start moving.

"That's... amazing," she finally said.

He flipped the notebook shut and tucked it back into his pocket. "You say that like you're surprised. You *are* aware I'm the court artist, aren't you?" At her blank look, he straightened. "Well, I suppose you wouldn't be, since this *is* your first time in our fair land." He placed a hand on his chest. "I am the artist. My sister is the warrior."

Curiosity overcame Alice's desire for him to leave. "You say that as if you're the only ones."

He shook his head, clearly amused. "You misunderstand. As the king's children, we assume headship in whatever our affinities are." He waved his hand. "My sister ensures the security of the Kingdom while I see to its beauty—both creating it and collecting it."

Alice decided to ignore the way he eyed her when he said that last bit. "Does it bother you that your sister is the warrior?"

Indigo tilted his head. "Why would it? She has to do all that hard work while I get to play." Then he scowled. "Mostly."

"Do you mean the centerpiece everyone keeps asking you about?"

He crossed his arms, and Alice bit her lip to keep from smiling. He looked very much like a toddler denied a sweet. "You'd think I haven't given them the most spectacular pieces year after year, the way they continually pester me about it."

"Well, I wouldn't want to keep you from your work." She moved towards the opposite side of the cage, but he stopped her with a hand on her arm.

"But you make such a lovely distraction, my sweet."

She held up her hands. "Oh no, you're not going to blame me. I've got enough problems as it is, without your father thinking I lured you in here."

Indigo shrugged and leaned his shoulder against the bars. "You wouldn't be the first to seek out my company, my darling pet."

Alice couldn't help snorting. "You seem to forget that I don't actually want your company, and I'll tell your father that if he asks."

"He'll never believe you."

Alice couldn't help rolling her eyes. "You're telling me nobody's ever turned you down? That's rather hard to believe."

"Not since I was about twelve when I hit maturity and grew into my current magnificent self."

Alice couldn't help the laugh that spurted out. "Well, you certainly don't suffer from a lack of self-worth." She shook her head. "You know, it's not good for anyone to always get what they want."

He paused, his mouth curving into a wicked smile. "Is that a challenge, my sweet? If so, I gladly accept."

"For heaven's sake, you daft gongoozler. I'm not challenging you. I just want you to leave already." Alice couldn't keep the exasperation out of her voice.

Her words didn't seem to faze him at all because he merely chuckled. "Now that's one I haven't heard." He leaned forward and pulled on one of her curls. She tried to swat his hand away, but he caught it in his. When she attempted to pull it away, he held fast, using it to pull her a few steps closer.

Alarm speared through Alice. This was more than mere teasing, and she didn't like it. "That's enough, Indigo. Let me go," she snapped.

His smile turned doting as a cool wave washed over her, smothering her annoyance. Her eyelids suddenly weighed almost too much to keep open, and she wanted nothing more than to allow the tranquility humming along her skin to soak into her frayed nerves.

Indigo's silver eyes gleamed as he tucked one of her curls behind her ear. "Better, my pet?"

Alice didn't remember why she had wanted him to leave now. In fact, all she really wanted was to put her head on his shoulder and let him make everything better.

A loud creak made Indigo stiffen, and his head whipped towards the sound. He muttered an unfamiliar word under his breath. Alice blinked, her thoughts suddenly clearing as if a strong wind had blown away the fog in her brain.

She reached to push him away, but his body shimmered and shrank. In the next moment, the ferret was standing on its hind legs chittering while his lacy wings fluttered.

Hide, I need to hide.

Alice crossed her arms and looked down at him. "Well, I'm not going to hide you, not after you used your charm on me like that."

The ferret wrinkled his nose. *You were upset.*

"It doesn't matter. I didn't give you leave—" But the ferret turned his head back towards the tower door as if she weren't speaking.

Azalea appeared there, a scowl on her face. "Indigo? Father sent me to find you."

Indigo wiggled under her blanket, but Alice pointed at him. "He's over here."

Traitor.

She glared at him. "At least I'm not a mind skulker."

Azalea shook her head. "Father is already unhappy with your progress on the centerpiece. Do you really want him to find out you have been wasting time with the prisoner when he told you to leave her alone?"

The ferret stuck his pointed face out from under the blanket and squeaked again.

"I can always throw him out the door if you'd like," Alice called down to Azalea.

That won't be necessary. The ferret gave her a cheeky grin before he scrambled up the bars and out onto the top of her cage. He leapt off, his wings spread out as he glided smoothly to the door.

By the time he landed, he'd returned to his human form. Azalea whirled and marched out of the door without a word. Indigo followed her, but at the last minute, he turned and blew Alice a kiss. "Don't fret. I'll be back soon, my pet."

Alice watched until the door closed again and then sank down to the floor. She let her head fall back against the bars. She'd learned precious few things except for how annoying Indigo was. He certainly wouldn't be any help. She could only hope his project kept him away.

Chapter 11

THE HORDE OF SELBYS milled about the floor of the library, darting around Citrine's feet so she almost lost her balance. At her promise to investigate the odd animal deaths at the Red Palace, they had all started chattering until it was so loud she found it difficult to even think. She moved towards the bellpull, but a tug on her trouser leg stopped her.

When she looked down, she found Hegbert still there. He was trying to say something, but with all the noise, she couldn't hear him.

She crouched down, and he raised his voice. *I meant to ask, Your Majesty, might you have an idea of what's doing this? I'm sure Piggle would thank me if he understood what manner of creature to watch for.*

Citrine shook her head. "I'm afraid I don't, not with any certainty. There's any number of creatures that are capable of tearing up a small animal."

But does they drain the blood?

"That's another thing for me to explore. You can tell Piggle the Pearl Queen has made a promise."

This seemed to satisfy the little selby, and he bobbed his head. *My thanks, ma'am.*

Citrine smiled and then stood up. She waded through the creatures to the bellpull and gave it a sharp tug.

Their news had done nothing to settle her nerves. What she told Hegbert was true. She didn't know for certain what kind of animal might do this, but she had several ideas, none of them good. However, the last thing she needed was for this selby pack to overhear those ideas. They were industrious creatures and could build a small city for themselves in less than a day, but they were also known for their chatter—and their lack of accuracy.

Mind made up, she clapped her hands, and the selbys stopped chittering and turned as one to glance at her.

"I appreciate your visit. As I told Hegbert, I will investigate this immediately, but I must ask you to leave so I can get started. Bliss?" She motioned to her steward, who had appeared at the door, an expression of long-suffering on his sober features.

He bowed his head. "Does Your Majesty require something?"

"Please tell Cook to give the selbys a barrel of nuts and one of berries to thank them for their trouble." The chattering started again, this time higher pitched and more excited. She turned her attention to the creatures milling around the library. "If you'll follow Bliss, he'll take you out and make sure you get your food."

It took several minutes, but eventually the last selby slipped out into the hallway, trailing after Bliss like an extremely long line of ducklings.

Citrine blew out a breath. *Now then.* She strode over to the far side of the room where she kept her selection of bestiaries and thumbed through her favorite volume. Only a few of the creatures she found in its pages were blood drinkers and capable of the savagery described by the selbys, but all of them sent a chill down her spine. She set it down with a heavy heart.

Something brushed against her ankles, and Marmalade's sudden appearance surprised her. She hadn't even heard him leave his shelf. *Bad news, Your Majesty?*

"You mean, besides all the animal deaths?" Citrine drew in a breath. "I'm sorry, Marmalade. I didn't mean to snap at you, and to answer your question, it seems there is a lot going on at the Red Palace at the moment, and none of it is good."

Marmalade sat back and blinked up at her. *How long will you be gone this time?*

Citrine put her hands on her hips. "What makes you think I'm leaving?"

The enormous orange cat quirked an eyebrow.

Citrine sighed. "All right, I am leaving, but I'm not going to the Red Palace. At least not yet. I need more information about that formula, and I'd like a second opinion on what this creature could be, too."

You know what it is?

Citrine grimaced. "I'm hoping I'm wrong about the possibilities."

Then why go at all?

"Because if I am right, this will affect the people at the palace." Citrine pushed up her spectacles and let her gaze wander over the shelves. "And as much as I hate to admit it, I don't think I'll find the answers here."

Several cats on the shelves sat up and hissed.

A smile forced its way onto her face. "Don't be like that," she said. "The formula was created by an Alchemist. Since I am not one myself, that means I need to talk to someone who is It's not an aspersion on the library."

Several the cats flopped back down, but Isla still bristled. *Where will you go, Your Majesty, to find these answers, if not the Red Palace?*

Citrine smiled. "You should know who it is since you're the one who suggested him in the first place. I'm going to Sir Lapin, of course." She scooped up the book she'd been reading, as well as the notebooks she'd taken from Sacklepenny's laboratory. "Hopefully, as he's such a skilled Alchemist, he'll have some answers for me about this creature as well."

Isla sniffed. *I suppose he is decent at it, for a giant rabbit.*

Citrine let out a huff of laughter. "It just bothers you he's a rabbit at all."

The black-and-white cat lifted a dainty paw and licked it. Citrine gave the cat a fond smile. As she slipped out of the library so she could pack for her trip, she wondered if Zander knew the crisis that might be brewing in his own garden.

Chapter 12

CHESS ROLLED OVER AGAIN, the covers tangling around his legs. Exasperated, he kicked them off and climbed out of bed. For the thousandth time, he picked up the smooth stone—the twin of the one he'd given Alice—from the table by his bed. He rubbed a thumb over it, willing it to glow. He'd promised himself he wouldn't contact her first.

What was she doing now? Was she happy back with her family? Had her father given Hadley the heave-ho yet? From what Alice had told him about her Papa James, it seemed like the he wouldn't take the young man's pushiness kindly. Had she even given Chess a thought?

Chess dragged a hand through his hair and set the stone back on his bedside table. What if he went there and visited? He'd toyed with the idea of visiting Alice in her world more than once lately. He wondered what her Papa James would have to say about him.

Chess grinned to himself. He wasn't known for his charm for no reason. The smile melted away. But would

Alice want that? It was one thing when they had found themselves in a life or death situation, but now that she had returned to her own family and friends, back in her normal life, would she even want to see him?

He ran a hand through his hair. Even if he wanted to go through the Looking Glass, with everything going on at the palace, he couldn't leave Zander right now.

But he *could* get a snack from the kitchens. Certainly, pacing around his room torturing himself with thoughts of Alice wasn't helping him get back to sleep.

His mind made up, he slipped into the dark hallway and paused. Quiet hung over the place, everyone having gone to bed hours ago. Avoiding the well-known creaks, he padded down the hallway and towards the back servants' stairs that led to the kitchens. No need to traipse through the entire palace.

He trotted down the stairs and slipped into the kitchen, looking around the dimly lit room. Neat piles of vegetables waited on one of the long tables for tomorrow's meals. He passed a basket of eggs and another one with glowberries in it. He grabbed a handful and popped one in his mouth, the juice bursting over his taste buds. His nose twitched, and he followed the smell of cinnamon and vanilla.

Cook had made her famous breakfast tartlets. He snagged one and bit into it, crumbs scattering on his chest, which he absently brushed off as the flavors danced over his tongue. He finished it in three bites and grabbed another one before opening the cold larder and pulling out a bottle of milk. With a half dozen more in there, he didn't feel guilty as he drank straight from the bottle.

He finished the last bite of tartlet and looked at the rest regretfully, but he knew even his charm wouldn't save him if he left Cook in the lurch. She had a soft spot for him, but if she came downstairs to find the better part of the breakfast she had prepared, eaten, he didn't want to be around for the repercussions. He drained the last of the milk and looked at the bottle in his hand.

Even though he was a favorite of Cook's, that didn't mean he wanted to leave any evidence. Cook kept a tub of water out back to rinse the bottles, so he nipped through the back door to the courtyard that spanned the space between the back of the palace and where the horses and griffons were kept. It wasn't a place anyone but the staff frequented much.

Sure enough, he found the water tub, already filled for the morning breakfast dishes. Chess dipped the bottle in and then dumped the water onto the ground. He did this several times and then turned to put the bottle in a crate that held the ones ready to be used again.

He'd just tucked the bottle inside when a sound caused him to whirl around. Someone stumbled around the corner, coming from the direction of the stables and the griffon atrium. From here, he couldn't make out the person's identity, but he was too big to be Will, the stable boy. Chess knew the head groom had gone home since his wife was having a baby—or perhaps she'd already had it. The person seemed to sense him and turned in his direction.

Chess ducked down and, in a moment, was in his cat form, and none too soon. The person stared towards where he'd just been standing, but the moonlight cloaked the person's features in shadows. Chess slunk around the back of the pile of crates and crouched, his black fur melding him into the darkness.

After a moment, the person started walking again, his gait oddly familiar, before disappearing from view. Chess blew out a breath, his mind spinning. It couldn't be who he thought it was, yet when he went back over the past few days, it made a horrible kind of sense.

Somehow, he doubted he'd be visiting Alice any time soon.

Chapter 13

THE MOONLIGHT TRICKLED DOWN through the branches, and all was tranquil and hushed. Alice waited until the noises from Tweed's cage stopped, and she was reasonably sure nobody would enter the tower.

Still, she looked around, her eyes searching the shadowy beams and her ears straining for any sounds.

While she wouldn't be surprised by another sneaky entrance from Indigo, the realization came to her after he had departed that the only access to the tower was through the doors located at each landing. That left only two options. Either he had come in as she slept, or he'd slipped in when the faeries had brought her dinner.

What a git she was to let his sudden appearance shake her up so much. It wasn't as if he had magically appeared out of thin air. He'd had to sneak in which meant she could be on her guard when it was likely he'd try again. Alice pulled the stone out of her pocket. A bit of moonlight glinted off the shiny blue-green surface.

She turned the stone over in her palm, and she tried to recall Chess's instructions. They remained hazy in her mind, but she thought she remembered the steps.

Turning the shiny side back up, she rubbed the stone with her thumb and concentrated on Chess's face.

Nothing happened.

She drew in a long breath and let it out slowly. She could do this.

She stared at the object and squeezed her eyes shut.

Chess's blue eyes and smile loomed up in her memory.

She peeked at the stone.

Still nothing.

She tried again, but this time she called his name softly.

The stone merely lay inert, its shiny exterior opaque.

Was it like a telephone and he wasn't answering?

Alice blew out a breath. His instructions had sounded so easy when he told her, but she didn't really know how this type of magic worked.

She blinked back tears. What if he had placed the stone somewhere or forgotten about her?

Alice wiped at her eyes, impatient. How ridiculous. She'd probably done something wrong.

Carefully, she placed the stone on her leg and ran her thumb over the object once more. "Chess, Chess, please answer," she whispered.

But nothing happened.

Alice pressed her lips together to stop their trembling and slid the stone back into her pocket.

She'd try later. It was late, after all. He was most likely in bed, asleep. She'd have to try during the daytime when there was a better chance he'd respond.

Alice pulled the blanket up to her chin and laid down, staring up at the vine-covered canopy above her head.

Everything would be fine. Even if she couldn't reach Chess, the Fae King would have her tested and then he'd send her on her way. She only needed to be patient, and she'd get out of here.

But no matter how many times she repeated this to herself, Alice didn't quite believe that.

Chapter 14

THE COMMANDER AND THE King left the breakfast room as Zander pushed back his own plate. "Those tartlets are some of Cook's finer creations."

"Mm-hmm." Chess avoided eye contact and toyed with the food on his plate.

Zander frowned. Chess usually loved the tartlets, but several bites of his pastry still sat untouched. He had also been abnormally quiet this morning. A pang of sympathy squeezed Zander's chest. He understood how his friend felt. "Well, there's nothing keeping you from going to see her."

Chess looked up at him. "Alice's only just returned home. I don't think she'd want me to show up on her doorstep unannounced this quickly."

Zander bit back a smile at the fact that Chess hadn't even asked him to clarify who he was talking about. He hadn't realized quite how deep his friend's feelings ran. "Alice might be happier to see you than you think. She..."

A commotion outside the breakfast room interrupted him. He exchanged a glance with Chess, and they both got to their feet. Chess was first through the door. Zander followed on his heels, apprehension making his stomach clench. What now?

They reached the front entrance to find the Commander on one knee in front of an almost hysterical stable boy. The King hovered behind him. The morning light revealed a drawn expression on his face and pronounced dark circles under his eyes.

"Lad, you need to get ahold of yourself. I can't understand what you are saying." The Commander's voice was firm as he gripped the boy's shoulders.

The boy drew in a shuddering breath and then another before he tried to speak. "I was feeding the griffons, sir, likes I always does in the mornings after the horses, so's they ain't spooked. Simpkin says I haves a way with 'em—the griffons, not the horses, although I does fine with them too—Simpkin's gone cause his missus is having another little one and they can be right fractious when they's hungry. The griffons, I mean." The boy paused and tilted his head. "I suppose little 'uns can be fractious too when they's hungry. My little sisters—"

"Just tell us, boy," the King snapped.

The boy turned wide eyes on the King, and his breath sped up again. A flicker of annoyance passed over the Commander's face before he suppressed it. "Simpkin told me you've been very reliable, but I need you to tell me what's happened. Can you do that?"

The boy nodded so hard, his hat flopped off his head onto the ground. "I... I always saves Verros for last." His eyes darted toward the King, and he cowered at the ferocious scowl on the King's face.

"Spit it out." The King's face was turning red, and the Commander shot a quelling look at his brother before he turned back to the stable boy.

"And then what happened?"

Zander watched his father's face turn a mottled purple, the veins at his temples throbbing. He'd rarely seen his father lose his temper and certainly never over something like this. He'd always treated the staff with great kindness. Moving closer, Zander put a hand on his shoulder only to have his father shrug it off.

The boy's stuttering voice pulled his attention away from his father and back to the story he was trying to tell. "Well, sir, the first thing I noticed was the door to the griffon atrium. It was open, and then when I got to Verros's stall, I didn't see him." He paused and took a shuddering breath. "I thought he'd gotten out. He's right smart and I wouldn't puts it past him to learn how to unlock his door. Although he'd have to be a right genius to open the big atrium door."

"Did you leave the door open, and he got out? Is that why you're so upset because you think you'll be in trouble?" The Commander patted the boy's shoulder. "He'll come back. It's well-known he's a bit of a rascal and—"

"No, he was there all right." The boy interrupted him. "But he was all tore up." His voice ended in a wail.

The Commander squeezed his shoulder before he fished a large handkerchief out of his pocket. He thrust it into the boy's hands and stood up, leaving the boy to bring himself back under control. He caught Zander's eye. "We'd best check this out. I'm sure there's a reasonable explanation." He gestured at the boy. "Come along and show us."

"I don't like this," Chess said, his tone tight.

"I don't either. I'm afraid of what we're going to find. Do you think it's like those animals Dugin's been finding?"

Chess's lips tightened into a thin line. "Well, we won't find out standing here."

Together they followed the Commander, the King, and the boy into the griffon atrium. It was in a separate building from the horses, about twice as large and about three times as tall. Three of the four griffons housed there moved restlessly in their individual aviaries, some swooping close to the sides of the individual enclosures, and others clawing at their doors.

Hesperus, the Commander's griffon, had her head out of the window built into the side of all the atriums, her sharp eyes watching the parade of people going past. Chess gave the griffon a wide berth. She had never been overly fond of him.

Zander paused in front of her, his gaze assessing. Her intelligent eyes looked back at him and she chirruped, tilting her head. Then she craned her neck to gaze down the center aisle before looking back at him. He grimaced. "I'm sorry, Hesperus. I wish I could understand you." He held up his palm, and she butted her beak against it. "If either Citrine or Alice were here, they'd understand what you were trying to tell me," he murmured before moving to stand with Chess outside Verros's atrium.

The Commander gestured at the stable boy and the King to stand back as he pulled open the door. Zander sucked in a breath, his stomach turning at the sight in front of him. The griffon was lying crumpled on the ground, one of his forelegs at an unnatural angle. Long gashes exposed muscle and sinew. A large bite wound on the griffon's neck still seeped blood, staining the animal's feathers a deep blue. The beast's eyes were closed, and its breath rasped in and out.

The King cried out and dropped to his knees next to his griffon and laid a hand on its neck feathers. Verros's eye slitted open, and it seemed to take the creature a moment to register who was there.

Suddenly, the griffon let out a shriek and snapped, its beak catching the side of the King's leg and drawing blood. The King scrambled away, his face drawn in shock and hurt.

The Commander helped him to his feet. "We'll have one of the Palace Healers check that. I'm sure it's because he's in pain."

The King ran a hand over his face, and Zander noticed it wasn't completely steady. "Yes, I suppose you're right." The King's shoulders sagged. "Do you think he's too far gone? Can we save him? I hate to see him in pain like this."

Zander turned his gaze away from his father's tortured expression. He seemed completely distraught. Not that the situation wasn't upsetting, but his father's reaction was... too extreme. He'd always been steady during any crisis.

The Commander lifted one shoulder in a gesture that was eerily similar to Chess. "We'll send for a Palace Healer, but I don't know if he'll be able to get close enough." He motioned to Anders, who had trailed them to the atrium. "Go get Collins. I think he's around some-where." Anders gave a nod of his head before he sprinted off towards the palace.

Chess stepped closer. "It's too bad we don't have someone with the Creature Gift. They could soothe the beast and perhaps find out what did this." His blue eyes watched the King.

The King's face paled noticeably. Then his expression twisted, and he whirled towards the stable boy, who had been standing silently off to the side, twisting the Commander's handkerchief in his hands. "This is your fault, boy."

The boy's eyes widened, and he shook his head, back-ing away from the King.

"You allowed this to happen to my beloved griffon. What were you doing?" He grabbed the boy's arm and shook him. "Did you sneak off somewhere? Answer me!"

The boy opened his mouth, but nothing came out. The King shook him again. "You'll pay for this. Lock him in the dungeon." He shoved him away, and the boy stumbled against the wall. His small face crumpled into sobs as he rubbed his shoulder. "I... I... I'm sorry, Sire. I... I... never left. I swear."

The King's arm reared back, and Zander shook off his shock in time to step in front of the boy. He caught his father's arm and dropped his voice. "Father, please, get ahold of yourself. I know you're upset—"

The King jerked away, his hand curling into a fist and his lips twisting into a snarl. Zander almost didn't recognize the man in front of him.

"Stop it!" Zander's voice rang out sharply, and his fa-ther froze. His face went slack and his eyes lost focus. A shudder ran through him before he blinked and looked around, as if confused.

The Commander put a hand on the King's shoulder. "We should return to the palace. The Council is meeting in less than an hour. The Healer will take care of Verros or put him out of his misery." He pointed to a man in a dark tunic and trousers that was rushing up the aisle.

The King nodded. He reached towards the griffon and then paused, his hand hovering in the air. With a sigh, he pulled it back and shuffled towards the entrance. "Yes, yes, you're right. We need to get ready for the Council meeting."

The Commander gave Zander a long look before he guided the King out of the atrium. His father didn't even acknowledge the Healer as the man hurriedly bowed before rushing towards the injured griffon.

Zander briefly explained to the Healer what was wrong and then moved out of the way to allow the man to work. He hoped they wouldn't have to put Verros down.

He turned to find Chess crouched next to the boy, who was sniffling into the handkerchief. "I don't want to... to... go to be... be locked up."

"The King was only upset, Will. You aren't headed for the dungeons." Chess looked up at Zander. "Tell him."

"But... but the King said." Will wiped his nose with his sleeve.

Zander smiled down at the boy. "Well, I'm the Prince, and I'm telling you that nobody is taking you to the dungeons, but I would suggest you stay out of the King's way for a few days." He ruffled the boy's hair. "Now, don't you have some work that needs doing?"

The boy scuffed his toe against the floor. "I... I... guess. If you're sure. I don't want to get any more trouble than I'm already in."

"You won't," Zander assured him.

After a brief hesitation, the boy ran off towards the horse stables. Chess rose to his feet. "This has to be related to what Dugin told us yesterday."

Zander pressed his lips together. Chess was right, but he wasn't sure how much more he could handle.

Chapter 15

ALICE BLINKED BLEARY EYES at the stone lying in her palm. She hadn't slept well, worry waking her repeatedly through the night. Even though she kept telling herself the King would let her go once he found out she was telling the truth, doubt flared every time she looked at Arthur's cage. Would that be her in five years?

When the first rays of the sun had peeked through the vines above, she had given up on sleep. She had tried the stone multiple times, but nothing had happened, but it was very early.

Now she pulled it back out and set it down, rubbing her eyes. She just needed to concentrate. She glanced around. Rustling noises came from Arthur's cage, and its gentle swaying showed he was awake. If she wanted to try again with no one seeing, she needed to hurry.

Alice took a deep breath and leaned over. Rubbing her thumb along its smooth greenish- blue surface, she carefully brought Chess's face to mind. Her heart twisted as she remembered his smile.

She whispered his name so that Arthur didn't hear her.

"That won't work in here." The tiny voice made Alice jump.

She closed her hand over the stone and whirled towards the sound. Poppy and Thistle hovered outside the bars of her cage, a basket between them.

"Erm, how did you... where..." Alice stammered. How had she not heard the door opening on the nearest landing?

Poppy pointed towards the distant floor of the tower. "Down there."

Alice squinted into the gloom below but couldn't make out any of the doors near the ground. "But why wouldn't you..."

Poppy anticipated her question. "It's easier to fly through the tower than make all the turns up those stairs. One time, we were in a hurry—Foxglove and me—and we banged the basket on the wall and lost half of Arthur's supper. Bluebell was so angry—"

Thistle raised her voice, talking over her sister. "May we enter?"

Alice nodded and slid the stone back into her pocket, hoping Poppy would forget about it. "What did you bring me this morning? Last night's dinner was delicious."

They set the basket down. Thistle set to work unloading it, but Poppy wasn't so easily distracted as Alice had hoped.

She pointed at Alice's pocket. "Was that a communion stone? The tower mutes those kinds of objects so you can't use them. Of course, that only makes sense because you don't want prisoners escaping or hurting someone or—"

"I wasn't trying to—"

Poppy giggled. "Yes, you were. I saw you. Who's Chess? Is he your sweetheart? Is he more handsome than Prince Indigo? Is that why you don't want to be his pet? Violet said he's been grumpy all morning, and when he found out about—"

"Poppy," Thistle said, interrupting her sister's stream of words, "come help me."

Poppy huffed out a breath but zipped over to join Thistle. She pulled out a bowl of pink berries and set them in front of Alice while Thistle unloaded some kind of pastry along with a glass bottle of water.

Alice picked up a berry and then prompted, "Found out about what?"

Poppy paused in tugging out another bottle, this one filled with pale-green sparkling liquid. With a quick glance at her sister, she blurted, "Another dead Fae, which proves you didn't kill the bumble, which I always knew. I told Violet and Foxglove that it couldn't be you even though Foxglove—ouch!" Poppy dropped the bottle into Alice's lap and rubbed her arm where Thistle had pinched her. "Why'd you do that?" She glared at her sister .

Thistle's face twisted with guilt and worry. "I'm sorry, Poppy, but we can't—"

"No, please, I need to know," Alice said, getting up on her knees. "Will they let me go now?"

Thistle's eyes widened. Even her halo of white curls seemed to bristle. "I truly have no idea." When Poppy opened her mouth, Thistle shook her head. "You don't either, Poppy." She turned back to Alice. "Nobody tells us important things like that."

"Maybe not, but they always talk around us like we aren't there. You can learn ever so much that way," Poppy said, a mischievous grin on her face.

"We should go," said Thistle, flying over to the basket. "Mr. Tweed still needs his breakfast."

Alice laid a hand on the basket. "Can you at least tell me if they'll do that testing today?"

Thistle hesitated. "Perhaps, but everyone will be busy with the Feast. They might wait until after."

Alice's stomach dropped at this news. "But that's three more days."

Thistle frowned. "If they wait until after the Feast, it will be longer than that." She started counting on her fingers. "The Feast itself lasts two days, but then everyone lies about for at least two more after that."

Alice's shoulders slumped. "You mean I could be stuck in this cage for another week, even though they know I'm innocent?"

Thistle's mouth turned up in a timid smile. "We'll take good care of you, and I'm sure they'll let you go—"

"But that's not all," interrupted Poppy and flew to hover in front of Alice. "After they found this last one, someone came forward." She dropped her voice to a conspiratorial whisper. "She said she spotted—"

"Poppy!" Thistle picked up her end of the basket. "Come on, we have to get this to Mr. Tweed. Bluebell will wonder what's taking us so long."

"But this is the best part, Thistle."

Thistle gave her a long look. "Do you want to help Foxglove empty the chamber pots?"

Poppy made a face and flew over to the basket, picking up her end of the handle. As they flew towards the cage door, Poppy twisted back and blurted, "It was a Jabberwock. They saw a Jabberwock!"

Alice jumped to her feet. "Wait!"

But Thistle pulled on her end of the handle, hurrying her sister along. "I'm sorry. We have to go."

The two buzzed out the cage door and circled upward towards Tweed's cage. Alice sank back onto the floor and picked up the pastry, her mind turning over what she'd learned. What had she stumbled into?

Chapter 16

CHESS WATCHED WILL RUN towards the stables, replaying this morning's events, especially the King's odd behavior and what he'd witnessed during the night. He didn't want to believe the conclusion he'd come to.

"I don't understand this." Zander thumped his fist against his thigh. "What could do this?"

Chess didn't want to voice his suspicions until he had tangible proof to show Zander, so he shrugged. "Unfortunately, Verros and the rest of the griffons are the only ones who could tell us that. We need someone with the Creature Gift." He gave Zander a pointed look.

"I can guess what you're going to say, and the answer is no." Zander turned and started walking.

Chess hurried after him. "At least send her a raven. Let her know what's going on."

Zander didn't stop walking. "No! The last thing I want is Citrine coming here right now."

"Zan, she'd want to help. Verros could tell her what happened last night."

Zander glanced back to where the Healer was kneeling outside the griffon's stall. "He lost so much blood, he probably won't make it, anyway. No use having her travel all this way for nothing."

Chess finally caught up. He needed to convince Zander so they could know. "Even if he doesn't, Hesperus or one of the others probably saw what happened too. I realize you're afraid…"

Zander whirled towards him, lifting his hand to point back at the stable doors. "Yes, I'm afraid. Something vicious enough to almost kill a griffon is loose. Of course I don't want Citrine here."

Chess crossed his arms. "You act like I don't care what happens to Citrine. She's been my friend for as long as she's been yours."

"Would you want Alice here? She's got the Creature Gift too. Maybe you can shove her down the Rabbit Hole again."

"Hey, I did that to save your hide." Chess blew out a breath. "If you're asking if I'd want her in danger, I think you know the answer to that, but I'd give her the choice to help. It's what I should have done the first time around."

Zander's head drooped until his chin almost touched his chest. "It's only… I have enough to worry about without bringing Citrine into this mess."

He looked so weary, Chess hated to push him, but he did it anyway because it would be better to know—for all of them. "You can't let this go. We have to find out what—or *who*—is doing this."

"Nobody is more aware of that than I am." Zander ran a hand over his face. "Can you at least let me get through this Council meeting? Who knows, perhaps Beecher will convince the others to throw me out, and it won't even be my problem anymore."

Chess rolled his eyes. "Someday, he's going to give himself apoplexy with all his blustering. You can't let that windbag get to you."

Zander snorted. "Easy for you to say. He's not after your head."

"All the more reason that you need help."

Zander shrugged and started walking again, and Chess fell into step with him. "Who do you suggest? I don't want to bring in someone I'd have to explain all this to."

Chess turned over the possibilities, discarding one name after another until finally it hit him. "Sir Lapin. He's steady and already knows about everything, and he's also an Alchemist and a Scholar. He might not have the Creature Gift, but besides Citrine, he's your best bet in helping to solve this."

Zander nodded. "He's a good choice. I'll send a raven after we're done with this Council meeting." He grimaced, and Chess felt a pang of sympathy for him.

"It'll be fine, Zan. The King's on your side, and I've got your back too." The words felt like a lie as soon as they crossed his lips, but he couldn't tell Zander what he suspected was the truth. Not right before the man had to meet with the Council. He only hoped the delay wouldn't come back to haunt him.

Chapter 17

Alice completed her last lap around the cage and plopped down on her cushion. She uncorked the glass bottle of water and took a long drink before setting it down again.

Above her, the sound of footsteps echoed, and Arthur's cage swayed gently.

After a few minutes, they halted, and Arthur's face appeared. "Did you finish your exercise, too, Miss Alice?" he called down to her.

"I did!"

"Excellent. I've found if you merely sit, it depresses the spirits. Movement helps tremendously."

"You're right. I do feel much better."

"Very good. I'm going to take a rest now. I find if I stick to a routine, it helps me to stay positive. You might want to try putting your own routine together."

"That's a good idea," she said and waved. He waved back, and then his face disappeared again.

She sighed. While the burst of exercise had helped, the rest of the day stretched out in front of her. Honestly, how the man had kept his wits after five years was beyond her. It was only the third day for Alice, and she was ready to scream with frustration and boredom.

Besides Arthur, her only visitors had been the three faery sisters. Foxglove had returned to meal delivery this morning. Alice smirked. She'd been very polite. Apparently, she hadn't enjoyed her chamber pot duties.

At this point, she'd almost welcome Indigo's company so she'd have something to focus on, something besides being stuck in here. She flopped back and cushioned her head in her clasped hands and stared up at the canopy of vines and flowers. Clouds scudded by, interspersed with sunshine.

A breeze rocked her cage, and the scents of flowers and vanilla wafted through the tower. Her eyelids grew heavy. Maybe Arthur was onto something and she should take a nap. It wasn't that she was tired, exactly...

"Time to wake up, my sweet." Indigo's voice startled Alice, and she shot up to a sitting position.

Indigo lounged on a nearby beam, and she immediately took back her former wish. She didn't want Indigo here, especially when she still hadn't cleared the sleep cobwebs from her brain. She pulled the blanket into her lap as if it would somehow shield her from him.

"What are you doing here?"

"I assumed you'd be happier to see me since I've managed to get your testing moved up. You did say that's what you wanted, isn't it?"

Alice examined his face warily, afraid to get her hopes up after his last visit. "I'm not sure I believe you."

Indigo frowned. "That hurts, my flower. It truly does. Here I went to all this trouble—when I'm quite busy getting ready for the Feast myself—and not only don't I get a thank-you, but you doubt me."

"Well, after the last time—"

"No, no"—he waved a hand and rose gracefully to his feet—"if that's the way you feel, I can go tell Father we can wait until after the Feast. It's a tremendous disappointment to me, of course. I had hoped to take you to the festivities as my guest, but Father really is quite busy." He turned and walked along the beam away from her.

Alice scrambled to her feet and hurled herself against the bars. "Wait! I'm sorry. I only—"

He whirled back towards her and tilted his head. "What was that?" He cupped a hand to his ear. "You'll have to repeat it because I didn't quite hear what you said."

Cheeks burning, Alice forced herself to say, "I'm sorry... for doubting you."

Indigo beamed at her. "That's what I thought you said. Now, I'm sure you'd like to thank me for doing you this great kindness."

"Of course. Thank you. I do appreciate it."

He *tsk*ed at her. "I don't think that's an adequate thank-you for this kind of favor. Do you?"

Alice crossed her arms. "In your opinion, what is adequate, Indigo?"

A smile slid across his face and his silver eyes gleamed even as he tapped his chin with a finger. "Let's see..." He snapped his fingers. "A kiss from your lovely lips would do."

Alice narrowed her eyes. "If you think—"

The creak of a door interrupted her, and she spun towards the sound. Azalea stood in the tower door. She pulled the lever, and the cage lurched forward. Alice yelped and grabbed onto the bars to keep her balance as it slid downward. The cage moved smoothly until it bumped against the stone ledge.

Azalea's face twisted into annoyance, and she scowled. For a minute, Alice wondered what she'd done to upset the other woman until she realized Azalea wasn't looking at her. Alice followed the other woman's stare and blinked.

Indigo, in his ferret form, scampered down the vine attached to her cage, his little blue face scrunched in concentration. He leapt onto the top of her cage and slithered through the bars.

He grinned up at her, his silver eyes shining. Even as she watched, the creature shimmered and stretched until Indigo stood next to her. He winked. "Admit it, you find my ferret irresistible, don't you?"

Azalea gave an irritated sigh. "Ignore him, and come along. It is time to test your signature."

Dread curled in Alice's stomach and it must have showed on her face because Indigo's expression softened. "Don't look so glum. I'll come with you and hold your hand, shall I?" As if to underscore his words, he grasped her hand, but she pulled away from him.

Azalea gestured at Alice impatiently. "Do not dawdle. King Thorne wants this done right away, so it does not interfere with the Feast." She pointed a finger at Indigo. "You do not need to come with us. You have work to do."

Indigo's mouth pulled into a frown. "But I want to. I have to see—"

The Fae woman didn't give him time to finish. "I do not have time to argue with you. Come or go, it is your hide with Father." She spun on her heel and started down the stairs, her wings rustling.

Once again Alice followed Azalea, the narrow staircase forcing Indigo to fall behind her.

At least this time, they were going in the right direction. She sincerely hoped she would never see that cage again. She paused, guilt nipping at her, as she remembered Arthur. Perhaps she could speak to King Thorne about him.

Indigo stepped up behind her, his hair tickling her cheek as he leaned down to speak in her ear. "Don't be nervous, pet. The testing won't hurt—much."

She swatted his hair out of her face, but a shiver of apprehension slid down Alice's spine. What did that mean?

They reached the bottom of the stairs to find a huge Fae man waiting. He was easily a foot taller than Alice and about three times as wide. His skin was a deep brown and his eyes and hair were both black. His tufted ears pushed up on the sides of his head in two triangles. She stopped and took an involuntary step back, only to run into Indigo's chest.

He put his hands on her shoulders and leaned down. "Don't be afraid, my sweet. Fariar is not as scary as he looks." Indigo's chuckle tickled her ear, and she scrunched her shoulder up. "In fact, he's probably much kinder than the rest of us."

Alice looked back at Indigo. "I should thank you for arranging this. I really do appreciate it."

Next to her, Azalea snorted. "This is not Indigo's doing. Fariar is making a trip after the Feast. If he did not test you now, it would be weeks. Father did not want there to be trouble with the Red Palace, if your story is true."

Alice turned and glared at Indigo, her hands curling into fists.

Indigo held up his hands. "Now, now, I'm the one that reminded Father of Fariar's trip."

"You deliberately misled me."

Indigo shrugged. "I might have exaggerated a tiny bit, but if it weren't for me, you'd have been in that cage for weeks. Tell her, Azalea."

A faint smile tugged at the Fae woman's lips. "It is always best to assume my brother is not telling you all of the truth, and what he is telling you is for his own benefit."

Fariar interrupted, holding his hand out to Alice. "Come. I must test you." His deep voice reverberated up her spine, but his tone was gentle.

Still, Alice's feet refused to move until Indigo gave her a little push. She stumbled forward, and Fariar caught her elbow to steady her. He scowled over her head as Indigo stepped closer to Alice. "I do not need your help, Indigo."

"But I promised my pet I would come with her. She already doesn't trust my word. I can't go back on what I said now."

Alice didn't even look at Indigo but directly at Fariar. "I don't need anyone to come with me."

Fariar looked down at Alice and smiled. It transformed his fearsome appearance. "You have my word that I will not hurt you. The test is not completely painless, but it is nothing to dread, either."

Alice's gaze swung to Indigo and then back to Fariar. "Let's get this done, then."

"But you need me, pet." Indigo moved to follow them, but Azalea stopped him.

"Fariar does not need your help, brother, and the woman does not want you."

Alice bit back her smile as she followed the big man down an adjacent tunnel. She suspected Azalea had enjoyed that a bit too much. As they walked further, her nerves jittered. She squared her shoulders. No matter what this involved, it didn't matter because it was her ticket home.

Chapter 18

BY THE TIME THEY reached the meeting room, most of the Council was already there. Chess felt dismayed when he spotted Baron Belier.

He was talking to Lord Beecher.

The moment Zander caught sight of them, his step faltered, and he paused. Chess nudged him with his elbow. "I see the two blowhards found each other."

"Keep your voice down. I have enough problems without them hearing you."

Chess lifted a shoulder. "It's not as if they can think any less of you."

Zander winced. "Thanks for pointing that out."

Chess grinned and winked. "Any time I can be of help."

A small smile hovered on Zander's face.

Good. Mission accomplished. Zander needed to be more forceful with the Council, but his blasted Drifter Gene made him fear men like Beecher and Belier. While it wouldn't do to underestimate either man or his in-fluence, he wished Zander would remember he was a prince and didn't need to kowtow to the likes of either man like that.

Both men turned to watch Zander and Chess. Lord Beecher's mouth puckered like he'd tasted a lemon. "It's a shame that such a promising lad is now useless."

Zander stiffened beside him, but he nodded at both men as if he were oblivious to the comment. "Lord Beecher. Baron Belier. It's good to see you both."

Chess wasn't sure how Zander could get those words past his lips. Chess hadn't even said them, and they still left a nasty taste in his mouth.

Belier gave a bow, but Beecher stared at Zander and thumped his cane. "Don't think suave manners are going to do anything to change my mind, Your Highness." The old man lifted his quivering chins. "I plan to propose your dethronement today. I believe it's only fair to warn you." He thumped his cane again to underscore his words.

Belier shifted uneasily next to him, his gaze darting between the Prince and Beecher. Chess had to give the old man points for sheer brazenness.

Beside him, Zander's hands clenched, but his expression remained neutral. "You must do as you see fit, Lord Beecher. That is why you're on the Council, after all."

"Don't think I won't." His mouth twisted. "Pah, how the King allows you to stay within the palace walls. Now that it's known you're a Drifter, that only shows his judgment is also suspect."

Zander's body stiffened. He opened his mouth to respond, but Chess jumped in. "Careful, Lord Beecher. That sounds awfully close to treason, wouldn't you say, Baron Belier?"

The other man ran a finger around his collar. "Well... that is, I don't..."

Beecher frowned at the baron and elbowed him so hard the other man staggered. "Stiffen that spine of yours, Baron. Nobody likes a wet noodle." The Baron's face flushed, and he muttered at his shoes, but Beecher ignored him, focusing his beady eyes on Chess. "I don't know who you think you are, Felinas, talking to me that way, but I'd watch yourself. You're nothing but a half-flit."

Chess grinned. "Better a half-flit than a full blowhard."

He only had a moment to enjoy the older man's spluttering before a heavy hand landed on his shoulder. "If you'll excuse us, Beecher. I need to talk to my son."

Chess resisted the urge to roll his eyes more because he didn't want to give Beecher the satisfaction. Instead, he spun around to face his father, dislodging the hand on his shoulder. He kept his grin firmly in place when he spoke. "Lead on, Commander. You know how I love our father-son chats."

His father's face remained neutral, but his jaw ticked. Chess couldn't deny the sense of satisfaction it gave him.

Zander hesitated, looking between Chess and his uncle. The Commander waved him towards the room. "You best get in there. The King will want to start soon."

Zander hesitated, but then nodded and stepped into the meeting room. The Commander drew Chess down the hallway. Once they were out of earshot, his displeasure bloomed across his face. "What do you think you're doing?"

Chess lifted one shoulder. "Putting that old man in his place." He lifted an eyebrow. "Which someone should have done a long time ago."

The Commander frowned. "Even if that was true, it's certainly not your job to do so. The King and Zander are in a precarious situation at the moment. You antagonizing their biggest detractor isn't helpful."

Chess crossed his arms. "So, what? I'm supposed to let the man insult Zander to his face? He even was questioning the fitness of the King. If anyone should shut up, it's him, not me!"

The Commander's expression softened for a fraction of a second before closing down to that neutral nothingness that made Chess crazy. "I appreciate your loyalty to your cousin and your uncle, but your jabs won't help them. Worse, they might hurt them."

Chess shifted restlessly. "Fine, I'll keep my thoughts about Beecher and that spineless wonder Belier to myself." He gestured towards the meeting room. "But shouldn't we get in there? I promise I'll let you lecture me later."

The Commander's lips pressed into a thin line. "Actually, Chess, you won't be attending this meeting. Your words only prove that you're a liability to both the Prince and the King."

Hurt flared in Chess's chest, but he pushed it down. "You can't..." He trailed off as he realized what this meant. He made his tone petulant. No use making the Commander suspicious. "All right. Fine. I'll stay out here."

The Commander narrowed his eyes. "Just stay out of trouble. We have enough of it already."

Chess rolled his eyes this time. "I heard you." He made a shooing gesture. "You should probably get in there. The King and Zander need at least one person on their side now that you've kicked me out."

The Commander gave Chess a hard stare. "I'll be leaving right after this meeting. I trust you won't stir up trouble while I'm gone."

Chess smirked. "I'll miss you too."

The Commander's mouth thinned. "Try to limit the damage you do with that mouth of yours." With those parting words, he turned on his heel and headed into the meeting. Chess waited a long minute until the door to the meeting room closed before he trotted off towards the King's royal quarters. He wouldn't get a better chance to look for that proof. Who knew the Commander would be the one to give him the opportunity?

Chess padded into the King's chambers, his nose twitching. He'd had to sweet talk more than one maid to get down here, and he had to slip into his cat form when he'd almost run into Anders.

He prowled the perimeter of the room. On the surface, everything appeared normal. Someone had made the massive bed and tied back the surrounding curtains. Nothing appeared out of order. Which didn't surprise him, really. The King leaving things lying around that could cast suspicion on the himself would be the height of idiocy, especially with servants in and out of this room.

But that didn't mean there wasn't something here to find. Chess's nose twitched again. He smelled something faint, but—he wrinkled his nose—putrid.

He followed the scent trail under the bed, a massive dark cavern. Chess pressed on, crawling further and further until he reached where the wall and headboard met. Puzzled, he strained his eyes, searching for what he had smelled. He saw nothing, but the smell was potent now to his heightened cat senses. He followed the trail until his nose pressed against the wall. What in the world?

He lifted his muzzle, pressing between where the bed and the wall met. Aha! He reached up with a paw and clawed at a piece of fabric, caught in the bed's frame-work.

A small piece of white fabric became visible, and he seized hold of the object with his teeth, tugging until one of the King's nightshirts came loose.

The smell was so overpowering it caused him to gag. He resisted the urge to retch and instead pulled the material out from under the bed to examine it in the light.

The nightshirt was in sorry shape—ripped in several areas and stained with stiff, dark-brown splotches. Even not in his cat form, Chess would have known those stains for what they were—blood.

He lifted his nose again and took a deep breath to clear his nasal passages and froze. He padded away from the King's clothing and sniffed again. There was some-thing else.

He cocked his ears, but no sounds came from the hallway. He followed his nose to the large armoire. Regardless of the scent's source, he couldn't open it as a cat.

Chess glanced towards the hallway again and trotted over to nudge the door closed. Hopefully, nobody would notice and investigate.

Certain that the coast was clear, he shifted back into his human shape, and then hastened to the armoire and flung the doors open.

After several minutes of digging around, he found nothing. Obviously, he needed his cat senses. With another shimmer, he stood on all fours again. He slipped inside the armoire, and the smell turned pungent in the enclosed space. In short order, he found another nightshirt, smelly and stiff, shoved inside a tall boot.

He almost got his head stuck inside the boot shaft trying to get it out and was considering a return to his human form when a sound made him freeze.

Footsteps sounded in the hallway outside. He looked towards the door and then back at the bloody nightshirt lying in the middle of the floor. He darted out and bit down on a corner, dragging the voluminous material into the armoire with him, the fabric brushing against the doors and pulling them partially shut as the bedroom door opened.

"Och, and who shut this door?" Chess recognized the housekeeper's muttering voice, and he wanted to smack himself. "How many times have I told that Gemma to keep these rooms opened so they can air out?"

He silently apologized to the sweet housemaid he'd gotten in trouble. He would need to make amends with her somehow.

The footsteps grew closer, and he pressed himself back between two pairs of boots. If she opened the armoire, the housekeeper might not see him, but she'd spot the nightshirt. Thankfully, she merely pushed the doors shut, her muttering still audible but muffled.

After several long minutes, the muttering disappeared. He counted to a thousand once, and then again, before he pushed against the armoire door. It proved too heavy for his cat form, so he shifted back to a human and nearly brained himself in the tight space.

He cracked the door and peered out. The room was empty. Still, he waited for a long minute, his ears straining, but nothing stirred.

He slid out, the two nightshirts clutched one in each hand. He looked down at the one he'd found in the armoire and grimaced.

The stiff stains were a deep blue. Only one creature he knew of had that color of blood—griffons.

Chapter 19

ZANDER STRODE OUT TO the stables. He needed to move, to experience the wind on his face.

Before he had made it halfway across the courtyard, someone yelled his name. He let out a breath when he recognized Chess. He'd been half afraid Lord Beecher had come after him to berate him some more.

"Zander, I'm glad I caught you." Chess looked around. "Has the Commander left yet?"

"He left as soon as the meeting ended. I'm sure he's already tracking the Queen by now."

Chess let out a breath. "Good. I need to talk to you."

"As long as you can do it on horseback, I've got time." Zander resumed walking, and Chess fell into step with him.

Will, the stable boy, must have been watching for him because he ran out to greet them. He dipped into a clumsy bow before looking at them, his expression eager. "Your Highness, Sir Chess, do you need me to get your horses ready?"

Zander glanced down at the boy and nodded. He usually saddled his own mount, but the boy looked so eager he didn't have the heart to disappoint him. The lad had been overly zealous in trying to be helpful ever since Zander had saved him from the dungeons. He supposed nobody liked to feel indebted.

"Should I ask how things went in there?" Chess leaned against a stable door, his leather coat buttoned to his chin. Zander thought it odd with the mild weather, but he had other things to worry about than Chess's choice of attire.

He ran a hand over his face. "Imagine the worst possible outcome and then multiply that by, say, ten."

Chess winced. "That bad, huh?"

Zander nodded, unsure of what he would do next. A few Councilmembers appeared to be on his side, but who knew? Maybe they were just more polite than the others. Well, except the Duchess. He didn't doubt her honesty since she always spoke her mind, but the others...

"Was it mainly Beecher who gave you problems?"

Chess's voice startled Zander back to the present. "He was certainly the ringleader, but the others were nearly as bad. Lady Perma looked at me like she was genuinely afraid of me."

He rubbed at his breastbone. That one still hurt. She'd known him since his infancy and had always favored him.

"Surely, the whole Council wasn't against you. You had to have some support—besides your father and the Commander, of course."

Zander closed his eyes and leaned his head against the stable wall. He didn't want to tell Chess that, while the Commander hadn't spoken against him, he certainly hadn't spoken for him either. "The Duchess told them they were being idiotic." A smile played around his mouth. "It was rather amusing to see Beecher bluster when she called him a doddering old fool who wouldn't recognize common sense if it bit him on his bum."

Chess chuckled. "Leave it to Leticia to tell it like it is. I've always admired that woman, and not only for her face and figure."

Zander quirked an eyebrow. "Is Alice aware this great admiration of yours?"

Chess lifted one shoulder. "The woman is old enough to be my mother. Besides, Alice is not the type to get jealous because I appreciate a beautiful face and form. It's like art, really."

"I'll leave you to explain that to her and wish you good luck." The smile slid from Zander's face. "But it wasn't only the Council. My father... he wasn't himself. Several times, he almost lost control." Zander looked up and met Chess's gaze. "If the Commander hadn't been there, it wouldn't have surprised me if a brawl had broken out."

Chess grimaced. "I'm sorry, Zander." He opened his mouth and then shut it again as Will came out, leading Zander's and Chess's mounts. He gestured. "Let's get out of here."

Zander couldn't agree more and swung himself up on the horse. Chess did the same.

The two walked their mounts out of the courtyard and around the back of the stable, where a trail led to the meadows beyond the palace. Zander touched his heels to his horse's sides, and Hart broke into a canter. Zander let the wind blow back his hair and tipped his face to the sun's warmth. He heard Chess behind him, and he breathed in a lungful of crisp air. If only life could always be this peaceful.

After several minutes, he slowed Hart to a walk. The path widened ahead but became more meandering and bumpy. Chess pulled up alongside of him, and they rode in companionable silence for another minute.

Zander finally spoke. "You said you had something you wanted to talk about."

Chess nodded, but his normal grin had disappeared. Instead, his lips pressed together, his expression tight.

"I guess I should start with last night, the night something attacked Verros."

Zander looked at Chess, but the other man was staring straight ahead. "Well, you can't just leave me in suspense like that. What happened?"

"It was late and I couldn't sleep, so I went down to the kitchens for a snack." Chess stopped talking, and a muscle in his cheek jumped. Finally, he sighed and looked at Zander. "I'm just going to say it because there's no easy way to break this to you. I saw someone last night coming from behind the stables, limping, and the only thing out there is the griffon atrium. I'm fairly sure it was your father."

"What? That makes no sense. Why would he be back there?" Zander's mind buzzed with confusion.

Chess unzipped his coat and pulled out a crumpled piece of white cloth that had big splotches of dark blue. "And I found this in your father's room."

Zander still couldn't get his buzzing brain to accept Chess's story, so he latched onto the more obvious issue. "What were you doing in my father's bedroom, of all things?"

Chess let his hand with the cloth drop onto his lap. "Looking for clues because, as you've said, the King is not himself, and Verros attacked him. It made little sense unless... he viewed your father as a threat."

"So what? You think my father did this? That he attacked Verros? Why would he do something like that?"

Chess shook his head, his expression grim. "I don't know, but all the evidence says he did it." He paused, his muscles tightening. "That curse is still affecting him."

"What are you saying?" Zander asked, his whole body recoiling from the answer he knew was coming.

"I saw the King in the labyrinth and what he was capable of." Chess drew in a deep breath. "I have no idea how or why, but that monster is still there, and it's overpowering your father, Zan."

The words punched into his gut, and Zander shook his head. "That's not possible. Alice broke the curse. The Palace Healers said—"

"I know what they said, but they're obviously wrong." Chess hands tightened on his reins. "If we don't do something about this, he might attack a person next."

Nausea boiled up in Zander's throat. He didn't want to believe it, but Chess was right. He just didn't know what he was going to do about it.

Chapter 20

FARIAR DABBED A DAMP cloth over the small wound on her temple. When he was done, the lingering sting was gone. He sat back and smiled. "There now. We're all finished. I hope that wasn't too terrible."

Alice smiled and let him help her sit up from the half-reclining position of the chaise lounge. "I hardly felt it."

And it was true. She'd almost fainted when Fariar explained how he was going to pull out her magical signature from her temple with what looked like a very sharp crochet hook. However, he'd wielded it skillfully, and there was only a pinch of pain before he pulled a glowing strand from her temple.

The big man patted her arm. "You were cooperative, and that helps." His smile dimmed. "I try my best not to hurt anyone, but if the person struggles, I'm sure you can imagine the difficulty."

Alice didn't want to imagine, so she changed the subject. "Will it take long—for the results, I mean?"

He collected the glass vial that held the silver and gold strand he'd extracted and stood up. "We'll have them in about an hour, I'd say, perhaps a little sooner."

Alice pleated the fabric of her skirt between her fingers. "I've already told everyone I tried to heal the little Fae. I'm not sure why you have to test for a signature since you know you'll find mine."

He patted her shoulder. "Yes, but we can tell more than merely who the signature belongs to, Miss Alice."

"Like what?"

"Well, we'll be able to tell if the magic used was malignant or not, for one thing. We can also make a reasonable guess as to the strength and skill of the magic wielder."

Alice's shoulders relaxed. If the test was that sensitive, it would prove she was innocent and they'd have to let her go. "That's good."

Fariar moved towards the door. "You can wait in here, if you wish."

Alice nodded, and the big Fae slipped out with hardly a sound. Once the door shut behind him, Alice looked around the room. She'd been so nervous when they came in here, she'd barely registered anything.

She sat at one end of the room, her chair's back adjustable. Since her first glimpse of the hook Fariar had used made her feel like she was going to pass out, Alice supposed a chair that could lay back might come in handy. She let her gaze wander around the room. A tree grew in one corner, its trunk divided into cubbies holding books and journals.

Across from it was a table pushed against one wall. On it sat a large wooden chest. Since Fariar had taken a glass vial from one of them, Alice assumed the other dozens of small drawers must also hold supplies.

As much as she'd like to investigate the room, this was her chance to use the communion stone. She didn't want to waste it. After another glance at the door to ensure it was shut, she slid her hand into her pocket and pulled it out. She gripped it in her palm and, closing her eyes, she brought Chess's face to mind.

"Chess, please answer me."

She rubbed her finger along the stone again as it glowed.

The door creaked open.

Closing her hand over the stone, she leapt up, certain her face telegraphed her guilt. "I was just..." The words died on her lips when she saw who it was.

The Advisor slid into the room. "Were you talking to someone, my dear?"

Alice shook her head. "No, I was, erm, humming to myself."

"Humming, you say?" His eyes dropped to her hand, and he raised an eyebrow. Alice followed his gaze, horrified to see the glow leaking through her fingers.

When she lifted her eyes, the Advisor was smiling in a way that made her skin crawl.

"What do you have there?"

Alice put her hand behind her back. "Nothing. It's... it's a..."

The Advisor shook his head sadly. "Fariar is too trusting, and he's always been soft when it comes to women. He knows he should secure all prisoners, especially when left alone, and I'm afraid that includes you."

"He—he said I should wait here."

"Did he say you could use magical items, or did you steal that?" Solus flicked a finger at her fist.

"I didn't steal anything! It's mine."

"Ah, so you *do* have a magical item, then. I thought as much." He held out his hand. "Give it to me and perhaps your punishment won't be as severe."

Alice skirted around the chaise lounge, trying to put more distance between them, but he followed her. "I said, come here."

A heavy compulsion pushed against Alice's mind. Unlike Indigo, nothing about the Advisor's charm was subtle, and she staggered under the assault. She mentally shoved against it even as she scuttled towards the bookshelf. The insistent buzz followed her, beating against her will until her head throbbed, but she fought against it with all of her will.

He stopped, breathing hard, and pinned her with a frigid stare. "I should have known you'd be willful."

Alice's own breath hitched from the effort. "I'm only waiting, as Mr. Fariar asked me to."

"I don't think he told you to use a communion stone, did he?"

Alice curled her clenched hand to her chest. "He didn't say not to. Nobody did!"

"I'm telling you to get over here and give it to me." The heavy hum of persuasion cut off abruptly, and he stalked across the room towards her. Alice's frantic gaze landed on the door and she darted towards it, grabbing the handle. She tugged, but it wouldn't open.

His hand closed over her wrist in a punishing grip, and he laughed as she tried to pull away. "Do you think I foolishly left it unsealed? I'm not nearly as trusting as

Fariar." His face abruptly blanked. "Now give me the stone."

Alice shook her head, and he squeezed her wrist, making her cry out in pain. With his other hand, he tried to pry her fingers up.

She drew back her foot and kicked him in the shin, hard. He yelled, abruptly letting go of her. She skittered away from him, putting the chaise lounge between them. His topaz eyes glowed with rage, and Alice bit her lip. Maybe kicking him hadn't been the best idea.

Then her gaze landed on a long wooden rod lying across the room. She looked back at the panting Advisor. A lock of auburn hair hung in his face, and he pushed it back before straightening his tunic.

"There's nowhere for you to go. You may as well give me the stone and let me secure you before I am forced to truly hurt you."

Alice stared at him for a long moment. There was no way she was giving up either the stone or her freedom. A desperate idea formed in her mind, but she'd only have one chance. She let her head droop and made a show of taking a reluctant step in his direction. A smile curled over his face, and he held out his hand.

She took one more step and then lunged towards the rod, grabbing it, but pain seared through her scalp. The Advisor had caught a fistful of her hair. She blindly swung the rod, but he grabbed her wrist and twisted. Pain shot up her arm as the rod dropped to the floor.

"I told you not to cross me," the Advisor said. Using her hair to pull her tight against him, he dragged her towards the chair.

Suddenly, the door flew open. "Why did you seal the door, my pet? I wanted to see how you..."

Indigo's frozen expression was visible over the Advisor's shoulder so she saw when it changed to something feral.

Indigo strode across the room and plucked the Advisor up like he weighed nothing. The smaller man's feet dangled several inches off the ground.

Indigo held the Advisor at eye level. "And just what are you doing, Solus?"

The smaller man didn't flinch, but scowled up at the Fae prince. "I was securing the prisoner. Fariar left her to wander around. She also has a communion stone she was attempting to use when I stopped her."

Indigo lifted one eyebrow, his tone languid. "It appeared like you were doing more than 'securing.'"

The man crossed his arms, which looked rather ridiculous since he was still hanging mid-air in Indigo's grip. "She wasn't cooperating."

Indigo sniffed. "I can imagine. Your charm is about as subtle as a hammer."

"We can't all have as much practice as you do with all your little pets." The Advisor's face twisted into a sneer.

"You, my dear Solus, have no chance of reaching the subtlety of my charm no matter how much you practice. Now, I certainly hope you weren't trying one of your little experiments again. You know Father would rather you didn't, especially after the last unfortunate incident."

"She attacked me. She deserves to be punished, not allowed to wander around loose."

"She's my pet, not yours."

The Advisor's eyes narrowed. "You forget, Your Highness, I was in the room when you talked to your father. He hasn't given you leave to make the girl your pet. That means—" The man's words cut off when, with a flick of his wrist, Indigo flung the Advisor away from him. The man sailed through the air and slammed into the wall with a grunt before he slid down to sprawl on the floor.

"Consider this my only warning—stay away from her." Indigo's smile was all teeth when he turned it on the Advisor. "You know I hate to share."

The Advisor stumbled to his feet and shook himself like a dog before straightening his tunic. "We'll see what the King says about that."

Indigo made a shooing gesture. "Yes, go see what Father has to say about hurting one of our guests and upsetting the Red King. That should go well for you."

The Advisor didn't respond. Instead, he spun on his heel and attempted to stride out the door, but his limp made it less than impressive.

Indigo watched him leave before he turned back to Alice.

She had backed against the table while the two men were arguing, but now she sagged against it, her clenched hand almost numb. Indigo walked over to stand in front of her, his eyes scanning her. He frowned and gently lifted her clenched fist.

"I'm sorry he hurt you." He rubbed a thumb over her fingers, and they uncurled without her permission to reveal the communion stone.

She tried to pull her hand away, but he tightened his grip. He plucked the stone from her hand. "No, that's mine."

He held it up and inspected it. "This is good quality. Who gave this to you?"

"A... a friend." Alice glared at him. "Now, I'd like my stone back." She tried to speak firmly, but her body trembled in a delayed reaction. Then her eyes prickled.

Indigo's expression softened, and he slipped the stone into his shirt pocket before he pulled her to his chest, wrapping his arms around her. She should push away from him. He was just as dangerous as the Advisor in his own way, but she couldn't breathe properly and her whole body shook. "I'm f-f-fine... I only need a minute..." She swallowed against the tears that were building behind her eyes.

He ran a large hand over her hair and down her back. A sense of calm and peace flowed into Alice. "I knew I should have come with you. I'm always right about these things."

His hand smoothed down her back again, trailing a comforting warmth, and her shaking subsided. As her breathing eased and the band around her lungs loosened, she suddenly realized what he was doing.

Hastily, she stepped out of the circle of his arms. "Thank you, but I'm fine now."

"I don't mind, my sweet." Indigo opened his arms, a gleam in his silver eyes.

She took another step back. "Well, I find I rather do. Mind, that is."

His arms dropped back to his sides, and he tilted his head. "But you're distraught. You need soothing."

"I said I'm fine." She held out her hand. "Now, please give me back my stone."

He patted his pocket. "Perhaps I will—if you tell me who gave it to you. Was it the Red Prince?"

Alice tried to hang onto her patience. He had helped her out of a sticky situation with the Advisor, after all. "No, it wasn't, although why it matters to you, I have no idea."

He wrinkled his nose. "You genuinely can't fathom the reason behind my curiosity?"

"No, I can't, but I'm sure you're going to tell me anyway." She crossed her arms.

He fished the stone out of his pocket and held it between his thumb and forefinger. "It should be obvious. I want to know who is giving you expensive gifts. It's only fair I'm appraised of my competition."

Alice forced herself to speak evenly. "There is no competition, Indigo, and while I appreciate what you did with the Advisor, it's none of your business who gave me that stone."

Indigo tapped the end of Alice's nose. "Don't be silly. Of course it's a competition, one I plan on winning. By the time Father lets you go, you'll beg to stay."

"Fine. Tell yourself whatever you want. Now, can I have my stone back?" She held out her hand again, wiggling her fingers.

Indigo held it above her palm. "You can have it—when you tell me who gave it to you."

Alice rolled her eyes. "If you must know, it was..." But the door opened before she finished her sentence.

Indigo growled and tucked the stone back in his pocket.

Alice sighed. Her chance to get the stone back was gone for the moment, but maybe, it wouldn't matter.

With any luck, she'd be going back to Wonderland soon and could talk to Chess in person.

Fariar motioned to her. "We have the results. The King wants you to be present when he reads them."

Chapter 21

Zander stood outside his father's study, clenching and unclenching his hands. Before he could talk himself out if it, he knocked twice.

"Come in," said a voice from inside.

Zander pushed the door open. His father sat behind his large desk, hands clasped across his stomach. When he spotted Zander, he smiled, but it didn't reach his eyes which only highlighted the dark smudges underneath them.

Zander offered his own smile and stepped into the room, carefully shutting the door behind him. Now that he was here, his mouth felt dry and the words he'd rehearsed had fled from his mind.

His father waved him closer. "Come sit down, son. What brings you here now? I thought you needed some air after that meeting." He grimaced.

Zander walked across the room and stopped behind a chair. His expression must have showed something because the King frowned at him. "Is something the matter?"

Zander gripped the back of the chair and forced himself to meet his father's gaze. "I need to discuss something with you."

Impatience flitted across his father's features, and he waved his hand. "Well, don't hover there like some kind of vulture. Sit down and get on with it," the King snapped. Catching himself, he rubbed a hand down his face. "I'm sorry, son. I can't seem to catch up on my sleep since I've been... back. Please, sit down and tell me what's on your mind."

Zander perched on the edge of the chair, his hands clasped loosely in front of him. He stared at the edge of the desk and cleared his throat. "I'm not exactly sure how to start." He rubbed his hands on his trouser legs. He had the overwhelming urge to get up and pace around the room.

The clock's tick sounded loud in the heavy silence of the room. Zander tried to gather his thoughts, to remember the words he had practiced all the way over here, but he couldn't seem to find them. When he glanced up, his father was staring not at him, but through him, his gaze far away.

This, more than anything, propelled Zander to speak. "Father, do you remember anything about last night?"

His father started. "Wh-what?"

Zander straightened and stared right into his father's hazel eyes. "I said, do you remember anything about last night?"

The King frowned. "I... I was sleeping. What is this about? Why are you asking me that?"

Zander pressed his lips together and took a big breath. "It's come to my attention that you... you might have... something to do with what happened to Verros."

The King surged up from his seat, his face turning an alarming shade of red. "What?" His voice echoed around the room.

Zander stood, too. "Someone saw you coming from behind the stables. The only thing back there is the griffon atrium. Can you explain that, Father?"

The King opened his mouth and then closed it. Anger etched his features, and his eyes narrowed. "Now look here. I don't know who told you such a pack of lies, but—"

Zander held up his hand. "No, Father. The source is reliable, but I want to hear from you. What were you doing at the stables last—"

Zander cut off as his father's face twisted into a snarl. "How dare you accuse me!" Red glowed from his hazel eyes... and was that *steam* coming from his nose? Zander backed up a step. His father dropped his gaze and gripped the edge of the desk, knuckles turning white.

After several moments of tense silence, the King's grip on the desk loosened and his whole body sagged. When he looked up, the red had faded from his eyes and was replaced by weary resignation.

"Father?" Zander's voice was cautious.

The King dropped into his chair and put his head into his hands. Zander dropped next to him and touched his father's shoulder, feeling it shake beneath his palm. "Tell me what's going on."

The King kept his head in his hands, slowly shaking it back and forth. When he spoke, his voice was small, lost.

"I... I don't know." He looked up and there were tears in his eyes. "I've found..." He swallowed. "I've found strange things in my room, and I've woken up and not been... in my bed."

"When you say *strange things*, what do you mean?"

The King sat up and stared at a framed painting across the room and not at Zander. His voice was barely a whisper and Zander had to lean in to hear him. "I found blood on my nightshirt and on my mouth. More than once. And—" He looked down at his hands again and slowly curled them into fists. He finally looked at Zander, a haunted expression in his eyes. "Last night. I... I found myself outside the atrium. I was by the door and when I looked down, there was blue blood all over my nightclothes, the taste of it in my mouth." He shook his head, the tears spilling down his cheeks. "I'm... I'm such a coward. I didn't check. I just fled. Back to my room. I hoped it was... a dream, but then this morning..." He let his head fall back into his hands.

The pain in his father's gaze made Zander's chest squeeze. "At least the Healer was able to save Verros."

His father looked up and gave Zander a wan smile. "I'm glad about that, but he'll have scars for the rest of his life. I doubt he'll let me near him again either."

Zander wanted to comfort his father, not press him to remember what had happened, but there wasn't a choice anymore. "Do you remember at all how you got out there?"

His father shook his head again. "It's like I'm sleep-walking and then I wake up. I tried locking my room, but..." He shrugged helplessly. "I was going to put a chair under the doorknob tonight, but I don't think it will help."

"You don't have to face this alone anymore, Father. I'm going to help you. We'll figure this out." He squeezed the King's shoulder, and the King placed his hand over Zander's.

"You've grown into a good man, but I'm afraid that whatever is wrong is getting worse. These gaps in my memory and the wandering, they're getting more frequent."

"Maybe we should talk to the Palace Healers again. I know they said you were well, but they might have missed something."

The King stood up and paced back and forth. "I was all right. When your friend Alice released me, I was whole, but something has happened since then. I think. It's all rather muddled, I'm afraid, but it's definitely been getting more frequent, and it seems I'm getting more dangerous, not less." He stopped and looked at Zander, his expression determined. "You're going to have to lock me up for everyone's safety."

Zander shook his head. "No, I'm not putting you in the dungeon. You're the King, for Wonder's sake!" He stood up, running a hand through his hair. His mind whirred.

The King interrupted his thoughts. "Zander, we have to do something. I'm afraid..." He closed his eyes briefly before opening them again. "I'm afraid the next time, I might hurt a person. My own griffon was bad enough, but I won't be responsible for anyone else's death." The pain in his voice reminded Zander of the Queen's brother Leander. There had only been pieces of the man left after he challenged the Minotaur... and lost. How much of that did his father remember? Well, he certainly wouldn't ask, especially right now.

"There has to be another solution than locking you in the dungeon. Everyone would want to know why, and what would we tell them?"

The King's shoulders slumped. "Then what do you propose? I barely kept control of myself just now." The King's eyes turned distant again. "The monster is so close, but I can keep it at bay during the day. It's when I sleep that he takes over. I've been trying to stay awake but I couldn't last night. That's why…" He trailed off.

"That's it… maybe."

"What do you mean?" The King looked so hopeful, Zander almost didn't want to voice his idea, afraid he'd get his father's hopes up for nothing.

"Well, it seems as if when you sleep, the monster takes over and wakes you up. That's how come you're wandering around, right?"

The King nodded for him to continue.

"Well, what if you slept so deeply, even if the monster takes over, you wouldn't wake up?"

The King's face lit with hope. "That…that might work."

"I can guard your room, make sure you don't leave." He looked up at his father. "Are you willing to try it? If I can find a strong enough sleeping draught?"

The King clutched at Zander's arm. "Yes, I'll do anything. I can't hurt someone again."

Zander put his arm around his father's shoulders, suddenly feeling the weight of what might happen. If this failed… No, it would work. It had to. If anyone found out about this, it would be a disaster.

"I'm... I'm going to bring Chess in on this, Father. He already knows some of it. We should also get a message to the Commander."

The King tucked his chin down. "Not yet. I don't... I can't let my brother know. What would he think of me?"

"This isn't your fault."

The King closed his eyes. "No matter the cause, I'm the one doing these things, Zander."

The anguish on the King's face broke Zander's heart. "All right. Do you think you'll be all right this afternoon?"

His father let out a shaky breath before he straightened. "Yes, I'm fine during the daytime."

Zander hid his uneasiness. He had to leave to get the sleeping draught. His father would have to be fine for the few hours he was gone.

"All right, then. Chess and I will go, but we'll be back before tonight."

With a last squeeze to his father's shoulder, Zander hurried out the door. He only hoped this would work.

Chapter 22

ALICE FOLLOWED FARIAR BACK up a tunnel, Indigo next to her. She rubbed her palms down the sides of her dress. She was innocent, and if that test was as detailed as Fariar said, there was nothing to be nervous about. This logic did nothing to still the jitters in her stomach.

Indigo was uncharacteristically silent, absently patting his shirt pocket periodically, which only made her more nervous.

They took a left at an intersection and then climbed a short flight of stairs before turning again down a side passage that ended at a nondescript door set into the wall, vines and flowers dripping over its edges. Fariar pushed it open, and it took Alice a moment to realize they were back in the same room where she had met King Thorne the first time. She wondered if all the rooms had multiple entrances, or if it was only this one.

The King straightened from where he'd been bent over a long table, Azalea next to him. They both turned to face the newcomers. Alice dipped into a curtsey even as she searched the shadowy corners for the Advisor.

Her shoulders loosened when she didn't spot him any-where.

The King's dark eyes ran over Alice. "You are well?"

Alice gave a brief nod. "I am, Your Majesty." It wasn't strictly a lie because there was nothing wrong with her physically. Mentally and emotionally was another story, but she didn't think the King cared about that.

He turned to Fariar and held out a hand. "You've the results?"

Fariar passed a sheaf of parchment to the King. He shuffled through them, nodding and humming to him-self.

Alice shifted from one foot to another, trying to keep her nerves from showing. The King finally came to the last page. His eyes scanned over it and then frowned. Her stomach knotted. The King quickly turned back to another page and tapped his lip.

Warm fingers pried open her fist. She hadn't even realized she'd been clenching her hands. Indigo thread-ed his fingers through hers and squeezed gently. Once again, comforting warmth flooded through her, this time running up her arm and loosening her knotted shoul-ders. It felt wonderful.

"Stop it," she hissed at him and snatched her hand away.

Hurt and surprise flickered over his face, but a smug smile quickly replaced them. "I'm going to win, my sweet, but don't worry. I never gloat. It's one of my best qualities."

The King's voice interrupted them as he addressed Fariar. "This report appears quite thorough. Do you have anything to add?"

Fariar's deep voice rumbled through the room. "The young miss's magical signature is clearly present on the bumble, but it's not malignant. She has quite a strong Healer Gift, which aligns with her story of trying to help the Fae. She also has a very strong Creature Gift, which she did not use on the Fae at all."

The King stabbed a long brown finger at the papers. "What about this other signature?"

A frown crinkled Fariar's dark face. "That one, Your Majesty, is clearly malignant, but it doesn't belong to this girl."

"Is it the same as you've found on the other two?"

Fariar's expression turned grim. "I'm afraid so, Your Majesty."

The King closed his eyes as if in pain. When he opened them again, they burned with anger. "Is there any way to trace this malignant signature?"

Fariar shook his head. "Unfortunately, no. Without someone to match it to, the only thing I can tell you about it is that it's malignant. I'm sorry, Your Majesty."

The King leaned a hip against the table and sighed. Alice wanted to say something, to remind him she needed to go home, but she clamped her lips shut.

Finally, the King looked up, his gaze landing on her. He blinked, and she was pretty sure he'd forgotten she was there. "Well, that leaves us with what to do with you, child."

Alice straightened. Her heart beat faster in her chest as she waited for what he would say.

A warm smile curled across his face. "I think this clearly shows you had no ill intent. I don't see any reason you shouldn't be free to go." Alice's rigid muscles unclenched at this news, and she swallowed down the sudden urge to cry. The King clapped his hands together. "Now then, we should get you—"

"Forgive me for interrupting, Your Majesty, but are you sure that's wise with what Zephyr told us just this morning about the goings-on at the Red Palace?" The familiar voice made her entire body go rigid as Solus stepped out of the shadows.

How many doors did this blasted room have, anyway? Alice was sure she had checked every corner, and he hadn't been here. One side of the Advisor's mouth tipped up as he caught her gaze and held it. Alice felt like a mouse under the stare of a particularly hungry cat.

"I think you should be aware I caught her earlier trying to use a communion stone. I believe your son has possession of it." The King's brows went up and Solus continued. "It might all be as she says—but with her having the Creature Gift too"—he shrugged—"we must ask ourselves if it is possible the Red King sent her to spy on us."

"You can't be serious?" The words burst out of Alice, anger burning away her caution. "What kind of git would send me as a spy? What could I possibly find out as a complete stranger here?"

Indigo shifted and his shoulder brushed Alice's. "She makes a good point, Advisor." He raised his eyebrow. "It makes one wonder if you have other reasons for wanting to keep her here besides the good of the Faelands."

The Advisor sniffed and turned his back on Indigo to address the king. "Surely, you can see that anyone who has an even passing acquaintance with the prince would understand someone so pretty and novel would be an irresistible lure to him. He often brings his pets into Underhill and gives them free rein." He waved a hand at Alice. "She'd have any number of opportunities to gather information."

Alice resisted the urge to scream and instead turned to the king, trying to keep her voice calm and reasonable. "Your Majesty, I don't mean any offense, but I have no idea what information could possibly be of enough interest to King Zane to send me here." She glanced at Indigo." And nobody has ever mentioned the prince, at least not in my hearing."

"Well, that's disappointing," Indigo murmured.

The King frowned, looking between her and his Advisor. "I can't agree with you on this, Solus. While it's a bit unusual that she has a communion stone, it's quite a leap to this young girl being a spy."

The Advisor's mouth thinned. "Why else would she have it, if not to communicate with someone back at the Red Palace?"

Indigo snorted. "That *is* what a communion stone is made to do, Solus—communicate."

The Advisor ignored Indigo, keeping his attention on the king. "If she was going home to the Mirror World as she claims, why would she need one?"

A tense silence stretched over the room as everyone seemed to give this argument weight. It was Azalea that finally spoke. "It is a simple matter to ask her who gave it to her and why, is it not?"

The weight of everyone's gaze pressed down on Alice, but she kept silent since nobody had asked her anything yet.

Finally, the King raised his eyebrow. "Did either King Zane or Prince Zander give you this stone?"

Alice shook her head. "No, sir."

"Well, who did then?" A touch of impatience colored the King's tone.

Alice's face heated. "It was a friend."

The King frowned. "Does this friend have a name?"

Alice swallowed. "Yes, sir. It's Chess."

The name dropped into the room like a rock in a still pond, and King Thorne's eyes widened. "Chess Felinas? The Red King's nephew?"

Alice nodded, her face heating. "Yes, sir."

The Advisor waved an arm at her. "You can't tell me that's a coincidence, Your Majesty." He whirled towards Alice. "Why did he give it to you?"

Alice's shoulders hunched, and she leaned away from his looming presence. "I... I... don't know. To keep in touch, I suppose?" She looked from him to the King.

The Advisor gave a nasty chuckle. "And why would he want to keep in touch with a girl from the Mirror World? Did you form a romantic attachment with him?"

Alice's face burned as the kiss she'd shared with Chess in the labyrinth rose in her mind. She wasn't sharing that with any of the people in this room, though. She crossed her arms. "I don't see why that's any of your business or what it has to do with all this."

"But we'd all like to know, my pet." Indigo's voice had turned silky. He fished the communion stone out of his pocket and examined it. "I wondered why you had a stone of this quality. Now it's obvious."

Alice wasn't sure what Indigo thought was obvious, but she didn't like what she heard in his tone.

The Advisor's lip curled as he looked down his nose at Alice. "The prince is right. We're all curious because if you aren't romantically involved, what other reason could the Red King's nephew have to give you a communion stone before sending you practically to Underhill's doorstep?" He didn't give Alice a chance to answer, but turned back to King Thorne. "The Red King has been indisposed for over a year, and has no idea what is going on in this corner of Wonderland. The mainland citizens already don't trust us. Of course, he's behind this, and who knows what she will go back and tell him? With all the strange happenings lately, can we really take that chance?"

The King frowned. "She's a beautiful young woman. I find it much more plausible that the Felinas boy would be interested in her than that she's a spy." He pointed a finger at the Advisor. "And don't think I don't know why you'd want to keep her around either, Solus."

The Advisor ran a hand through his burnished hair and smoothed his tunic. "I only have the Faelands' best interests at heart. You know me well enough to understand that, too."

"Regardless, I don't see any reason to keep her here. The last thing we need is to create enmity with the Red Palace."

Indigo stepped forward. "Perhaps it wouldn't be a bad idea to extend her stay, Father. As our guest, of course." He draped an arm over Alice's shoulders. "I could show her around the island, give her something good to take back to the Red King if information is what she's after. If she is a spy, why not use it to our advantage?"

Alice shot Indigo a hostile look as she stepped out from under his arm and addressed the King. "Your Majesty, my only desire is to go home." She gestured at the communion stone Indigo still held. "The truth is, Chess and I faced some difficult things together and became friends. That stone is a way to keep in contact. Nothing more."

Solus's mouth thinned. "There's nothing to stop her from lying to us, Your Majesty. As your son said, it would be wise to keep her contained."

"That's not—" Indigo said, but the King held up his hand to quiet him.

Then he looked from the Advisor to Alice to Indigo and then back again. He tapped his lip, and Alice thought she might scream if he didn't say something soon. Finally, he spoke, his voice heavy. "There is a lot to think about here." He looked at Alice, an apology in his eyes. "I'm sorry, child, but things have been rather unsettled of late, and with the Feast coming up, I cannot take any chances." He waved his hand at Indigo. "Return her to her cage."

Alice's stomach plummeted, and the only thing that kept the tears at bay was the Advisor's presence. She refused to give him the satisfaction.

Beside her, Indigo stiffened. "Surely, Father, that's unnecessary. I'll ensure she doesn't go anywhere she shouldn't."

The Advisor narrowed his eyes at Indigo. "Your Highness, I understand you mean well, but do you really have time to oversee her? Don't you still need to finish the centerpiece for the Feast? Besides, we're all aware of your penchant for your pets, aren't we?"

"And we all know what your interest is in humans, Solus." Indigo's tone turned mocking. "You can hardly claim a lack of bias after what I witnessed earlier."

"She attacked me—unprovoked, I might add." The Advisor stepped towards the Fae prince, his genial expression gone, replaced with a snarl.

Indigo lifted Alice's wrist and held it up so the King could see. "I suppose she gave these bruises to herself, then."

"She was an unsecured prisoner." The Advisor's words came through gritted teeth. Alice was pretty sure if Indigo hadn't been a prince, the other man would have hit him.

As it was, the King chopped a hand through the air. "Enough! The both of you squabble like children sometimes." He pointed at Indigo. "Take the girl back to her cage. Make sure she has whatever she needs. I will untangle this mess after the Feast."

The Advisor gave Indigo a smug look, but the King turned towards him. "And you, leave her in peace. The last thing we need is to create enemies where there aren't any."

The Advisor bowed stiffly. "As you wish, Your Majesty. If you'll excuse me, then." He turned and walked towards the door. He brushed past Alice and his gaze held a promise she didn't like.

Chapter 23

"Go away and leave me alone." Alice once again sat in the middle of her cage, her back to Indigo.

He was currently lounging on the closest beam. He hung his head upside down so he had a better view. "But don't you want me to join you? You appear to be in need of a hug."

Alice ignored him and picked at the edges of the blanket. Indigo's tone turned wheedling. "Everyone says my hugs are wonderful."

Alice snorted. "You're a prince. Of course they tell you what you want to hear."

Indigo swung himself upright and glared down at her from his perch. "That's not true. Plenty of people tell me the truth."

Alice sighed. "No. They don't."

"And what, pray tell, is this truth?"

Her temper frayed, and she spun to face him. "If you truly want to know, fine, I'll tell you." She held up a hand and began ticking things off on her fingers. "You have the attention span of a hummingbird. You view people as toys for your entertainment. You only care about yourself and what you want, never mind anyone else's thoughts or feelings. You have too high an opinion of yourself, and you have a childish inability to understand the word *no*."

Indigo's face twisted into a scowl. "You're an ungrateful little baggage. I saved you from the Advisor, didn't I?"

Alice crossed her arms. "Only because you view me as some sort of"—she groped for the right word—"belonging, and you don't want to share. It's not as if you actually care about what I think or feel. You made that perfectly clear just now with the King. It's your fault I'm still in here."

Indigo eyes widened in outrage. "You're blaming me for your predicament? That's completely unfair. I tried to convince him to let you stay as a guest."

Alice gritted her teeth to keep from screaming at him. When she finally spoke, her voice was strained. "You should have told your father to send me home, but no, you suggested I stay here and gave him a reason to keep me locked up." Alice's voice cracked on the last word and she blinked back tears, annoyed with herself. It wasn't as if the bloody bloke cared how she felt.

Indigo's features softened, and he tossed something through the air. The communion stone landed with a clink in front of Alice. "Think of this as a peace offering, pet."

She picked it up, her hand closing around its smooth surface. Indigo beamed at her, but Alice simply stared at the stone in her palm. "This doesn't change anything, Indigo."

His smile faded. "I never intended for you to be back in that cage. I only wanted you to stay longer."

"Well, you got your wish, didn't you?" Alice glared at him.

"Don't be so cross. I'm sure I can convince Father to release you—perhaps in time to come with me to the Feast."

"No, thank you! I've seen what your help is worth."

"I told you that wasn't my fault!"

"Yes, it... Just go away." She turned her face away from him. "I may be in a cage, but I can still decide who I want to talk to." Despite her best efforts, Alice's voice wobbled at the end, and tears pressed at the backs of her eyes. Was it too much to ask to cry in peace?

Warm tingles spread over her back and shoulders, and the pressure on the backs of her eyelids eased.

"Stop doing that!" she snapped.

He shrugged. "I'm only trying to help you. It pains me for you to be so sad."

Alice narrowed her eyes. "No, the only thing that brings you any pain is not getting your way. You're no better than the Advisor."

For the first time, Indigo's eyes sparked with anger. "That was uncalled-for. I think I'll leave you alone so you can realize how much you'll miss my presence."

He looked at her as if waiting for her to speak. When she didn't, he shrugged. "I'm going now. Who knows when I'll be back."

After a brief pause, he leapt onto the next beam, shimmering into his ferret form. She watched him scamper away until he finally disappeared from view. She let out a long breath. Finally, she was alone. Above her, Arthur's cage swayed, but he said nothing, for which she was grateful. She only wanted to forget for a little while. With this intention, she laid down on the pillow and pulled the blanket up to her shoulders. Trying to shove the events of the past day out of her mind, she closed her eyes.

Chapter 24

THE KING HELD UP the bottle and eyed the viscous liquid inside with skepticism. "Do you really think this will work?" He sat on the edge of his bed in his nightshirt. He looked surprisingly small with his pale legs and bare feet sticking out.

Zander nodded. "Cata... that is, the person I got it from assured me this would knock out a hippogriff. As a precaution, I'll stay close by."

The King frowned. "Won't people notice something odd if you're hanging around my room all night? I thought the purpose of this was to avoid all that."

"I don't plan on sitting outside your door. I'll stay in Mother's rooms. There's an adjoining door. If we keep it open, I'll be able to hear whether you're trying to leave or moving around."

"That might not be a good idea, Zander. What if I attack you?" The King stared down at his hands. "I... I'm not sure I'll be able to control myself."

The words splashed over Zander like cold water, and he tried to hide his reaction. "Don't worry. I don't plan on sleeping tonight."

"You shouldn't be doing this on your own." The King's eyebrows furrowed. "You're putting yourself at risk, and I'm not sure how wise that is under the circumstances. If I'm... unable to rule, you're my only heir."

Zander swallowed. He'd lost his father once, and hearing him talking like this, like his time was limited, made the pain of remembered grief choke him. He squeezed his father's shoulder, which felt bony through his nightshirt. "Try not to worry. We'll find a solution to all of this." He tapped the bottle. "And this is the first step."

"I realize you want to keep things quiet, and I do, too. But it would ease my worry if you had someone else with you."

Zander hesitated. "It's too bad the Commander already left. He seems like the best option."

The King vehemently shook his head. "No. I'm glad he's not here. He's the last person I want to learn about this."

"But—"

"I said no!"

Zander held up a hand. "All right, if you feel that strongly about it, I won't bring him into this. What if I ask Chess, then? He already knows, and I agree, I'd rather not tell more people than we absolutely have to."

After a pause, the King gave a sharp nod. "But he mustn't tell the Commander."

Zander resisted the urge to snort. "You won't have to worry about that."

The King exhaled a long breath. "All right, then. I suppose this is the best option we have."

Zander gave his father an encouraging smile. "I'll be right here, Father. You don't have to worry."

"I sincerely hope you are right," said the King, and then he tipped the contents of the bottle into his mouth.

Chapter 25

DESPITE HER DESPERATION TO disappear into sleep, Alice found she couldn't. She flopped onto her back and stared up at the canopy above her. Watching the sunlight filtering through the leaves, despair welled up in her. How had she ended up here? She had been so close to going home. Again.

Tears prickled, and she did nothing to stop them as they leaked down her cheeks. She pushed the blanket against her mouth to stifle her sobs. She didn't know how long she cried, but when her tears finally slowed, drowsiness pulled at her eyelids.

As she drifted off, her cage lurched into motion. Alarmed, she sat up and peered towards the tower door.

Her stomach dropped when she saw who was standing there.

It was the Advisor.

Alice crawled to the far side of the cage. She used the bars to climb to her feet. She looked around the cage, but if she picked up the chamber pot, she'd lose any element of surprise.

As her cage moved inexorably closer, Solus's face came into focus. His smile chilled Alice. She pushed her lips together to still their trembling and braced herself.

Maybe if she surprised him, she could get away or at least get help. She peered over her shoulder, regretting the fact she'd sent Indigo away. She didn't think he'd be back anytime soon, either.

The cage bumped against the landing, and Alice didn't wait. She launched herself at the door, swinging it open.

The Advisor's eyes widened as she rammed it into him, knocking him back a step. She whirled towards the stairs, but a hard yank on her skirt made her stumble.

Before she could find her footing, his hand closed over her arm, squeezing painfully.

"This will go a lot better for you, my dear, if you cooperate." He jerked her closer. His charm buzzed over her, heavy and sticky, and she pushed against it. "Come with me." There was a compulsion in the command, but there was no way she was going anywhere with him. She closed her hand into a fist and swung. Her knuckles connected with his nose with an audible crunch.

Solus yelled and dropped her arm, covering his face. Alice stomped on his foot, and he yanked his leg back, throwing him off balance. She shoved him hard, and he fell against the wall. She darted onto the landing and ran down the stairs, almost tripping in her haste.

"You won't get away," the Advisor said, his voice muffled and nasal. "There's nowhere for you to go!"

Ice skated over her skin as she remembered the locked door waiting for her at the bottom. Still, she rushed down the stairwell, hoping against hope he hadn't bothered with a key.Footsteps sounded behind her, and she glanced over her shoulder. The Advisor was gaining on her.

Alice put on a burst of speed, trying to keep her balance on the tightly twisting stairs. She raced around another turn and skidded to a stop, almost slamming into Azalea.

The Fae woman skipped down a few steps to avoid a collision. Her eyes darted from Alice to the shadows behind her. "What is going on here?"

"I... He..." Alice put a hand on her side, her breath coming in gasps, as much from fear as exertion. "He was trying to take me somewhere."

The Advisor rushed down the dozen steps that separated them and Alice pushed her back against the wall, trying to put as much distance between them as she could.

A smear of blood marred the Advisor's cheek and a hank of hair hung in his eyes. He smoothed it back. "Ah, Princess Azalea, your timing is very fortunate. I'm afraid the prisoner was trying to escape."

Alice opened her mouth to protest, but Azalea held up a hand. "That does not explain what you are doing here, Advisor Solus."

"I was only checking on the prisoner."

Azalea raised an eyebrow. "Why?"

The Advisor smoothed a hand down his tunic. "She's from the Mirror World, and she demonstrates Gifts. Of course, I would like to find out why, but she attacked me and then tried to escape."

Azalea's gaze narrowed. "King Thorne did not give you permission to examine her."

Solus drew himself up and stared down his nose at the princess. "It would be a tragic waste if she is released without allowing me to do any tests."

Azalea stared at him for a long moment, and then drew her sword, the tip pointing at his Adam's apple. The Advisor swallowed, his gaze fixed on the blade. "I am not questioning your purpose, Advisor Solus, but King Thorne specifically told you to leave her alone. Is there a reason you are defying his direct order?"

Solus smoothed his tunic again. "I had no intention of hurting the girl. I merely wanted some information. It would be good for all of us to understand this phenomenon better."

"Perhaps that is true, but it does not change what the King told you." She nodded her head towards the staircase behind her. "I suggest you leave now, or I will have to bring you before my father to explain your disobedience."

The Advisor scowled and then caught himself. He bowed his head. "As you wish, Your Highness."

With a last, menacing look at Alice, he slid past Azalea and glided down the stairs.

Azalea kept her eyes on him until he disappeared before she turned her attention back to Alice, sliding her sword back into its sheath. "Are you all right?"

Alice nodded her head, suddenly finding herself too shaky to speak.

"I must apologize for the Advisor's behavior. I will make sure it does not happen again." She nodded towards the stairs behind Alice. "You had best return to your accommodations now."

Alice didn't move. Instead, she cleared her throat. "What if he comes back and you're not here?"

Azalea frowned. "That will not happen. I promise you."

Alice hesitated and then decided to push the issue. "I'm not sure you can keep that promise. Are you going to watch him continually?"

"Well, no, not continually. I have other duties."

Alice lifted her chin. "Then what guarantee is there that I won't find myself at that man's mercy?"

Azalea's face softened. "You have my word that you will be safe here. Father would severely punish him if he hurt you, and he knows that."

Alice's mouth quirked. "That's hardly reassuring."

Azalea shrugged. "It is the best I can do under the circumstances." She gestured towards the stairs. "Now, you need to return."

Alice didn't move. "You realize that the Red King and the Red Prince will be furious if anything happens to me?" While she was sure Zander would be, she actually didn't know how the Red King would feel, but he rather owed her, didn't he?

Azalea met her gaze. "I am aware of that, and I will do my best to ensure nothing happens to you." She rested her hand on her sword's hilt. "Now, I must insist you return to your accommodations."

Reluctantly, Alice turned and climbed back up the stairs. Azalea followed her until they reached the landing. The cage door had bounced shut again, and Azalea leaned around her to open it just as Alice reached for it, too. They bumped into each other and Alice almost fell, trying to find her footing.

"Oh, I'm sorry. Did I step on you?" she said as Azalea steadied her elbow.

"No, I am fine." The other woman held the door as Alice stepped back into her cage and then shut it behind her with a clink of metal on metal.

Alice held onto the bars of her cage with one hand, her other clenched at her side, and watched the landing get farther away until the cage stopped moving. Azalea lifted her hand in a brief wave before the tower door shut with a loud creak.

Alice opened her hand and looked down at the key in her hand and smiled. It had been a long time since she'd picked anyone's pockets, but her skills proved only a little rusty. She turned the key over in her hand and her smile faded. No matter what Azalea promised, Alice didn't plan on sticking around long enough to give the Advisor another chance.

Chapter 26

SIR LAPIN BLANC PUFFED on his pipe and considered Citrine. They were sitting in his cozy kitchen. "Well, my dear, just because you *can* do something doesn't mean you should."

"What do you expect the effects might be?" Citrine wrapped her hands around the teacup, letting it warm her chilled fingers.

"It's difficult to determine, but aside from the fact that Gifts tend to be hereditary, our understanding of their origins and mechanisms is limited."

Citrine took a sip of the tea before she spoke. "I'm wary myself, but I promised Zander I'd investigate. He has to be concerned." She pursed her lips. "Not that he has told me that, but I've heard enough from others to be aware that the Council hasn't been very accepting of his Drifter Gene."

Lapin shook his head. "The whole ban is foolishness, and I can't, in good conscience, recommend you create this formula." He tapped the notebook she'd brought. "Besides, it looks as if getting rid of your Gift requires a royal artifact from the Fae, but it doesn't indicate what kind. Even if it did, the chances of anyone in the Faelands handing over any artifact is highly unlikely."

Citrine frowned at Lapin and took another sip of her tea. "But isn't King Thorne more reasonable than most in the Faelands?"

"He is—for a Fae—but his interest in humans is nonexistent, and there are others around him, including several clan leaders, that hate them." Lapin shook his head. "No, I'm afraid it's very unlikely they would loan us an artifact." Lapin took another long pull on his pipe and blew several smoke rings towards the ceiling before he spoke again. "And as I told you, stripping one's Gift might permanently alter the person's mind, or soul, even."

Citrine set her cup on the table with a clink and slumped back in her chair. "I suppose you're right. If the Council was more open-minded, Zander wouldn't even consider doing this. I don't suppose you would talk to them?"

Lapin smiled. "I'd be happy to offer whatever support I can for the Prince, but I'm afraid your confidence in my influence might be misplaced. Although I'm flattered."

Citrine fiddled with the napkin on her lap. "There has to be some way to help Zander. I hate to think of him having to put up with everyone's suspicions when he's done nothing to deserve them."

A touch on her hand startled her. Lapin's white paw covered the back of her hand. "There will always be ignorant people, and fear makes us say and do terrible things."

Citrine stared into her tea for a minute before straightening. When she spoke, her tone was brisk. "Yes,

I suppose you are right." She reached into her satchel and pulled out the bestiary she'd brought. She set it on the table with a thump and patted it.

"This is the other reason I came by. I need your opinion on something."

Lapin leaned forward, his eyes bright. "Now you've piqued my curiosity."

"Recently, I had some visitors—a pack of selbys. Once I got them to calm down, they told me a rather alarming tale."

Lapin lifted his eyebrows and took another puff of his pipe. "Go on, my dear. You have my full attention."

"Apparently, something has been ripping up small animals around the palace in recent days."

Lapin frowned. "That's a shame, of course, but any number of predators are a possibility."

Citrine leaned forward. "Yes, but all the victims were found drained of their blood."

"That puts a different spin on it."

She pulled the book towards her and flipped to the first page she had marked. "I found a few options, but all of them are quite large—not something that would hide itself easily." She pushed the book towards Lapin.

He read the first page and then flipped to the other three. He said nothing as he read each entry, puffing on his pipe as he did so. When he'd finished, he shut the book and pushed it back to Citrine.

"Any of them could be your culprit, but as you said, it's almost unfathomable that one of them is running about the palace grounds without being sighted by someone." Lapin puffed on his pipe. "Did anyone tell you about the King's curse?"

A loud rapping on the window prevented Citrine's answer, and they both turned towards the sound. A large raven stood on the window ledge, peering in at them. Lapin pushed himself up from the chair and opened the window. The raven hopped inside.

Your knowledge is known far and wide. The Prince asks for your help, that you come to his side. Caw!

Before Citrine could interpret the raven's words, Lapin removed the scroll from the raven's leg.

"Let's see what the message is," Lapin said as he absently scooped up a handful of seeds from a small bowl on his countertop and handed them to the raven, who pecked at them greedily.

Citrine peered over Lapin's shoulder. He finished reading and handed the parchment to her. She scanned the contents and then met Lapin's gaze.

"What are we going to do?"

Lapin lifted an eyebrow. "That message didn't say anything about *we*, my dear."

Citrine narrowed her eyes. "Well, you can't expect me to go back to the Pearl Palace and just wait around for more news." She lifted her chin. "Besides, it's my duty as the Pearl Queen to investigate this."

"I didn't realize your duties extended all the way to the Red Palace." Lapin's tone was mild.

"I promised the selbys I would look into what was going on there." She gestured towards the parchment. "If it's the King, that would explain a lot."

Lapin took his pipe out of his mouth and looked at her in question.

"In response to your earlier question, I am familiar with the King's curse. Even though I'm rather removed from things, birds are the worst gossips. They see and hear everything." She shook her head. "But I don't understand it. If Alice broke the King's curse, what's happening here? Surely, someone didn't place another curse on him."

Lapin frowned and scanned the parchment again. "I can't say for certain until I get there and talk to the King, but that seems unlikely." He puffed on his pipe a few times, the wheels turning in his brain almost visible. Finally, he spoke. "A curse is a powerful thing, and it has many tendrils that sink into a person."

Citrine clutched his arm. "What are you saying?"

Lapin patted her hand. "I'm only guessing at this point. Let's wait until after I talk to the King before I answer that." He turned and began clearing the table. When she didn't move, he glanced over his shoulder. "I suppose you'll be joining me on my trip to the Red Palace?"

Citrine crossed her arms. "You can't stop me from going."

Lapin picked up her cup and winked. "I wouldn't dream of it, my dear."

Chapter 27

Pounding footsteps coming from the hall brought Zander off the bed in an instant. Chess was already on his feet, and the two of them sprinted through the connecting door.

Zander only had enough time to take in his father sprawled across the bed, his nightshirt crusted in blood, before someone was pounding on the door. The King blinked open his eyes and sat up, rubbing his face like a child. Blood smeared his lips and cheek.

"Wha...?" His voice was bleary as he looked around in confusion. Then his gaze dropped to his nightshirt. He moaned and gripped both sides of his head. "No, no, no."

The knock came again. "Your Majesty!" The crack in Anders' voice was audible through the door.

Zander exchanged a wild-eyed look with Chess, but Chess was already moving. He reached the King and gently pushed him back onto his pillow. "You need to lie down, Your Majesty."

The King struggled to sit back up, but Chess's voice took on a soothing sing-song quality that Zander recognized. His friend's charm buzzed over his skin.

He glanced back one more time as he reached the door. Chess had managed to get his father lying down, the sheet and blanket pulled up to his chin. The King's eyes were already half-mast as if he might drop off to sleep at any moment.

Taking a deep breath, Zander braced himself and opened the door.

Anders' wispy hair stood on end, his eyes wide. "Your Highness, I need to speak with King Zane. Right away." He tried to peer around Zander, but Zander shifted to block his view.

"I'm afraid my father is not feeling well." He stepped into the hallway, pulling the door shut behind him, thankful now that he'd taken to sleeping in his clothes at night as a precaution. A shudder ran up his spine. What if he hadn't stayed one more night in Mother's rooms? Although how the King had gotten out without either him or Chess knowing, he couldn't fathom.

"Your Highness?" Anders' voice cut through Zander's thoughts.

"I'm sorry, Anders. I'm afraid I'm still clearing the cobwebs. What's happened?"

The steward wrung his hands. "It's one of the flower maidens and a footman. They're both..." He glanced in both directions and leaned closer, his voice barely a whisper. "They're dead, Your Highness." He swallowed, his Adam's apple bobbing. "Some kind of attack. The young man was still alive when Dugin found them. He was raving about a beast man."

Guilt choked Zander. This was the second flower maiden to die under his watch. The Queen had been responsible for the last one, and he still remembered Buttercup's face when he'd told her he found her sister, but she hadn't survived. Now more people under his protection were dead.

A moan behind him made ice skate over Zander's skin as a new fear emerged. "How many people overheard?"

Anders frowned. "Well, sir, Dugin was shaken up and began shouting, which brought Simpkin out, so I'm afraid the stable boy also witnessed what happened." Anders shook his head. "Poor lad. He took it hard. He was familiar the flower maiden, you see."

"We'll worry about him later. Where did you put the bodies?"

The sound of something hitting the floor made both Zander and Anders look at the closed door.

Anders gestured towards the King's room. "Perhaps we should inform the King about what is going on now. I can..." Anders trailed off at the sound of scuffling.

Zander jumped in, talking louder than strictly necessary. "No, he's quite ill. He mustn't be disturbed, especially with something like this." He straightened his shoulders. "I'll take care of it, Anders."

The steward bowed his head. "As you wish, Your Highness."

"Now, where are the bodies?"

Anders stood straighter. "I had Simpkin and Dugin carry them into the second cold cellar. I thought it best to put them somewhere out of the way."

"That's good. Very good. I'd like to see them."

"Shall I fetch one of the Palace Healers?"

Zander shook his head. Inside, panic clawed at him, but he ruthlessly shoved it down, keeping his voice steady and even. "Not right now. They can't help either of them, after all."

Anders gnawed on his lip. "Erm, I meant for His Majesty."

"No, he's resting right now." Zander strode down the hall and Anders hurried to his side. Zander didn't slow down as he gave instructions. "But I would like to talk to Simpkin and Dugin. Fetch them and have them wait for me in my father's study." As an afterthought, he added, "The stable boy can come along too. I'm sure he won't want to be out there by himself right now."

"Very good, Your Highness." Anders bobbed his head and scurried down the servants' hallway to carry out the orders.

Zander waited until the man disappeared around the corner before he turned back to the bedroom door.

He opened it and blinked.

Chess stood by the bed, the bloodstained nightshirt crumpled in his hand. The King was under the covers, the sheet and blanket pulled up to his chin. His face was clean, and he was deeply asleep.

"Well, what happened? I couldn't hear from in here." Chess gestured towards the sleeping King. "Not to mention, I was rather preoccupied."

Zander ran his hands down the sides of his trousers and tried to steady his breathing. "One of the flower maidens is dead, along with a footman. Anders said something attacked them both. The man was alive when they found him." He swallowed. "He was talking about a beast-man."

Chess let out a low whistle. "That is not good, my friend."

Zander ran a hand through his hair. "You're telling me." He waved at his father. "What happened here? Did he get violent?"

Chess shook his head. "No, but he was extremely distraught when he saw all the blood on this." He shook the nightshirt in Zander's direction. "There was no way he would have been able to hold any kind of normal conversation in the state he was in, so I persuaded him to take one of the sleeping draughts."

"I hope you're going to get rid of that." Zander gestured towards the nightshirt.

"I'll take care of it, but this is the least of your worries right now. What are you going to tell the Council? I don't think your father will go along with any fiction you come up with. He was beside himself."

Zander let out a sigh that seemed to come from his feet. "I honestly don't know. I'm going to view the bodies now. Hopefully, something will come to me between now and when I address them." Zander paced back and forth. "Nobody can find out the King did this."

"Can you put off speaking to the Council? At least until we figure out what to do for your father?"

Zander wanted to hug Chess for saying "we." "Not for long. Word will get out. As it is, I'm sure the staff will know before the day is out, no matter how hard Anders tries to stop the whispers. And I suppose eventually I'll have to tell the Fae King one of his flower maidens is dead, too. If he finds out my father did this..." Zander grimaced. "That won't go well."

Zander dropped into an armchair and put his head in his hands. "What am I going to do, Chess? Half the Council would be happy to see the back of me because of my Drifter Gene. What are they going to do if they find out my father is turning into a rampaging beast?"

Chess closed the space between them and squeezed his shoulder. "Unfortunately, I don't think you'll be able to keep this quiet for long, at least not among the palace and the Council." He frowned. "And to be honest, I'm not sure you should." He waved a hand in the King's direction. "I know it's not his fault, but he's a danger to himself and to everyone in this palace right now."

Zander squeezed his eyes closed, his shoulders slumping. "I know, but if I could only buy some time so we can find out what's happening to him, or so Citrine could figure out how to get rid of my Drifter Gene." He looked up at Chess, his chest squeezing with panic. "If the Council finds out all this now, our family could lose the throne, and then what will happen to Wonderland?"

Chess's expression softened. "It won't come to that. We won't let it." His tone turned brisk. "Now, what do you need me to do?"

Zander drew in a deep breath. Cowering in here would not change things. That was up to him, and his first action needed to be viewing the bodies and dealing with them. He pushed to his feet. "Can you stay here with Father? Make sure he doesn't leave this room until I come back?"

Chess smiled. "Of course. He's safe in my hands."

Zander blinked several times to clear the moisture in his eyes. "Thanks, Chess. I owe you one."

Chess waved a hand. "I stopped keeping score a long time ago. Why bother when you can never repay me?" Chess winked and then made a shooing gesture. "You'd better get going."

Zander nodded and turned towards the door. With a little luck, he might stave off disaster, at least for a little while, but he'd have to hurry.

Lapin offered his paw to Citrine as she alighted from her carriage. Usually, a groom came to take care of her gargoyles, and she'd assumed that wouldn't change now that she used her flying horses, but nobody seemed to be around. How odd.

Worry niggled at her, and she exchanged a glance with Lapin. "I hope things aren't worse than we feared."

Lapin patted her hand. "Let's not borrow trouble until we need to." A smile curled across his face, and he pointed behind her. "See? Here comes one of the stable lads now."

The young man ran up and took charge of her horses and the carriage. She watched for a moment to make sure he could handle them. They could be spirited, but he had no problem with either one.

Turning back to Lapin, she nodded towards the front entrance. "I suppose we'd best get on with things."

They climbed the front steps and stepped in front of the main door. Usually, by now, Anders would be welcoming them, but nobody appeared. After an awkward moment, a soldier on the left bowed to her and pulled open the door. She and Lapin entered the Red Palace to find the entryway completely empty.

She hesitated on the marble floor. The lack of activity at this time of morning was almost eerie. "I do hope nothing has happened."

Even as the words left her mouth, Anders appeared, two staff members trailing behind him. She recognized Simpkin, from the stables, but not the other man.

Anders had almost passed her when he pulled up with a start. "Oh, Your Majesty! When did you arrive? I'm so sorry, and Sir Lapin too. I..." The usually unflappable steward wavered between what he had been doing and his need to attend to the new guests. Finally, he held up a hand. "If you'll excuse me for a moment. I must deliver these men to their destination. I will return momentarily."

He snapped his fingers at the men. "What are you waiting for? Let's go! Prince Zander needs to talk to you both immediately."

The men pulled their curious gazes away and followed Anders down a side hallway that led to Zander's study. Well, she supposed, it was his father's now.

Lapin pulled out his pipe from his pocket and clamped it between his teeth. "Hmmm, interesting."

"It certainly is," said Citrine.

The minutes ticked by as they waited for Anders to return. When he finally did, he looked flustered. "Ah, I apologize again. It's been... a morning, I'm afraid, but if you'll follow me, I'll take you to the west parlor."

"Citrine!" She turned at the sound of her name. Zander hurried towards her.

Part of his hair stood up. He must have been running his hands through it again, a sure sign he was upset. He crossed the entryway. His fingers were like ice when he took her hands, his expression puzzled.

"I sent a raven to Sir Lapin. What are you doing here?"

Citrine ignored his accusing tone. "I was with Sir Lapin when he received your message. I thought I'd tag along since I had news for you."

Seeming to notice Lapin for the first time, the Prince gave the rabbit a distracted nod. "It's good of you to come." He turned back to Citrine, a light sparking in his eyes. "When you say news, do you mean..."

Citrine nodded, but held up a hand. "I did find some answers for you, but it's not that simple."

The rigid muscles in his shoulders relaxed. "Simple or not, you don't know how glad I am to hear that."

Unease slithered up her spine at his words. "What in the world has happened?"

Zander glanced between her and Lapin. "I don't have time to explain right now, but I will." He gestured at Anders. "Make sure they're comfortable." He stepped away from Citrine. "I need to speak with some of the staff, but as soon as I'm done, I'll tell both of you everything."

Before she could respond, Zander whirled and was gone. Citrine and Lapin fell in step with the steward. She was dying of curiosity, but one glimpse of Anders' shuttered expression, and she knew it was pointless to question the faithful steward.

When they reached the small, cozy room, Anders ushered them inside, where two armchairs flanked an enormous fireplace. Across from the two chairs was a plump settee, and a low coffee table sat in the middle of the snug setting. "If you'll wait here, I'll send someone in with tea shortly."

Without waiting for an answer, he bustled back out the door.

When he departed, she exchanged a prolonged glance with Lapin. "Whatever do you think has happened?"

Lapin chewed on the end of his pipe. "We'll have to wait for the Prince to find out the answer to that question." He paused and met her gaze. "But I would brace yourself, my dear."

Chapter 28

AN HOUR LATER, ZANDER and Chess joined Citrine and Sir Lapin in the cozy parlor.

"Am I glad to see the two of you!" Chess hugged Citrine and clapped Lapin on the back before he plopped down on the settee.

Zander had barely sat down next to him before Citrine leaned forward, her grey eyes intent. "Now, tell us what's happened. I've been about to burst with all this secrecy."

A smile tugged at Zander's mouth at her eager curiosity.

"What I'd like to know is, where is the King? I haven't seen him since we got here." Lapin's eyes held Zander's, leaving no room for prevarication.

He and Chess exchanged a look, and Chess spoke up before Zander had the chance. "Well, right now, he's fast asleep chained to his bed, and hopefully, that's where he'll stay for a while yet."

Citrine pushed up her spectacles and scrunched her nose. "You'd better explain why that is, Chess."

Chess grinned. "Because I drugged him."

Citrine gaped at him, and Zander rolled his eyes at his friend. "What Chess neglected to say is that we've been drugging the King for the last two nights now—with his permission—for his and everyone else's safety."

Lapin exchanged a glance with Citrine, and they nodded at each other. "It's as we suspected," the rabbit said. He turned back to Zander. "Why don't you tell us exactly what's going on? We have some ideas, but we need to hear the details from you."

With a sigh, Zander related recent events to Citrine and Lapin. "And now, I'm trying to buy some time to figure things out, but I'm not sure how long I can keep this under wraps," he finished.

There was a long silence where the only sound was the crackle of the fire and the ticking of the clock on the mantle. Finally, Citrine leaned back in her chair. "You are in quite the pickle, aren't you?"

"That's putting it mildly, my dear." Lapin turned his sharp gaze on Zander. "From what you've told us, it seems even though Alice seemed to have broken the curse on the King, it's still somehow controlling him. It seems odd that it's only at nighttime."

"That's not as strange as you believe," Citrine interrupted. Her gaze went to Chess. "You said when he was in the labyrinth, he was a Minotaur-type creature?"

Chess nodded.

Citrine turned back to Lapin. "They're nocturnal." She pursed her lips. "And they also have an almost insatiable thirst for blood, which explains the dead animals in the garden."

Lapin's expression clouded. "Does he show any unusual behavior during the daytime?"

Zander looked at Chess before he answered. "Not... exactly. He's been more snappish, and he loses his temper more frequently, but his lack of sleep might explain that. A few times, it's seemed as if..." He paused, not sure if he was going to sound crazy or not.

Chess filled in the silence. "It's the King's eyes. Sometimes they... glow red." At Zander's surprised glance, he shrugged. "They did that in the labyrinth, too, but let's not forget the most important part here—two people are now dead."

Zander shifted in his chair. "But he doesn't have control over himself."

Chess held up his hands. "You don't have to defend him, Zan. We're trying to help here."

Zander slumped back against the settee's cushions. "I know, but I'd hate for anyone to think of him as a monster... even if he's acting like one at the moment."

Citrine had said nothing and was instead staring off into space, a finger absently tapping against her bottom lip.

Lapin nudged her knee. She started. "What is going through your mind, my dear? I can almost see the wheels turning in that brain of yours."

Citrine sat back. "I'm wondering if the curse is only a link, and someone is controlling him through it."

"Why do you say that?" Lapin asked.

Citrine spread her hands. "When Alice broke the curse, at first he was fine, so we know it wasn't some type of damage like with the Jabberwock's Curse and the previous prince. The problem there was that he had been under the curse too long, and his mind was permanently affected. That doesn't seem to be the issue here."

Lapin nodded for her to continue. She looked at all of them, her gaze landing on Zander's face last. "Additionally, if the curse itself was still affecting him, it would be a more constant problem, right? You're an Alchemist, Sir Lapin. With the episodes so sporadic, doesn't it seem as if someone is instigating them, so to speak?"

Lapin absently chewed on his pipe for several minutes before he spoke. "That's true, but what you're suggesting is not only complicated spell work but would require something organic from the King—his blood or hair or some such item."

Zander clenched his fists. "The Queen has to be behind this somehow. After all, she's the one that cursed him to begin with, but she flew off. I mean, she attacked him, so I suppose it's possible that she took something from him then. It all happened so quickly, though, I'm afraid I didn't notice if she did. I was relieved to see the back of her."

Chess stood up and moved to lean against the fireplace mantel. "If the Queen is doing this, is there any way to stop her—if the Commander finds her, that is?"

Lapin slowly shook his head. "I'm afraid not, at least not while she has whatever item she took. Of course, we're still speaking hypothetically here. Nothing is for certain. However, if someone retrieved the item from her, it would break the connection. I think. But these things are tricky business."

"Would breaking the connection hurt my father?"

Lapin's face creased with concern. "I can't guarantee what would happen, and if she destroys the item, well then..." He shrugged a furry shoulder, letting the words hang in the air.

"Well then, what?" Zander asked, his hands shaking.

"That's the problem—I don't know. There are several possibilities." Lapin's chin sank onto his chest as he chewed on the end of his pipe. "But none of them are good, I'm afraid." He raised his eyes to meet Zander's. "I understand you want to protect your father, but drugging the man forever isn't a proper solution."

Zander scrubbed his hands against his thighs. A dull headache throbbed behind his eyes. He almost wished he could take the same draught as the King and forget all about this. He sighed. "I need more time."

"What will time give you?" Lapin leaned forward.

"If I can't help my father, maybe I can get rid of my Drifter Gene. That will at least protect the throne if my father..." Zander swallowed and forced the words out. "That is, if my father is unfit to rule."

Lapin frowned. "Yes, Citrine told me what she found in Sacklepenny's lab, but, Sire, I'm not sure that's any less risky than trying to break the connection this curse has to your father. I've not heard of anyone getting rid of their Gift." He paused, his eyes unreadable. "Your personality might be permanently altered."

Zander's gut knotted, and he pushed to his feet to pace around the small room. "What choice do I have? Half the Council wants me gone as it is. If they find out about Father..." He didn't finish the sentence. He didn't have to.

Citrine stood and crossed the room. She put a hand on his arm. "Surely we can convince the Council that you aren't a danger to anyone. We even know of a Mirror

World resident that can come break another Jabber-wock's Curse, if it comes to that."

Zander closed his eyes and let the warmth of her hand anchor him in the storm raging around him. "You weren't at the Council meeting. A few of them would probably listen, but men like Lord Beecher—I'll never convince them."

Chess snorted. "He's so old, surely you won't have to worry about him that much longer."

A gasp of laughter escaped Zander, but he quickly sobered. "It won't be soon enough to help me. The Commander is tracking the Queen." He frowned. "We should have heard from him by now."

Chess waved a hand. "He's the last person you need to worry about right now. He's nearly oblivious to anything else when he gets on a trail."

Zander still felt uneasy, but he went back to what he'd been saying. "If he finds her, we'll learn if she's involved—but it might not be in time to save the throne." He looked into Citrine's eyes. "I need to figure out how to get rid of my Drifter Gene. It's the only way."

"But, Zander—"

"He's right, Citrine," Chess interrupted. "As much as I hate the risks to Zander, it might be the only way to keep the Council from booting the whole family."

"Not the whole family. Your father would be next in line." Lapin pointed out.

"You know what I mean," said Chess, and then rolled his eyes. "Besides, I would make a terrible prince. All that duty." He gave an exaggerated shudder.

Citrine glanced between Zander and Chess. "It's not as easy as you believe. You have to obtain a royal Fae artifact, and we're not even sure if the formula requires a specific one. King Thorne wouldn't be eager to give us one of those under normal circumstances, but now that a flower maiden has been killed..."

Chess raised an eyebrow. "It's not as if we have to tell him—at least not until after we get the artifact. From my own experiences, the Fae pretty much keep to themselves."

Zander winced at the note of bitterness in his friend's voice. Although he rarely talked about it, Chess had never forgiven either of his parents—his mother for leaving him when he was hardly more than a child or his father for failing to stop her.

Zander rubbed the back of his neck. "But if they find out from another source, I'm sure they'll be furious." He dropped back into the chair and put his head in his hands. "This is hopeless. Maybe I should just give up the throne and be done with it."

Chess clapped him on the shoulder. "You give up too easily, friend. I'll go to the Fae court. After all, my mother is the King's sister, so he'll have to at least see me." He grinned. "Besides, everyone loves me."

A flicker of hope lit in Zander's chest, and he tried to smother it. "I can't ask you to do that." Chess hadn't seen his mother since he was fourteen, and Zander didn't want the first time to be tied to this mess.

Chess winked. "You didn't ask. I volunteered."

"Are you sure?"

Chess lifted one shoulder. "Why not?" He continued before Zander could speak. "While I'm gone, perhaps Sir Lapin and Citrine can help you find some answers for your father."

Zander shook his head and turned toward their guests. "Citrine, you need to go home. It's too dangerous for you here. You too, Lapin. I should have never asked you to come."

Citrine scowled at him. "For Wonder's sake, I can take care of myself, Zander Alivaras." She lifted her chin, a stubborn glint in her eye. "Besides, you need my help."

Zander didn't want to admit how much he wanted her to stay, so he tried again. "But Citrine, my father killed a girl here last night. What if he gets out again?"

"Don't be ridiculous, Zander. Chess just said you chained him to his bed, and he's drugged into oblivion. Besides, I'm not so foolish as to wander around alone where someone can attack me. Honestly!"

"And I'm not going anywhere, either, Sire." Lapin patted the arm of his chair. "Monsters don't scare me." He glanced at Citrine. "Besides, I might have an idea for a potion that will help the King keep his mind. I'll need your help, though, dear." He pointed his pipe at Citrine, who nodded eagerly.

Chess slapped his hands on his thighs and looked around at everyone. "Well, then it's settled. I'll go to the Fae, and you three will contain the King and look for a way to sever whatever this connection is."

Warmth bubbled up in Zander's chest as he looked around at these people who would risk so much for him. The muscles in his shoulders and neck loosened. There was no guarantee he wouldn't be run out of the Kingdom, but he wasn't alone. With his friends' help, at least there was a chance now.

Chapter 29

"Are you sure you don't want to take anyone with you? I can send a small contingent of our soldiers." Zander's face creased with concern, which had become an almost constant expression for him.

Chess shook his head and patted the satchel that was slung over his shoulder. "Are you kidding? With the palace's famous health elixir and Cook's baked goods, the Fae will welcome me with open arms." He grinned. "You know how they love gifts."

The worry didn't leave Zander's face. "Things have been strained between Wonderland and the Faelands for a while now. I just don't want anything to happen to you."

Chess smirked. "Zander, I'm the nephew of both the Red King and the Fae King. They have to be nice to me." He lightly punched Zander's shoulder. "There are legitimate things for you to worry about, but I'm not one of them."

Sir Lapin nodded. "He's right, Sire." The big rabbit smiled. "The only thing we should worry about is the Fae King wanting him around for a longer visit."

Zander gave a sharp jerk of his chin. "You're right. I hope... That is, you should take the opportunity to... erm, even though we are in somewhat of a hurry, don't feel like you can't visit... everyone you want to," he ended lamely.

It was obvious who Zander was referring to, but Chess still hadn't decided how he felt about seeing his mother again. It had been over seven years. He assumed she'd be somewhere around the palace, but perhaps not. He swallowed. She might have remarried and had more children, or not even live near the King. The Faelands covered an entire island. It wasn't as if she *had* to live at the palace. He shook off the tightness that had coiled in his neck and shoulders. He'd have to see how things went.

"You should still be careful." Citrine's voice pulled him out of his thoughts. She stepped up and hugged him, as she whispered in his ear, "You should definitely talk to her. I'm sure she misses you."

He only smiled in response. Hitching the satchel higher on his shoulder, he tipped his head towards the mirror. "Well, I'm not accomplishing anything standing here jawing with you lot." He nodded at Zander. "I'll get that artifact for you, even if it requires stealing."

"Chess—"

He didn't stay to hear the rest of Zander's statement. Instead, he strode through the Looking Glass.

It spit him out in front of a large hill. He couldn't have planned that better if he tried. Although he'd never been here, he'd seen the maps. He grinned at Underhill and waited.

It didn't take long.

The outline of a door shimmered into view and then split open. A tall woman with blue skin and silver braids intermingled with feathers strode out of the opening. Based on the armor she wore and the half a dozen similarly garbed Fae behind her, Chess assumed this was palace security.

She stopped about a dozen feet away and pulled her sword from the scabbard at her waist. "Who are you, and what do you want?"

Chess held up both his hands and gave the woman his most charming smile. "You might want to work on your welcoming skills, love. It's almost as if you aren't happy to see me."

The woman's expression didn't waver. "I do not have time for games. State your business."

Chess let his hands drop to his sides and straightened. All right, then, she was going to play it that way. He could adapt. He formally bowed his head before he spoke. "My name is Sir Chess Felinas, and I am here to visit my uncle, King Thorne, on official Red Palace business."

The silver eyes narrowed and assessed him. He kept his posture relaxed, but as the seconds ticked by he wondered if he had made a mistake coming here alone.

Finally, she gave a sharp nod and re-sheathed her sword. "Yes, you have the look of Aunt Larkspur." She pursed her lips. "It is interesting that you visit now, after all this time." She gestured with one hand, and one of the Fae warriors stepped up to her side. "Notify the King of our visitor's presence."

The tall man bowed his head and took off at a lope to deliver the message.

She spun on her heel and headed back inside, gesturing impatiently. "Come along, then."

He lengthened his stride to catch up so he could fall into step with her. "You realize, it's considered rather rude where I come from not to introduce yourself." He let his charm out. "After all, I told you my name."

She huffed out a breath. "Your genes are very obvious."

He gave her a puzzled look. "You mean, my... Aunt Larkspur?"

She shot him an impatient glance. "No, not because of your mother, but because there are too many similarities between you and my brother."

He ignored her emphasis on the word *mother* and asked the more obvious question. "And why would I be at all like your brother?"

"Because you are our cousin." She lengthened her stride and threw the next words over her shoulder. "I am Azalea, by the way."

As he hurried to catch up, Chess hoped the fact that his newly acquainted cousin being named after a poisonous plant wasn't a sign of things to come.

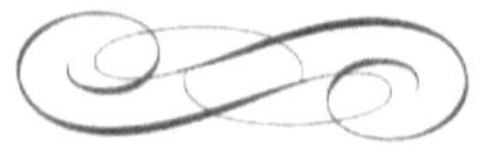

Chess paused outside the throne room, while Azalea announced him to her father. The life force in the walls seemed to breathe in and out.

Numerous small Fae flitted in and out of the leaves and branches that formed the walls and ceiling. The King lounged in an enormous woven swing-like chair. Besides his height and the color of his skin, the man looked nothing like Chess's mother, and he lacked her willowy build.

Noting the large antlers on the top of the King's head, Chess decided his grandparents must have not come from the same Fae clans. Of course, the only things he knew about the clans were what his mother had told him as a child—which wasn't much. His eyes scanned the room, delving into the shadowed corners, but it appeared empty besides the small Fae.

"Come." By her tone, Chess realized it probably wasn't the first time Azalea had spoken to him.

He straightened and walked into the room, his posture purposefully relaxed. A bubble of disappointment surfaced when he realized his mother wasn't here, but he would examine that later. His attention turned to his mission.

Chess stopped about a dozen feet from where the King sat and executed a courtly bow. "I bring greetings from the Red Palace, Your Majesty." He slid the satchel from his shoulder. "And gifts."

The King straightened in his swing-like chair and his dark eyes drilled into Chess as if he were trying to read his soul, reminding him of Azalea's earlier assessment. It took all of Chess's willpower not to squirm under that gaze and to keep his snarky thoughts to himself.

Finally, the King spoke. "So, you're Larkspur's son."

It was a statement, not a question, but Chess answered, anyway. "Yes, Your Majesty, I'm the son of the flower maiden Larkspur and the Red King's brother, Commander Zavier Alivaras."

The King's mouth quirked, and he rose to his feet. Slowly, he circled Chess, as if he were examining a horse.

Chess kept his stance loose and let a smile play around his lips. "Would you like to examine my teeth next, your Highness?"

The King quirked an eyebrow, but instead of answering him, he turned to Azalea. "Where did you find him?"

Azalea, who had been standing next to Chess in rigid silence, relaxed a fraction. "He was outside the entrance to Underhill. A lookout alerted me to his presence."

"Did he say what he wanted? Is he here about the girl?" The King's mouth creased into a frown.

Azalea shook her head. "He only said he was here on official Red Palace business. He didn't say what that business was."

Chess briefly wondered who this *girl* was, but decided to jump in before things got too far off track. "As I'm standing right here, I'd be happy to answer your questions directly, Your Majesty."

The King's gaze swung back to Chess, and the weight of his power fell on him like a smothering blanket. Chess gritted his teeth and kept his posture straight. After a tense moment, a smile curled across the King's face. "So you *have* inherited more than your looks from Larkspur. All right, then—what did you say your name was again?"

Chess bit back a retort. He knew the man knew his name, but repeated it anyway.

"Ah, yes, Chess. Such an unusual name. I wonder what Larkspur was thinking. It doesn't follow our naming conventions at all."

"Well, she had my father's wishes to consider, and I don't think he would have been pleased if she'd named me after a flower."

The King snorted. "We do not name our males after flowers. Not only do you have a ridiculous name, but you know nothing of our ways, either."

Chess gave a lazy grin. "I'm afraid you'll have to take that up with my esteemed parents, as blame for that oversight can't be laid at my feet, Your Majesty."

The King *tsk*ed. "You not only have the look of Larkspur, but you have apparently taken after her in tongue as well."

Warmth seeped into his chest, and his smile widened.

The King frowned. "Do not take that as a compliment. Flower maidens are supposed to be sweet and compliant, not sharp-tongued and contrary. I blame it on all the time she spent with the humans."

"To be fair, Your Majesty, I'm sure my mother had little choice but to grow a spine, living with my father." As soon as he said it, Chess wished he could suck the words back into his mouth. The last thing he wanted was to discuss his home life with this man.

The King surprised him, though, by letting out a deep laugh that sounded like tree branches rubbing together. "I do not doubt it, my boy." He turned his attention to the satchel. "Now, you said you brought gifts?"

Chess swallowed a chuckle at the King's eager expression. Instead, he pulled out the polished box that contained three bottles of the health elixir and a larger box that contained Cook's best pastries. He handed them over to the King, who walked to a nearby table.

The King waved a hand in his daughter's direction. "Come, see what your cousin has brought us."

She stayed where she was and folded her arms. "I doubt these offerings will make up for his long absence or the pain he has caused Aunt Larkspur by his willful avoidance all these years."

The King pinned his daughter with an intense stare. "Azalea, now is not the time."

Azalea's expression closed. "Regardless, I have no interest in my cousin's gifts, as they do not make up for his long silence."

The injustice of her words opened a wound long scabbed over. Chess faced Azalea and smirked. "It *was* too bad of me to leave my mother like that." He snapped his fingers. "Oh, wait, that's right. *She* was the one that left *me.*"

Azalea shifted, her posture stiff. "She had no choice, and you refused to communicate with her."

"There's always a choice, Princess, and I'm not sure why you're holding me responsible when she never contacted me either."

Azalea's eyes narrowed, but her father, having finished a pastry, interrupted the exchange. "Azalea, why don't you go check on Indigo? Make sure he's making progress. The Feast is tonight, after all."

With a last searching look at Chess, Azalea nodded at her father, whirled, and disappeared out the door.

Chess chided himself for letting his emotions get the better of him. His mother wasn't why he was here. He only hoped that the King wouldn't pick up where his daughter had left off, but when he turned back to the King, the man was starting on another pastry.

"Cook makes the best tartlets in Wonderland."

The King nodded. "Perhaps also in the Faelands, too. Please give her my compliments."

"I'm glad you're enjoying them. Now, about that business…"

The King waved his tartlet in the air, sending crumbs flying. "That can wait. Our Luna Feast is tonight. You will join us, and then we can talk about your business when it's over."

"Your Majesty, things are rather urgent back home. I really must insist that—"

The King interrupted him. "Nothing is urgent enough to worry about on a Feast day. Your business can wait, nephew. Today is a day for good food and dancing." A smile curved over the older man's face. "Besides, we must celebrate your first visit to the Faelands."

He turned and clapped his hands. All the small Fae in the room came to attention, their small bodies vibrating with anticipation. He pointed at a slender girl with out-sized feathery wings and a curly pale blue halo of hair. "Bluebell, take my nephew to an honored guest room."

The tiny girl dipped into a curtsey. She zipped over to hover in front of Chess and made another curtsey. "Please come with me," she said, her voice chiming like a bell.

Chess hesitated, but the King was busy polishing off a third pastry. Pushing his uncle today wouldn't further his cause, so with a shrug, he followed the Fae girl out the door. As he followed Bluebell through the twisting tunnels, he couldn't quite decide if he hoped his mother would attend this party or not.

Chapter 30

A LITTLE WHILE LATER, Chess sprawled out on the bed in his room. He had to hand it to the Fae. They knew how to do comfort. His bed sat in an alcove. The filmy draperies framed a living headboard, its intertwined branches lush with leaves and budding flowers. Their scents of spiced vanilla and heady gardenia perfumed the room.

A skylight covered in colored glass cast a pattern on the plush rug on the floor. He wasn't sure how that worked underneath a hill, but he appreciated the fact that his bedroom didn't feel like a cave.

His satchel sat on the thick cushion of a deep blue cup-shaped chair, and a small table next to it held bottles of sparkling liquid and a plate of iced cakes. He licked a trace of icing off his finger. Well, it *had* held cakes.

A soft knock on his door made him sit up. He swung his legs over the side of his bed and walked to the door, wondering if more time had passed than he realized.

Surely, it couldn't be time for the Feast already. The sun was still shining.

When he opened the door, Azalea stood on the other side, her posture stiff. Chess leaned his shoulder against the doorjamb. "On an errand from your father, or did you forget something you wanted to berate me for?"

"I have questions. You will answer them."

Chess raised an eyebrow. "I will?"

She gave a decisive nod. "Yes, you will."

Chess crossed his arms. "I have nothing to hide. Ask away."

She straightened her shoulders. "I am very close to my Aunt Larkspur, and your silence has hurt her deeply."

When she paused, as if expecting an answer, he said, "That isn't a question." He'd tell her what she wanted to know, but he wasn't going to make it easy for her either. She's the one who'd come to him, after all.

Azalea's gaze studied the room behind him as if she could find the words somewhere inside. "She sent you many letters. Aunt Larkspur believed your silence was purposeful, but, what you said to my father earlier—you seemed to imply she did not contact you." She looked at him, and he bit back a sigh.

"That is also not a question. What is it you want to know?"

She huffed out a breath. "Why did you say that? It is not correct. I saw some of her letters and presents myself, but your voice did not ring with falsehood."

Chess straightened. "That's because what I said was true. My mother left when I was fourteen, and I never heard from her again." He kept his voice even and his expression neutral, but inside, the old hurt he thought had long since scarred over throbbed with remembered pain.

Azalea studied him for a long moment and then asked, "Did you want to hear from your mother?"

A laugh huffed through his lips. "What do you think?"

She tilted her head. "I do not know. That is why I am asking."

Chess stepped back from the doorway. "You may as well come in. I'm not having this conversation in the hallway."

Azalea stepped past the threshold and halted, watching him. "You did not answer my question."

"The answer is yes, Azalea. As a young boy, I adored my mother. Of course, I wanted to hear from her after she disappeared." He ran a hand through his hair, pacing back and forth. "I didn't understand... That is, nobody ever gave me a genuine explanation of why she left. One day she was there and then she was... gone. The Commander—my father—told me it was because she missed home." He finally looked at his cousin, a bitter smile curving his lips. "You can imagine my surprise, since I believed *we* were her home... that I—" He broke off and swallowed down the wave of emotion. He should have realized coming here would bring up all the old hurt and pain. Stupid of him.

A soft touch on his shoulder brought him back to the moment. "I am not privy to why she left. I was very young when she returned, but I owe you an apology. It seems I have wronged you all this time, cousin. I blamed you for hurting Aunt, but the separation hurt you, as well." She hesitated and then nodded, seeming to come to some inward decision. "I could explain more, but I... that is, would you like to visit Aunt Larkspur?"

Chess had heard the expression of *time stopping*, but he'd never experienced it before. For a long moment, he just gaped at his cousin, his mind a furious whir of jumbled thoughts and emotions.

Until one thing crystalized in his mind. "Yes, I would. In fact, I can't think of anything right now I'd rather do than see my mother."

Azalea's rigid posture relaxed, and a smile brightened her serious face. "Then I will take you to her." She turned towards the door. "Come."

Chess blinked. "Right now?"

Azalea looked back at him, her brow wrinkled. "Did you not say you wanted to see her, right now?"

"Well, yes... but..."

"Is there something else you must do first?"

Chess took a deep breath and blew it out. "No, you're right." He gestured at the door. "Lead on, cousin."

Chess followed Azalea out of Underhill onto a well-marked path that ran into the surrounding forest. "She doesn't live with the rest of you?"

Azalea shook her head. "No, since she returned, she has preferred her own company."

She turned down a side path. The trees pressed in from both sides, the flowers and plants crowding their footsteps. Chess rubbed his damp palms along his trouser legs, his mind strangely blank.

Despite turning the upcoming encounter over and over in his mind, he had yet to come up with any words that didn't make him sound bitter or embarrassingly needy. "Maybe we should have given her some warning she's going to have company," he said.

"I already did. She is expecting you."

"Were you so sure I'd say yes? I mean, what would you have done if I turned you down?"

Azalea shrugged, her wings fluttering with the motion. "You did not. Besides, the odds were good, based on your behavior earlier."

"I'm not sure if I should be impressed by your insight or slightly terrified." Azalea snorted but kept walking. Chess didn't ask what he wanted to—what did his mother think of this upcoming visit?

After a few more minutes, the trees thinned, and Azalea drew to a halt. Nerves jittered through him as he stopped next to her. She pointed up ahead to where a chimney was visible through the leaves, puffs of lazy smoke wafting from the top.

"It is past this ring of trees. I will take you through. When you are ready to come back, send one of the bumbles. There are always several tending her gardens."

"Thank you, Azalea. I appreciate this," he said. "I'm... I'm not sure I would've come here on my own."

She tilted her head. "Then I am glad I spoke. Aunt Larkspur will be happy to see you at last."

A lump rose in Chess's throat. Was Azalea right, or did his mother resent him for not contacting her? He drew in a deep breath. It was time to find out. "Let's go then."

Azalea paused at a tightly bunched ring of silvery birches. She drew several glittering symbols in the air. They hung there before slowly dissipating. There was a loud groan and two of the trees bent away, creating an opening into the clearing.

Azalea stepped through and he followed. At the center stood a small stone cottage, its door painted a vibrant blue. An explosion of flowers of every size, shape, and color surrounded the house, and tendrils of flowering vines climbed its rough walls, draping over a dormer window set into the high peaked roof. Tiny Fae darted in and out of the foliage. Several stopped what they were doing to watch him.

Chess stared at the little house, his feet rooted to the ground. Before he could convince himself to knock on the door, it swung open. A figure filled the doorway, and his throat closed as he blinked back the sudden moisture in his eyes.

The silhouette was still the same. Tall and slender, she stood with her familiar brilliant blue hair waving around her smooth brown face, the features made indistinct by the distance. The simple, robe-like dress she wore fluttered around her legs, its greens and blues blended like a watercolors.

"He came, Aunt Larkspur," Azalea called to the woman.

Chess wondered if his mother still recognized him by sight or if almost ten years had changed him enough to make him unrecognizable. There was a profound silence for several long moments. Even the trees seemed to still as if they understood something important was transpiring.

Finally, she waved an arm. "Come in, then." It was the same musical voice he remembered, but her tone gave away none of her feelings. He again wondered how she really felt about this visit. He rubbed his hands down the sides of his trousers and glanced at Azalea.

A smile tugged at her mouth. "You will not see her, standing out here."

He took the first step and together they crossed the clearing and went up the three moss-covered steps.

The front door was open, but his mother had retreated inside.

Azalea stopped at the threshold. "I'll leave you, then. Remember, send a bumble when you are ready to return. The Feast begins at sundown."

Chess swallowed, tapping at his leg. "Thanks."

"It is good for you to visit her." With these last words, Azalea trotted back down the steps and out of the clearing.

With a shaky inhale, he entered his mother's home.

He paused a few steps inside the door, letting his eyes adjust from the bright sunshine outside to the cool dimness inside. He had an impression of plants and color, but his attention narrowed onto the figure standing next to a small round table in the middle of the room.

Her brilliant blue eyes watched him silently, traveling over him as if taking inventory.

Just when he thought maybe he wasn't welcome here, she broke into a wide smile.

"It's about time you came to visit, Chess Felinas." In two strides, she crossed the room and wrapped her arms around him.

For a moment, Chess stood completely still, a riot of emotions running through him, and then his arms came up and he hugged her tightly. Her familiar scent surrounded him. He had forgotten how she always smelled of flowers and something earthy, like soil left in the sun.

More memories ran through his head, ones he had pushed down deep. Pressure built at the back of his eyes, and he swallowed painfully, blinking his eyes to keep the tears from falling.

His mother stepped back and framed his face in her palms. Her own eyes, on a level with his, shone with unshed tears. When she spoke, her lips trembled slightly. "I have missed you, son. Even though it has taken many years, I am glad you've come."

He had to clear his throat to speak. "I'm glad to see you too, Mother."

She stepped back and waved him to the table while she walked to a wood stove in a corner. She began gathering various herbs and flower heads, throwing them in a pot that was filled with water. "Sit. I will make us some tea."

He pulled out a chair and sat. "I don't want to put you to any bother."

His mother glanced back at him. "Nonsense, it's no bother at all."

He leaned back in the chair, looking around, while she returned to her preparations. The home was comprised of one large room. On one side was a sitting area and an enormous fireplace with shelves flanking it, filled with books and plants. A set of steep stairs curved upward from the corner. On the other side was a kitchen area.

Heaps of herbs and flower heads covered most of the surfaces, except the table where he was sitting.

"This is a nice place, but I'm surprised you don't live in Underhill with everyone else."

Larkspur shrugged her slim shoulders. "I wanted the quiet. Underhill is... I don't know how much you've seen, but there's much activity all the time."

Chess traced the table's woodgrain with a finger. "Isn't one reason you came back here because you missed your family, your home?"

Larkspur's hands paused in their tasks before they resumed expertly adding plants to the simmering pot. "Let me get our tea ready. I can see you have questions. I want to answer them, but not until we are face to face."

Chess bit back the questions that clamored to be released, and an awkward silence fell over the room. His mother cleared her throat.

"What brings you to the Faelands? It's obvious that you didn't come to visit me."

The words seemed to carry an undertone of blame, and Chess pushed aside the guilt that his mother's words provoked. It wasn't as if she had sent him so much as one raven in all the time she'd been gone. "I came on palace business. I needed to talk to King Thorne."

"Ah, that sounds serious. I hope all is well at the palace." She glanced at him, and he gave a sharp nod.

Larkspur turned back to her task as another silence fell over the kitchen. Chess shifted in his chair while she gave the contents of the pot a swift stir. She then pulled a teapot from a cabinet, placed a cloth over its opening and poured the liquid over it. With a deft twist of her hand, she tied up the cloth that now held a heap of plant matter into a little bundle and dropped it in the teapot.

She pulled two cups from the same cupboard and placed it all on a round wooden tray. With that done, she walked to the table and set down her burden before settling herself across from him.

"So what do you need from the King? Or aren't you allowed to say?" She carefully poured the tea into the cups and pushed one towards Chess. Fragrant steam wafted up to Chess's nose, and he took an appreciative sniff of ginger and something sweet before he spoke.

"It's rather complicated, but the short answer is a royal artifact."

Larkspur regarded him over her cup and took a sip of her tea. "My brother won't part with one of those easily. Can you tell me why you need it?"

"That's a very long story."

Larkspur's mouth curved into a smile. "I think it is rather obvious I have nowhere pressing to go."

Chess sighed, not sure where to begin and what he should divulge. After all, she was the King's sister. It was clear her loyalty was here and not at the Red Palace, but this was easier to talk about than the past.

Taking a deep breath, he explained the situation. At times, it was as if he was talking in circles, but she listened intently, only interrupting to clarify something.

He finally drew to the end of his tale. "The King is not doing well at all, and if we don't bring back that artifact, the Prince might lose the throne permanently." When he finished, he leaned back in his chair and picked up his cup. He grimaced and set it back down. It had gone cold.

"Poor Zane," Larkspur murmured, her hair waving around her head. She glanced up at him and then back at her cup. "What does your... the Commander say about all this?"

"He's gone at the moment, looking for the Queen."

Another silence blanketed the room, and Chess shifted in his chair. The only sound was the crackle of the fireplace and the faint whistle of the breeze blowing through the open windows.

"I should—" Chess started.

"He said—" Larkspur said.

Chess lifted a hand. "I'm sorry. What were you going to say?"

Larkspur hesitated and then lifted her chin to look him directly in the eye. "I understand you didn't come to the Faelands for the sole reason to visit me, but you're here." She covered his hand with hers. He stared down at the long brown fingers so similar to his.

"We really don't need to—"

Her grip tightened. "No, I think we do." A smile played around her mouth. "You've never liked unpleasant conversations. Even when you were a tiny thing, whenever I would scold you, you'd try to make me laugh instead."

Chess's mouth slid into a half grin. "Did it work?"

"Probably more often than it should have, but don't try it today. I don't know how long you'll be here or... even if you'll be back, but I don't want to waste this chance to settle things between us."

Chess swallowed, but he didn't look away from his mother's intense gaze. Instead, he leaned forward. "All right then. We can start with why you seemed to believe it was my job to contact you when you were the one who left me... us."

His mother blinked at him and shook her head. "I never thought that."

"Then why did Azalea tell me how hurt you were when I never communicated with you? I was barely more than a child when you left, and it wasn't as if you sent me so much as a letter. It was like..." Chess's voice cracked with emotion. "...you'd died."

Her eyes widened. "But I did. I sent many letters and gifts." Her gaze dropped to the table, and she twisted her fingers together. "They were all returned—unopened. Finally, around your eighteenth year, your father sent me a letter with my last gift. He said you wanted nothing from me." Her chin dipped to her chest and her shoulders curled inward. "He said you were ashamed of your Fae heritage and you wanted to forget it... and me."

Chess's heart ached at those words. "I never got any messages, and certainly no gifts." He shoved away from the table and stood up. "I can't believe he was lying all this time."

Larkspur hunched over the table and shook her head, her hair writhing like angry snakes. "I don't understand. Why would he do this? He loved me, of that I have no doubt. It was painful for him to send me away. He said he only did it for you, that it was the only way."

Chess froze as what she said filtered into his brain. "Wait, you're saying he sent you away?"

"Yes." She stood and began gathering the tea things.

"But... he said you... you left. That we should be happy you stayed as long as you did."

Larkspur stilled, and when she raised her head, there were tears in her blue eyes, the slits contracted to small vertical slivers. She crossed to him and put her palm against his cheek. "I would have never willingly left you, Chess. You are my son, and even then, I could see your Fae heritage pushing to the surface."

Chess could barely pull in a breath. "He said it wasn't your fault, that you couldn't stay away from here, and then you never wrote or visited. I thought... that I wasn't... that you needed this place more than you needed me."

Tears spilled down his mother's cheeks. "Oh, Chess. It breaks my heart—all this time you believed..." She covered her mouth with a trembling hand.

Chess's thoughts churned, his eyes burning with unshed tears. He couldn't make sense of what he was hearing. Pain and anger and a deep relief mixed until he was unsure how he felt. All he knew was that it changed everything.

"I can't believe... all these years I thought you left us, left me." Anger burned through him, and he clenched his fists. "And he let me, the liar."

A touch on his arm made him start. "I can't pretend to understand why your father did this, but he loves you."

Chess snorted. "After everything he's done, he doesn't deserve you defending him."

She shook her head. "I'm not defending him. I'm telling you the truth." She gave a tentative smile. "Besides, no matter what your opinion of his actions, we have a chance to start over. I don't want to waste it on anger or blame. Do you?"

Chess realized his mother was right. He'd deal with the Commander later. Right now, he had his mother back. He pulled her into a fierce hug, and she squeezed him back. "I missed you, Meemee."

Chapter 31

ALICE STOOD IN THE middle of her cage and stared first at the key in her hand and then at the tower door across the expanse of empty space. She suppressed a shudder.

She was fairly sure King Thorne would let her go—eventually. If it weren't for the Advisor, she would give it some more time. As it was, she'd been on tenterhooks since last night, afraid he'd be back, that this time Azalea wouldn't be there to stop him.

Of course, even if she did get out of this tower, she had no idea how to get out of Underhill or back to Wonderland.

"Arthur?" she called.

"Yes?" His bespectacled face appeared at the bars.

Alice's eyes strained to peer into the shadows as she looked around the tower. She hadn't seen Indigo since yesterday, but she wouldn't put it past him to sneak in here and lurk out of sight. Reasonably sure they were alone, she asked, "If you got out of your cage, do you think you could find your way out of Underhill?"

He blinked at her. "I... I don't know. I rarely leave my cage."

"But if you did, if I could get us out of here, would you be able to find your way out?"

Arthur's beard quivered, even as he shook his head. "I believe I could find the way out if we had some time." His mouth trembled. "I would give anything to leave this place, but... I don't know... a fall would be fatal from this height, Miss Alice. We are very high up."

Alice rubbed a hand over her face. "You don't have to tell me that." She got to her feet and paced across the cage floor, sending it swaying slightly. She'd found after the first day, she'd gotten used to the movement. It was a lot like being on board Papa James' ships when she was younger.

"There has to be a way, though, Arthur." She pointed above her head. "This vine goes to the tower door. If we can figure out a way to pull that lever or get the cage to slide down..." She trailed off, her mind turning over the possibilities.

Arthur pushed up his spectacles. "There's nothing in my cage that would be heavy enough to cause the lever to move, even if I were able to hit it. I'm afraid I don't have very good aim."

Alice stared down at one of the cages below her. From this spot, she had a clear view of a chain with a golden loop connecting the cage to its corresponding vine, but she couldn't discern how the lever set the cage free. "Do you think there's a way to make the cage move without using the lever? Maybe I can make it swing hard enough to get going."

Arthur shook his head so hard, his glasses slipped down his nose. "That's much too dangerous. The cage might come loose and crash down to the floor."

Alice grimaced. Definitely not the outcome she wanted. She turned over various ideas in her head, the only sounds the faint breeze that always seemed to blow through the tower and a few birds twittering.

Perhaps it would be possible to go hand over hand down the vine. It wasn't that far. Her gaze travelled along the plant's length and then to the dark shadows below. She took a step back from the bars. No, there was no way she'd make it across.

She let her head fall into her hands, despair weighing her down. She just wanted to go home. Was that too much to ask?

"Miss Alice, I might have an idea."

She looked up at the older man. "I'm listening."

"Well, there must be some kind of mechanism that releases the cage, probably near the loop where it's attached. You might be able to manually do what the lever does." He paused. "But it would mean you'd need to climb onto the outside of the cage."

Alice stared at him. It was a good idea that had a decent chance of working. She glanced down again and swallowed. If she didn't fall to her death, of course. She squeezed her eyes shut. Was it worth the risk, or should she wait a while longer? The Advisor's face loomed in her mind. No, in her gut, she knew he would try again, and she might not be so lucky next time.

"Miss Alice, did you hear me?"

"Yes, I did. I was… thinking." She gripped the bars, her hands suddenly damp. "What do you think about getting out of here tonight, when they're all busy at that Feast?"

Arthur's Adam's apple bobbed up and down, and he sniffled. "That sounds… capital, just capital."

Alice finished her dinner and then watched as the light that filtered through the latticed ceiling slowly dimmed. Lanterns along walls flickered on as the tower darkened. She stood to her feet, a knot of ice heavy in her stomach.

Carefully, she tucked the key into the bodice of her dress. With a last look around her prison, she moved to the door and pushed it open. For a moment her mind blanked in blind panic, and her fingers gripped the edges of the doorway.

Above her, Arthur's face pressed against the bars, his eyes blinking behind his spectacles. "Are you sure about this, Miss Alice?" His voice wavered. "I won't blame you if you'd rather not risk yourself."

She drew in a deep breath and gave a sharp jerk of her chin. "I'm sure. We're leaving here tonight, Arthur, one way or another."

Even though she sounded confident, her hands shook as she positioned herself in the doorway. Her glance fell down to the dim shadows below. She swallowed. All right… she wasn't so sure.

Then she remembered the promise of retribution in the Advisor's eyes as he'd tried to staunch the blood flowing from his nose. She shook her head. No, she didn't have a choice. Not really.

Gripping the doorway with both hands, she swung herself out of the opening, her feet finding purchase on the bars on the side of the cage.

She squeezed her eyes shut as the cage swung back and forth. For a long moment, she couldn't force her paralyzed limbs to move.

"I say, are you all right down there?"

"Yes," Alice squeaked out. The cage finally stilled, and she slid her hands up the bars and pulled herself towards the top.

Her heart hammered so hard in her chest, she was half afraid that it would vibrate her right off the cage. Slowly and carefully, she eased her way upward. Alice's breath came in gasps, and cold sweat made her skin clammy by the time she made it to the top of the cage.

It was then that she realized the worst was yet to come. She was kneeling, but in order to reach that golden loop, she was going to have to stand up.

Her hands felt numb as she clenched the top of the cage. Her confidence wavered, but the idea of trying to climb back inside was equally terrifying.

Tears welled up, and one trickled down her cheek. She was too afraid to wipe it away, and it slowly made its way down to her chin before it dripped off.

"Miss Alice, you're almost there. All you need to do is stand up." Arthur's voice floated down to her.

Alice blinked furiously, not wasting any energy answering him. She needed to get ahold of herself because the only other alternative was unthinkable. In her mind, the faces of Rommy and Papa James flashed through her mind, and then there was Chess, his eyes laughing at her with that grin that simultaneously made her want to kiss him and smack him. She suddenly knew she wanted to see that grin again, almost as much as she wanted to reunite with her family.

It gave her the courage she needed. Pressing her lips together, her knuckles white where she clung to the chain, she forced her legs to stand. The cage swayed underneath her, and she let out a cry of alarm before clamping her lips shut. Above her, Arthur gasped.

She loosened her hold slightly and turned her attention to the loop that attached the cage to the vine. If there was a mechanism, it should be there, but she couldn't quite see. Gritting her teeth, she pushed herself up on her toes, thanking fortune that she was tall. She glimpsed a thin rod attached to a squeeze handle before her foot slipped and plunged between the bars. She screamed as the cage whirled in a crazy circle.

"Miss Alice!"

The metal bit into her hand as she clung to it, and her breath came in pants of panic as the cage bucked beneath her.

It took too long for the cage to stop its crazy spinning, and by the time it was done, her heart hammered in her ears.

"Miss Alice!" Arthur called again, his face so tightly pressed against the bars that his beard looked like it was in three pieces.

"I'm all right," she called as she extricated her foot while keeping a tight grip on the chain. She pushed to her feet again, but this time, she wrapped one leg around the chain. Using it for balance, she pushed up on her toes again. The rod pierced the vine, and the loop rested against it.

Alice stared at the contraption for a minute before she figured out how it must work. The lever at the door must pull the rod down, releasing the loop.

Fingers trembling, she let go with one hand and reached for the rounded end of the rod. She barely got ahold of it. She pulled, but it didn't budge.

Gritting her teeth and using the chain to leverage herself higher, she got a better hold of the end of the rod. Unfortunately, that also meant her foot barely grazed the bars of the cage. Alice gripped the end and pulled with all of her might.

Nothing happened.

Then the rod jerked downward, and with a creak, the cage slid forward. Alice barely remembered to let go of the vine above so the chain didn't pull her from her perch as she glided towards the tower door.

Above her, Arthur let out a whoop, but Alice was too busy trying to hold on as the cage picked up speed. As the tower door got closer, she realized they'd left out one important thing in their plans—how to slow down.

Chapter 32

THE CAGE BARRELED TOWARDS the door, and Alice gripped the chain with both hands, her leg still wrapped around it, and braced herself.

The jolt reverberated through Alice's entire body as the cage hit the stone lip that jutted out from the doorway, and the sound echoed through the tower. The cage bounced backwards and hit again, more softly this time.

Finally, it juddered into stillness. Alice cracked her eyes open and took stock. Besides some soreness in her hands from gripping the chain so tightly, she seemed to be in one piece.

Gingerly, she unwrapped herself from the chain and peered down. While the front of the cage was up against the stone lip, there was nothing but space around the rest of the cage. A sense of vertigo washed over her, and she swayed.

"Miss Alice?"

It took her a minute to get the words out, and they wobbled a bit. "I'm fine, Arthur."

She took a moment to get her balance and then leaned over to survey the situation. She'd have to climb down and swing herself onto the stone lip. There wasn't a lot of room between the cage and the door, either.

With a prayer that she wouldn't have made it all this way only to fall to her death now, Alice lowered herself down until she was once again kneeling on top of the cage. Gripping the bars, she stretched out flat and felt for a foothold, letting out a breath when she found it.

It took longer for her to go down than it had to climb up, but she finally found herself even with the stone ledge. She edged as close as possible, the cage swaying with her movements.

"You're so close, Miss Alice! Just step onto the ledge."

Alice rolled her eyes. Easy for him to say. He wasn't the one who had to make the leap. But she couldn't stay here forever. Her fingers cramped and her body trembled, more from anxiety than fatigue. The foot of space between herself and freedom stretched like a canyon.

Alice breathed in deeply and leapt towards the ledge, letting go of the bars. The cage swung away from her and she careened into the wall, her hands smacking the stone. She took a step backwards from the impact, and her heel came down on nothing. Flailing, she threw herself forward onto her knees, the stone stinging through her skirts as the cage bumped back against the ledge.

"Are you all right?" Arthur called.

For a long minute, Alice knelt where she was, her heart thundering in her chest and her breath coming in ragged gasps. She couldn't even force herself to nod. Finally, she managed a yes.

With great care, Alice got to her feet, hugging close to the tower wall. It would be horribly ridiculous if she made it all this way, only to trip over her own feet and fall to her death. She edged up to where the cage and door almost met. Shoving at the cage, she wiggled her way through. The space was so tight, she barely had room to fish the key from her bodice. It fit easily into the lock.

She looked back to where Arthur stood, his face pressed against the bars of the cage he'd been in for five long years.

For a fleeting moment, she doubted the idea of bringing him with her. She would have a hard enough time trying to get out of here on her own, and he'd admitted he really didn't know how to get out of here. He would certainly slow her down. She smothered the thought. She wouldn't leave him behind, not after she'd promised to let him out. Besides, he deserved to see his family again as much as she did.

"I'll come let you out. Just give me a moment." The temptation to hurry was nearly overwhelming, but she hadn't almost become a pancake for nothing. She leaned her ear against the door and listened. When the silence stretched, she eased it open a crack and peered out. Everything was still and dark on the tower landing.

She slipped through the opening and pulled the lever, sending the cage back to its place in the tower. Then she shut and locked the door behind her. It wouldn't buy them much time, but if someone came, it wouldn't be immediately obvious she'd flown the coop.

Unfortunately, Arthur was above her, so it would cost her time to let him out, and she also wasn't sure which landing was the right one. Putting her hand against the wall, she ran up the stairs, pausing now and then to listen. She counted two landings before she stopped. This should be the right one... but when she checked, it wasn't.

It took four more tries before she found the correct landing. Once she had the door open, she paused, straining her ears for any sounds. When the silence reassured her she was still alone, she pulled the lever. The cage slid downward. Each second that ticked off seemed to last forever. Alice resisted the urge to tap her foot.

Finally, it bumped against the small ledge in front of the tower door. Arthur Tweed hardly waited for the cage to stop moving before he shoved himself out of the cage and collapsed at Alice's feet. Alice reached down to help him up, but the man clung to her legs, great sobs shaking his body. "Th-thank... you!" he said.

Alice looked over her shoulder. Did she hear something? She patted his shoulder. "You're welcome, but we need to go."

The man continued to blubber at her feet. Above his sobs, something clanked down below. She reached down and shook his shoulder, harder this time. "Your breakdown is going to have to wait. If you want to stay free, we must leave now."

The man finally clambered to his feet, tears still streaming down his face. He gulped and rubbed a dirty sleeve across his face. When he made to grab her hands and thank her again, Alice backed away and started down the stairs. "You can thank me later. Right now, we need to get out of the stairwell. We're easy marks here."

The man visibly paled and, with great effort, pulled himself together enough to follow her. They hurried downward, passing the landing after landing, including the one that led to Alice's cage.

Alice was sure they had to be near the bottom of the staircase when she heard foosteps. Alice stopped and held up her hand. She put a finger over her lips as a cold snake of fear slid up her spine. The footsteps were getting closer. She pointed back the way they had come.

When the Arthur stood rooted to the spot, Alice grabbed his shirtsleeve and pulled him after her. When they reached the landing they'd passed moments ago, she quickly unlocked the door and stepped out onto the ledge. It wasn't overly wide, less than a yard, and the emptiness yawning at her feet almost made her dizzy. She jerked her eyes up and moved over so Arthur had room to squeeze in next to her. Then she pulled the door shut behind them.

"What—"

Alice shook her head, her voice barely a whisper. "There's someone coming."

They stood like statues on the ledge for what seemed like hours. Finally, Alice heard the footsteps pass their landing. She counted to a hundred—twice—before she eased the door open again. The stairwell was empty. She slid out, pulling Arthur behind her. They'd barely gone down a dozen steps when someone shouted above her.

Whoever it was had realized the prisoners were gone. The two raced down the remaining steps, trying to make as little noise as possible. They reached the bottom, and Alice tried to fit the key into the lock with trembling fingers.

"Hurry!" Arthur glanced over his shoulder, pushing at Alice's back.

"Stop it! You're not helping!"

The lock turned, and she shoved open the door. Arthur crowded out behind her. The tunnels stretched out on either side of her, and Alice dithered until Arther grabbed her hand and yanked her to the left. They ducked into another side tunnel just in time. The door to the tower slammed shut with a bang, and the Advisor's voice echoed after them. "You may as well come out. You'll never find your way out of these tunnels on your own."

Chapter 33

"Now that you have reunited with your uncle, will you be visiting more often?" The Fae woman on his right side had been blatantly flirting with him the entire evening. Now she leaned towards him, her ruby red hair falling over his arm in a silky curtain.

Chess leaned back in his chair so that his arm no longer had its hairy covering. "That depends, Orchid."

She smirked up at him, her green cat-like eyes gleaming in the flickering light of the small Fae whose only job seemed to be to light the room as they flitted among the woven branches that formed the ceiling of the feast hall.

"On what?" She tilted her head, and a dimple peeked out on her smooth golden-brown cheek. It reminded him of Alice, and he felt a pang in his chest, but he pushed it aside.

Instead, his lips curved into a smile. "A lot of things."

Orchid drew a sharp-tipped nail down his arm and then let her hand cover his on the wooden plank table. "Dance with me and I'll convince you." There was a mild compulsion in her words, but being half-Fae himself, her charm had no effect on him.

He pulled his hand away from hers. "It's tempting, but I would rather observe." He winked. "Although I'm sure your dancing skills are excellent."

Chess only half paid attention to the woman's response. Instead, his eyes scanned the clusters of Fae that now crowded onto the middle of the floor, dancing with abandon around a fantastical fountain made up of wavy circles of clear glass rings. Inside each ring, the artist had etched flowers and insects in exquisite detail, the colors glowing in the flickering lights of the feast hall. The water shot up a cylinder in the middle and flowed down the circles, changing colors during its journey. Periodically, the water would shoot a colorful spray high into the air, spattering the crowd with a rainbow mist.

He'd met the creator of the fountain, his cousin Indigo, earlier. For no reason, Chess could discern his Fae cousin had been rather hostile. At that very moment, King Thorne whirled by, and Chess shook his head, a smile tugging at his mouth. He couldn't imagine Zander's father doing that.

The scrape of a chair brought his attention back to the Fae woman. Orchid was standing now. She tossed her long hair over her shoulder. Her smile had lost the dimples and turned sharp. "Don't expect me to make the offer again."

Without waiting for his response, she walked out onto the floor, hips swishing, to join the dancers. Even as he watched, a tall man with horns grabbed her around the waist and swung her into a line of dancers that were ringing the fountain. Every so often, someone would stick a glass into the flowing water and down it in a large gulp, and everyone else would cheer.

Three tall, willowy men played what looked like fiddles in the corner, their long, many-jointed fingers moving too fast for him to follow over the strings of the instruments.

"I didn't think you'd know enough to avoid Orchid's clutches." Azalea made this observation from his left side, and he turned to face his cousin. She had set aside her bow and one of her swords in honor of the festive occasion, but she still wore a uniform, although the material was a shimmery pearl color. He wondered if she ever allowed herself to be completely off duty. They were part of the few still sitting. She said the words in an even tone with no judgment coloring them, but her top lip curled ever so slightly.

"You don't like the woman?"

Azalea shrugged. "I didn't say that. She possesses remarkable beauty and demonstrates exceptional hunting skills when she chooses to do so. But it's probably wise that someone like you doesn't get too close to her."

"Someone like me?" Chess smirked at her. "You mean a half-flit?"

Azalea flinched at the word. "I didn't mean to offend, but you aren't familiar with our ways, and Orchid is quite... predatory."

Chess shrugged one shoulder. "You'd be surprised at how similar royal courts can be." He smiled. "But I appreciate that you are looking out for your clueless cousin from the mainland."

A small smile curled the corner of her lips. "I have a feeling you are anything but clueless, cousin."

"And here I thought I was the reason you're still sitting here rather than enjoying the festivities with everyone else." He nodded towards the seething sea of bodies. "I even spotted that Advisor of yours somewhere in that throng."

It was Azalea's turn to shrug. "You are not entirely wrong, but it is merely a good excuse. As the King's daughter, it is not just dancing for me."

Chess nodded towards Indigo, who whirled by with three women clinging to him. "What about your brother?"

Her gaze followed his path until he disappeared back into the crowd. "That is different. It is Indigo."

Chess raised his eyebrows, but Azalea's expression had closed. He turned back to the crowd and his eyes scanned for a familiar face. He had hoped his mother would come. After their reunion this afternoon, he wanted more time with her.

"She doesn't come to these things unless Father makes an issue of it, and not always then, either."

Chess turned to Azalea, his lips parting in surprise. "I'm not sure I like the way you can read me so well."

She shrugged. "It is not difficult. You have been looking for someone all evening." She fiddled with the hilt of one of her daggers. "I hope your reunion turned out positively."

Chess pushed some crumbs into a line with his thumb. "It did. It was rather illuminating."

Azalea's brows pulled down. "I am not sure I—"

A shrill scream interrupted her words, and she and Chess both turned to the throng of dancers. A ripple of commotion spread across the floor like a wave, with dancers scrambling and shoving to get out of the way of... something.

A laugh burst from Chess's mouth when he saw what, or rather who, was causing all the panic. A blur of turquoise blue fur scuttled towards him at stop speed.

Azalea drew back, horror washing over her face. "I thought we killed that creature."

Chapter 34

ARTHUR AND ALICE EXCHANGED looks as the footsteps went past their hiding spot. When the sound faded, the older man's shoulders slumped. "He's most likely right, you know. We'll never be able to find our way out of here."

"Do you want to go back to your cage, then?" Alice couldn't keep the snap out of her voice.

Arthur shook his head, his spectacles sliding down his nose.

"Then we can't give up."

The footsteps came back, and Alice put her finger over her lips and pointed to a set of steps off to the right.

Together they crept up them and turned into another, much shorter tunnel that ended abruptly with a door. The footsteps got closer. Alice gripped the door handle, and it turned easily in her hand.

The Advisor's voice was so close it made Alice jump. "I have more than one way of finding you both, you know. Don't make me set the King's hunters out. Trust me when I say you will not like it if they find you before I do."

Arthur's eyes bugged out, his spectacles magnifying them, but they didn't have time for him to have a meltdown. Alice opened the door and shoved Arthur inside. As she pulled it shut, she glimpsed part of the Advisor's tunic.

She held her breath, hoping he hadn't seen them, since, with her luck, this would be the only room in the entire Underhill that only had one entrance. She turned around to see where they had ended up. The room was dim, the only light coming from a fireplace. The flames were banked low. A perfectly round hassock sat in front of the fire, the firelight shimmering off its deep green color. The rest of the room was shrouded in shadows. She could make out a low bed and a chair, but they were thankfully empty.

She walked towards the far corner, intent on finding another way out or some place to hide. As she moved further inside, she wrinkled her nose. The room had a sharp, musky smell.

Arthur was still frozen by the door.

"Arthur," she whispered, "come away from there. If the Advisor comes in, he'll run right into you. We should probably hide somewhere."

"Miss... Miss... Alice." His voice stuttered, but he wasn't looking at her.

"What?"

He lifted his arm and pointed towards the fireplace.

"Yes, I know there's a fire, but there isn't anyone..." Alice's voice trailed off.

What she'd thought was a hassock was slowly uncoiling itself from in front of the fire. She had no name for the creature. Its head resembled a cat with pointed ears, almond-shaped eyes that looked black in the dim light, and whiskers. A frilly collar of fur surrounded its head. It stretched back on two front legs, tipped in sharp claws. When it yawned, it revealed four large fangs that glistened in the firelight. The rest of its body was long and sinewy, resembling a large snake. It was easily as big around as she was, but instead of scales, silky, dark green fur covered its body.

Once it had completely uncoiled, its multiple sets of legs came into view. It shook itself, and its tail unfurled, showing a nasty-looking barb on the end.

It turned its enormous eyes on Arthur, who let out a yelp and promptly crumpled onto the floor in a dead faint. The creature sniffed his still form.

Most entertaining. The creature stretched out each syllable of the word, and the drawn out "s" rattled uncomfortably in Alice's head. It then settled its long body, propping its head on a paw, and turned its stare on Alice as if waiting to see what she'd do.

"Oh dear. We didn't mean to intrude. If you'll just let me rouse my companion, we'll leave you alone." Alice crouched next to Arthur and patted his cheek, keeping a wary eye on the creature as she did so. So far, it had only seemed curious, but she didn't think it had fangs and claws only for decoration, either.

Don't rush away on my account. The voice was undeniably feminine.

"That's very kind of you, but we don't want to be a bother."

The creature's eyes widened. *You are a fauna speaker. Excellent.*

Alice jerked her head up at the creature's words. "I have the Creature Gift, if that's what you mean." She paused. "I'm Alice, by the way."

The creature dipped its head in acknowledgement. *You may call me Seela. I am King Thorne's hunter.* She preened. *His favorite.*

Wonderful. Alice tried to keep the dismay off of her face. "I appreciate your patience, Seela." She slapped Arthur's cheek harder, and his eyes fluttered. "Wake up, Arthur. We need to leave."

Seela slithered closer, peering down at Arthur. Up close, the creature's musky odor made Alice's eyes water.

Is this your servant?

"No, he's a... a friend."

Arthur's eyes cracked open, and he blinked up at Alice. "I... are we..." Then he caught sight of Seela and let out a garbled yell before his eyes rolled back and he fainted again.

Your friend has an extremely weak constitution.

"I'm afraid he's had a rather rough time lately. I hope you'll excuse him."

I suppose it's understandable. I make even the large Fae nervous.

Alice resisted the urge to ask why. Though this hunter seemed friendly enough, Alice didn't want to push her limits. Arthur's eyes fluttered again, and Alice turned to the creature. "I hate to ask, since this is your room and all, but would you mind backing away a bit? I'm afraid if he sees you, he'll just faint again."

Of course. Seela slid backwards, her body undulating in a way that made Alice slightly queasy.

She forced a smile. "Thank you."

Seela dipped her head but kept her eyes on the two of them.

Arthur blinked up at Alice. "Where... what's..."

"I need you to stay with me, Arthur." She put her arm around his back and helped him to sit up. His body stiffened as he caught sight of the hunter, but Alice gripped him tighter. "No, Arthur, don't faint again. This is Seela, and she's been most kind. There's no need to be afraid."

"But Miss Alice... that's... that's a..."

"I know, but she's been quite understanding about us bursting in on her like this. Now, do you think you can stand?"

Arthur gave a shaky nod, and Alice helped him to his feet. Seela observed all this, her eyes bright with curiosity.

"I'm surprised you aren't at the Feast with everyone else," Alice said as she walked towards the door.

I dislike all the noise and crowds. There are too many Fae in one place to tempt me to leave my fire.

Alice cracked the door and peered out, and then shut it again hastily. "Erm, I don't suppose you would let us stay here for a few minutes longer—just until Arthur gets his legs under him?"

Seela narrowed her eyes. *That is not why you want to stay. Who are you running from?*

Alice swallowed, her back against the door. "I... that is..." She licked her lips. "What makes you say that?" Arthur edged over next to her so they were standing shoulder to shoulder.

It is obvious someone outside has alarmed you. I can hear your heartbeat, and it has quickened.

Well, that wasn't creepy at all.

Alice debated. If she told Seela the truth, would she turn her over to the Advisor? Or would she get the King? While she didn't want to go back in her cage, she was reasonably sure the King wouldn't do anything to her, not with her connection to the Red Palace. Still, after all of this, she didn't know if she could take being put back in that cage.

In the few seconds Alice was trying to decide what to do, Seela slid within a few feet and rose so her head was even with Alice's, balancing herself on the back half of her body. Alice shrank back against the door, and Arthur whimpered. She kept a firm grip on his arm, hoping he wouldn't pass out again.

Seela's open, curious demeanor was gone, and her eyes were steely. *Tell me who you are and why you are here.*

Alice took a shaky breath. There wasn't any choice now. She had no doubt Seela would use those fangs and claws if Alice didn't answer, but that didn't mean she had to spill all the beans. Selecting her words carefully to avoid anything untruthful, she said, "I'm trying to avoid the Advisor, and I'm afraid I got rather turned around."

Seela peered at Alice before nodding as if in confirmation. *Why is he interested in you?*

Alice didn't look away from the dark eyes. "He has a rather unhealthy interest in my Gifts, I believe."

Seela's rigid body posture relaxed. *Solus does not make many friends with his obsessions.* The hunter sighed. *I will take you back to the Feast. I assume you will be safe enough there.*

Alice glanced at Arthur. "Seela kindly offered to take us back to the Feast." The poor man was shaking, but after a brief pause, he nodded. It wasn't exactly where she wanted to go, but if the Feast was as noisy and chaotic as everyone seemed to imply, surely she and Arthur could slip away once they got there.

"Thank you. Again. You are most kind."

Seela gave a shimmy that seemed like a shrug. *I dislike Solus, and it amuses me to thwart him.* She made a shooing gesture with her front leg and Alice moved out of the way.

Seela turned the handle and slid out the door. She glanced back at them before she tipped her head. *Come along. I do not want to be away from my fire for long.*

Alice started to follow, but Arthur gripped her sleeve. "What are we doing?" he whispered.

"She's going to help us get back to the Feast."

Arthur's eyes widened. "But..."

Alice squeezed his arm and gave a tiny shake of her head. "She promised to help us avoid the Advisor, and that's the main thing right now. We'll worry about the rest later."

Seela was at the stairs now and looked back at them, her eyes narrowing. Alice smiled. "We're coming. I just needed to tell Arthur the good news that we'll be back to the Feast in no time."

Seela gave a soft hiss and bumped down the stairs. Alice followed, pulling Arthur along behind her.

They walked down one tunnel after another, and they went up and then down several staircases, twisting and turning until Alice had no idea where they were. She fought the sinking feeling that they would never find their way out of this place.

"Do you hear that?" Arthur whispered to her.

Alice paused. Then she heard it too. The sound of music floated faintly in the air. "We must be getting close."

"What will we do then?" Arthur chewed his lip, a crease between his brows.

"I'm not sure," Alice admitted.

The sounds of revelry got steadily louder. As they approached an archway, Seela stopped. Music and laughter washed over Alice. Beyond the hunter was a sea of color and movement, with a throng of people dancing and celebrating.

A shudder rippled over the hunter, and she turned to Alice. *I'm sure you will be able to avoid the Advisor here. I will leave you now.*

Alice still wasn't sure why the hunter had helped her, but she was grateful to the creature. "Thank you. You have been very kind to interrupt your own evening to help us."

Seela's dark eyes twinkled. *It is worthwhile to disappoint the Advisor.*

With a bob of her head, the hunter slithered back down the tunnel, leaving Alice and Arthur at the edge of the party.

A loud cheer brought her attention back to the partygoers, and she glimpsed flying silver hair. There were probably plenty of Fae with with that color hair besides Indigo and Azalea, but she didn't want to take a chance on anyone spotting them.

Alice backed away from the arch and retreated down the tunnel until they could no longer see the Feast or its attendees.

Arthur pushed up his spectacles and cleared his throat. "What do we do now? I am afraid I am completely turned around."

"I'd be happy to help with that."

The familiar voice sent ice skating across Alice's skin, and when she turned, the Advisor had a smug smile on his face.

Alice gripped Arthur's arm and backed away, but Solus wagged a finger at her. "I'm afraid there's nowhere to go, my dear. You'll never find your way out of here."

"I'll take my chances, thank you."

The Advisor advanced towards them, his golden eyes glowing. "I never thought that hunter would leave, but I have to know—how did you get her to help you? She's usually unfriendly."

"Maybe it's just you she doesn't like. I found her to be quite kind."

The Advisor let out a startled laugh. "I've never heard anyone call one of our hunters *kind*, but I have to admit to being even more intrigued. Few of the humans that stumble onto our island have Gifts." He flicked a finger in Arthur's direction. "He was a complete disappointment, but yours are quite strong."

Alice's mind raced even as she continued to back away. A shout came from the gathering a short distance away, and she stopped. Any hope of help was in there, if she could only get past him. Surely the King would be upset with the Advisor for going against his orders, and it might help her persuade him that the cage was unsafe.

Alice stopped and raised her chin. "If you touch me, I'll start screaming, and what will King Thorne say, then?"

The Advisor paused, and his expression darkened. "Don't be ridiculous. If you believe the King will be happy to find out you've escaped your cage, think again. He'll make sure it doesn't happen again, and trust me when I say you probably won't like his methods."

Alice crossed her arms. She couldn't back down or show weakness with this man. "The King didn't even want to put me in that cage. It was you that convinced him. Besides, he doesn't want any trouble with the Red Palace, and trust *me* when *I* say neither King Zane nor Prince Zander will be merciful if something happens to me."

The Advisor's face paled for a moment, but then his expression cleared. "You're quite right, my dear. Nobody wants an incident with the Red Palace." His gaze flicked to Arthur. "But nobody cares if something happens to him."

Beside her, Arthur stiffened, and Alice narrowed her eyes. "He's harmless, and everybody knows it. You're the one who imprisoned him, and you forgot all about the poor man."

A smile curled across the Advisor's face and Alice shifted, not liking the expression in his eyes. Next to her, Arthur moved forward jerkily, and she grabbed his arm, but it was like he didn't even see her.

"You might be able to resist my charm, but he can't. It's all in the will. While you are too willful for your own good, I'm not sure if he even has one."

Alice watched, horrified, as Arthur hopped on one foot and then the other before patting his head.

"And nobody will find him harmless if he attacks someone during the Luna Feast." The Advisor made a sad face. "*What a shame. The poor man snapped and tried to kill the King or one of his children.*" His face twisted into a sneer. "And do you understand what will happen to him then? He'll die."

Arthur spun in a circle, his spectacles flying off his face, going faster and faster.

"Stop it!" Alice reached out to stop him, but Arthur was spinning too quickly, his face taking on a green hue. "Stop it and I'll go with you."

Arthur abruptly came to a halt. He stumbled over his own feet, groaning, and staggered up against a wall.

The Advisor straightened his tunic and smiled. "That's what I thought you'd say."

Alice held up her hand. "I'll come with you, but on one condition. Let Arthur go. He hasn't done anything, and you've locked him up long enough."

The Advisor narrowed his eyes. "You're not in any position to make demands."

Alice lifted her chin and tried to quell her trembling. "If you let him go, I'll come with you quietly and cooperate." When he didn't answer, she added. "You'll find it difficult to get what you want if I don't."

The Advisor stared at her for a long moment, and finally nodded. "Fine, he can go—I doubt he'll find his way out of here, though. Eventually, someone will stumble across his bones in some dusty corner, but he's worthless to me, anyway."

"No, Miss Alice. I can't let you do this." Arthur's gaze ping-ponged between the two of them.

"It's all right, Arthur. The Advisor said he only wants to do a few tests. I'm sure it will be fine."

The Advisor smiled. "At last, you're being reasonable. Come along."

Arthur protested, but the Advisor simply froze him in place before taking Alice's arm and pulling her down the tunnel.

Alice let him lead her, making note of their turns. After the second turn, she sprang into action. Jerking her arm away, she stomped hard on the Advisor's foot. She spun and raced back the way they'd come, yelling loudly, "Run, Arthur!"

Her only goal was to get to the Feast. A force knocked her to her knees, and an arm came around her throat. It squeezed harder, and spots flecked over her vision.

Then everything went dark.

Chapter 35

CHESS STARED AT AZALEA. "Where did you come across Wickle?"

Before Azalea could answer him, Wickle scrambled onto the table and hopped up and down in front of him. The small creature cheeped and whistled, clearly trying to tell him something.

Chess was so startled to see the snark, it took him a minute to put the pieces together. He felt a sudden shock as he realized the significance of Wickle's presence.

He stared at the agitated creature. "Is Alice here, Wickle?"

Wickle's eyes widened, and he bobbed his head before trundling towards the edge of the table and then back to Chess, like a dog wanting someone to follow it.

The breath squeezed out of Chess's lungs, and he turned to Azalea, trying to keep his voice level. "Where is she?"

Azalea gazed at him thoughtfully. "So she was telling the truth, then. I wasn't entirely sure."

The fact that his cousin knew who he was talking about made Chess's heart rate spike. "Where is she?" he repeated, his voice rising.

Her eyes widened at his sudden intensity. "First, tell me why Alice is here," she said, speaking slowly.

"I don't know. Something must have happened. She was supposed to go home." He clenched his hands to keep from grabbing his cousin and shaking the answers out of her. "But you still haven't answered me—where is she?"

Azalea frowned at him. "I told Father the Advisor was wrong about her. It made no logical sense that she was a spy."

"Spy? What are you talking about?" He waved a hand. "Never mind. I want to see her."

By this time, Indigo had slid from the crowd of Fae and was standing in front of them. His eyes narrowed on Chess, but his tone was lazy. "You seem awfully upset, Cousin. Just what is this girl to you, anyway?"

Chess jabbed a finger at Indigo. "That's none of your business."

Indigo smirked. "Funny, that's what she said, too, when I asked her about that communion stone you gave her."

Chess shot to his feet, causing Wickle to chitter in alarm. "I don't have time for your stupidity. Just tell me where she is!" he shouted.

Azalea stared at him, and Indigo's mouth dropped open. Chess drew in a steadying breath. When he spoke again he lowered his voice, barely keeping a rein on his temper. "I would like to see Alice. Now."

Indigo crossed his arms. "I fail to understand why you have any say over my pet."

Chess placed both palms on the table and leaned towards the other man. "What did you call Alice?"

Azalea put a hand on his arm. "Ignore him. Alice is not his pet, and he is rather disgruntled by her lack of interest." She glared at her brother but spoke to Chess. "I will take you to see Alice. There has been a misunderstanding."

Chess forced his muscles to unclench, and he straightened. "All right. I'm sure we can straighten this out." He held out his hand, and Wickle jumped into it and scrambled up to settle on his shoulder.

Azalea wrinkled her nose. "Must you bring that creature?"

Chess patted Wickle on his tiny head. "I'm not telling him he has to stay behind. Are you?"

Azalea gave the snark a long look before she turned and plunged into the crowd. He followed as she weaved her way out of the feasting hall and up a set of steps underneath one of the many archways that led into the space.

Indigo trailed behind them. "Azalea's wrong. Alice definitely likes me. She's just angry over a little misunderstanding."

Chess fell into step with Azalea. "Is he always like this?"

Azalea grimaced. "Yes, but to be fair, most females fawn over him."

"He doesn't seem the type to take no for an answer." Chess said the words casually, but Azalea must have heard the implied threat in them.

She glanced back at her brother, and the pause before she spoke made Chess's gut churn. "He is persistent when he wants something, but not completely reckless."

Chess didn't think that was much of an answer, but he would deal with Indigo later if he found out the Fae had hurt Alice in any way.

"What is the girl to you?"

"She's..." He stopped, not sure what to say. They didn't have any kind of understanding, and he'd sent her home. In truth, they weren't anything to each other, but saying that felt like a lie. "She's important to me," he finally said.

"If she's so important to you, then why did you let her leave?" Indigo asked.

Chess ignored him, but Indigo repeated the question. He had a feeling if he didn't answer, his cousin would just keep pestering him.

"Because she needed to go home."

Indigo snorted. "Obviously, she must not mean much to you. If she were my pet, I wouldn't just let her go."

Chess whirled around, and Indigo almost ran into him. "Maybe that's because I view her as a person, not a... pet." He poked a finger at the taller man. "And I asked you not to keep calling her that."

Indigo stepped closer, looming over Chess. "Or you'll what, cousin?"

Azalea interrupted before Chess could answer. "She is in here."

Chess gave Indigo a last glare. "Don't push me or you'll find out." When he turned, Azalea was standing in front of a wooden door.

He hurried over to her. "What is this place?" he asked as Azalea turned the handle on the door. She frowned when it swung open easily.

She glanced at her brother before she answered. "It is our prison."

Chess bit back his anger. It wouldn't solve anything at this point. "You locked her up?"

Azalea shrugged. "We discovered her by a dying Fae, and it was not the first faery we had found in that condition. Of course, we had to question her."

Chess wanted to argue that any idiot should realize that Alice wouldn't do something like that, but with every second his impatience was growing. "Just take me to her."

Azalea climbed the stairs, and he followed, his heart picking up speed. He was going to see Alice. His mouth went dry, and worry gnawed at him. What state would he find her in? If they had hurt her at all...

Azalea paused and reached into her pocket, and then she frowned. "I left my key in my other uniform."

"How irresponsible of you, sister, but once again your luck holds out." Indigo pushed on another door and it swung open.

"I don't like this, brother."

Chess gazed past her, and his breath caught when he glimpsed the cages hanging throughout the inside of the tower. Azalea pulled a lever, and the cage closest slid towards them until it bumped against the stone lip of the small ledge that jutted out into the inside of the tower.

Chess stared at the empty cage, a feeling of bewilderment crowding out his earlier indignation.

Azalea's mouth thinned and her brow crinkled. "As I feared, it's empty."

"Is this some kind of prank?" he asked, heat rising in his chest.

Azalea ignored Chess and looked at her brother. His face turned grim before he spoke. "When was the last time you saw the Advisor?"

Chapter 36

ZANDER HADN'T REALIZED FEAR had a stink. He glanced over at the lump on the bed that was his father.

The entire room lay in shadows, a fire burning low in the grate. Zander considered snuffing it out as the room was already overly warm and stuffy, with the funk of stale sweat adding to the smell.

A grunt and clank behind him made him turn. His father's eyes were still closed, but he'd kicked off some of his covers and rolled over. The manacle around the King's wrist twisted his arm at an awkward angle. Zander's heart ached at the sight of his father—the King—chained to his bed and drugged into oblivion.

He walked to the bedside and, pulling the key from his breast pocket, unlocked the manacle from his father's wrist. The arm flopped lifelessly over the side of the bed. With a grunt of effort, Zander moved his father to a more comfortable position and, with a heavy heart, he closed the manacle back onto his father's wrist. He supposed this was better than locking him up in the dungeon, but still.

His hands clenched at his sides. If Lyssandra were here, he wasn't sure he could have resisted squeezing the life out of her.

A knock startled him out of his morbid thoughts. When he opened the door, Anders was standing there. "I'm sorry to disturb you, Sire, but two Councilmembers are here to see you. They said it was urgent that they speak to you."

It didn't escape Zander's notice that Anders was back to calling him *Sire*, and he almost corrected the man. Then, he glanced over his shoulder to where his father lay in a drugged stupor and decided not to. He pulled the door shut behind him and pulled another key, this one larger, out of his trouser pocket and locked the dead bolt that he'd had installed on the outside of the door earlier today. At least, he thought it was today. The days were running together.

He fell into step with Anders. "Who's here?"

"The Duchess and Lord Dordo, Sire."

"Did they say why they needed to see me so urgently?"

Anders shook his head. "No, Sire, and I didn't presume to ask. I put them in the, erm, your study, but I can move them if you'd like."

Zander clattered down the steps. "No, that's fine, Anders." When he reached the bottom of the staircase, he paused. "Perhaps you should have some tea brought. I'm afraid this might take a while."

Sympathy flashed across the man's face before he bowed quickly. "Of course, Sire. I'll have it sent immediately." Anders whisked down an adjacent hallway, and Zander watched until the man disappeared around a corner.

Then he turned towards his study and squared his shoulders.

When he strode into the room, the Duchess and Lord Dordo popped up from where they'd been sitting. The Duchess dropped a curtsey, and Lord Dordo bowed. "We're sorry to come so late, but I didn't think we should wait." The Duchess's voice was cool, but her fingers gripped the fabric of her skirts.

"Yes, yes. It's quite turgid." Lord Dordo's head bobbed in agreement.

The Duchess rolled her sharp green eyes, but for once didn't correct him. "I'm afraid we don't have good news for you, Your Highness."

A dull headache started up behind Zander's eyes. Of course it wouldn't be good news. When was the last time he'd heard anything good? He gestured at the two chairs and rounded the desk to take his own seat. "Please, sit."

He waited until they'd both settled themselves before he asked, "What's wrong?"

The Duchess exchanged a glance with Lord Dordo, and he nodded at her to speak. Zander thanked Wonder for small favors. He wasn't sure if he was up to interpreting Dordo's version of events.

As ever, the Duchess was direct and to the point. "I'm afraid Lord Beecher found out about the death of the flower maiden and that the King was responsible."

The words dropped into Zander's stomach like rocks. The Duchess's lips continued to move, but a buzzing had started in his ears that muffled her words.

Her lips stopped, and she peered at him as if expecting an answer. He shook his head. "I'm sorry. Can you repeat that?"

"I said, he's telling people the curse permanently damaged the king's mind. He's planning to host a gathering at his estate. I'm afraid he wants to gather support to get rid of both you and your father."

Zander clasped his hands on his desk. He didn't have to ask why Beecher wanted to be rid of him. "Do you know who he proposes should take our place?"

She hesitated, glancing at Dordo again before speaking. "From the rumors swirling about, he has your uncle in mind."

Something like relief washed over Zander and loosened his tense muscles. "I suppose it's not good news, but at least he's not bringing in some outsider to attempt a coup."

"This is an outage, it is," said Dordo, slapping a hand on the edge of the desk. "It's not up to the likes of Beecher to say who sits on the stone."

The Duchess pursed her lips. "By your lack of surprise or dismay over this news, I take it it's true that the King killed a flower maiden? I had hoped the story got exaggerated."

Zander gave a sharp jerk of his head. "I'm afraid so."

She tilted her head. "But why? Has the King truly lost his mind? He seemed perfectly lucid to me at the last Council meeting, if a bit short-tempered, but Beecher has that effect on everyone."

Zander drew in a breath, his mind spinning over how much to say. When he spoke, he picked his words carefully, aware that the wrong ones might cut short the time he had to fix this mess. "The King hasn't been himself since his time in the labyrinth. We believe the flower maiden somehow startled him, and he overreacted. It's unfortunate and tragic, but we... I've taken precautions so it doesn't happen again."

The Duchess gave him a long look, and Zander was afraid she would call him on his obvious blurring of the truth, but she merely gave a brisk nod and stood to her feet. "We will pass that explanation along. Now, we won't keep you any longer. It's late, and with all due respect, you look like you could use some sleep." She swept towards the hall but paused at the doorway. "I am not the only one who believes you would make an excellent king. You have friends who are on your side, Your Highness." With those words, she swept out of the study, Dordo following, nearly running into a maid who was bringing in the tea.

He waved at the girl. "Just leave it on the desk, if you don't mind, and then you can go."

The girl bobbed a clumsy curtsey, nearly spilling the tea on the floor before setting it on the desk and then fleeing back out the door.

Zander watched the steam rise from the spout of the teapot. If only he could run away like the maid had. He slumped back and let his head hit the back of the chair. Maybe Beecher was on to something, and he should just let his uncle assume the throne.

Chapter 37

ALICE BLINKED HER EYES open, not sure where she was or what was going on. Slowly, she took in her surroundings. Her gaze landed on bottles and beakers littering a long table, gold and silver strands twisting inside their glass walls, before moving to the other side of the room where herbs and potions, along with various books, filled several shelves.

Where was she? She pushed against the fogginess and confusion. Somewhere nearby a door creaked shut with a loud clunk.

Memory slammed into her, and she jerked upright only to find herself unable to move. A glance downward revealed a leather strap stretched across her shoulders. Her legs also wouldn't budge. Panic flooded through her and her breath sped up, the sound of her heartbeat loud in her own ears. She wiggled and bucked against her restraints, but there wasn't any give.

"Truly, you're overreacting, my dear."

She tried to locate the voice as something clinked behind her head. "I find being tied up tends to make me do that."

Solus came around and leaned over her. She cringed away from him, and he smiled. He probably meant to be reassuring, but his eyes were sharp and hungry. "There's nothing to be afraid of. If you cooperate, the pain will be minimal."

The fog in Alice's brain was now completely gone, and terror pooled in her stomach. She wiggled again, but that only confirmed she was bound fast. Solus picked up a wooden rod that had a hook on the end and moved towards her, and she swallowed. "What... what are you going to do?" She hated the wobble in her voice.

He stepped behind her, and she could only see the underside of his chin and one quivering nostril. "I only want a few samples of your magical signature, my dear. Nothing to be worried about." He lowered the sharp instrument, and she jerked her head to the side.

He stopped and sighed. "The less you fight me, the easier this will be, but I don't really care if this causes you pain or not." His lips pressed together. "I will get the samples one way or another."

He lowered the instrument again and paused. When she stayed still, he pressed the end against her temple. There was a prick against her skin and then a pulling sensation, similar to when Fariar had tested her magical signature. Her muscles relaxed a fraction. If this was all he wanted, maybe it would be over soon.

The Advisor brought up a small crystal knife and severed a glowing strand of braided gold and silver. He dropped it into a glass vial, stoppering it with a cork. He held it up and examined the writhing strand.

"Hmmm, I don't know that I've seen the gold and silver strands together, and its movement is quite a unique pattern, too." He looked down at her. "Have you always had Gifts, or did they only manifest when you came here?"

Alice pressed her lips together, not sure if she should cooperate or not. Before she could decide, the Advisor chuckled as if she amused him. "They all have this idea that a show of spirit will impress me. I can assure you it won't. I'll find out the answers I seek, whether or not you tell me."

He poked the instrument back into her temple more roughly this time, and she flinched. The strand he pulled out was longer, and the pressure in her head turned into a dull headache.

Solus turned back to her and paused. "I'll give you one more chance to answer me, but I don't have time to play games. I wouldn't put it past that dolt Indigo to seek you out tonight."

Alice took a bit of hope from the man's words. It didn't seem like he meant to kill her. She hoped, anyway. He lifted the instrument again, and she spoke in a rush. "I knew nothing about Gifts until I got here. I certainly wasn't able to talk to animals or heal anyone."

"Hmmm. And you had no inkling that you possessed these abilities when you were in the Mirror World?"

"Well, I've always had a way with animals, and I had a knack for figuring out what was wrong with them."

Solus absently patted her shoulder. "That aligns with my theory."

To take her mind off the pain pulsing in her head, she asked, "What theory is that?"

Solus looked down at her and raised an eyebrow. "You can't want to hear about all that now."

"It's not as if I have anything else to do."

His mouth quirked. This time when he put the instrument against her temple, she barely felt the prick of the tip.

"I am operating under the assumption that humans in the Mirror World do not hold any belief in magic; therefore, their abilities do not fully manifest."

Alice winced as he took a third strand, the pounding in her head getting stronger. What he said made sense. "I still don't understand what you need from me."

"That should be obvious. You are a human from the Mirror World who has manifested Gifts here. I want to compare your magical signature to others here with the same Gifts."

Alice still wasn't sure why that helped anything, but thinking was getting more difficult. He had pulled a fourth strand from her temple. A trickle of blood was running freely down her cheek, and she had to grit her teeth against the pain that pulsed through her skull.

He gathered the four vials and moved over to the table. He moved out of her line of sight, but she could hear the clinking of glass on glass. She closed her eyes and tried to breathe through the pulsing pain in her head.

His footsteps made her eyes snap back open. This time he moved to stand beside her, and instead of the hook, he had another wooden rod, but this one had a long, pointed end to it.

"I only need one more thing." His fingers were icy as he pulled down the neck of her dress to expose more of her chest.

Alarmed, she thrashed against her bonds, trying to get away from him. "Don't touch me!"

His lip curled in distaste. "You need not carry on so. I have no interest in your person. I merely need a small amount of your essence."

His mouth settled into a grim line. The panic that had settled somewhat reared back up again, and she squirmed.

"You've been quite cooperative, so I feel I should warn you. This will be a more unpleasant retrieval."

She wiggled harder now, and he frowned. "Fighting me will only make it worse." He shrugged thin shoulders. "But I am still going to get my specimen, regardless. Who knows when I'll have this opportunity again."

She stilled and drew in a breath, bracing for whatever was coming.

He pressed the instrument into her chest, and it poked through the skin. Blood trickled from the wound. She hissed out a breath at the prick of pain, but it wasn't as bad as she had feared.

And then he pulled. The pressure increased to a burning pain. The more he tugged, the worse it got. A whimper escaped her lips as her breath became labored.

"Just a bit more." He suddenly jerked, and a burst of agony turned her vision white.

When it cleared, the Advisor was gone, and Arthur was staring down at her.

Chapter 38

C ITRINE KNOCKED ON THE door to the King's bedroom. She hoped it wasn't too late. It had to be after midnight, but she'd lost track of the time. She hated to bother Zander, but the rawness of the King's skin from those manacles had rather alarmed Lapin.

There was a pause and then footsteps. The door creaked open, and Zander's face appeared. He looked haggard in the dim light, his shirt untucked and rumpled and large circles under his eyes.

He opened the door wider, rubbing a hand over his face. "What are you doing here so late? Did you and Lapin figure out a potion for Father?"

She shook her head. "We're close, but we're still missing a key ingredient that will bring the formula together." She pulled a pot of salve from her pocket and held it up. "But Lapin said the King's wrist was looking chafed the last time he was up here, so we mixed this up, too."

"Thanks. I'll get some of this on him and change the manacle to the other side." There was a deep sadness in his voice that tugged at Citrine's heart. She hated to see him like this.

When Zander held out his hand for the ointment, she brushed past him. She stopped and wrinkled her nose, her eyes taking in the dim shadows and the low banked fire. "When's the last time someone aired this room?"

Zander's chin came up. "I've been trying to take care of things myself." He deflated slightly. "I didn't want any of the maids in here. Not after what happened."

Citrine crossed to the French doors and opened them, letting in a wash of cool air. Then she moved towards the lump on the bed that was the King. "Has he been awake at all?"

Zander shook his head. "Not since I gave him the sleeping draught this evening. He took a double dose."

Citrine pursed her lips. "Is it really necessary to keep him drugged so heavily?"

She crossed over to the bed and reached for the King's arm. Zander blocked her hand. "What are you doing? He's dangerous. You can't go near him."

Citrine resisted the urge to roll her eyes. Poor Zander was so tired he was practically delirious himself. She nudged him aside. "Don't be ridiculous. He can barely move, and with the strength of that potion he's taken, even if he woke up, he'd be weak and disorientated." She held out her hand for the key.

Zander's lips pressed together, and he shook his head. "No, give me the ointment and I'll do it."

Citrine held his gaze for a long, stubborn moment, but finally, with a sigh, she handed it to him.

While Zander took care of his father, she moved around the room, picking up stray clothing and straightening the blankets and pillows on the settee in front of the fireplace. Clearly, Zander wasn't taking any chances and had moved into these rooms to keep watch. She gathered a cup, bowl, and plate, placed them on a tray, and moved it by the door. Then she knelt and banked the fire further. The room was stifling.

By the time she finished, Zander had moved the shackle to the opposite side of the bed and manacled his father's other wrist. She plucked the key out of his hand and laid it on the bedside table.

When he protested, she shushed him and, taking his hand, led him to the settee. She sat down and pulled him down next to her.

He gave her a startled look.

"When's the last time you slept? I mean, truly slept, Zander?"

"I sleep," he said, hunching his shoulders.

She raised an eyebrow.

After a moment, he broke eye contact. "I'm fine, Citrine."

"No, you're not, Zander. This would be hard by itself, but you've had one hard thing after another for too long now. It's a wonder you aren't a gibbering idiot."

A laugh burst from his mouth. "Don't hold back on my account."

Her lips tipped into a smile. "You know what I mean. I'm concerned about you. Can't you let someone else take over here, at least for one night? Surely, a soldier, or even a pair of them would watch over your father for that long."

He blew out a breath, frustration in every line of his body. "It's my responsibility, Citrine. Not anyone else's.

Mine." His eyes dropped to his hands clasped in his lap. "He's already killed one person. I can't let him do it again. He agreed to this." His voice hitched, and he closed his eyes.

Her heart cracked at the despair etched across his face. She wanted to fix this for him, but she couldn't. Instead, she pulled him into a hug. His arms slid around her waist, and she felt a deep sigh leave him as his face burrowed into the curve of her neck. They stayed like that for a long moment.

Then she shifted on the settee so that his head lay on her shoulder. Gently, she smoothed her other hand over his hair. He looked up at her. "What am I going to do, Trinny?"

"Nothing right now. You're going to rest. Everything seems so much worse when you're exhausted like this."

"Maybe it would be better to just let the Commander take the throne. He's a good man and a powerful leader."

She shook her head, and his wavy hair tickled her cheek. She pushed the hair off his forehead, and it flopped back into place. "That might end up being the right answer, but that isn't something to decide tonight."

"But..."

She covered his lips with her fingers to hush him. "Not tonight," she repeated firmly, trying to ignore the tingle that originated where her skin touched his.

He stilled, his eyes darkening. Then he shifted so his face was even with hers, his lips hovering a breath away. One of his hands slid up her back to cradle the back of her head, and she found breathing had suddenly become... difficult.

"Zander I don't think—"

"I'm tired of thinking, Trinny."

His lips brushed hers, the softest of touches. He leaned back and looked into her eyes, a question in his. Perhaps she was tired of thinking, too. She pulled his head down and their lips touched and then melded together, bringing both heat and familiar comfort.

He deepened the kiss, and her hands clutched at the back of his shirt. A distant part of her brain was listing all the ways this was a bad idea, but for once she ignored it. His fingers delved into her hair, and her hair slid free of its haphazard bun, forming a silky curtain around them. He trailed hot kisses from the corner of her mouth and along her jaw.

She needed to stop this. Right now. His mouth found the hollow behind her ear and she hummed softly. Maybe just a moment more.

A loud groan and the creaking of bedsprings made them both freeze. Zander pulled away from her and they both sat up, their eyes zeroing in on the bed. The lump shifted restlessly. After another groan, the King rolled over with a loud clank of chain. Then he was still again. After several long moments, the rhythmic sound of deep breaths once again filled the room.

Citrine set both feet on the floor so she was sitting primly on the edge of the settee. She reached down and picked up her hairpin from the floor. Holding it between her teeth, she coiled her hair back into its bun and jabbed the pin in to hold it in place.

When she finished, she glanced over at Zander. He was looking at her with a half-smile on his face, but there was still heat in his eyes.

He reached out a hand, but she stood up, and he let it fall back into his lap. Silence fell once again. After a few moments, he spoke, his voice low, "I'm... not sure what to say right now, but I won't apologize."

She sighed. "There's nothing to apologize for, Zander." Her mouth curved upward. "I think we both needed a bit of comfort."

He huffed out a laugh. "If that's what you want to call it."

She gave a decisive nod and her tone turned brisk. "I do. Now, you still need to rest." She picked up a pillow that had fallen to the floor and set it back on the settee. Then she patted it. "I'll stay and keep watch."

"There is no way..."

She held up a hand. "If your father so much as flicks an eyelash, I'll wake you. I give my word as the Pearl Queen."

He hesitated and then stretched out. "All right, but only for a little while."

She took a blanket and covered him with it, and he looked up at her. "This still doesn't feel right."

She brushed the hair out of his eyes and leaned down to place a soft kiss on his forehead. When she straightened, he caught her hand. She raised an eyebrow.

He gave her a sweet smile that made her toes curl, but she kept her expression placid.

"We can figure out a way to make this work, Trinny."

Her throat ached with sadness even as she shook her head. "We've gone over this, Zander—"

"No." He pushed up on one elbow. "It's different now. We have Alice."

"Alice? How can she help from the Mirror World?"

His grip on her hand tightened. "She has the Creature Gift and the Healer Gift, the same Gifts as your mother. She could help you, take some of the load."

A small hope unfurled inside Citrine, but her logical brain reminded her of a large flaw with his plan. "But she's not here, Zander, and we have no idea if she'll ever come back."

Zander's smile stretched into a grin. "I think she will if Chess has anything to say about it."

Citrine was afraid to let the hope bloom, so she gently pushed his shoulder until he laid back down. "You need to get some sleep, Zander. When this is all over, we'll talk about it."

She dropped down in front of the settee and leaned her back against it. His hand brushed against her hair. "I love you, Trinny."

"I know. I love you too. Now close your eyes and rest already."

He still had a smile on his face when he drifted off to sleep.

Citrine stared at the glowing remains of the fire. The kiss replayed in her mind, and she touched a finger to her lips. His idea had merit. But she couldn't forget it was only an idea. She let her hand drop. There was a long way between this moment and Alice actually agreeing to help her. Now wasn't the time, anyway.

Resolutely, she turned her mind to the formula she and Lapin had been working on, but she couldn't help the smile that stayed on her lips as she went over the various ingredients. Something was missing. The King needed to stay in his right mind, not let the monster take over. It was there, right on the edge of her thoughts.

The firelight was hypnotic, and her eyelids grew heavy and she let them close. Just for a minute.

She jerked awake when something brushed her shoulder, her heart pounding. She let out a breath when she realized Zander's hand had slipped off the settee. She didn't know how long she had dozed, but it was still night. She studied him in the faint moonlight that illuminated his face. His hair hung disheveled and shaggy around his sleeping features. How dear he was to her. If only there was a formula to make her not love him.

And then she blinked. That was it. She needed Love's Bane. She wanted to smack herself. Of course! It sheltered the mind and the emotions.

Quietly, she got to her feet, and then stopped. She couldn't leave. She'd promised. She glanced back at Zander. His face relaxed for once and wavered.

Love's Bane only bloomed at night. If she didn't get it now, she'd have to wait another whole day.

As much as she didn't want to wake him, she knew Zander would be upset if she didn't.

"Zander?" she called softly.

A grunting noise behind her made her whirl around.

The King was awake, sitting up, his form dimly visible in the shadowy room. She swallowed.

She leaned down to touch Zander's shoulder, and the King's glowing red eyes tracked her movements. An icy fist squeezed her heart.

"Zander?" she said again, a little louder this time.

The Prince didn't stir, and she shook Zander's shoulder.

The King climbed from the bed, and her heart sped up. The King tilted his head, almost as if he could hear it, and ice skated across her skin.

She shook Zander harder, but he was deeply asleep. The King stalked towards her.

"Zander, you need to wake up." She kept her tone conversational, afraid of agitating the King further, and tried to slow her breathing. She was still safe. The chain would only let him go so far.

He reached the foot of the bed, but he didn't stop. Her gaze flicked to the bed and landed on the manacle, lying open on top of the blanket, and then back to the King.

A chilling smile curved across his face.

"Zander!" she screamed, but the King moved with frightening speed and his talon-tipped fingers closed around her throat, cutting off her voice.

Chapter 39

THE SCREAM ECHOED FROM the room. Chess pushed aside Azalea and Indigo and shoved at the door. It didn't budge. He slammed both of his hands on the panels and shoved again.

A hand on his shoulder caused him to spin, his teeth bared. Azalea held up her hands. "It is sealed."

"Well, bloody well unseal it!" Chess snarled.

Azalea stepped in front of him and traced several shimmery figures in the air. Before they even faded, Chess tried to step around her, but she held out her arm to block him. "No, let Indigo and me go in first."

Azalea had barely opened the door when Chess rushed by her.

And stopped.

A small man with wispy hair was bent over a woman. His body hid her face, but he knew who it was. With a growl, he reached the man in only a few strides and lifted him bodily away from the prone form.

The man blinked at him, his eyes owlish behind over-sized spectacles.

"Who are you?" Chess demanded, shaking the man.

"I... I..."

"Chess, stop it! He's rescuing me!"

He whirled towards the voice, letting go of the man, not even caring when he hit the floor and fell to his knees. Alice filled Chess's vision. His gaze ran over her, taking in her disheveled hair and snagging on the blood running down the side of her face and soaking into the neckline of her dress.

He stepped over the man still on the floor in order to reach her. "Alice." It was all he could manage. His hands hovered, afraid to touch her in case she was hurt worse than she looked. Her scream still rang in his ears.

A smile lit her face, and she struggled to sit up, but the strap across her chest was only half unfastened. "As happy as I am to see you, could you to undo these restraints before the Advisor wakes up?"

A smile tugged at his mouth as his fingers fumbled with the straps. Indigo moved to her legs, undoing the leather restraint that held them.

"Here, let me help you, pet." Indigo moved to her other side and put a solicitous hand behind her shoulder.

Chess narrowed his eyes, and Wickle hissed. Alice's eyes widened at the sight of the snark, and she swung her legs around to sit, holding out her hands. The snark trilled and leapt into them. Alice brought the blue fluff up to her cheek.

"Oh, Wickle, I thought you were dead." Her voice cracked on the last word, and her lips trembled. Chess sat next to her and put his arm around her shoulder only to knock into Indigo, who had seated himself on her other side and was also trying to put his arm around her.

Wickle hissed at the Fae, and Indigo drew back, frowning. A smug grin curled across Chess's face as he tucked Alice into his side and pulled out his handkerchief. He gently dabbed at the wound on her temple. "Are you all right, love? When I heard you scream..."

A shudder ran through Alice's body, and she snuggled closer to him and set Wickle in her lap. "I'm all right. I think." As if to belie her words, she began to shake, and he wrapped his other arm around her as she buried her face in his shoulder. Wetness seeped into the fabric, and he had the sudden desire to kill the person who had hurt her.

Indigo scowled at them. "You should let me soothe her."

Chess glared at him over the top of Alice's head. "I think she's had enough of your lot."

Indigo ignored him and reached out to touch Alice's shoulder, but Wickle bared his fangs and snarled. Indigo snatched his hand away.

Meanwhile, Azalea was standing in front of Arthur. "How were you involved in this?"

Despite her calm demeanor, the man cringed away from her, nervously eyeing all of her weapons. "I... I ... was... That is..." He licked his lips. "Miss Alice. That is to say. The Advisor... he..." His gaze skittered to the man lying on the floor, who groaned.

Everyone stared as the Advisor staggered to his feet. Blood ran down the side of his face, and he still looked rather bleary. He put a hand out to steady himself before he pointed at Arthur. "This man attacked me. He needs to be dealt with appropriately."

Belatedly, Arthur seemed to realize he was still holding the book he'd used to knock the Advisor on the head, and he dropped it as if it burned him. It landed with a resounding thwack. Azalea looked from the book to the Advisor and back again.

"Did you hit him with this?" she asked, her hand resting on the hilt of her sword.

"Erm... Yes. That. Is. He—" Arthur stuttered, hunching in on himself.

Alice pulled away from Chess and scooped up Wickle before she hopped to her feet. "Don't hurt him. He was protecting me." She swayed and Chess put his arm around her waist to steady her even as Indigo reached out, too.

She whirled towards the Fae man, almost losing her balance. "Stop it! I told you I don't want you charming me."

"I'm only trying to help. You need soothing." Indigo's voice deepened, and he ran a hand down her arm. Alice flinched away and her face turned white.

Chess knocked Indigo's hand away. "She said she doesn't want you charming her. You're clearly not helping."

Indigo crossed his arms. "I'm not the one who sent her away."

Chess leaned towards Indigo, pointing his finger at the man. "I didn't send her anywhere. She wanted to go home, not that it's any of your business. She said she doesn't want—"

The Advisor spoke over him. "I don't understand why you are worried about her. I was the one who was attacked. You need to take—"

"Miss Alice!" Arthur reached out both hands as Alice crumpled.

Chess reached for her at the same time as Indigo, and they caught her before she hit the ground. Chess glared at his cousin. "I've got her."

Indigo scowled back at Chess, not willing to let go either.

The Advisor stepped towards them, his gaze intent on Alice. "Neither of you should have custody. She's a prisoner, and—"

A blur of blue fur sailed through the air, and Solus scrambled backwards, his hands held out in front of him. Terror etched on his face. "No... no, stay away from me!" The Advisor's voice climbed to a high-pitched screech. Startled, Indigo let go long enough for Chess to swing Alice up into his arms. By the time Chess turned around, the snark had latched onto the man's arm and sunk in his fangs.

Solus screamed and tried to shake off the snark, but Wickle held on. The man sank to his knees, still wildly flailing his arm. Wickle finally let go and landed on the ground with a loud hiss.

The man stared at his arm, which swelled bigger and bigger. The stitches on the sleeve near his shoulder popped as the swelling moved up his arm and towards his neck.

"No, no, I can't..." He choked on his words as his neck distorted and cut off his air. He fell to his side, his body twitching and convulsing as his face turned blue and foam dribbled over his lips.

He gave a final jerk, his body bowing and his eyes nearly bulging from their sockets. Then he fell still, staring at nothing.

Silence dropped over the group like a thick blanket. Wickle trundled back to Chess and cheeped. Indigo looked from the snark to the Advisor's still body before he took an enormous step away from Alice.

The snark jumped onto Chess's trousers and scrambled upward until he perched on Chess's shoulder.

Azalea frowned at Wickle. "Their venom has a reputation for working quickly, but I have never seen it." Her hand went to her sword and Chess edged away from her, not sure what she planned to do. He only knew that Alice would never forgive him if he let anything happen to the little snark, and to be honest, the Advisor rather deserved his fate.

"He was protecting Alice. You can't blame him for this. It's your Advisor that's at fault here."

Azalea stood for a long moment before she responded. "I can see the creature is loyal to her, and I am sorry that she has suffered at the hands of the Advisor. I hope you consider that debt has been paid."

Wickle trilled and chittered. He seemed to agree.

Chess looked down at Alice, her pale face still and her body limp. He wasn't so sure about that, but he had more pressing problems. "I don't give a miter about your Advisor. I'm concerned about Alice right now."

Azalea nodded. "Yes, of course." She turned to Indigo. "Tell one of the Healers they are needed, and take her to an honored guest room." She looked back at the Advisor and grimaced. "I will take care of the Advisor and the other prisoner."

Chess had forgotten all about the man. Arthur hunched against the wall, watching them with blinking eyes oddly magnified behind his spectacles. Chess sighed. He really wanted to take care of Alice, but he instinctively knew she would be furious if anything happened to this Arthur person. "I hope you'll put him in a guest room too, rather than back in one of those cages."

Azalea sighed. "You are right. I no longer know why they put him in prison, and the person who knows..." She shrugged. "He is beyond caring now."

Indigo strode to the door. "Are you coming? Or did you want to discuss more business with my sister?" His tone bordered on hostile, but Chess didn't care. He just wanted Alice to wake up and be all right. If that meant he had to put up with his cousin, he'd do it.

Chess gathered Alice closer and nodded his head. "I'll follow you."

Together, they hustled out the door and down another tunnel.

Chapter 40

A SCREAM JERKED ZANDER from a deep sleep. He blinked in confusion. Two bodies thrashed on the floor and rolled into a small table, knocking it onto the floor with a crash.

Zander stumbled to his feet, still clearing the sleep from his brain. He struggled to make sense of what he was seeing.

"Zan—" The voice choked off, but he recognized Citrine's voice.

He blinked again, and his vision sharpened. His father's hulking figure was pinning Citrine to the floor. Horror paralyzed him for a moment. Then Zander launched himself at the man's back, trying to rip him off, but the King threw him off and whirled towards him.

Zander glimpsed blood and Citrine's still body before the monster attacked him, his talons ripping at Zander's flesh. Zander tried to get a hold on his father, but the King was impossibly strong. They grappled with each other, Zander's feet sliding across the floor.

"Father!" Zander shouted in his face, but there was no recognition in the wild, red eyes. Instead, the man's mouth twisted into a snarl and he let out a bellow that made Zander's ears ring.

His father shoved him away, and Zander staggered back, nearly losing his balance. Behind him, Citrine stirred, and the King's wild eyes swung in her direction.

"Run, Citrine!" Zander yelled as he threw himself at the King, but the King absorbed the blow, throwing Zander off-balance. He struggled to stay upright, his mind churning. His Jabberwock could handle this, but there wasn't room to shift in here. The King turned back to Citrine, who was dragging herself towards the door on her hands and knees. He fell on her with a grunt, and she screamed.

Zander rammed into him, knocking him off Citrine. His father rolled across the floor and Zander kicked him, knocking him closer to the French doors. He hoped Citrine would take the chance to get away. The King staggered to his feet, his face not even recognizable anymore. Letting out another bawl of sound, he lowered his head and charged towards Zander.

His heart twisting, Zander rushed towards the assault, using his own momentum to send them towards the balcony. They burst through the partially open French doors, shattering some of the glass from the force. His father flew over the railing even as Zander dove after him, shifting as he moved.

His father landed with a sickening thud but lay still for only a moment before he leapt back to his feet. Zander roared as he landed, and the creature turned to face him, its eyes glowing red in the dark and steam rising from his nostrils.

In the moonlight, he was a nightmarish blend of the King and what Zander assumed was the appearance of the monster in the labyrinth. He had swelled in size, and while he retained his normal features, they were twisted so that Zander hardly recognized his father's face.

The creature threw back his head and let out a bellow that bounced through the air like a challenge. Zander opened his own mouth and roared again. Behind him, several windows lit up, but that was the least of his worries right now.

He charged his father. The King leapt backwards and just avoided the snap of Zander's jaws.

The beast's gaze darted back towards the balcony. When the King tried to circle around, Zander turned with him. The King suddenly lunged to the side. He was impossibly fast, and it took all of Zander's focus to block him, even with his bigger size and strength.

The beast seemed almost crazed with bloodlust as he tried to get around Zander and back to Citrine. With a low growl, Zander knocked into his father's chest with his head. The King staggered back and fell. Zander pinned him with a large foot. His father bared his teeth and tried to claw Zander.

Although his scales were too thick for the claws to do any actual damage, it still hurt. He roared into his father's face, but it didn't do any good.

The sound of a voice made him twist his long neck around. A light flickered behind the broken French doors, and he heard Anders' voice, the sound of footsteps, and then Lapin's familiar tones. What he didn't hear was Citrine.

Zander looked down at his father, who was still struggling, and back towards the window, wishing he had the ability to ask what was happening to Citrine... but he couldn't let go of the King.

"Sire..." Anders appeared on the balcony, rumpled, his wispy hair standing on end and his robe only half on. His eyes bulged a bit when he spotted Zander and the King, but he pulled himself together. "Sire, I've sent for a Healer for the Pearl Queen, and the palace guards should be to you shortly."

He'd hardly gotten the words out before the sound of running feet crunching on the gravel path sounded. The palace guards were moving swiftly in his direction.

The metallic scent of blood drifted on the breeze, and he had to fight the overpowering urge to leave his father and go to Citrine.

The guards slowed as they got closer, and he willed them to hurry. Underneath his talons, his father's body suddenly went limp.

Zander watched the King's body deflate, and his claws slowly retracted and then disappeared.

The soldiers stopped several yards away, surrounding them. Zander breathed a sigh of relief until a spear almost jabbed him in the eye.

That was when he realized the soldiers weren't looking at his father at all.

They were all staring at him with their weapons drawn.

Zander quickly shifted back into his human form and held up both his hands. "I need to..." He gestured towards his father, who was struggling to stand.

"I'm sorry, Your Highness, but please step away from the King."

The words snapped Zander out of his shock. He batted the spear away from him and moved to help his father.

The soldier blocked him again. "Halt!"

Beyond them, the King struggled to his feet, lucid but unsteady. Zander knew he should take care of his father, but he couldn't. A sob rose in his chest and he swallowed it down, as he tried to push through the ring of soldiers. "I have to go to Ci— the Pearl Queen."

A hand gripped his shoulder, and he swung around, his voice a growl. "Get out of my way!"

The soldier cringed backward, but to his credit, lifted his spear again in shaking hands. "You need to..."

"I do believe you've the wrong man, my good chap," said Lapin as he hurried up the walkway towards them. "The evidence speaks for itself."

The King tottered a few steps. His eyes were wide and horrified. He slowly lifted his hands. In the moonlight, the bloodstains on his hands and forearms were plainly visible. Blood painted ugly splotches across his crumpled nightshirt.

Realization dawned on the soldier's face even as the King groaned and covered his face with his hands. "No, no, not again."

Lapin stepped up to the King and put an arm around the man's shoulders. "Steady on, Your Majesty. We'll get this sorted."

The guard captain looked from the King to Zander. "Your Highness, should we..."

Zander closed his eyes for a moment, trying to pull himself together. He nodded at three soldiers that were clustered together. "You three, take the King back to his rooms—"

"No," the King interrupted. He straightened, his shoulders back and his head lifted. "You must put me in the dungeons."

"But, Father..."

"No, he's right, Your Highness. It's for the best right now," said Lapin.

The guard captain stepped forward, clearly hesitant, and looked at Zander. Reluctantly, Zander nodded. "You're probably right."

He should see to his father, make sure he was as comfortable as possible, but all he could think about was Citrine and all the blood on his father.

As if reading his mind, Lapin spoke up. "I'll see to the King. You go. Let me know if she's... how she is." For the first time, Lapin's expression faltered, and an icy knot formed in Zander's stomach, a sense of urgency pushing at him.

A soldier took the King's arm to lead him away, and Zane's gaze met Zander's, full of anguish and sorrow. "I'm... I'm so sorry, son. I..."

Zander didn't have words, but he nodded at his father. "I know, but I need to go."

He didn't even look back as he hurried up the path towards Citrine, hoping he wasn't too late.

Chapter 41

A LARGE HAND PRESSED against her chest, and coolness flooded into her. She almost didn't want to open her eyes, but pushed up her heavy lids, anyway.

Her gaze flicked from Fariar's familiar face to Indigo lounging against a flower-festooned pole to Chess's face. Her eyes burned and tears welled up. She hadn't been hallucinating. He was really here.

She tried to speak, but only a croak came out. She tried again. "Chess?"

He straightened, and his tight expression eased. "I'm here, love." He stepped forward, and a ball of blue fluff hopped up and down on his shoulder, twittering loudly. The big Fae waved him back.

"Not yet." Fariar turned back to her and smiled. "I'm glad you're awake. That's a good sign."

Pain pulsed behind her temples, and a spot in the center of her chest burned. "I'm not so sure. I still feel as if someone trampled me."

Fariar chuckled. "I'm sure you do." His expression sobered. "I'm afraid Solus took some of your essence."

He ran a light finger over the spot that burned, and Alice had a brief flash of the white-hot agony before Arthur had knocked the man out.

"Is that why I passed out?"

"Most likely."

She struggled to sit up, but Fariar gently pressed her back against the pillow. "Patience. I need to finish my assessment."

Alice gave a huff, but settled back against the pillows. Fariar returned his large hand to just below her collarbone and closed his eyes again. After a long moment, he sat back. His gaze encompassed the three of them. "The good news is that the Advisor did not take too much."

Indigo crossed his arms. "Only because we arrived to stop him."

"Be glad that you did. As it stands, I don't think he took enough to cause permanent damage." Alice felt faint at his words. Seeing her expression, he shook his head. "Don't worry. I will go in and heal the effects of his carelessness." He made a shooing gesture at Chess and Indigo. "You two need to get out of my way."

He waited until Chess and Indigo moved off the dais before he turned back to Alice. First, he pulled out a white cloth and a bottle from a bag and poured some liquid on the cloth. He gently cleaned off the blood on her temple and chest. Alice winced once or twice, but overall, it wasn't painful. Once he had finished that, he placed his hands on both sides of her head and closed his eyes. Her own eyes drifted shut as coolness flowed from his fingers. She sighed as the pain in her head eased.

Then he moved on to her chest. Fariar took longer this time, and his face creased with concentration. When he finally lifted his hands, she was surprised that the puncture wound was gone. Fariar pulled another bottle out of his bag, this one containing a sludgy-looking liquid. He uncorked it and downed it in one long swallow, grimacing.

He gently pulled the blanket back up and tucked it beneath Alice's chin before he stood. "You should be fine, but you'll need to rest."

Alice made a face. "For how long? I feel much better now."

Fariar smiled. "You're replenishing your essence. You'll need to rest at least until tomorrow evening." He pulled yet another glass bottle out of his bag, this one with a shiny silver liquid inside, and set it on a small table by her bed. "Make sure you drink this after you take a nap. It's a tonic that will help with some of the aftereffects of this kind of shock to your body."

"Does it taste bad?" Alice wrinkled her nose.

"Not as bad as you'll feel if you don't take it." Fariar stood up.

"How long do you think until she's healed completely?" Chess asked.

"If she isn't feeling markedly better by lunch tomorrow, let me know. But I wouldn't worry. She's young and healthy. There's no reason she won't fully recover."

With those words, Fariar patted Alice's shoulder and walked out of the room, leaving Chess and Indigo staring at Alice.

She struggled to sit up, and both men rushed to help her, almost knocking each other over. She rolled her eyes. "I'm fine," she said and pulled herself up without help.

Indigo covered a yawn with his hand. "All this care-giving is exhausting."

Behind him, Chess snorted.

Alice waved a hand at him. "You don't have to stay. You heard Fariar, I'm fine."

Indigo's gaze cut to Chess. "Well, I can't let my cousin show me up, now, can I?"

She sighed. She longed to have a minute alone with Chess without Indigo glowering at them, but she had no idea how she'd get rid of him. He was nothing if not persistent, and she doubted he'd leave if Chess was here. He'd probably view it as another challenge.

At that moment, Azalea materialized in the doorway, and Alice wanted to hug the woman, but she had to be satisfied with a smile instead.

The tense expression on the woman's face loosened. "I see the Healer has done his work. Are you well?"

Alice nodded. "I already am much better, and Fariar said I should be as good as new by tomorrow. I only need to rest."

"I am glad," Azalea said, a faint smile curving her mouth.

Alice bit her lip, Arthur's face rising in her memory. Perhaps she should wait to ask, but she had to know. "Where's Arthur? Is he all right?"

Azalea's gaze flicked to Chess. "My cousin demanded he be given a guest room, and I spoke with my father. He will be returned to the Mirror World as soon as we can arrange it."

Relief washed through Alice. "I'm glad. He deserves to go home." She had no wish to offend Azalea, but it wasn't right, what they'd done to Arther, or to her for that matter.

Azalea frowned. "Yes, he does." Then her expression smoothed back out, and her gaze went to Indigo. "Father wishes to speak with us."

Indigo gestured at Alice. "I can't leave. She obviously needs me to take care of her."

Azalea pursed her lips. "I'm sure our cousin is more than capable of sitting with the girl while she sleeps."

"But…"

Azalea caught Alice's gaze and her eyelid dropped in a quick wink, so fast Alice wasn't sure if she imagined it. Turning to Indigo, Azalea's expression turned stern. "You can come back later. You do not want to anger Father right now. He is already upset over what Solus has done."

"I suppose if I must," Indigo drawled. He leapt up the steps and leaned down to press a kiss to Alice's forehead. Before she could protest, he disappeared out the door.

Chess turned to her, his eyes twinkling. "It appears that you have an admirer, love."

"I thought he would never leave." Alice wrinkled her nose. "He can be quite persistent."

Chess walked up the shallow steps and perched on the edge of her bed. "Are you saying you wanted to get me alone, Miss Cavendish? How shocking!"

Alice's face heated, and she shoved at his arm. "Don't be daft. We couldn't have a proper conversation with him hovering."

She shifted against the pillows and winced. Seeing this, Chess's expression sobered, his gaze zeroing in on her face. "Conversation can go hang, at the moment."

Then he had his arms around her, pulling her close, his cheek resting on the top of her head. "You gave me the worst fright, love. I'm pretty sure I lost one of my nine lives when I heard you scream, and then when you passed out..." His arms tightened.

Alice relaxed into the warmth of his embrace, letting the safety of it soothe her.

Beside her, Wickle twittered. *Mate make you feel better.*

Her face heated, but she didn't disagree. Chess's presence did make her feel better. Not that he was her mate or anything, of course. But he was here, and when she'd said goodbye to him she didn't expect she'd ever see him again, but he came—when she needed him most. She pressed her burning face against his shoulder, glad he was unable to see how flustered she was, thanks to Wickle.

After several moments, he eased her back, his hand coming up to cup her cheek. The intensity of his gaze caused her stomach to do a slow swoop. "Are you truly all right?"

She let out a breath of laughter. "Well, I still feel a bit like someone beat me with a stick, but Fariar did his job."

A chuckle rumbled through his chest, and he reached behind her to adjust her pillows. She slanted him a glance under her lashes. "I could get used to this."

He paused in what he was doing, his face inches away from hers. "Do you want to get used to it, Alice?"

Goosebumps pebbled across her skin, and her breath caught. "I..."

He leaned forward, so close his breath feathered across her lips when he spoke. "Because I could."

His blue eyes burned into hers, and she couldn't look away. Slowly, tentatively, she touched her mouth to his. She felt his smile before his lips moved against hers, both his hands coming up to cup her face. Her eyes slid shut, and her world narrowed to where their mouths met.

She slipped her hands up his chest and around his neck, letting her fingers play with the silky curls at his nape. He explored her mouth softly, and one arm slid around her waist. Heat shimmered through her. There was nothing but Chess, the touch of him, the spicy, faintly woodsy scent of him.

He slowed the kiss and then pulled away. She made a sound of protest, tightening her grip.

He breathed out a laugh and put his forehead against hers, loosening her hands and pulling them down to hold in his own. "As delightful as this is, you're supposed to be recovering, love."

Alice's face flamed in embarrassment and she tucked her chin down. What was wrong with her? She'd never been that forward in her life. She sat back and tried to pull her hands from his, but he held on.

He lifted one to his lips and pressed a kiss to her palm. A tingle worked its way up her arm. "Don't," he said. "Whatever you're thinking right now, you're wrong."

She pulled her hand away this time and swatted at him, covering her confusion with a tart tone. "What gives you the impression that you know my thoughts? You can read minds now?"

He grinned and traced a finger down her heated cheek. "Not minds, love."

She shifted higher against the pillows, putting some space between them so she could think straight. Now would be a good time to change the subject. "So, how did you even know I was here? The communion stone wouldn't work in that tower, and then Indigo took it from me."

He frowned at the mention of Indigo. "That's a rather long story, but the short answer is I didn't. I came here for another reason entirely. Getting to see you was an added bonus."

Mate come and save you. Wickle fix bad man.

She looked down at the snark, who was nestled on top of the blanket. "What bad man? Do you mean the Advisor?"

Wickle cheeped and chittered, but didn't answer, so Alice looked at Chess who shifted, his eyes avoiding hers. "What does he mean, he 'fixed' the bad man?"

Chess took the bottle of tonic off the small table and thrust it at her.

"Here, you need to drink this first."

Alice ignored the tightness in her chest and took it from him. "Wasn't I was supposed to wait until after I took a nap?"

Chess lifted one shoulder. "Trust me, you'll want that first, love."

"Just tell me!"

"Drink that, and I will."

With a frown, she pulled out the stopper. Then she hesitated and looked at the contents again. "I'm only doing this because I know how stubborn you are."

"Like recognizing like, love." He winked.

She tipped the bottle into her mouth, and the cool liquid slid down her throat, erasing the dry ache. It tingled as it made its way to her stomach. The tingling expanded through her limbs until it spread to her fingers and her toes. A sense of calm washed over her, and some of the aches in her muscles eased almost immediately.

She turned back to Chess and raised her eyebrows. "Now, tell me—what happened?"

Some of the calm receded, though, when Chess didn't answer right away and instead picked up her hand and twined her fingers with his. Wickle climbed into her lap, letting out a loud purring noise.

"You have to remember Wickle was protecting you."

Alice looked from the snark back to Chess. "Now you're worrying me. Just spit it out already."

Chess pressed her fingers. "Wickle killed the Advisor."

The words hung in the air. Alice stared down at the ball of blue fluff in her lap. Yes, everyone had kept saying snarks were dangerous, but she hadn't truly believed it. Even now, she couldn't imagine Wickle hurting anyone, but apparently he had. For her.

Worry clutched at her chest. What if the Fae wanted revenge? What if they actually killed the snark this time?

"Wickle, what have you done?"

Wickle looked up at her, his blue fringe hanging over his enormous eyes. *Bad man. Hurt Alice.*

Alice lifted her stricken gaze to Chess. "Will they come after him?"

Chess shook his head. "Probably not, or they would have done it already. Besides, the man went out of his way to hurt you. Azalea seemed to think the Advisor's death evened things out. I'm not sure I agree with that, but I suppose I'll have to be content with the fact that he's dead."

Alice shook her head. Guilt and relief warred inside of her. "What he did was awful, but I didn't want him… dead."

Alice sad?

She stroked the blue fur. "I know you were only protecting me, Wickle, but you can't just go around killing people."

Wickle blew out a breath, making his fringe flap upwards. *Bad man can't hurt Alice now.*

Chess leaned forward and rubbed her shoulder. "He didn't go after the man until the Advisor started acting aggressively. If he'd only kept his mouth shut, he'd probably still be here."

Alice opened her mouth to say something, but a yawn almost cracked her jaw.

Chess chuckled and gently pushed a strand of hair off her face. "You should rest. You're still recovering from what that bloody idiot did to you."

Alice started to protest, but Chess held up a hand. "I promise, I'll catch you up on everything—after you sleep for a while more."

Alice reluctantly agreed, and Chess helped her get comfortable. She expected him to leave, but he settled himself in one of the cup-like chairs. When she looked at him questioningly, he winked. "Don't worry, love. I won't tell you if you snore."

Chapter 42

ZANDER STOPPED OUTSIDE THE partially open door of the guest room. He took several deep breaths before he pushed it open as the Healer straightened from Citrine's prone form. His stomach plummeted at the somber expression on the man's face.

"How is she?" Zander asked.

"I've repaired the damage internally, Sire, but she lost an incredible amount of blood."

Zander came to stand by the man. Citrine's face was the same bleach white as the pillow, and her dark red hair spread around her reminded him too much of the blood on his father's hands and nightshirt. The steady rise and fall of her chest reassured him. "But she'll recover, right?"

The Healer hesitated before he answered. "Under normal circumstances, with someone who is young and seemingly healthy, I'd say yes." He paused again, and Zander wanted to pull the words out of the man. "But with her heart defect—"

"What defect?"

The man's face fell. "I assumed you knew. The Pearl Queen has a defect in her heart. She was most likely born with it, and it doesn't seem to give her any trouble. However, it may delay or impede the healing process."

"You're a Healer. Can't you fix it?"

The man shook his head sadly. "No, I'm afraid that's outside my abilities. It would be quite a delicate thing. Sometimes, with these maladies one is born with, it is better to leave them be than start mucking about, especially with someone's heart. It's rather necessary for existence, after all."

"But... you said you repaired the damage, so she has to get better." Zander could hear the desperation in his own voice.

The Healer placed a hand on his shoulder. "I hope so. I truly do, but an artery was nicked, and she lost so much blood. Normally, the body, given enough time and rest without further trauma, can replace lost blood, but with her weak heart, I'm just not sure. I've given her the best chance I can. We'll just have to wait and see now."

Zander's legs gave out, and if there hadn't been a chair nearby, he would have most likely fallen on the floor.

The man gathered up his satchel and moved towards the door. "I'll check on her again in a few hours. If there's any change or you're concerned at all, please don't hesitate to call for me."

Zander closed his eyes, a lump rising in his throat. This was all his fault. He should have made her leave last night, not been so selfish.

He still didn't understand how his father got out of those shackles without either of them hearing him.

Then a sliver of memory prodded him. Citrine plucking the key from his hand. But he must have gotten it back.

He sat up and frantically patted the shirt pocket he always kept it in.

It was empty.

It was possible it had fallen out when they'd been fighting, but he didn't remember putting it back. He threw himself back in the chair, his hands covering his eyes. How could he have been so incredibly stupid?

A knock came then, and after a pause, Lapin poked his head into the room. "I came to inform you we got your father settled, and to check on you both."

Zander waved him in, not moving from his chair. "Thank you for doing that. I needed..." He trailed off, his gaze going back to Citrine's still face.

Lapin entered the room and came to stand next to Zander's chair. "I saw the Healer leaving. What did he have to say?"

Zander slumped back as he related the Healer's mixed report.

Lapin hooked his thumbs into his lapels and rocked back on his heels. "She's very persistent in whatever she puts her mind to, and that has to work in her favor here."

A tired smile crept across Zander's face. "You're right about that."

They stood in silence for several moments, and a deep weariness washed over Zander. All he wanted to do was lie down next to Citrine, gather her up in his arms and sleep until this was all over.

"You'll need to tell the Council. You can't hide this from them any longer." Lapin didn't look at him when he said the words. "I understand you hoped to help the King first, but…" He looked down at Citrine.

"Beecher already knows." The Duchess and Lord Dordo's visit from last night seemed like weeks ago now.

"All the more reason to call them together. If you don't, you'll only give that old fool more fuel for the fire he's trying to start."

Lapin was right, but the idea of facing Lord Beecher and the rest while Citrine lay here hovering between life and death and his father sat in a locked dungeon cell was almost too much. He pinched the bridge of his nose and closed his eyes, drawing in a deep breath.

Lapin laid a hand on his shoulder. "I can send the message while you get some rest, if you'd like. I doubt they can all gather until after lunch, at the earliest, and that will give me some more time to work on that potion for the King. We were very close."

A sob worked its way up Zander's throat and he swallowed it down. "I don't want to leave her."

"I know, but you need to be prepared for this meeting. She would want you to take care of yourself."

Lapin was right. His exhaustion was part of the reason Citrine was in this position, but he didn't want to leave her alone. He gently took her limp hand in his and pressed it to his cheek.

"Would you like me to have one of the flower maidens come sit with her?"

Zander swallowed past the lump in his throat, touched by the rabbit's thoughtfulness. Wordlessly, he nodded and pushed to his feet, letting go of Citrine's hand. His body felt so heavy he could barely move, but he needed to have his wits about him if he was going to deal with

Lord Beecher and the rest. He desperately wished the Commander were here, or Chess.

Or Citrine. She always thought about these things so logically. A sob broke free, and he pushed his fist against his mouth, trying to gain control. He took several deep, shuddering breaths.

"I'll send someone in so you can rest." Lapin squeezed his shoulder in sympathy. "She'll be all right. You'll see," he said before he quietly left the room.

Zander watched him go, not sure he believed the rabbit this time.

When Zander reached the meeting room in the early afternoon, everyone was already assembled, along with Lapin, but the King's presence surprised him. They had shackled his hands and feet together, and he could barely shuffle. Two guards stood on either side of him.

"That's completely unnecessary," Zander snapped. "Take off those leg irons at once."

The King, his gaze lucid, shook his head. "No, I told them to do it." His mouth pressed into a thin line. "It's for everyone's safety, including mine. I can't guarantee"—he paused, his throat working—"that I can stay in control. I won't have anyone else hurt on my account."

"You've been fine during the day. There's no need for that right now."

His father shook his head. "Please don't argue with me. My mind is made up."

"Well, at least sit down," Zander said as he rounded the table to take his seat next to his father's. The King shuffled sideways.

"No, Zander, you take my seat. It's obvious I am not fit to rule at the moment. I'm afraid you'll need to take charge." He must have seen the argument building on Zander's face because he held up his hand, the chains clanking. "At least for right now. I have not lost hope that we can solve my problem."

Zander waited until the King made his way around the table. A guard pulled out the chair and helped him sit. Lord Dordo shifted uncomfortably when the King sat down next to him, and Zander's heart pinched with sympathy when he realized his father hadn't missed the reaction.

"This is a disgrace!" Lord Beecher didn't even wait until Zander sat down before thumping his cane to drive home his point. "Neither of you is fit to rule this Kingdom." He pointed a gnarled finger at the king. "You've lost your mind, and you—" His finger swung towards Zander, his face turning purple. "And you're a Drifter. You should have been drowned at birth. That's how we used to take care of this problem when I was young."

Next to him, Lady Perma gasped, clasping her hands in front of her. "Wilfred, that's a horrible thing to say to the young Prince. It's not his fault he's part monster."

Zander kept his expression neutral, but inside he withered. If she thought he was a monster, what hope did he have of keeping the throne?

The Duchess sighed. "Henrietta, you aren't helping matters."

"I only meant, the Prince is such a nice young man. He can't help his affliction."

The Duchess rolled her eyes and then turned to face Zander. "Your Highness, I for one have no issue with your Drifter Gene, as long as you can keep your animal form under control. And since we've only just realized it, I can't see the problem."

Lapin smiled and nodded at the Duchess. "That's an excellent point. I've always said—"

Beecher slammed his cane on the floor. "I don't care what you say. You're a giant rabbit. What do you know beyond carrots and lettuce? What are you doing at this meeting, anyway? You're not on the Council."

Lapin didn't react to this insult, but merely continued as if Beecher had said nothing. "The response so long ago to the Drifter Gene was an overreaction, in my opinion. The Prince is fully in control of his Jabberwock, and I see no reason he can't assume the kingly duties until we get His Majesty sorted." His expression sobered, and he continued. "The young Pearl Queen and I were working on a tonic for him so King Zane can better keep control of himself, and the Commander is tracking the Red Queen. I know this was a very unfortunate incident. I am, of course, greatly saddened by the Pearl Queen's injury, but we can't lose sight of who the real enemy is here."

"Poppycock! The real problem is that our ruler and his progeny aren't fit for the throne." Beecher waved his cane in the air, almost taking out the Duchess, who glared at him. "I say we put the Commander on the throne. He's got a level head and isn't liable to turn into some kind of creature every other minute."

"I say, that's a catalyst idea!" Lord Dordo cast an apologetic look in Zander's direction. "I don't think it is wise to have someone with the Drifter Gene on the throne."

Lady Perma wrung her hands. "But the Prince is a good man, and as much as I like the Commander, he's part of the family line too, isn't he?"

The King's face looked grey in the morning light, but he straightened under the weight of his chains and spoke. "My son inherited his Drifter Gene through my wife's line. As I recall, the Queen was much beloved." He looked around the table, and Dordo dropped his eyes to his lap.

Beecher didn't back down, though, and continued to glower. "Another secret? How many more are you keeping, Your Majesty?" He banged his cane again. "This is why we need someone different on the throne. Someone we can trust."

The words hit Zander hard, and he struggled to keep his expression neutral. The man probably thought emotions were a weakness, and he didn't want to give Beecher any more ammunition.

Still, he needed to stop this. He stood. "What if I could get rid of my Drifter Gene? Would you want me on the throne then?"

"Since you can't, it doesn't really matter, does it?" Beecher jutted out his chin. "You're—"

"Do shut up, Wilfred," the Duchess interrupted. She tilted her head in Zander's direction. "Is that something you'd be willing to do?"

Zander sank back into his chair and gave a sharp jerk of his chin. "I would consider it—if we can get what we need to create the formula."

Lady Perma twisted the pearl beads at her neck. "Does such a thing even exist? Could it be possible?"

Lapin held up a furry paw. "I've seen the formula. The Pearl Queen found it in Sacklepenny's laboratory, and it looks entirely possible." At the name of the legendary Alchemist, a soft murmur went around the table. The rabbit ignored it and continued. "I'm just not sure it's the best idea."

The King stared at Zander, wide-eyed. "Son, I have to agree with Sir Lapin. I know you said you're only considering it, but—"

"He needs to do more than consider it." Beecher narrowed his eyes at Zander. "Promise you'll do it, or I'll trumpet you and your father's defects to the entire Kingdom."

Zander looked away from his father and instead met the Council's collective gaze. "If we can get what we need, I am willing to... rid myself of my Gene."

Beecher harrumphed. "I suppose that would be acceptable." He pointed his cane at Zander. "But if you fail, don't expect me to support you as the next king or to keep quiet about all this. I'll do everything in my power to thwart you."

Zander gave a wry smile. "Oh, I don't doubt it, sir."

Chapter 43

THE NEXT AFTERNOON, ALICE sat cross-legged on her bed, a pile of pillows mounded against the flowering headboard. She ran her fingers through her hair, trying to undo the tangles and knots, Wickle asleep in her lap.

Indigo lounged nearby. "You should let me help you with that hair of yours. It's giving me a headache watching you," he said.

Alice acted like she hadn't heard him, and instead asked, "Do you think King Thorne will see Chess today?" This was the third time Chess had tried to see the King since last night, but with no success.

Indigo shrugged. "I have no idea, my sweet. The Advisor's most fortunate demise has stirred up a bit of a maelstrom. I would imagine my father is rather busy at the moment." He lifted his eyebrows. "In fact, it could be days and days before he sees my cousin."

Alice's fingers stilled on the knot she was working on. "I hope you're exaggerating."

"One never knows." He stood and wandered around the room, stopping periodically to touch a flower or poke at a vine.

She let out a huff, and Wickle stirred in her lap. "You'd think after everything that's happened, you'd at least try to be helpful."

His hand stilled on the flower. "I'm here keeping you company, aren't I?"

Alice resisted the urge to roll her eyes. "Nobody said you had to do that."

"How could I possibly live with myself if I wasn't here with you in your hour of need, my sweet?"

Alice snorted and Wickle stirred on her lap. "Funny, you had no problem leaving me in a cage."

Indigo whirled to face her and placed a hand on his chest. "You sent me away, my sweet. I was merely heeding your wishes."

"Then maybe you should heed them now and go away."

He turned a mournful gaze on her. "Tell me you don't mean that, my pet."

Alice looked up at him, a sense of warmth spreading over her. It was true. She didn't really want him to go, and he was trying so hard to... She shook her head. "Stop it!"

He smirked, unrepentant. "But it's so amusing. Most don't even recognize my charm, and it's such a bore. You, on the other hand, are a delightful challenge."

She glared at him. "I am not here to amuse you, Indigo, or give you practice on manipulating people."

"Oh, I beg to differ, my sweet." He walked up the steps of the dais and stopped at the foot of the bed. He loomed over her, but Wickle sat up, hissing, his fur puffing up. Indigo hastily stepped back, almost catching his heel on the first step. He scowled down at the snark. "Why must you keep that nasty thing in here?"

Alice ran a hand over the blue fluff. "I much prefer his company to yours."

Indigo opened his mouth, but Alice interrupted him, pointing at the door. "I believe it's time for you to leave. Chess should be back soon, anyway."

He wrinkled his nose, eyeing the snark. "You have questionable taste in companions. First a snark, and then my mongrel cousin."

"Don't call him that." Alice's hands curled into fists, and Wickle grumbled low in his little chest.

Indigo's eyes narrowed as he studied her. "You're terribly protective of my cousin. Now why would that be?"

Alice's face heated. "Of course I'm protective of my friends." She scooped up Wickle and cuddled him against her cheek.

"Oh, I think he's more to you than a friend." Indigo's lip curled on the last word.

Alice lowered Wickle. "Chess and I have been through a lot together, and he's saved my life more than once."

Indigo crossed his arms. "I saved you from the Advisor—twice—and you don't blush over me."

Alice shifted, so she was higher against the pillows. "Once. You saved me once," she corrected, "and I already thanked you for that."

"Not properly." Indigo's eyes suddenly took on a gleam Alice didn't like.

She gave him a stern look. "Don't start that again."

Indigo slouched against a wooden pillar, playing idly with a pink flower. "And how did you thank my cousin? I'm sure it was with more than a prim 'thank you.'"

"Not that it's any of your business, but Chess isn't like you. He doesn't expect people to pay him for his help."

"What a paragon he is." Indigo's tone turned mocking, and his eyes glinted with temper.

Alice suddenly remembered how he had thrown the Advisor against the wall like he was a sack of flour, and she was very glad Wickle was with her. She ruffled her fingers through the snark's fur, eliciting a rumbly purr from the little creature that filled the room.

"So, my sweet, tell me what's so wonderful about my cousin that makes you defend him and causes you to blush so prettily?"

Alice wished Indigo would just go away, but she doubted he'd leave even if she asked nicely, so she shrugged. "He's my friend, and he's important to me. That's all."

"Well, I'm a prince."

She sighed, not sure what that had to do with anything. "Yes, but you're not Chess."

Indigo pointed an accusatory finger at her. "You love him."

The words hit her in the chest, and Alice dropped her gaze to Wickle. He stared up at her with big eyes. *Alice love mate.*

She realized Wickle and Indigo were right, and she couldn't deny it any longer. She lifted her chin and met Indigo's gaze squarely. "And what if I do?"

"You do what, love?" Chess asked and strolled into the room.

Alice froze, an icy knot forming in her stomach. How much had he heard? She searched his face, but it was clear Chess's mind was on something else.

"We were discussing you, as it so happens." Indigo pushed off of the pillar and sauntered over to Chess, twirling a small pink bud in his fingers.

Chess frowned. "Me? What about me?"

Alice's lungs compressed, and she went cold all over as Indigo stopped in front of his cousin. His gaze didn't leave Alice's face when he answered. "We were just discussing how long you'll both be enjoying our hospitality." He threw himself into a nearby chair. "It'll probably be weeks."

Wickle hissed in Indigo's direction. *Blue man make Alice upset. Wickle bite him?*

Alice ran a shaky hand through Wickle's fur. "It's all right, Wickle." She shot Indigo a narrow-eyed glare before turning back to Chess. "I'm sure Indigo is exaggerating. Did you have any luck?"

Chess ran a hand through his curls, making the ends stick up. "The King refuses to meet with me. He's given me every runaround there is." His blue eyes rested on Indigo. "Do you know why he's avoiding me?"

Indigo shrugged, examining a nail. "I haven't the foggiest of notions. Perhaps he's concerned about your response to what's happened to Alice."

Chess frowned. "Well, I'm not happy about the fact that you locked her up or what happened with the Advisor, but he's dead now. There's nothing else to be done at this point." He blew out a breath. "Can you talk to him? Get him to meet with me?"

Indigo studied the flower bud in his hand. "That depends. Once you do, will you both be leaving right away?"

Chess nodded. "We need to get back as soon as we can. Things are a bit... urgent back at the Red Palace."

Indigo smirked and glanced at Alice. "Then I don't think I'll help you. Besides, Father will see you eventually. It might be a fortnight or two, though."

"We don't have that kind of time!" A muscle in Chess's jaw ticked. "You don't seem to understand the severity of the situation."

"That's not my problem." Indigo pushed to his feet and stepped closer to Chess. "There's nothing preventing you from going back empty-handed, Cousin."

Alice glanced between the two men, the tension shimmering in the air between them. "We're leaving one way or another, Indigo. Stalling won't help anything."

Indigo spun away from Chess and, leaping onto the dais, he ducked under the flowered bower that enclosed her bed. He ran a hand over her head, leaving a trail of warmth. "I'll be back later, pet, and I'll bring something to entertain you."

He skirted by Chess and lightly punched him in the shoulder. "I'm certain our paths will cross again, cousin."

Chess shook his head as he watched Indigo saunter out the door. "I can't fathom the fact that I'm related to that bloody idiot."

Alice's face heated. "I'm afraid it's my fault. If he wasn't so determined to get me to stay, he'd probably help you, if only out of curiosity." She bit her lip. "Perhaps I could be a bit friendlier." She didn't fancy giving

Indigo any encouragement, but if it got them out of here quicker, it might be worth putting up with Indigo.

"Sorry, love, I'm not willing to offer you up as a sacrificial lamb even if Zander is in a world of trouble." Chess pulled the chair next to her bed and sat down. "You'd think the King would meet with me even if it was only so he could smooth things over. Not run away and hide like he's five years old. And that one—" He gestured towards the hallway. "He's even worse."

"I can't decide if he's malicious or just horribly spoiled."

Chess sighed. "Probably both."

Alice's fingers worked at another tangle, her mind turning over ideas. "Have you talked to Azalea? She seems to have more common sense even if she is a bit... terse."

Chess shook his head. "She's been dealing with the mess with the Advisor. I guess it's caused a massive upheaval among the clan leaders. That's another reason I want to get what we need and get out of here—I don't want to get caught up in whatever happens with that." His glance landed on Wickle, who twittered sleepily, and then back at Alice. She met his gaze. Absently, she pulled another section of her hair over her shoulder, trying to undo the tangles in the back.

"Do you want me to find you a brush or something?"

Alice's thoughts immediately bounced back to Indigo's offer to brush her hair, and she glanced at Chess. Warmth flooded her cheeks at the idea of him brushing her hair.

He tipped his head. "Are you all right, love? You look flushed."

This only made her face get hotter. "I'm fine," she choked out.

"Are you sure? I can get another tonic from Fariar if you need it, or even have him come check on you again." His expression clouded with concern, and she allowed a small bloom of hope that he might feel the same way she did. He had showed he cared in so many ways, but that didn't mean he loved her.

She dipped her chin down, hiding her face. She gathered her hair and started braiding it, grasping at the first thing that popped into her head. "Did you hear anything about Arthur? Did they send him back yet?"

Chess rubbed his hand over the back of his neck. "I'm embarrassed to say I forgot about the man, but if I ever get in to see the King, I'll ask about him."

Alice let out a puff of air. "I'm worried about him. He's already been stuck here for five years, and I can envision everyone forgetting about him again for another few."

Chess tapped her knee under the blanket. "I'll make sure he gets home, even if I have to take him myself."

She reached out and clasped his hand. "Thank you."

He smiled. "It's only fair the chap gets to go home." His expression sobered. "Of course, that all depends on if I can ever get an audience with the King."

An idea took shape in Alice's mind. "You said you saw your mother, right?"

Chess had caught her up on the events at the Red Palace, and why he was here. He also mentioned he had seen his mother, although he hadn't shared many details except that it had gone well.

Chess leaned forward, steepling his hands under his chin. "I did, but I'm not sure what that has to do with anything."

She shook her head. "Since she's the King's sister, she could help you."

He pushed to his feet and wandered idly around the room. "I don't know."

"You said she was happy you were here. Surely, she'd want to help you with this."

Alice watched him finger a blossom at the foot of her bed. Emotions flickered over Chess's face, and his expression settled into a frown. "I guess I'm not used to having my mother in my life. I don't want to seem..." He lifted a shoulder. "I don't know... like the only reason I visited her was because I needed something from her."

The doubt in his voice tugged at Alice's heart. He returned to studying the vine. Silence trickled into the room and settled over them.

When she finally spoke, she chose her words carefully, her fingers nervously pleating the blanket in front of her. "You know, Chess, from what you've told me, I think giving your mother a chance to help you would be as much of a blessing to her as to you."

He lifted his head to look at her. "What do you mean?"

"She missed out on so much of your time growing up. There were so many things she couldn't help you with. I think giving her a chance to do that now would be a kindness, not a burden."

Chess said nothing for a long moment, his gaze returning to the flowering vine as if it were the most interesting thing in the world. What if she'd presumed too much?

When he finally looked at her, his eyes were shiny. "Maybe you're right."

Alice's muscles loosened, and she grinned. "I thought you'd figured out I'm always right."

She'd meant to tease him, and she expected a chuckle, or at least a smile, but he crossed to sit on her bed and took her hands in his. "I'm learning, Alice."

The words felt weightier than they should, and her breath lodged in her chest. He leaned forward, eyes glowing, and she swayed closer, pulled to him like metal to a magnet.

"Oooh, it's her sweetheart! I told you she had a sweetheart!"

Alice jerked away from Chess, her face turning hot, her eyes darting towards the voice. "Poppy!"

"We can come back later," said Foxglove, her smile sly. "We don't want to... interrupt."

Thistle elbowed her. "We've brought you some things so you can get cleaned up." She glanced at Chess shyly. "Fariar said it was all right, if you'll give us a moment."

Chess rose to his feet and dropped a kiss onto the top of Alice's head. "I'll leave you to it, then." He seemed unfazed by the previous moment, while Alice was still trying to calm her hammering heart. But that wasn't the important thing right now.

"You'll go visit her, then?" she asked.

He paused at the door and winked at her. "I thought I'd wait until you were ready and then we can go together."

Warmth filled her chest, and she smiled at him. "I'd like that."

Chapter 44

CHESS FOLLOWED THE PATH he'd taken with Azalea the first time he'd visited his mother. This time, though, Alice padded silently next to him, Wickle tucked into the pocket of the loose vest she wore over the matching cream robe-like dress the Wildflower sisters found for her to wear. She had assured him she'd remind the little snark not to pop out and scare his mother half to death, but she'd refused to leave him behind. He supposed he didn't blame her, for a variety of reasons.

While Alice was getting cleaned up, Chess had tried once more to talk to the King, who stonewalled him again. He only hoped his mother had some kind of sway over the man.

The trees pressed in from both sides, the flowers and plants crowding their footsteps, and Alice's shoulder brushed his. He appreciated that she seemed content to simply walk next to him. Chess rubbed his damp palms along his trouser legs, his mind strangely blank.

Despite his previous meeting with his mother, and her happiness at his arrival, he didn't want to come across as using her.

Absently, he reached out and caught Alice's hand, twining their fingers together. It felt as natural as breathing, and he only hoped she didn't mind. He glanced down at her, and she met his gaze.

She squeezed his fingers. "Take a breath. She knows why you're here, after all."

He gave a half smile. "It's one thing to understand that and another for your long-absent son to come around demanding favors."

Alice's expression softened even as she rolled her eyes at him. "I seriously doubt she'll think that, Chess."

"If my father hadn't been such a blighter, this wouldn't be so... fraught." He scowled, his feet scuffing the leaves that littered the path.

Alice bumped his shoulder with hers. "You might want to get out some of that famous charm of yours. Your current expression is rather frightening."

Chess couldn't help grinning at her, and she smiled in return. "There, that's better. Now you won't scare your mother."

Their hands swung as they walked in companionable silence. Around them, the forest was alive with creatures rustling through the trees and the twittering or droning of them calling to each other. Small Fae, almost indistinguishable from birds or insects, darted through the branches or amongst the flowers.

After a few more minutes, the trees thinned, and they drew to a halt. Chess pointed. "Her house is through that ring of trees in the clearing." As before, puffs of smoke rose from the stone chimney. Then he remembered and wanted to smack himself. "The last time, Azalea opened the ring of trees. I should have thought of that. Now we'll have to go back and get her."

"You give up too easily. Surely, the woman gets visitors that can't open her, erm, trees." Alice let go of his hand and walked over to the closest birch tree. The tree beside it sidled closer to its neighbor. She merely raised an eyebrow and then cupped her hands around her mouth. "Helllooo! Miss Larkspur, you have company!"

The sound of Alice's voice was startlingly loud in the forest, and all the birds and insects grew quiet in response.

Chess couldn't help the laugh that escaped. "I'm not sure it works that way, love. This isn't..." His words cut off when the two trees rustled and bent away.

Alice shot him a triumphant smile and held out her hand. "You were saying?"

Chess let her pull him through into the clearing. "I stand corrected."

He was still chuckling when his mother trotted down the steps to meet them, her arms outstretched. He went into them without thinking, squeezing her tightly. All of his earlier worry melted away as she stepped back and framed his face in her hands. "I'm so happy you're here." She let go and turned towards Alice, and her smile widened. "And you have brought your mate. Welcome."

Chess's face heated, and Alice's flushed a charming pink. "No, Mother. This is Alice. She's..." He paused, not sure what he should call her. The words he wanted to say sat on the tip of his tongue, but they hadn't talked about a future or...

Alice stepped forward into the awkward silence and dropped a curtsey. "I'm a friend of Chess's. We've only recently met through a series of rather interesting circumstances. I'm so pleased to meet you."

Chess blinked at Alice. He was so used to seeing her in nontraditional settings that he sometimes forgot she would have navigated social situations back home all the time.

His mother turned to Alice and clasped her hand. "I doubt very much you are only a friend, but I won't say any more about that." She waved them towards the door. "Come in, and I will make us some tea."

Chess hesitated and then took Alice's hand before he followed his mother into her cottage. His mother gestured them to the round table, and they sat down while she bustled to the counter where a teapot already sat, steam wafting from its tip. "You have excellent timing. I was getting ready to sit down with a cup." She reached up and pulled out more cups and set them on the same wooden tray from the last time.

Alice's hand came over his to still his tapping fingers. "Your home is quite cozy," she said.

Larkspur brought the tray to the table. "Thank you. I am quite content here." She set it down and then settled herself into a chair. She picked up her cup and looked at him over the top. "I suppose you'll need to leave soon. Is that why you've come—to say goodbye, then?"

Chess ran his fingers over the grain of the table's wooden surface. "No, not yet anyway. I was actually hoping... you could do me a favor?"

She leaned forward, her eyes bright with curiosity. "Of course I will. What is it you need?"

Pressure built at the back of his eyes, and he blinked it away. She hadn't even asked what the favor was. She'd simply agreed. Alice's hand tightened on his as if she sensed the impact of his mother's offer on him. He cleared his throat. "I need to speak to the King, and he keeps avoiding me." He spread his hands out. "I don't understand why, though." He glanced at Alice. "Well, I have an idea, but it makes little sense why he's acting this way."

Larkspur frowned and took another sip of her tea before carefully placing it on the table. "Is this about the artifact?"

Chess nodded. "Like I told you, the King is not doing well at all, and I need to get that artifact back to the palace soon, or it might be too late." He leaned back in his chair and picked up his cup. The fragrant steam smelled of lemon and something reminiscent of fresh grass.

Larkspur's blue hair waved around her head. "Is the Prince quite sure he wants to do this? Stripping yourself of your magic is something we do here as a punishment."

Alice frowned at the words and looked at him. He shrugged. "He needs the leverage, at a minimum. The Council... Well, suffice it to say, he doesn't have a lot of backers at the moment." He glanced up at his mother. "King Zane is in a bad way."

"Are you positive the Queen is the one manipulating the King?" Larkspur stirred her tea. "That is difficult spell work. Only a powerful Alchemist can do things like that, and even then, the person would most likely need some kind of magical help."

Chess shrugged. "I agree, and Citrine mentioned something about the Queen using Fae wings, but I didn't follow exactly what she was talking about."

Larkspur became still, and even her hair stopped moving. "She used the clippings from the flower maidens."

Her voice was so low, Chess almost didn't hear her, and his stomach turned as the implications of her words sank in. Before he could say anything, though, Alice's hand tightened on his arm, her face suddenly pale. Alarm spiked through him. "Are you all right, love? If you're feeling poorly..."

She waved a hand. "No, I'm fine. It's just...I didn't mean to interrupt."

"If you're sure, love."

Alice nodded, absently patting his hand. When he continued peering at her, she smiled. "Don't worry about me. You came to see your mother. I'm fine."

Chess's gaze moved back to his mother. "Do you think it's possible for you to arrange for me to meet with the King?"

Larkspur gave a decisive nod. "Yes, leave it to me." She leaned over and patted his cheek. "Don't worry, I will get your uncle to see you." Her eyes glinted. "He will talk to you this very evening if I have my way."

A short while later, Chess and Alice waved at Larkspur, and then walked hand in hand through the ring of birch trees.

"Well, that went better than I expected," said Chess.

Alice smiled up at him. "I told you your mother would be happy to help you."

Chess lifted her hand to his lips and kissed it. "That you did, love." Then he frowned. "But even if she does get the King to see me, I don't like my chances of getting my hands on one of his artifacts. The only thing I have to give him in exchange is the goodwill of the Red Palace, and I don't know if that will be enough." He kicked at a rock that lay on the path.

Alice slowed her pace, her brow furrowed. They walked a ways in silence before she finally spoke, her voice low."Do you think information on who's killing his people would persuade him?"

Chess stopped, bringing Alice to a halt next to him. "What?"

"I think—no, I'm positive it's the Queen that's behind everything—the Red King's problems, the killings and disappearances here, all of it."

Chess glanced over his shoulder at the surrounding forest and then back at Alice. "Lyssandra's definitely capable of all that, but we need to be absolutely certain before giving that information to my uncle, especially in exchange for something like an artifact. What made you decide it's her?"

"It was when your mother mentioned the flower maidens. I don't know anything about spellwork or potions, but if she was using pieces of their wings to boost her magic in some way, wouldn't she need more eventually?"

Chess ran his hands through his hair, trying to think it through. "That's true, but we don't have any idea how much she had to begin with, or how much she needs. Coming here and nabbing Fae, even the small ones, would be a huge gamble. Would she be foolish enough to take that kind of risk?"

"Chess, she has to be desperate at this point. Besides, one of the faeries that brought my meals told me there was a Jabberwock siting near where they found the last victim. That can't be a coincidence."

Chess stared down at Alice as the pieces clicked into place. He couldn't believe he hadn't seen how the problems at the Red Palace and in the Faelands fit together so neatly. He took both her hands. "I think you're right, but listen to me. We need to keep this in our back pocket and only bring it out if we absolutely have to."

Alice bit her lip. "I know I said we could use it as leverage, but shouldn't we tell them before we leave—at least drop a hint to Larkspur if nothing else?"

Chess's mouth thinned and he shook his head. "Maybe once we get back to the Red Palace, but right now, I don't want my uncle asking too many questions about flower maidens. I honestly have no idea how he'll react to finding out the Red Queen is the reason for all his current problems. We might both end up in a cage."

Alice stared at him for a minute before she nodded. "All right."

Chess brought one of her hands up and kissed the palm. "Thank you, Alice."

She ducked her head, her cheeks turning pink. "I don't know that I helped all that much."

He stepped closer. "You've helped me more than you know, and I don't just mean right now." He let go of one of her hands and brought his palm up to her cheek. "You've—"

He broke off at the sound of loud giggles. A trio of bumble faeries along with another one that had wings like a dragonfly were peeking out from behind a nearby tree, avidly watching Chess and Alice, their eyes alive with curiosity. He hoped they hadn't heard too much of the conversation.

Alice's mouth twitched. "We should get back to Underhill before we give the locals any more entertainment."

Chess chuckled. "I suppose you're right."

Together, they started back down the path, Alice's hand tucked in his. Maybe it was selfish of him, but he hoped she wouldn't be going home for a while yet.

Chapter 45

ZANDER SHIFTED ON THE chair he'd pulled up next to Citrine's bedside. Even as he watched the slow rise and fall of her chest under the sheet, part of his mind was on his father. Sir Lapin had stationed himself outside the King's cell in order to keep him company, and Zander told himself it was enough.

Earlier, a maid had banked the fire in the grate, and now moonlight spilled through the glass doors that led to the small balcony. He wasn't sure if he'd ever look at the French doors again without remembering the fight with his father.

He picked up Citrine's long, white hand that lay on the covers and brought it to his cheek. Something about its limpness made his chest ache. Maybe it was because her fingers were rarely still. There was usually either a pencil or a book in her hands. Her mind was always working, observing and learning how things worked, or the *why* of something. To see her so lifeless, her spirit appearing snuffed out, opened a chasm in his soul.

It was worse knowing that with Alice's help, they had hope for a future together, but he would give all that up just to know Citrine was out there. She anchored him in a way nothing else did. If she didn't... His mind closed off the thought.

The wind whistled outside, and he distantly noted that the annual storm that marked the end of Wonderland's summer months was probably brewing. It didn't matter.

Something banged outside the window, making him jump. He let go of Citrine's hand and stood up.

Then froze.

On the balcony, the moonlight outlined a figure. He moved closer, his heart picking up speed.

A few steps from the glass doors, he realized who it was—the Queen.

Only the panes of glass separated them. Something in his chest twisted, and a darkness rose inside him. It was within his power to bring an end to this right now.

If he opened this door and snapped her neck, all of his troubles would be over.

All the pain she had caused, all the upheaval. He reached for the door, but he paused.

The woman standing on the balcony wasn't the same. While her pale hair fell in a perfect braid over her shoulder, and her simple dress was pristine, her face held a gaunt quality, and shadows formed half-moons under her dark eyes.

He paused, not sure if he was looking at the ruthless woman who had played them like an expert harpist or one that was desperate and on the run.

He brushed off the question and grasped the door handle more firmly.

And still he hesitated.

Then Zander shook his head. What was he doing? Whether ruthless or desperate, the last thing he wanted to do was let her in the palace, into Citrine's room with her lying there helpless.

He turned to call the guards, but the Queen banged on the door. He spun back. She held something up. It glinted gold in the moonlight.

Her brown eyes widened, and she beckoned him outside.

The wisest course of action would be to call the guards, but some dark part of him needed to know why she was here.

Besides, he was twice her size. Surely he had the ability to overpower one woman, and then this would be all over. He glanced back at Citrine and his heart stuttered. Well, maybe not all over.

Taking a deep breath, Zander stepped out onto the balcony, leaving the door ajar so he would hear Citrine if she needed him. The wind whipped at his clothes and blew loose strands of white-blonde hair across Lyssandra's face. The faint scent of jasmine and vanilla permeated the air.

"I should kill you." It wasn't what he'd meant to say.

Lyssandra's pale face got even paler, and she held up a shaky hand. "I know. You should."

He blinked in surprise. It wasn't what he expected from her. Gone were the coquettish glances and artifice that generally marked the Queen's behavior. Instead, her expression was bleak.

"Give me one good reason I shouldn't call the palace guards right now." He took a menacing step closer, but to her credit, she held her ground.

Her chin came up and her eyes sparked. "You and I both know they'd never get here in time. I'd shift and be gone before they reached the main staircase."

She had a point. "I'm still not sure why you're here. Have you come to gloat? Is that it?"

Lyssandra shook her head. "No, I... I came because..." She toyed with the end of her long braid, her eyes studying the tip as if it held the answer to all the world's problems. Finally she looked up at him, her dark eyes shiny with unshed tears. "I don't know how to stop all this."

Zander let out a snort. "That's easy enough. I should kill you now and put us both out of our misery."

She swallowed. "I deserve that."

"You've done nothing but cause havoc and chaos." He ticked each item off in his fingers. "You cursed my father and made everyone think he was dead. You cursed me and almost got me killed. You fixed it so that the throne was up for grabs, so two people I care about had to risk themselves." He pointed a finger at her face. "You caused your own brother's death, and because of you, Citrine might die too." His voice had risen with each accusation while she seemed to shrink smaller and smaller.

She rubbed her arms. "I've made a mess of things. I only... I wanted..."

He looked at her coldly. "You wanted power and control. It doesn't take a genius to figure that out."

Anger flashed over her features. "Yes, I did—I do. I won't deny it, and I'm not ashamed of it."

Disgust welled up in him and he turned towards the door. Listening to her was a mistake. He should go in and call—

Lyssandra sprang forward and grabbed his arm. "It's so easy for you to sit in judgment of me. You have no idea what my life was like before I became the Red Queen."

Zander jerked away. "No, I don't, but nothing you can tell me will excuse what you've done."

Tears tracked down her cheeks. "I wasn't lying when I told you about my father."

Zander stilled at the memory of her halting words that hinted at the abuse she'd suffered at her father's hands. He hardened his resolve. "I'm sorry your father wasn't a good man, but he's dead now. Whatever he did, it isn't an excuse for all the pain and destruction you've caused."

She dashed the tears away with the heel of her hand. "Do you think I don't understand that?" When she looked up at him, there was anguish in her eyes. "I loved my brother, and to know he died, how he died..." A shudder wracked her slight frame. "And I was the cause."

A wave of weariness washed over him, and his shoulders slumped. "Why are you here? What do you want from me?"

Something like hope sparked in her eyes, and she reached for his hands. He backed away to avoid her touch. She pulled her arms in towards her middle, twisting her hands together. "I came..." She stopped and licked her lips. When she spoke, her words came in a rush. "I came to ask you to leave. With me."

He opened his mouth, and she held up her hand. "Wait, before you say no, listen to me. Nobody in this Kingdom is going to accept you. People like Lord

Beecher will fight you until you take your last breath, even if you make it onto the throne. You and I are alike, Zander. We both have the Drifter Gene, and our animals are powerful." Her mouth twisted. "Aren't you tired of hiding what you are? Of living in fear that someone will find out? That everyone will turn on you because of it?"

Her words hit a sore spot, but he didn't want to reveal that to her. "It's my duty to take care of the people of Wonderland. It doesn't matter if some of them won't like me."

"But doesn't the unfairness of that twist your gut sometimes? I mean, look at you. You're almost sickeningly noble, if you don't mind me saying so."

Despite himself, his mouth quirked up. "Oh, please do."

Her eyes narrowed and some of the cunning returned. "Besides, I am nothing if not observant."

He shifted uneasily. "What does that mean?"

"It means I've seen that the throne isn't something you truly desire."

He protested, but she talked right over him. "Oh, you'll rule. You'll do the right thing. I don't think you can help yourself, but you won't love it, not the way your father did. And you'll have to do it alone."

The words were like a knife in his heart. When he spoke, his voice was thin even to his own ears. "That's a big presumption on your part."

Her gaze went past his shoulder to where Citrine lay in the bed, and she raised an eyebrow. "You have to remember that you were my father's first choice as a husband for me, but you rejected that idea even though your precious Pearl Queen had already broken your engagement."

Fire flickered to life in his chest at the reminder of what Lyssandra had done, but the Queen either didn't realize or was too reckless to care how close Zander was to losing his thin hold on his temper.

"And you're still at her side, after all these years, like one of her pathetic creatures. You'd probably..." Her voice choked off when Zander's hand closed around her throat and squeezed, a red haze blocking his vision.

She could have fought him, shifted even, and broke his hold, but Lyssandra covered his hand with both of hers, and her lips curved into a mocking smile.

They stared at each other until her lids fluttered and her lips parted, searching for air that wouldn't come. He wanted to make her pay for all the pain she'd caused him and those he loved, but even as he thought about it, his grip loosened. He couldn't do it. He couldn't take a life like this, even if it was hers. Perhaps in battle, but not when she wouldn't even fight back.

Abruptly, he let go, and she staggered against the railing, gasping in air. He spun away from her, intent on calling the guards.

Like he should have done when he first saw her.

"Wait," she wheezed.

He paused. "I almost killed you. I wanted to."

"But you didn't."

He turned slowly back towards her, almost against his will. "There was just as much chance for you to lose that gamble."

"Oh, but I knew you wouldn't do it, not in the end." Even as she said the words, the red marks from his fingers stood out on the white skin of her neck. Numbness swept away any regret he might have felt.

"How could you have known that when I didn't?"

She smirked. "Because at your core, you have to do the right thing—even if it's killing you."

He ran a weary hand over his face. "Why are you really here, Lyssandra?"

She took a step towards him, her expression suddenly earnest. "Come with me through the Looking Glass. Leave all of this behind. The people of Wonderland don't deserve you or your loyalty. They'll turn on you the first chance that they get, all because of some benighted bigotry about something you were born with."

His shoulders bowed under the weight of her words. Her bitterness was palpable, but she wasn't wrong. Zander understood he'd deal with the people's prejudice for the rest of his life once they found out about his Drifter Gene. Some would never accept him, no matter what he did.

As she saw his doubts, she pressed. "We can leave, right now, or"—her glance strayed to the room behind them—"in a little while. In the Mirror World, nobody even believes in the Gifts. All this weight you carry, you can leave it behind you."

For the briefest of moments, the idea of running away held an almost hypnotic pull. He fought against it. "But I can't leave Wonderland with nobody to rule." He glared at her. "You're the reason my father is unfit."

She pulled something shiny from her pocket. It was a golden ring, the kind put into a bull's nose to control it. Something dark stained parts of it. She held it up. "He doesn't have to be."

Zander stared at the object, his body tensing. "What is that?"

She tucked it back into her pocket. "Let's say it still controls the beast." She glanced up at him. "Come with me and I'll give it to you. You don't have to live like this, Zander. Neither of us do."

Shame and desire warred inside of him. How was it possible for him to even listen to anything she said after everything she had done? He'd been seconds away from killing her only a few minutes ago. Was he losing his mind?

But she was right. Even in the best possible scenario, some people would never accept him. He'd always have to hide that part of himself or rip it out. "And you expect me to trust you? After everything you've done, I'm supposed to believe, what—you want to ride off into the sunset with me?"

"I know you have no reason to trust me, but"—she blew out a breath—"I want to be free of this place."

"Nothing's stopping you from leaving. Nobody's stopping you from going through the Looking Glass tonight and never coming back. You don't need me."

She drew in a breath. "But I'm tired of being alone... and I think you are, too."

He flung out his arms. "So you'd simply trust that I wouldn't turn on you? With all the reasons you've given me?"

A half smile tipped her lips. "It's possible, but not probable. Like I said before, you can't help doing the right thing." Lyssandra took a step towards him and pulled a delicate ring off her middle finger. Its ruby stone glistened in the moonlight, and faint magic pulsed from it.

When he only stared at it, she moved closer. "This is a promise ring. Once you put it on, it would seal our word to each other. Neither of us could break it."

She held out the piece of jewelry, and he stared at it, hypnotized by the hope of relief, a way out of all of his problems.

"Z... Zander?" The voice from inside was low and scratchy, and it broke the spell the Queen's words had woven over him.

Zander jerked back from her, and his horror must have been clearly visible on his face because Lyssandra's expression flickered to reveal a hungry darkness before her mask slid back in place. But it was too late. He'd seen the truth. He slapped at her hand, sending the ring clattering to the balcony floor.

She gave a cry and scrambled towards it. Behind him, Citrine called his name again, and all he could think about was protecting her. He kicked the jewelry, and it clattered against the rails before disappearing from view. The Queen scorched him with a hateful glare before she leapt onto the balcony railing, looking more animal than human. "Don't forget I gave you a chance, but you sealed his fate."

Then she launched upward, shifting as she went. The moonlight glinted off her ruby scales as she flew away.

Chapter 46

TRUE TO HER WORD, Larkspur had gotten them an audience with her brother that very evening. Alice and Chess stood side by side, the King's heavy gaze on them. She'd left Wickle in her room to be on the safe side. No need to remind anyone about the snark.

"Well, nephew, you asked to see me, and here I am, so get on with it." The King slouched in his swing-like throne; his legs tossed over the side. In his hand, he held a small green orb that he ran through his fingers over and over. Alice wished she could ask what it was, but she doubted he would appreciate that. His whole tone and posture showed he wanted this meeting over sooner rather than later.

Chess glanced at Alice and then stepped forward. "I don't come on my behalf, Your Majesty. I am coming on behalf of the Red Palace, and Prince Zander in particular."

The King waved a dark brown hand. "Yes, yes, you're here on official business. Get on with it." A small Fae buzzed around his head, and he swatted at it.

"Stop bothering me," he muttered. With a high-pitched squeak, it flitted to the other side of the room.

"As you wish, Your Majesty," Chess said.

The King let out a gusty sigh. "I thought I told you to dispense with all that formality. Call me Uncle. We are family, after all."

"All right then, Uncle, since we are family, I would like to request the loan of a royal artifact."

The King's head lifted from his study of the orb in his hand, and he turned his piercing gaze on Chess. "Why?"

Chess paused, and Alice could almost see him examining and discarding a variety of responses. Finally, he gave a small nod, as if he'd decided something. "The truth is, Prince Zander is in a precarious position. The Red King is... unwell, and the Prince has the Drifter Gene."

The King swung his legs down and leaned forward. "I thought your people had driven away or killed anyone with that Gift." His mouth pursed, making it clear what he thought about that.

"The general opinion about the Gene has softened with time, but the Council is not confident the citizens would accept a ruler with that... erm, issue."

"Fools! They should be glad to have someone with that kind of power on the throne. What's his form?"

Chess looked at Alice a bit helplessly. They were throwing all of Zander's secrets out for the Fae king to see. She shrugged. They were in this deep, and they needed the artifact.

Chess looked back at the King. "It's a Jabberwock."

"I don't see why anyone is complaining. They'd have a king who could protect them."

Chess's mouth pressed into a thin line. "People are fearful of someone with that much power, Your... Uncle."

The King lifted a shaggy eyebrow. "Yes, I'm aware." His tone was dry. "Still, that doesn't explain why you need one of my artifacts."

Chess paused, his chest rising and falling before he finally spoke. "Someone found a formula that allows a person to rid themselves of a Gift, but it requires a royal Fae artifact to work."

"So that silly Council wants your Prince to divest himself of his Gift?" The King fell back into his chair. "They are stupider than I credited them. Do you have any idea what shedding a Gifting can do to a person? You'll be lucky if the Prince isn't a gibbering idiot by the time you're done. Even if he doesn't end up a hollow husk, he'll change. You might not want what's left on the throne."

A chill slid up Alice's spine, and she could see the King's words had upset Chess, too. "Are you saying it isn't possible to get rid of a Gift without permanently damaging a person?" he asked.

The King tossed the orb up in the air and then caught it. "I'm saying it's an enormous risk."

"But it *is* possible?" Chess pressed.

The King shrugged, and when he spoke, it was reluctantly. "I suppose, in theory, it's possible." He sat up again and pointed a long, gnarled finger at Chess. "Do you realize we strip Gifts from people as a punishment? I can hardly countenance someone doing it willingly, with all the dangers involved."

"Well, I suppose that decision is up to the Prince, Uncle. If you loan us the artifact, I will return it safely to you, and whatever happens to the him, nobody will lay that at your doorstep, if that's your concern."

The King snorted. "So many promises, but how do I know you'll follow through?" He waved a hand at the stormy expression on Chess's face. "I'm not questioning you, nephew. I suppose you mean what you are saying, but if we are being honest here, you aren't in charge, are you?"

Chess's cheeks darkened in a blush. "I can assure you, I am speaking on behalf of the Prince and his father."

"If he doesn't survive this process, what then? You said that the King is unwell. That would leave that Council of yours in charge." The King stabbed a finger at Chess. "And I don't trust those flibbertigibbets!"

Alice rather agreed with the King on that point.

"Your Majesty—"

"Uncle," the King interrupted.

"Uncle, then, I was tasked with bringing back an artifact, and I can't go back empty-handed."

The King stared down at the green orb and rolled it between his hands for several long moments. Finally, he looked up, regret in his expression. "Even if I didn't believe stripping a Gift was a mistake, I can't loan out an artifact. The clans would raise a ruckus, as well they should. It's far too dangerous. I'm sorry, nephew."

Chess's shoulders slumped, and his mouth tightened. Alice looked between him and the King. It looked like they needed to delve into their back pockets after all.

She stepped forward and dropped a hasty curtsey before straightening. "Your Majesty, what if we told you we had a good idea of who is responsible for the dead and missing Fae?"

The King glowered at her. "If you were aware of that, why didn't you mention it when my daughter first brought you here?"

"I didn't have the complete story." She gestured at Chess. "Once I heard about the King's, erm, illness and how the Queen might be behind it, it was easy to understand she needed more power."

"What has that got to do with us and the small Fae?"

She glanced at Chess, a question in her eyes. He nodded at her to continue, and she turned back to the King, clasping her hands. It was a risk to share this information. He might become furious, but it was their only hope at this point. "I'm not sure how to put this delicately, Your Majesty, but the Queen used dust made from Fae wings to power her spell work. It's why I'm pretty sure she's the one behind all the killings and disappearances here. She needs a magical boost, if you will."

The King stopped moving the orb in his hands as he digested her words. He focused those dark, fathomless eyes on her, and Alice suppressed a shiver. "Why would you think this would change my mind? I have even less of an incentive to help anyone at the Red Palace now."

Alice swallowed, her throat suddenly dry. "Your feelings are understandable, but that still doesn't solve your problem. What if we could bring the Queen to you?" She felt more than saw the startled look Chess gave her, but she continued. "Would you be willing to exchange the artifact for her?"

A long silence stretched out and Alice held her breath, hoping against hope the King would agree. "I can send my own warriors after her. Why do I need you two?" he said.

"Because we know her far better than you do, and we've defeated her before." She lifted her chin. "Besides, you owe me."

The King sat up, and his expression darkened. "Owe you?"

"It was your Advisor who hurt me, and that was *after* you put me in a cage for something I didn't do, correct?"

The King glowered at her for a long moment before his head drooped. "Oh, all right. I suppose I'm agreeable to your proposal since it saves me a lot of trouble if you two go after her."

Alice let out a rush of air, and her shoulders relaxed. "Thank you..."

He held up his hand. "But you won't be going alone. Azalea will accompany you, and whoever she sees fit to bring along."

"I have no problem with that," Chess said quickly. "Do we have your word that if we bring you the Queen, you'll give us an artifact?"

The King gave a sharp nod of his head. "Yes, you do."

"I need you to say what you are promising... out loud," Chess said.

The King raised an eyebrow. "I thought you didn't know our ways," he muttered, and then louder he said, "I promise that if you return with the Queen, I will give you a royal Fae artifact."

Something in the air shimmered and settled.

"We should start soon—" Chess began, but the King held up his hand again.

"I want the woman brought in alive." His eyes narrowed into two burning black pits. "She will answer for what she's done to those under my care, and death will be a mercy she won't receive."

Alice swallowed and edged closer to Chess. He took her hand before he bowed his head. "Yes, Uncle. We'll bring her to you for justice."

The King's expression cleared, and he waved a hand at them. "Go away now. I'll let Azalea know."

"But, Your... erm, Uncle, I must impress how little time—"

"Yes, yes, you humans are always in such a blasted hurry. You certainly can't leave tonight. Azalea won't be ready until morning at least..."

Chess exchanged a glance with Alice and then bowed his head again. "As you wish, Uncle."

As they turned to go, Alice paused. "Erm, Your Majesty?"

"What is it now?"

Alice twisted her hands together, nerves dancing in her stomach. "I only wanted to find out. Did Mr. Tweed get home safely?"

The King frowned. "Who?"

"Arthur Tweed. The man you imprisoned here and then forgot about." From the way the King's eyebrows climbed towards his hairline, Alice realized she hadn't hidden her irritation very well.

The King waved a hand. "Oh, him. Someone will take him back when it's convenient."

Alice lifted her chin, trying and failing to keep her temper. "With all due respect, Your Majesty, the man has been waiting for years, and based on my own experiences, I'm sure he deserved to be in that cage about as much as I did."

The small Fae in the room stilled as the King rose to his feet, a terrifying expression on his face. His power pressed down on Alice, and she locked her knees to keep from throwing herself prostrate before him. The tension in the room thickened, and Alice's stomach sank as she realized she might have ruined Chess's chances for the artifact.

Then, a familiar, languid voice spoke from a shadowy corner of the room. "For Wonder's sake, I'll take care of it. Nobody wants that wispy little man around here any longer than necessary, anyway. He fainted yesterday when Azalea asked him a few questions."

The King's gaze swung to where Indigo materialized from a gloomy corner. "And why would you bestir yourself to get involved?"

Indigo sauntered closer to the King. "I'd think that would be obvious, Father. It pains me to see my pet upset." Indigo winked at Alice, and beside her, Chess stiffened.

King Thorne's expression morphed from anger to amusement, and the icy knot in Alice's stomach loosened. "You and your pets. All right, take care of it. It's not as if I want the man in my guest rooms indefinitely." He turned back to Chess and Alice. "You are both dismissed. Azalea will come find you when she's ready."

"I hope you aren't leaving too early. If I'm to go on a quest I need a good night's rest first," said Indigo as he examined a fingernail and then buffed it on his shirt.

Chess's posture turned rigid. "You don't need trouble yourself on our behalf, cousin."

Indigo's smile held an edge. "It's no trouble at all. After all, I can't let my pet go wandering into danger without me."

"We really don't need you to—"

The King interrupted, a smug smile on his lips. "That's an excellent idea, Indigo. Just be ready to leave. I doubt they'll wait for you."

Chess gave a stiff nod and pulled Alice towards the door. Guilt bubbled up in Alice as they slipped out of the room. If she hadn't made the King angry, Indigo probably wouldn't be going with them, but she couldn't be sorry she spoke up for Arthur. She only hoped Indigo's presence wouldn't prove to be a problem for all of them.

Chapter 47

ZANDER STARED AT THE space where the Queen had just been on the balcony. Had he been hallucinating? That couldn't have just happened.

Citrine called out again, and he hurried back into the bedroom, locking the door behind him.

When he reached the bed, her grey eyes were open. She lifted her hand off the bed, but the action looked as if it cost her, and she let it fall back to the covers.

He dropped next to her and smiled. "You're awake."

She didn't smile back. "I... heard her." She lifted her hand again and rested it against his chest. "You'll be a great king. I know it. The people... will learn..."

Then, as if the effort was too much, her eyes slid closed again and her hand fell limply back on the bed.

"Citrine?" He gently shook her shoulder, and her eyelids fluttered open.

He gently brushed her hair off her face. "I should call the Healer, and for some food. You must be hungry. You..."

She clutched his hand to stop him, her grip weak. He stilled and looked down at her.

"Don't call anyone. I only... want you." Each word seemed to be a struggle, and Zander's stomach dropped when her eyes shut again, briefly, as if it took too much strength to talk.

He leaned in closer. "You're going to be all right. I mean," he let out a shaky laugh, "you're finally awake. Lapin will be so happy to hear this."

Her chest rose as she drew in a breath. "I... I'm so sorry, Zander." She paused again. "I'm always disappointing you, it seems."

Zander shook his head. Tears welled even as his mind resisted the truth his heart had already accepted. "You've never disappointed me. I've been so lucky to have your love and your friendship."

A shudder ran through her and she closed her eyes. "And you've... been a gift... to me."

"Please, please don't leave me."

Her hand rose from the coverlet, and she put her palm against his cheek. "I... I wish I didn't have to."

Her hand fell away, but he caught it and pressed his mouth to her palm, a tear dripping onto her skin.

Her eyes had closed again, and her breathing was so shallow, fear gripped him like a vice. "Citrine? Citrine, stay with me."

Her eyelids fluttered open with effort. "I'm not gone yet." A frown creased her face. "And we have things to discuss."

"Don't talk. Save your strength."

She squinted at him. "No, listen. I don't..." She stopped and caught her breath before she continued. "The Pearl Kingdom. Spar... is gone."

"Your brother might come back, but until he does, I'll find someone, Citrine. Don't worry about that now."

She frowned. "But I have to... someone has to..." She struggled to sit up, but the movement left her gasping.

He gripped her shoulders. "Please don't. I'll take care of it. You have my word."

She grabbed his hand in a suddenly forceful grip. "Alice. Like you said... Alice can do it. Promise you'll ask her."

Zander nodded, although he wasn't sure she would come back. Another tear tracked down his cheek. Citrine would be past caring by then.

"Give me paper. I have to... Grenmar."

It took him a moment to remember the water dragon that lived in the pond in front of the Pearl Palace. He wasn't sure why Citrine wanted to write to the creature. It had almost eaten Alice when they retrieved the dragon blood lily. Still, he stood up, his gaze flitting over the room as he turned in a helpless circle. "I don't have any."

She pointed, her hand trembling. "My satchel."

Zander rummaged through it until he found the paper and pen she'd requested and brought it over to her.

"Write what I tell you."

He sat on the edge of the bed and placed the paper against his knee and wrote what she told him. Then he helped to prop her up so she was able draw the symbol of the Pearl Kingdom. She pursed her lips at the shaky scrawl. "It... will have to... do."

Then she shivered. "I'm so cold."

He pulled the bedcovers back up, but her head moved back and forth against the pillow. "I need you."

It took Zander a moment to realize what she wanted. Carefully, he climbed onto the bed and stretched out next to her, gathering Citrine into his arms where she fit perfectly.

"Will you stay?" Her grey eyes looked up into his, but he didn't see any fear in them.

He pressed a kiss against her forehead. "As long as you need me."

She let out a sigh and pushed her face into the crook of his neck. Her breath made soft puffs of air on his skin, and he tightened his arms as it were possible keep her here if he could only hold on hard enough.

"I love you, Trinny. I don't think I can do this without you."

He felt her words as much as heard them, her lips the barest brush against his skin. "You can. I know it."

"I think you've always believed more in me than I ever did in myself."

Her lips formed a smile.

Zander wasn't sure how long they lay there, but he realized the breaths against his neck were getting farther and farther apart. He loosened his hold so he could look at her beloved face. It was still and very white, but so beautiful.

Her eyes fluttered open, her gaze clear and lucid, and when she spoke, her voice was strong. "I love you, Zander. Don't forget, but don't let it keep you from a future." The previous breathlessness was gone and, for a moment, a wild hope sprang up in his chest.

Then Citrine's lips curved into a brilliant smile, and she let out a long sigh. Her eyes slid shut and her body went limp, her head lolling over his arm.

"Citrine? Please! Citrine?!"

But she didn't answer.

She was gone.

He crushed her limp form to his chest, burying his face in her thick hair. A sob ripped out of him, and the tears that had been threatening tracked down his face in a torrent.

He wasn't sure how long he held her before he finally laid her gently back down on the bed. Her skin was ice cold when he pressed his lips to hers and sat up.

He rubbed away the wetness from his face with the heels of his hands. A wave of grief and weariness crashed down on him. He couldn't do this.

Zander knew he should tell someone, but his body refused to move. He kept staring at her face, willing her to open her eyes, to speak, to tell him this was only a horrible nightmare.

He drew in a ragged breath, still unwilling to leave her.

If he told someone, it would make it true.

And it couldn't be true.

Because a world without Citrine wasn't a world worth living in.

So, he took her icy hand in his and kept his own private vigil as the night slowly lightened and the pink edges of dawn kissed the horizon.

When he finally stood, his body was stiff and sore from staying in one position so long. He gently brushed a long strand of hair off Citrine's cheek and dropped a kiss on her cold forehead.

Then he turned and walked out the door to the reality that refused to be ignored any longer.

Chapter 48

THE SUN HAD BARELY peeked over the horizon, when Chess found himself on the now familiar path to his mother's home. He slid his hand into Alice's as they walked through the trees. When it was still dark, a small Fae had brought a message from Larkspur saying that she wanted to see him before he left. In truth, he was glad for another excuse to visit her, and for something to do. He'd never been good at waiting.

Azalea had sent word to him they would leave later in the morning. He was thankful his cousin seemed unwilling to waste time, either, but every hour that passed made him nervous. He didn't know what was happening back at the Red Palace or if the King was worse or...

"Hey, stop worrying." Alice's voice interrupted his thoughts. "You can't make this go any faster. We're lucky the King agreed to this."

"I'm wondering if it's worth it, honestly. After what everyone keeps saying about the dangers, I can't imagine Zander getting rid of his Gift."

Alice sighed. "Maybe I shouldn't have bargained with the King. Then you could have gone back and honestly said they wouldn't give it to you."

Chess lifted her hand and kissed the back of it. "No, you were brilliant, love. At least if we succeed, Zander might have some leverage with the Council. He needs something to at least shut up Lord Beecher."

Alice's mouth quirked into a smile. "From the little I know of the man, I think the only way Zander can shut him up might be stuffing the artifact *in* his mouth."

Chess chuckled. "Yes, well, that would be a good way to get thumped with that cane of his." He sobered. "I've been thinking though. Zander wouldn't actually have to go through with it. The option should be enough... hopefully."

They had reached the ring of trees, but before he could say anything, two of the trunks groaned and creaked before opening to let them through. Larkspur stood at her door and waved at them. "I'm glad you've made time to stop before leaving on your quest."

Chess shook his head. "How does she find out these things living way out here?"

Alice pointed to the small Fae flitting around the flowers and plants. "I think it's the Fae version of *a little bird told me.*"

Chess and Alice had barely made it up the steps when Larkspur hugged him. He couldn't help smiling. He had missed his mother's hugs.

When she finished with him, Larkspur pulled Alice into a hug, too. When she drew back, she put both hands on either side of Alice's face and stared at her for a long moment. Then she smiled. "You've recovered your essence. I'm so glad."

Turning, she motioned them inside and moved over to her tea kettle, steam already coming from its spout. "Sit. I'll have our tea ready in a moment."

"I'm not sure we have time for a long visit," Chess said, taking a seat at the table.

She flapped a hand at him. "Nonsense. You aren't leaving for hours yet. There's plenty of time." She studied them for a long moment before moving to her bundles of dried plants. Her long fingers expertly picked through the selection until she had some that pleased her. She dropped them in the teapot and poured the hot water over them. She already had cups on a tray, and she placed the teapot next to them before bringing the whole thing over to the table.

"We'll let that steep for a moment, shall we? Now, tell me about this quest of yours." Her brilliant blue eyes were bright with interest.

Chess smirked. "Well, it seems you already know all about it."

Larkspur tilted her head, her hair waving about her face. "But I want to hear the details from you. Second-hand isn't the same thing. I am assuming Azalea will accompany you."

Chess made a face. "I don't mind her coming along. She'll be a help, but I could do without her brother."

Larkspur's eyebrows rose. "Indigo is going with you? That is rather surprising."

Alice's cheeks turned rosy. "I'm afraid that's my fault. He's become rather... fixated on me."

Larkspur patted her hand. "That is also not surprising. You are a beautiful young woman and, if I am not mistaken"—her glance slid to Chess before returning to Alice's face—"you are immune to his charms."

Alice wrinkled her nose. "That doesn't seem to stop him from trying to use them on me. I wish he'd stop already. It's a bloody nuisance."

Larkspur sighed. "I'm afraid he's terribly spoiled, and like his ferret form, he likes to cause mischief. I've tried to tell my brother his son needs his attention, not indulgence, but he can hardly bear to be in Indigo's company."

Alice frowned. "Why not?"

Larkspur pushed the cup back and her expression turned serious. "Thorne's wife died shortly after Azalea and Indigo were born."

"Oh, I didn't realize they were twins." Alice leaned forward, her interest obviously piqued by the story.

"Yes, it's not very common among us, and the twins not only resemble their mother, but Indigo is just like her. She also was a court artist, and she had that same wild spirit. But where she tempered herself, I'm afraid nobody has curbed Indigo."

Chess raised an eyebrow. "So, he's a spoiled prince? Sorry, but that doesn't elicit any sympathy from me." He reached out and covered Alice's hand with his own. His mother's eyes followed his gesture, and her mouth twitched as if she wanted to smile. His face heated under her scrutiny.

But she didn't comment, and instead said, "Indigo's a good soul underneath. What he needs is something bigger than himself to burn away that selfish shell he's built up. He might accompany you for Alice's sake, but this will be good for him."

Chess snorted. "It's not our job to help him grow up."

"You can afford to be generous, son." Before he could ask her what she meant by that, she changed the topic. "Now, what exactly are you hoping to do on this quest of yours?"

Happy to leave the subject of Indigo, Chess leaned his forearms on the table and clasped his hands. "As you've probably already heard, we have to find the Queen and bring her back to King Thorne. She's likely the one that has been killing your small Fae."

"Are you sure it is her?" Larkspurs frowned.

Chess looked at Alice and then back at his mother. "There are too many coincidences for it not to be, and she's more than capable of it. After all, she cursed the Red Prince and her husband."

"It's hard to believe she still has her freedom after all that," Larkspur said.

Alice leaned forward. "She has the Drifter Gene, and her form is the Jabberwock."

Understanding dawned on Larkspur's face, "That explains so much," she said.

Then Larkspur's mouth tightened, and she covered Chess's hand with hers. "If she is that powerful and she can do complicated spell work, even if you do find her, how will you bring her back without killing her?"

Chess shrugged. He didn't want to admit that he had no idea. The task of finding her was going to be challenging enough.

At his non-answer, Larkspur *tsk*ed. She poured tea into the cups and pushed one towards each of them.

"You will get yourself and this lovely girl killed without a plan."

"We've been rather faffing about ever since I arrived here, ma'am, and it's worked so far." Alice sat back and took a sip of her tea.

A smile curved over his mother's lips. "I appreciate your defense of my son and his lack of planning, but if you hope to bring this woman back alive, you'll have to have more than merely a few hopes." She stood and walked over to a cabinet. Standing on her toes, she rummaged through the contents before pulling out a vial that contained a clear liquid.

She sat down and set it on the table. Alice picked it up and examined it. "What is it?"

"It will bind the Queen's magic."

Alice set it back on the table. "You mean she won't be able to shift or..."

"Yes, that's exactly what I mean." Larkspur tapped the glass side. "If you can get the entire vial into her, it should last for at least a full day, perhaps longer. It rather depends on her size."

Chess closed his hand over the vial and slipped it into his pocket. "Thank you."

She laid her palm on his cheek. "You are my son. I have only recently found you again. It would be extremely disappointing if something happened to you now." She winked at him before turning to Alice. "Now, then, tell me about yourself. How did you come to be in Wonderland?"

Alice shot him a look, and Chess's face heated. "I'm afraid that's my fault, Meemee."

They spent the next hour chatting and laughing. It filled something in Chess that he hadn't even realized was missing. When he got home he would have to confront his father and all his lies, but at this moment, in this place, he had his mother back. And it was enough.

Finally, they stood to leave. Larkspur followed them to the door, and Chess leaned down to drop a kiss on her cheek. "If we're successful, I might not have time to visit again before we have to leave for the Red Palace. But... I hope... I can come for a more relaxing visit next time."

Larkspur's eyes grew wet. "I would like that very much." She gripped his arms. "I am proud of you, son. You will be successful in this quest."

Chess moved towards the door, blinking back tears. Behind him, his mother stopped Alice, placing her hand on Alice's cheek. She murmured something he couldn't hear, but Alice's face flamed red. She nodded and Larkspur pulled her into a hug. Then she pushed Alice towards the door.

Once they were outside, he looked at Alice. Her face was still pink. "Are you going to tell me what my mother said?"

She gave him a mysterious smile. "No, I don't think I will just yet."

Chapter 49

INDIGO POKED HIS FINGER at Wickle again, causing the snark to hiss at him.

"Will you please stop harassing him?" Alice said for what felt like the hundredth time, and walked to the other side of the King's throne room where Azalea and Chess were studying a model of the island that served as a map.

Indigo followed her. "I don't understand why he doesn't like me."

"Probably because you keep poking at him. You'd assume, considering what happened to the Advisor, you'd leave him alone."

His brow furrowed in concentration, and he approached the snark again. "I will get him to like me. You know how I love a good challenge, my sweet." He held out his hand to the small creature perched on Alice's shoulder.

Wickle crowded against Alice's neck, trying to hide under her hair. *Not mate. Make go away. No like.*

Alice sighed. "Don't you have somewhere else you need to be?" She gestured at Azalea, who was in the process of turning the floating model of the island that comprised the Faelands so Chess could get a better look. "They obviously don't need you here."

Indigo's hand fell back to his side, and he made a face. "Father insisted I attend. Something about learning planning skills." He rolled his eyes. "It's tediously boring."

"Well, it's tediously annoying that you keep pestering Wickle."

Indigo's eyes gleamed. "Are you feeling neglected, my pet?"

"Most definitely not," Alice said and moved to stand next to Chess. He absently put an arm around her shoulder, squeezing her in a half hug before letting go and turning back to the map.

"Where did you find the latest victim?" he was saying.

Azalea pointed to an area that had the word *Boglands* in gold script hovering above the three-dimensional map. "This was where they found the last one, a grundy."

Chess raised an eyebrow, and Azalea explained. "It's a type of nixie—lives in the Great Bog but comes out to sun itself."

Alice leaned in to get a closer glimpse of the area Azalea had pointed to.

"How many Fae have you found dead?" Chess asked.

Azalea tilted the map so it was more vertical. She gestured to the half a dozen pulsing lights, mostly clustered in one section. "These are the deaths, though more have been reported missing."

"Are the missing ones from this area, too?" Alice pointed at the blinking lights that were just north of the Greening.

Azalea shook her head and gestured at a forested region east of the Greening near the foot of a mountain labeled Obsidian Mountain. "The first reports of anyone missing came from the Greening, but the last few are closer to this area." Then her finger moved closer to the Boglands. "They have also found one dead in this territory."

Chess frowned. "Who is the clan leader of the Boglands? We should talk to him—or her—first."

Indigo sauntered over to join them and reached out his finger to touch Wickle again, but snatched it back when the snark showed his fangs. He turned to Azalea. "Lord Zaba wouldn't have necessarily told us if his people were being killed or gone missing. He has a tendency to make his enemies disappear."

Azalea frowned. "Yes, the only one he mentioned was the grundy, but that does not mean much."

The two exchanged a glance, and Alice narrowed her eyes. "What aren't you saying?"

Indigo and Azalea exchanged another significant gaze before Azalea finally answered. "The... hierarchy here is not as set as in Wonderland, and some of the other leaders accept my father's rule more readily than others."

"But your father is the King of the Faelands, isn't he?" Alice asked.

"What my sister is trying to say without spelling it out is that the clan leaders often squabble like children and some of them don't like to share—especially power."

Alice wrinkled her nose. "Surely if someone is killing their people, they'll cooperate, though, won't they?"

Indigo shrugged. "Perhaps... probably. Depends on what they think they can get out of it by not cooperating."

Chess rolled his eyes. "Wonderful."

Azalea frowned at her brother. "Indigo is being dramatic. As you said, they will want to help us. There are only a few that might be... difficult."

While they were talking, Chess examined the map again, his eyes narrowing. Watching him, Alice sighed. She hadn't realized quite how large the Faelands were, and knowing that some of the other leaders would make things harder... well, the idea of trying to find the Queen was beginning to feel like an impossible task.

"Don't worry, pet. We'll find this queen of yours." Indigo tugged one of her curls, ignoring Wickle's hiss. "And think of all the fun we'll have looking."

Alice absently swatted at his hand. "But what if we don't?" She didn't realize she had said the words out loud until Indigo ran a hand down her arm, leaving warmth and a sense of well-being in his wake.

She pulled away from him. "That's not as helpful as you seem to think it is."

Indigo grinned, but Alice scowled at him. "I mean it, Indigo. Stop it."

He blew out a breath. "Fine, if that's what you want. I live only to make you happy, my pet."

Alice regarded him suspiciously, but when her emotions didn't change, she turned back to Azalea. "Poppy said something about a Jabberwock sighting. Is that normal here?"

Azalea nodded. "Usually a couple every year or two. They are not plentiful anywhere in the Kingdom of Wonderland anymore, though."

"Maybe this Zaba or someone from his clan has seen one?" Alice ran a hand over Wickle, who cheeped sleepily.

"This forest is dense and hides a number of large creatures. Most of the time, you will not know they are there unless they want you to see them—or if you are eaten."

She said it so casually it took a moment for the words to sink in, and Alice shivered. Indigo noticed and moved closer to her. He leaned down and spoke, his breath brushing her ear. "Don't worry, pet, I'll protect you from any of dangers."

Chess snorted. "You and what ferret?"

Indigo bristled, straightening to his full height. Tension crackled in the room, and Alice tried to divert everyone's attention back to the quest. "We need to ask around. I mean, obviously, a Jabberwock could hide in the forest, but it would be harder for something that size to go unnoticed in a bog, right? And the Queen's Jabberwock is ruby red, so she'd be hard to miss."

Chess caught her hand and kissed the back of it. "Brilliant idea, love."

Alice's face heated. She was still unsure about Chess. She knew her own feelings, and he'd been very free with his affection since he'd found her again. But he also had a reputation as a flirt. It seemed like he truly cared, but what if she was only seeing what she wanted to?

She pushed the thoughts away. There would be time to deal with whatever was between them later. Right now, she would enjoy the warmth of his hand holding hers She resolutely ignored the small voice that asked if the time would ever be right.

Azalea met Indigo's gaze. "We should go see Lord Zaba. One of his clan might have seen a Jabberwock." She turned to Alice. "You said she is ruby red in that form?"

Alice nodded even as Indigo made a face. "You can talk to him if you want, but I'll pass on that dubious pleasure, thanks."

"You asked to come with us, brother. Nobody forced you. If we must speak to Lord Zaba, it is wiser if we do it together."

Indigo let out a long-suffering sigh. "Fine. If you insist, but don't come crying to me if he decides this would be a perfect time to lessen the number of Father's offspring."

Unease snaked up Alice's spine, and she suddenly regretted her suggestion. Chess squeezed her hand and leaned down to speak in her ear. "Don't look so worried, love. I'm pretty sure the only one this Zaba will want to make disappear is Indigo."

Alice choked back a laugh and spoke to the siblings. "How far away is he?"

"It is a day's walk from here," Azalea answered. "Faster if we fly."

Alice wasn't sure how to ask, since she wasn't sure what the etiquette was regarding Fae wings, but Azalea seemed to be the only one of them that had any. "Erm, I don't want to offend you, but there are three of us and only one of you."

Azalea flexed her wings, and a small smile lifted her lips. "You are wrong. There is one of you, and also a cat and a ferret. In my animal form, I can carry all of you easily that way."

Alice didn't know if she should ask or not, but she couldn't help herself. "What *is* your animal form?"

"It is a griffon." Azalea's face broke into a full smile, its brilliance taking Alice by surprise since the woman's expression was usually stoic.

Alice grinned back. This might not be so bad after all.

Then Indigo poked at Wickle again. "You'll have to leave him here, my sweet. Lord Zaba will not be happy to see us, but if you bring the snark, we'll probably all die in the swamp."

With those encouraging words, Indigo strolled towards the door, and the rest of them trailed after him.

Chapter 50

AZALEA LANDED NEXT TO a large body of still water, its surface covered in patches of green fuzz. The sun glinted off the variegated silvery feathers that covered her head. Chess stood, careful not to let his claws dig beyond the darker grey feathers on his cousin's back. He had a feeling she would be less than understanding and didn't want to get on the wrong side of her sharp beak. He leapt down, the ground giving way under his paws, before he shifted back into his human form. Indigo didn't move from Alice's hold, so she gently tossed him onto the ground before sliding off herself.

Chess waited until both Fae siblings had shifted back into their human forms before he asked, "So, how do we let this Lord Zaba learn we're here?"

Indigo glanced around, his posture stiffer than normal. "Oh, I'm sure he already knows. Nobody from other clans can set foot in the Boglands without Zaba knowing about it."

"Will it help if I tell him I'm here on business from the Red King?"

Indigo smirked. "Perhaps. Or perhaps we'll end up sleeping with the fishes."

Azalea's glare should have scorched her brother on the spot, but Chess wasn't sure if it was because Indigo was exaggerating or because he wasn't.

Chess inspected their surroundings. The plants crowding the still water were thick and lush, and the heavy, earthy sent of rotting vegetation tickled his nose. There were no swamplands on the Wonderland mainland, and the thick air and spongy ground made his skin itch.

Azalea strode toward a stand of tall cattails. Tiny Fae droned around Chess's head, and he resisted the urge to swat at them. One landed in his hair, sending a prickling sensation along his scalp before it buzzed away. He reached back for Alice's hand, but Indigo stepped between them, throwing a muscled arm around Alice's shoulders and leaning down to say something in her ear. Chess gritted his teeth. He hadn't told her how he felt, he reminded himself, and they'd made no promises to each other. He had no genuine right for the hot burn of jealousy that churned in his gut, but he couldn't help his smile when Alice shrugged out from beneath the arm and rolled her eyes at the Fae man.

They followed Azalea to the edge of the murky water, giant lily pads floating on its scummy surface. Shadows darted beneath the water, making it ripple.

Alice stepped closer to his side and slipped her hand into his. "I sincerely hope we are not going in there," she said, her eyes trained on the water.

He pressed her fingers. "Don't tell me the woman that faced down a monster is afraid of a little water."

"I... I can't swim." Her voice was tight as she tried to jerk her hand away, but he held fast.

He angled his body towards her and tipped her chin up with his finger so their gazes met. "Look, I'm sorry. I was only teasing. You'll be fine. You rescued me from that merrow in the labyrinth pool, remember?"

She hugged herself. "That was different."

"Look at me, love." When she finally did, he smiled. "I told you I have your back, and I don't go back on my promises. No matter what, I won't let anything happen to you."

She tried to smile back, but her mouth trembled. "I... I don't think even you can promise everything will be all right."

"I'm not that foolish, but I *can* promise you any threats will have to go through me first."

She leaned into him. "I'm glad you're here."

A loud glub and splash made them both start. They watched as an enormous bubble bobbed to the surface. Inside were two clearly Fae men. They were both wide and squat, with broad faces and wide mouths with only a hint of lips. A toad-like skin covered their bald heads, the taller one more brown and the shorter one more green. They wore what Chess supposed was armor, but it looked more as if they had skinned a snake and wrapped it around themselves. They both held large spears, the tips lethally sharp.

Alice edged closer to him, and he slid an arm around her waist. As the men walked forward, the bubble bobbed along the surface, functioning almost as a strange wheel.

When it bumped into the stand of cattails, one man used his spear to pop the bubble. They sprang forward on powerful legs and landed before the group, bringing with them the smell of rotted vegetation and stagnant water.

The men nodded first to Indigo and then to Azalea. They completely ignored Chess and Alice as if they weren't there.

When the taller of the two spoke, his voice was deep and guttural. "Lord Zaba greets you."

"King Thorne returns his greeting." Azalea's tone was formal, her posture erect.

The two sets of bulbous eyes turned to Indigo. Finally, he must have realized they were waiting for him to speak. He waved a hand. "Oh yes, hello and all of that."

The two toad-men glared at Indigo before turning back to Azalea. Chess wasn't sure how the man's disrespectful attitude would help them.

"Lord Zaba wishes to know the reason for your esteemed visit."

"I bet he's trying to see if this is a good time to get rid of us," Indigo muttered a little too loudly.

Azalea shot him a glare before turning her attention to the Fae men. "We have come on account of the small Fae and hope to speak with Lord Zaba about the killing that occurred here recently. We have some new information that could help us find the perpetrator."

Chess noticed the way Azalea carefully framed her words so that nobody would be able to claim she had made any promises. He wondered what kind of person this toad-man was and if Indigo had been serious.

The two Fae men spoke in guttural grunts and odd trilling peeps that Chess didn't understand. The minutes ticked by as they continued to confer, their faces scrunched in concentration.

Azalea and Indigo didn't seem to recognize what they were saying either, but Azalea's body was rigid.

Alice leaned closer and whispered in his ear. "They're debating whether or not to take us to the clan leader."

He blinked down at her. "It's probably rude to eavesdrop, but under the circumstances..." Her mouth tipped into a smile. "I thought manners could go hang."

Chess bit back a chuckle as the two men turned back to Azalea. "Come, we will take you to Lord Zaba. He will want to hear what you have to say. It greatly saddens him that nobody has avenged the murdered Fae yet."

Beside him, Indigo bristled, but Azalea merely nodded. "Yes, it weighs heavily on King Thorne's mind and heart as well."

Clearly, Azalea was used to being a diplomat to the other Fae clan leaders.

Beside him, Alice stiffened as the two men marched back toward the swamp. His hand tightened around hers. He wanted to reassure her, but he rather thought the only way to reach Lord Zaba was to go into his swamp.

The shorter man held out his hand, his fingers long and spindly and with a few too many joints. A large lily pad slowly floated toward them. The man gestured toward it, and Azalea nimbly leapt into its middle. It sagged with her weight, the swamp water washing over its edges. Indigo went next, and it sagged even more.

The taller man joined the royal siblings, while the shorter man moved to follow.

"I'm afraid they are with us," Indigo said.

The Fae men stilled and once again spoke to each other in their guttural language before the smaller man finally turned back to Chess and Alice and made an impatient gesture.

Chess stepped toward the lily pad, but Alice didn't move. When he turned back, he realized her eyes were wide and staring, her face completely devoid of color. He gave her hand a gentle tug. "It's all right, love." He tugged again, and she stumbled forward a step. "See? We'll go together."

But she dug her heels in and shook her head, dark hair flying around her face. "I... I can't." She pulled her hand away and hugged herself, her eyes never leaving the still, algae-covered surface of the swamp. His heart clenched at the stark fear on her face.

He looked at the lily pad's occupants and then back at Alice. It would be dangerous to leave her here alone, but they needed to know what was going on. They didn't need Indigo at the meeting, but he was about as reliable as wet paper. The idea of leaving Alice with him set Chess's teeth on edge.

"She needs to be charmed, cousin. Are you up to the task?" Indigo's smile mocked him.

Chess crossed his arms. "I think Alice has made it clear that she doesn't want or need anyone's charm."

"I suppose there's always the option of knocking her unconscious, but that doesn't seem very gentlemanly."

Chess scowled at his cousin as the two toad-men waited. He glanced back at Alice, but if anything, she was whiter than ever, and he could see fine tremors moving along her body. There was no way she was getting onto that lily pad, but she'd made it clear how she felt about being charmed.

Before he could decide what to do, Indigo leapt back off the lily pad and reached Alice's side in one long stride, shouldering Chess out of the way. "Since you are apparently unwilling or incapable of helping her, I will."

Chess grabbed his cousin's arm and pulled him back around. "She said she didn't want to be charmed."

Indigo jerked away from him and waved a hand in Alice's direction. "She's not moving without some help, and I plan on giving it to her."

"She does need help." Chess's agreement made his cousin hesitate. "But you need to ask her."

Uncertainty spread over Indigo's features. "What if she says no?"

Chess crossed his arms. "Then I'll stay back with her, but I won't let you charm her without her permission, not after she's said she doesn't want that so many times already."

Indigo blew out a long breath. "I suppose it won't hurt to ask her." He moved towards Alice, but Chess was already in front of her. He bent so he could look directly into her wide, staring eyes. Fear had such a tight grip on her, it was like she didn't even see him—only the murky water.

"Alice, love, look at me." Her gaze flickered from the water to his face. Then, she blinked. Her face was still white but her gaze met his squarely now. "We need to go see Lord Zaba, but the only way is on that lily pad."

He hadn't even finished the words and she was shaking her head again. He cupped her cheek and she stared up at him, and he could feel her trembling. "I... I can't," she said, her voice hoarse. "I'm sorry, but..." She looked at the water helplessly.

He took her hands. "You can—if Indigo helps you."

Her eyes darted from his to the other man and then back to Chess. "But... I'd rather you do it."

Chess shook his head. "I don't think my charm is strong enough, not for this, love."

She swallowed, and he watched the battle flicker over her features. Finally, her mouth firmed and she gave a jerk of her head. "All right."

Chess moved back to make room for Indigo. With both of the toad-men glaring at them, Indigo trotted to Alice's side. Even as Chess watched, the tightness in Alice's expression eased, and her shoulders inched down from her ears.

Indigo slid his hand down her arm and took her hand. Chess trailed behind them, his stomach in a knot, as Indigo led Alice to the edge and slipped his arm around her waist. He jumped them both onto the lily pad.

Chess leapt after them, and as soon as he landed, the lily pad sank. Alice gasped as the water covered all of their feet, but Indigo's hand ran down her arm again, and her expression glazed over. Chess hated he wasn't the one to help Alice, but she was on the lily pad. And she was all right. That was the important thing, not his ego.

The water inching up to his shins interrupted his thoughts. Chess wasn't afraid of water, but he didn't like it, either. He especially didn't enjoy sinking into a swamp. Just when he was ready to return to the shore and bring Alice with him, the shorter man made an intricate sign in the air. Pale green and gold sparkles lingered before the sign slowly dissipated.

The sides of the lily pad stretched and grew, curving up over them like an enormous mouth until it had enveloped them completely. Chess wasn't sure he liked this any better, but at least the water around their ankles had drained away.

The small man tapped the sides of their leafy prison, and they turned translucent. Suddenly, he could see into the waters that now surrounded them as they sank beneath the swamp's surface.

Next to him, Alice blinked and straightened away from Indigo. He put a hand on her shoulder, but she shrugged it off, sliding closer to Chess.

Even as he put an arm around her waist and tucked her close to his side, he nodded at Indigo. His cousin returned the gesture and then crossed his arms and leaned against one side of the bubble, his eyes fixed on Alice's back as they descended to the bottom of the swamp.

Chapter 51

ALICE TRIED TO BREATHE slowly as the green bubble descended to the bottom of the swamp. She resolutely focused on Chess's warmth and his arm around her.

Indigo continued to watch her, his silver eyes narrowed. She didn't want to admit it, but she probably wouldn't have gotten onto this lily pad without him manipulating her fears away. She peeked up at Chess, wishing it had been him to help her, not Indigo.

As they sank lower, her ears popped, reminding her of how far away the surface was. She swallowed. To take her mind off of where she was, she turned her attention to the two toad-men. She sensed their caution and unease, but she wasn't sure it originated from being in the presence of King Thorne's children, or if was the coming confrontation with this Lord Zaba.

Around them, various creatures swam, darting this way and that in the shadowy depths. Some were what you'd expect in a swamp, like fish, but others were various kinds of Fae. Alice marveled at the variety from tiny ones that could be mistaken for tadpoles to much larger creatures that more closely resembled the toad-men in front of her.

A shadow moved over the bubble, and Alice tracked the movement of a long reptilian body as it swam above them. It circled back around, and her heart picked up speed. She wasn't sure how sturdy their mode of transportation was, but it only circled lazily a few times as if curious before swimming away and disappearing into the murk.

A few minutes later, a large rocky formation rose from the silty swamp floor. Parts of it speared upwards, roughly shaped like towers. Large torpedo-shaped fish swam around the perimeter, and as one passed close to their conveyance, Alice spotted jagged teeth protruding from its bottom jaw. She shivered.

"I hope we don't get an up close and personal introduction to any of them," Chess murmured in her ear.

She gave him a quick smile before the bubble bumped into a round opening of the castle, although that seemed a rather generous term for the rock formations clumped together.

Short toad-man waved his hand through the air once again. The walls of the lily pad became solid before they unfurled.

Alice braced, expecting to be doused in water, but they were in a dry passageway. The toad-men walked forward and gestured for them to follow. Azalea strode after them, but Indigo elbowed his way next to Alice, forcing Chess to walk ahead of them. Indigo slowed, so they fell behind. When she picked up her pace to catch up to Chess, Indigo put a hand on her arm.

"Before you run off, my pet, I need to speak with you." He spoke in a low drawl, but his silvery gaze darted around as if afraid of being overheard.

When Alice nodded, he leaned closer and dropped his voice. "Lord Zaba will most likely seem friendly, but he's dangerous."

Alice lifted her eyebrows. It was hard to imagine that the clan leader would risk the reprisal of King Thorne by harming one of his children. Of course, she had no idea about the politics in the Faelands.

Indigo continued, his voice soft. "He's not happy about the clans having to follow Father, but Azalea and I should be protected, as well as my cousin, since he's the nephew of two kings. Zaba won't want to stir the waters unless there's something in it for him."

"Why are you telling me this?" Alice asked, somewhat mystified.

"Because you lack any beneficial affiliations, it would be best, my pet, to avoid his notice. Don't speak, and try to stay out of his line of sight."

With that ominous warning, Indigo straightened and hurried to catch up with Azalea. Once he reached her, he bent down to speak into her ear. She shook her head at him, and Alice saw the other woman's hand rest briefly on the hilt of her sword.

"I don't like this," she said to Chess, who had slowed so they could walk together.

"I won't let anyone harm you, love."

Alice gave him a look of surprise. He winked. "I'm not above eavesdropping when it serves my purposes, and while I don't trust Indigo, I think he's probably telling the truth about this. When we get to wherever we're going, stay close to me."

"Don't worry, I will." She rubbed her arms and looked around at the damp walls of the tunnels. "This whole place is dodgy. If something goes wrong, we're stuck."

Chess frowned, but the two toad-men paused at a doorway and announced their presence. "Lord Zaba, the visitors are here."

Alice peered around the toad-men, curiosity warring with caution. Instead of the throne room she expected, it was some kind of training space. Several pairs of Fae were grappling with each other.

Beyond them, the far wall was translucent, giving a view into the swampy waters outside the palace. Two men, their hair bundled into braids, charged each other on what looked like enormous snapping turtles. Inside, one of the bigger men threw his opponent to the ground. When the man didn't get up, the big guy straightened, a triumphant smile spreading across his face. He grabbed a large leaf and blotted the sweat from his face before he reached for a tunic and pulled it over his head. It wasn't until their two guides bowed to him that Alice realized this was Zaba.

He resembled the toad-men, but was several inches taller, his sinewy muscles more pronounced. His face looked craggier and lined, and a shock of white hair made a crest down the center of his head. He clapped his hands loudly, and the other wrestling pairs paused.

"You will leave us." He didn't spare any of his men a glance, but they all quickly gathered up their belongings and exited the room.

The man kept his beady, mud-colored eyes trained on his visitors as the men filed from the room. Alice slid behind Chess, hoping to make herself as inconspicuous as possible. Zaba was not what she'd been expecting. He frightened her, as much as she hated to admit it.

Zaba walked towards the royal siblings, his gait a rolling hop-step. He slapped Indigo on the shoulder, but his show of hearty welcome was obviously false. The shrewd calculation in the clan leader's eyes made her stomach coil with unease.

"It's been a long time since you graced my humble palace with your presence." The words were welcoming, but the tone was not.

Indigo shrugged his big shoulders. "It's not as if you're on the way anywhere I'm going, Zaba."

The clan leader chuckled. "No doubt, since I have neither paints nor pets here for you to play with."

Indigo gave the man a lazy smile. "It's nice to know our subjects know us so well."

This reminder of his position didn't seem to sit well with the clan leader, and when he turned towards Azalea, his shoulder hit Indigo hard enough to knock the taller man back a step. "And you, warrior princess, my men tell me you finally arrived to see to the death of one of my people. I'm happy to hear you are taking action at last."

Azalea's expression tightened, but she dipped her head politely. "Thank you for seeing us, and we appreciate your patience."

Then the clan leader's gaze fell on Alice and Chess, and he grinned. "I see you have brought me presents to help my patience along."

Alice fought the urge to back away from the man as he did his odd hop walk towards them. He circled slowly, as if inspecting a horse, stopping in front of Chess. He sniffed loudly. "The boy is quite pretty, despite being only half Fae. He'll make an agreeable companion for my Rana."

Azalea stepped forward. "I am afraid there is a misunderstanding, Lord Zaba. This is Sir Chess Felinas. He is the nephew of both King Thorne and the Red King."

The clan leader put a hand on his chest. "My apologies." He gave a roguish wink. "Rana will be disappointed about missing out on such a handsome specimen, though, but I must admit I wondered about Larkspur's son. I should have known. You resemble her a great deal." He sighed. "Lovely woman, your mother."

Chess gave a charming smile, shifting to block Alice from view. "I am honored you think so."

Zaba turned his attention to Alice despite Chess's efforts. He gave another loud sniff, and his mouth stretched into a wide smile. "Now this one is fully human."

One of his too-long, spindly fingers lifted a curl from her shoulder, and she resisted the urge to wrinkle her nose at the stagnant-water stench rolling off him. "She's quite lovely. Too thin to produce strong sons, but she'll still make a delightful addition to my females."

Icy cold spread over her skin at his words, and some of her revulsion must have shown on her face because he leaned closer, his muddy brown eyes narrowing. "I can see I don't quite catch your fancy." He patted her cheek, his touch cold and clammy, and she flinched away from him. He gave a guttural laugh. "But don't worry, I haven't had any complaints yet."

Heat rose up her neck and flooded her face. "There's always a first," she muttered under her breath.

Chess stepped between them. When he spoke, his tone was steely. "She's not here for you."

Zaba's beady gaze went from Chess to Alice and back again. "Is she your female, then?"

Indigo stepped up next to her. "No, the girl's my pet."

Both Chess and Alice glared at him.

"No, I'm not."

"No, she's not."

They spoke at the same time, and Indigo crossed his arms. "Yes, she is. I claimed her first."

Chess rolled his eyes. "If we're going by that, then my claim should trump yours since I'm the one that found her before she even met any of you."

Alice whipped around to glare at him next, and Chess held up his hands. "I'm just saying if that's the criteria, I still win."

She narrowed her eyes at him. "I'm not some prize or pet or"—she turned her scowling gaze on the clan leader—"*present*, and I'll thank all of you to remember that."

The toad-man's muddy eyes drilled into Alice, but she refused to lower her gaze. She should have kept her mouth shut, but now she had no choice but to not back down. He licked his lips with an absurdly long tongue, his thin, rubbery lips twisting, and she fought down a shudder.

Just when she thought he was going to order someone to throw her in a dungeon or run her through with a spear, he threw back his head and let out a loud croaky laugh, clapping both Chess and Indigo on their shoulders. "I wish both of you good luck with this one." He leered at Alice. "If I were a few years younger..." He smacked his lips before sighing. "But I'm not. I'll leave it to the young tadpoles here."

Turning back to Azalea as if nothing had happened, he said, "Now, tell me, what new information do you possess?"

Azalea carefully explained about the bumble's death and the malignant magical signature that nobody recognized. She let Chess explain about the Red Queen. He finished and then asked the clan leader, "So, we need to know. Did you or any of your people come across a Jabberwock or any indications of its presence? She would be ruby red."

The clan leader gestured at the taller guard that had escorted them here. "Your brother Mezzo, he found Pinana, didn't he?"

The Fae nodded solemnly.

"Did he say anything about a Jabberwock or find anything that would show one's presence?"

The guard shuffled his feet. "The only thing he said was that poor Pinana was a husk when he found her."

"You're sure?"

The Fae thought for a moment and then held up a finger. "He mentioned that the area looked trampled, but we thought a struggle caused it."

Zaba pursed his lips. "It's too late now to search for clues. The swamp doesn't leave traces of anything for long."

Azalea's shoulders dropped a bit, but her expression remained neutral. "It is still something. A creature the size of a Jabberwock could have caused the trampled area. We thank you for your time and for the information." She nodded at their group. "Now, we should probably take our leave."

Zaba held up a finger. "I have heard a rumor that one of the missing ones turned up again."

"Was it one of your people?" Azalea asked.

Zaba shook his head. "Not mine. You should check with Duir, the Elder Oak."

"Thank you, Lord Zaba."

The Fae shrugged his big shoulders. "Eh, he spends half his time not moving. He might be petrified by now."

Azalea bowed her head. "We will seek him out next. Thank you again for seeing us."

Zaba grinned, his beady eyes finding Alice. "It was my pleasure."

He waved a long arm at the two Fae guards. "Take them back to the surface."

Azalea and Indigo followed the two guards out of the room. Chess followed them, but as Alice turned to go, Zaba laid a clammy hand on her arm, and she stopped. "If you tire of the foolishness of young men, come visit me again." He gave her an exaggerated wink.

Alice stared down at his hand, nonplussed by his blatant interest in her. "Erm..."

She started when Chess slid an arm around her waist and tugged her to his side. "That won't be necessary, sir." He winked. "I'm told my appeal far outweighs my foolishness."

The clan leader laughed and shook a finger at Chess. "You have your mother's charm."

Alice's face flamed, but she couldn't help being relieved when they left the squat clan leader and his leering face behind.

Chapter 52

AZALEA FLEW THEM TO the edge of a forest, and Alice breathed more freely once they stepped under its canopy of branches, despite the fact they'd have to continue on foot. If she never saw another swamp or Lord Zaba again, she'd be happy.

Azalea led, brushing aside flowers and buds so vibrant they glowed in the dim light of the forest. The trees crowded in around them, brilliantly emerald, forcing them to walk in a single-file line. Chess followed on her heels, and Indigo walked behind Alice.

"Do you think Elder Duir will help us?" Chess asked as he pushed aside a vine growing across their path.

Azalea nodded even as her gaze swept back and forth. "Duir is wise, and he is an excellent guardian of his people. He has lost the most Fae in these killings. He will want to help as much as he is able."

Chess opened his mouth to ask a question, but Azalea held up a hand. "It is better if we do not draw attention to our presence."

A shiver slid up Alice's spine, and she wondered who or what Azalea hoped to avoid. Behind her, Indigo moved closer. "Don't worry, pet, I'll protect you."

"I think I'll take my chances with whatever's out there," she muttered, but apparently not as quietly as she thought because Indigo tugged at one of her curls.

"I believe you protest too much, my sweet."

Azalea glanced back at them, her face tight. "You must be silent."

Behind her, Indigo snorted, but he said nothing more, and they trudged onward.

They walked until the sun was high overhead, its rays filtering through the thick canopy of branches.

Azalea obviously had a destination in mind, but as far as Alice could see, there wasn't a clear path. Several times, they had to climb over fallen trees, their trunks covered in shades of amethyst or turquoise moss, or skirt around tangles of vivid vegetation. Birds and small Fae flitted in and out of the surrounding branches, and once they passed a circle of mushrooms sheltered in the roots of a large tree. Tiny glowing creatures twirled and floated in the circle, keeping beat to a lively, infectious tune.

Finally, Alice couldn't stand it any longer. "Are we even close to finding this Oak King?" she asked.

Indigo sighed. "Elder Oak, my sweet, not Oak King. Only my father has that title."

"I notice you didn't answer the question." Chess twisted to look at his cousin.

Azalea paused on the path. "Nobody knows exactly where to find the Elder Oak, but he is often in the center of his land. However, there are many trees. If he is ruminating, it might take us a moment to identify him amongst them."

"Ruminating? Do you mean to say he's a… tree?" Chess coughed into his hand to cover a laugh.

Indigo smirked. "You *do* know what a dryad is, don't you, cousin?"

Azalea ignored her brother and glared at Chess. "Show respect. He is an elder dryad and one of the oldest beings in the Faelands, or Wonderland, for that matter."

Chess gave her a mock bow. "My apologies. I would hate to upset a tree."

Azalea blew out a breath and looked at Alice. "Maybe you can get your mate to behave."

Alice's face flushed. "He's not… that is, I… I don't think anyone can make him behave. At least, I haven't seen anyone accomplish it yet."

Chess grinned and put his hands over his heart. "Aww, that's the nicest thing you've ever said about me, love."

She pushed his arm, a laugh escaping. "Stop being such a git."

Chess grabbed her hand and tugged her closer. "That's a terrible thing to say about your mate."

Even though she knew he meant nothing by the words, her breath stuttered in her chest. She rolled her eyes, trying to cover her reaction. "Oh, I've heard lots worse about you!"

Chess winked. "I've no doubt." He squeezed her hand, and they shared a smile.

Indigo stepped between them. "Oh, do tell, my sweet. What are these things you've heard about my cousin?"

Alice glanced up at the Fae man. His mouth stretched into a lazy smile, but his eyes were narrowed. "Oh, I—"

"Quiet, all of you." Azalea held up a hand, her eyes still scanning the surrounding woods.

"Did you find Elder Duir?" Indigo asked, his gaze roving from tree to tree.

"No, but we are being followed." Azalea tipped her head towards a cluster of ferns at the base of a nearby tree. "Your bickering no doubt drew them."

If Azalea hadn't pointed the creature out, Alice doubted she would have seen it. Green scales that blended with the leaves covered the small body, and the white feathers on its head were barely visible as it peeked out at them. Once she saw one, she noticed several others.

"I didn't know you had chickens here," said Alice. "They're darling."

"Those are not chickens." Azalea drew both her swords and handed one to Chess. "They are cockatrices, and very dangerous."

Alice wrinkled her nose, wondering how something that resembled a chicken was dangerous. Of course, Wickle looked like an adorable ball of fluff.

Azalea's gaze remained trained on the surrounding forest. "Whatever you do, do not look into their eyes."

This did not clear things up for Alice, and only left her more confused. Azalea didn't wait for any questions, but handed Alice one of her daggers and a sharp-tipped arrow. She gave her other dagger and another arrow to her brother. She drew them into a tight circle so their backs all faced each other. Alice's unease grew.

"Aren't you going to shift into your griffon?" Alice asked.

Azalea kept her eyes trained on the forest around them. "No, it is more risky in my other form. I would have to use both my beak and talons. It puts me too close to their eye level."

Behind her, Indigo sighed loudly. "I hate cockatrices. Turning to stone is such a bother."

"Stone?" Alice said, but the swelling sound of clucking drowned out whatever else Indigo said.

The clucking came from all sides, interspersed with hisses. That's when she realized there was an entire flock and they had surrounded the four of them.

The rustling and hissing got louder as the flock tightened the circle. Alice tried to reach out to the chickens—or whatever they were called—but she couldn't connect with any one individual. All she could get was a collective sense of excitement and almost frenzied anticipation.

She swallowed, her hands clenching around her weapons as her back bumped into Chess.

"Whatever you do, avoid making eye contact with them, love."

Alice wondered how she was supposed to fight something she couldn't look at, but then one cockatrice darted towards Azalea. Its beak dripped with saliva and was honed to a lethally sharp edge. Azalea jabbed downward with her sword, skewering the creature on her blade like a green marshmallow.

Alice's stomach turned queasy as Azalea flicked the bird off her blade and turned to the next one. A clump of the birds scattered as the body landed amongst them. As if this were some kind of signal, the entire flock rushed forward. Alice glimpsed a churning sea of green and white, the glow of burning red eyes, and then the cockatrices were on them. Staring over the heads of the flock, Alice stabbed downward with her arrow. She pierced a small body, and the creature let out a pathetic squeak. Although Alice felt bad for killing the creature, when another one had darted in and driven its beak into her calf, she changed her mind.

She screamed and slashed downward with her dagger. This time she felt no guilt when the cockatrice squawked and died. The spot on her calf burned, and the blood sent the nearby animals into more of a frenzy. She struggled to keep them from landing another blow. Sweat beaded her brow.

Beside her, Azalea jabbed and flicked her sword in a steady rhythm, and a mound of small, scaled bodies grew around their feet. Their first attack thwarted, the flock backed off, milling around them.

"Will they go away?" Alice asked Azalea as she tried to catch her breath.

Azalea shook her head, her braids almost slapping Alice in the face. "We will have to kill the whole flock, or most of them."

Almost before Azalea finished her answer, the flock had reformed themselves and charged again. They seemed better prepared this time, dodging around weapons, beaks aimed at shins and calves. Alice jerked her leg out of the way and stabbed a particularly persistent one, while behind her Chess grunted in pain, and Indigo let out a string of unfamiliar words.

One cockatrice flapped into the air, and Alice turned her head to avoid its beady stare. She put up her hands to block the sharp talons that stretched towards her face.

She expected to feel those sharp points rip into her arm, but there was a squawk, and when she peeked out, the cockatrice was lying on the ground, its head separated from its body.

Azalea whipped back towards another bird that had flapped towards her.

Alice didn't have time to thank her as another clump of cockatrices charged at her. She risked a glance out over the flock and her heart sank. The animals seemed to have multiplied, and they just kept coming. Her arm burned as she stabbed another of the chicken creatures. How long could they keep this up? She used the back of her other arm to wipe the sweat out of her eyes.

She only hoped Indigo and Chess were all right, but she didn't dare stop to check on them. Another bird flapped up towards her face and she squeezed her eyes shut as she slashed at it. Stupid chicken things! It dodged her dagger, and she whipped her arrow up. It tore at her hand and she screamed. Something swished by her face, and the cockatrice fell in two halves to the ground.

Chess winked at her before whirling back to his spot next to Indigo.

"Look out!" she yelled as another bird flapped straight at his face.

Everything seemed to happen in slow motion. Chess whipped his head to the side, but it was too late. Even as she watched, his body stiffened, grey spreading across his limbs. His eyes met hers before they clouded over to stone.

"No! Chess!" Alice swung around and jabbed at the bird, but Indigo blocked her. His hand darted out, and he grabbed the creature out of the air by its long tail. It writhed around, its sharp beak and talons trying to find flesh.

"What are you doing? Kill it!" Alice yelled.

"We can't."

There was no time to find out why. Around them, the other birds sensed an opening and renewed their attack with lethal viciousness. Despair weighed on Alice, but she didn't have time to indulge in feelings. She kicked out and connected with a scaled body, sending it sprawling into several of its comrades. Behind her, Indigo yelled in pain. The cockatrice he held had hit its mark. Still, he didn't let go of the writhing creature as it hissed and fought him.

Pain blossomed in her calf, and Alice grimly slashed at her attackers. This wasn't working. They couldn't hold off these stupid chicken creatures forever, and Chess needed help. How long could you be a statue before you died? Was he suffocating in that stone? She choked back a sob and stabbed another of the creatures, flinging it into a clump of cockatrices.

Alice looked out at the still swarming sea of birds. She didn't care what Azalea called them. She didn't want to experience death by chicken, even if they had scales.

"Cease!" The deep voice echoed out over the animals like a wave, and the cockatrices all paused, their little white heads swiveling towards the sound.

Alice swung around, trying to find the source of the voice, and then her gaze snagged on a tree, and she blinked.

And then blinked again.

A man was emerging from its trunk, as if he were peeling himself out of it. His skin was brown and rough like bark, and his eyes were a warm hazel. When he finished, he shook his head, and several rust-colored leaves floated down, which grew from his head instead of hair.

Despite holding a large cockatrice in his hand, Indigo bowed deferentially. "Elder Duir, we are exceedingly happy to see you."

The man's face creased into a smile. "It is good to see you also, Indigo." He looked out over the sea of cockatrices, their numbers only slightly smaller than when the attack started.

He shook his head and gave a sigh before addressing the flock. "You mustn't attack visitors, especially not royal ones."

The birds ducked their heads, clucking nervously. He waved a large hand. "Go on now. Go back to your homes."

His soft eyes turned towards Chess and the cockatrice that Indigo still held. At Duir's appearance, it had stopped struggling and pulled its wings and neck inward, as if it were trying to shrink.

Its beady eyes stared at Duir, but he avoided its gaze and held out a hand. Indigo passed the bird to the dryad, who murmured something in its ear. After a moment, he set the bird on the ground. It hopped over to Chess and flapped up to perch on his frozen arm. The bird twisted its head and stared into Chess's eye with its own beady one.

After a long moment, a crack appeared along Chess's shoulder and then another. The bird hopped down as the stone statue shattered.

Alice gasped, reaching for Chess, but her hand found warm flesh instead of stone. He shook himself, and more stone tumbled from his hair.

"Are you all right?" She frantically patted his face and then his chest before she threw her arms around him, tears welling in her eyes. "I thought that stupid chicken creature had killed you!"

He staggered a bit, even as he hugged her back. "Would you care so much if it had?" he murmured in her ear.

Alice's voice caught on the lump in her throat as she pulled back enough to gaze up at him. "Don't be daft, of course I would. I…" She caught herself and hugged him tight once more. "Don't do that to me again!"

"I'll try not to, love," he said, a wry smile on his face.

Elder Duir cleared his throat. "Are you quite all right, sir? Being petrified can sap your strength."

Chess straightened away from Alice and nodded respectfully at the dryad. "Compared with being a statue, I'm just fine. Thank you."

The dryad smiled. "I am happy I could be of service to you."

Azalea stepped closer to Chess, her gaze running over him critically. "I am glad you are returned to us, cousin. Thank you, Elder Duir."

The man dipped his head, and a few more leaves drifted to the ground. "I am only sorry the cockatrices attacked you." He frowned. "They've been more agitated than normal lately with all the problems."

Azalea glanced at Chess again before turning back to the clan leader. "That is why we are here, Elder Duir.

We are trying to find the person behind the killings of the small Fae, and we were hoping you might help us."

Alice listened even as she kept an arm around Chess. He didn't seem to need support anymore, but she wanted to reassure herself he was truly all right.

Duir's mouth turned down as sorrow washed over his face. "I don't know what I can do to help you. It has pained me greatly to see members of my clan drained of their essence."

Alice could hardly stand the sadness on the dryad's face. Impulsively, she let go of Chess and laid a hand on his arm. "We think we know who's doing it, but we need help to find her."

Duir laid a gnarled hand over hers and smiled down at her. "Tell me then. Perhaps I know more than I realize."

After Azalea nodded at her to continue, Alice explained about the Red Queen, and why they thought she was the one doing the killings. She ended with Lord Zaba's news that one victim had escaped.

Duir listened carefully, and then slowly, like watching the sun rise, his face brightened. "Yes, there was a survivor, a coinin faery named Fia. She talked about a pretty woman who tricked her." He turned and began walking, gesturing for them to follow. "Come, we will talk to her."

For the first time, a glimmer of hope blossomed that they might just succeed in this quest.

Chapter 53

AFTER TRAMPING THROUGH THE woods for quite a while, they came to a small glade with a large tree at its center, its roots twisted high as if on tiptoe.

Duir held up a hand to stop them from going any further. "I'll ask Fia to come out. She's quite shy, and after the incident, she has become more fearful of strangers."

The group nodded and stayed at the edge of the glade as Duir made his way to the tree and tapped lightly on the trunk. Nothing happened for a long moment.

Then Duir bent over, his gnarled hands on his thighs. A small face was just visible, its expression pinched, peering from behind a large root. Duir spoke quietly to the small Fae, and her large eyes darted towards them. Finally, she nodded.

Duir straightened and waved them forward. As they got closer, Alice got a better look at Fia, who had emerged from her home to speak with them. She was small, only coming up to about Alice's waist. Her soft brown hair curled around her hunched shoulders, and she had a delicate face with a button nose that twitched, and long tapered ears poked through her hair like a rabbit's. Her tunic and leggings matched the soft brown shade of her hair.

Fia half-hid behind one of Duir's large legs and peeked out at them. Alice had the feeling that she was only one loud noise away from vanishing back into her burrow. Duir put a hand on the girl's shoulder. "These are the friends I told you about, Fia."

Fia's nose twitched, and she stared up at them with large doe-like eyes. When she spoke, her voice sounded lyrical and soft.

I was gathering berries for my supper, and a woman came...

It wasn't until Duir tapped Fia and she stopped that Alice realized none of the others could understand her. When she started on her story again, Fia's words came more slowly but no less musical.

"I'm sorry," Fia said and dipped her head, her small hands clasped in front of her, trembling. "I forgot."

Alice smiled at her. "It's all right. We only want to understand what happened."

Fia blinked up at her before she lowered her gaze back to her hands. "While I gathered berries for my supper, a woman approached. At first I tried to hide, but then she sat down right on the ground and started to cry. I couldn't hide when she displayed so much distress, so I asked her what was wrong. She said she had lost her way and pleaded for my help."

Fia paused and looked up at Duir. He smiled encouragingly, and the Fae continued her story. "I took her hand to lead her but..." Her face creased in confusion and her small nose twitched from side to side. "We didn't end where I meant to take her. I don't know how, but even though I led her, we ended up at a small cottage in the foothills of Obsidian Mountain." She fidgeted, her hands plucking at the fabric of her tunic. "I didn't want to go in, but I still followed her inside anyway."

A shudder shook her body, and she squeezed her eyes shut as if that would blot out the memory. Alice wanted to hug the girl but realized that would probably only frighten her more.

Azalea frowned down at the Fae girl, frustration and something like guilt on her face. "What did this woman do to you?"

At the venom in Azalea's voice, Fia shrunk back against Duir, her body tensed for flight. Her eyes widened as they darted around the circle of people that loomed in front of her.

Alice gave Azalea a look and a tiny shake of her head before she knelt in front of Fia, trying to make herself smaller and less intimidating to the Fae. "I understand it's hard to remember, but we need to know what happened." She gestured at the group behind her. "We want to catch this woman, so she doesn't do to anyone else what she did to you, but we need your help. Can you do that?"

Fia looked up at Duir, who nodded at her. "They mean you no harm, Fia. They only want to help. Remember, I told you these are King Thorne's children and their friends."

Fia dropped her eyes and brushed at the dirt with a bare toe. "All right," she said finally. Slowly, haltingly, the story of her time in the cottage came out. The woman had put her in a cage. Fia had been so frightened she thought her heart might burst. There were others, and a few were close to death. The woman had drained her essence, not all at once, but each time the process proved very painful and left Fia weak.

"I thought I would never leave that place alive." Fia's voice dropped to a barely audible whisper, and Alice took the Fae girl's hand in hers.

"That must have been so awful for you. How did you escape?"

Fia shook her head. "The woman became careless, or maybe she believed I had become too weak, but she left my cage unlatched. I only discovered it by accident while the woman was gone. I was afraid she would come back and catch me, but I worked up the courage finally and... I left." A world of terror pulsed in that pause, and Alice felt her own heart ache in sympathy. Fia shut her eyes again, and a shudder ran through her small body. When Fia opened her eyes again, they shimmered with tears. "I unlatched the other cages, but some were too weak to move on their own, and I had to leave them behind. I only managed to get a sparkle pixie and a bumble faery out. She hadn't drained the pixie much yet, but the bumble seemed very feeble."

Alice exchanged a glance with Indigo, and his expression tightened. It was entirely possible that the bumble Alice had tried to heal and the one Fia referred to were the same.

She turned back to Fia. "How many did she have in the cages?"

Fia's face creased in concentration. "When I was first captured, perhaps five or six? But when I escaped, there were only four of us left, and one was…" She closed her eyes again, a whimper escaping.

Alice squeezed her hand, desperate to comfort the poor girl.

Chess crouched down next to her and gave the Fae girl a gentle smile. "Do you know how long you were in the cottage, Fia?"

Her nose twitched and her face scrunched up. "I… I don't know." She looked up at Duir. "I lost time, so it was difficult to keep track of the days." Her eyes went back to Chess. "I am sorry. I cannot answer your question."

"Don't be. You've been so helpful, and you were very brave." He patted her shoulder.

The small Fae girl shook her head, and tears streamed down her cheeks. "No, I was not. The bumble that escaped—she was worse off than I was, but she tried to keep my spirits up. I was too weak to help her, and her wings were very damaged…" Her voice dropped to a whisper. "I fear she did not survive."

She covered her face and cried in earnest.

Now Alice knew the bumble she'd found had to be the same one, but she didn't want to tell the Fae girl that her instinct had been right, and the bumble hadn't made it.

Before she could decide what, if anything, she should say, Duir bent down again, his large hand smoothing the Fae girl's hair. "You mustn't carry this guilt with you, Fia. You are not the one who harmed your brothers and sisters."

"I… I… should have… helped… her, helped them all." Fia's words hitched with barely controlled sobs.

Alice couldn't stand it any longer, and she hugged the girl to her. To her surprise, Fia didn't pull away but clung to her. Alice put her cheek against the soft hair. Even as she held the Fae, anger twisted up inside of her. She knew the Queen was power hungry and ruthless, but to harm someone like this? Alice hugged the girl tighter.

"You aren't the villain here, Fia, and you were hurt and weak. Nobody faults you." She leaned back and looked into the Fae's face. The tears had stopped, but Fia still looked miserable.

Azalea cleared her throat. When Alice looked up at her, the other woman's expression was stoic, but her eyes were suspiciously shiny. She awkwardly patted Fia on the shoulder, almost knocking her over. "You did well, little one. I will let my father know of your bravery."

Fia straightened away from Alice's shoulder, her eyes widening. "You do not... that is... thank you."

"Do you think you could find this cottage again?" Azalea asked.

The girl's body trembled again, and she shrank back against Alice. "I... I do not know."

"We can't stop her unless we find her, and you're the only one who can help us do that." Alice's voice was gentle. "Do you think you can find your courage one more time?"

Fia looked at her for a long moment and then lifted her quivering chin. "I will try."

Chapter 54

ALICE GOT TO HER feet. "We should go before the Queen moves somewhere else."

Azalea stared down at Fia. "You said it was in the foothills of the Obsidian Mountain. That is over an hour's walk from here."

"Why can't we fly like before?" Alice asked.

"We can't risk being seen, especially if the Queen is in her Jabberwock form. We don't want to take that chance. Our only hope is if we can surprise her, I think." Azalea's face tightened into a grim expression. "If she sees us, she could disappear again or attack us. I am a fair warrior, but I don't know that I can defeat a Jabberwock."

Indigo pushed off the tree where he'd slouched. "Then I guess we better get going."

Azalea shook her head and gestured at the sun, which hung low in the sky. "I dislike the idea of walking blind to this cottage. We don't know how far this woman roams or which form she will be in. We must have a plan."

Chess nodded. "Azalea's right. This might be our only chance of finding Lyssandra. If she runs again, it could be days or even weeks before we find her again. I don't have that kind of time."

"Then what do you propose we do?" Indigo plopped down on a stump and kicked his long legs out in front of him. "I'm not all that keen to sleep on the forest floor."

Fia's eyes widened, and she shook her head so hard her hair flew around her face. "Oh no! You must stay with me." She motioned towards the tree. "You are welcome in my home."

Alice eyed the tree with a raised eyebrow. "While we appreciate your hospitality, I don't know that we'll all, erm, fit into your home." She gestured at Indigo and Chess. "Especially them."

A mischievous smile spread across the girl's face. "My home is bigger on the inside than it looks from out here."

Duir smiled. "She is right. You do not have to worry."

"All right." Alice knew her doubt was probably written all over her face, but honestly, how were they all going to fit into a tree trunk?

Fia turned towards the tree, Duir close at her heels. Azalea and Indigo followed. Alice looked at Chess, but he only shrugged.

"You can't seriously think we're all going to fit in there, can you?"

Chess winked. "I guess we're going to find out."

They followed the others, walking down between the roots of the tree. The others ducked through a door Fia held open for them.

Alice entered first, Chess at her back, fully expecting to crouch or even crawl wherever they were going, but the door opened into a wood-lined entryway, a large forked branch serving as a coat tree in the corner. Fia moved down a hallway, waving at them to follow.

As they walked further, the floor slanted downward beneath Alice's feet. They didn't travel far before the hall opened into a large room. At one end was a fireplace, and next to it was a rocking chair made of woven twigs, some of which still had flower buds on them. On the other side, a large cup-shaped chair sat with a bright cushion on its seat. At the other end of the room was a table with chairs. A countertop ran along one wall, and set in it was an old-fashioned-looking sink with a pump. A pot of something bubbled on the wood stove. The delicious smell made Alice's stomach growl loudly. She felt her face heat, and she clapped a hand to her middle.

Chess smirked at her. "Hungry, love?"

She gave him a sheepish smile. "Well, I haven't eaten anything since this morning, and we've been from one end of this island to the other."

Fia shooed them towards her table, much of her shyness falling away in the need to feed them. "You must all sit and eat." She bustled over to the counter and reached up into a cupboard, pulling out bowls and cups.

It didn't take long before they were all crowded around the little table, bowls of stew and cups of cold spring water in front of them. True, Indigo and Duir had to perch on overturned crates, but they all fit somehow.

Alice took a bite of the dish in front of her and closed her eyes as the flavors washed over her tongue. "This is wonderful, Fia. What is it?"

The girl leaned forward eagerly. "It's my acorn stew. I always make it this time of year, but the special ingredient is my pickled grubs."

Alice stopped chewing and stared at the Fae girl, who was looking at her expectantly. Beside her, Chess coughed.

Alice forced herself to swallow and patted her mouth with the cloth napkin. "How... unusual," she choked out, her stomach churning queasily.

She stared down at the chunks of what she now realized were grubs clinging to the bottom of her almost empty bowl, and she swallowed. She tore her gaze away, so she didn't gag. If she just didn't think about it, she'd be fine.

Fia hopped up. "I can get you some more if you are still hungry. There is plenty."

"Erm, no, I'm quite full. Thank you." Alice pushed the bowl away from her, and Fia sank back into her chair, looking uncertain.

Alice forced her mouth into a smile, willing her stomach not to rebel. "It was... delicious, Fia, but I honestly couldn't eat another bite." Alice only felt a twinge of guilt. What she'd said was true, after all—the stew had been delicious until she'd realized what she was eating, and now she really couldn't eat another bite. She suppressed a dry heave by coughing into her hand.

"I'll take some more." Indigo shoved his bowl in Fia's direction. "I'm still hungry."

The girl took the bowl eagerly and turned to the big pot and dished up more.

Alice closed her eyes, concentrating on breathing and keeping her meal in her stomach.

"Haven't you ever heard you shouldn't ask questions if you don't want to know the answers?" Chess's warm breath on her ear sent a tiny shiver through her.

Her eyes popped open. "I never thought..." She put her hand to her mouth and swallowed again.

Chess slid his bread over to her. "Here, eat some of this. It'll help."

She hesitated, not sure she wanted to put anything else in her already churning stomach. Chess pushed the bread into her hand. "Trust me."

When she still hesitated, he leaned in again to speak into her ear so the others wouldn't hear. "You don't want to hurt the girl's feelings by casting up your accounts all over her floor, do you?"

Alice grudgingly took the bread. "I suppose not," she mumbled and took a small bite.

Encouraged that it stayed down, she nibbled on the roll, pointedly avoiding looking at Indigo, who was downing the stew as if he hadn't eaten in a year. Another wave of nausea hit her when he sucked in a longer piece of grub into his mouth.

Chess's hand found hers under the table. "Look at me, love." She hadn't even realized her eyes had closed, and she opened them. His face was close to hers and all she could see were his vivid blue eyes. It would be so easy to get lost in them.

His mouth spread into a smile. "There you go. Think about my pretty mug instead."

She shoved his arm, a laugh escaping. "I'd agree with you, but I don't want to inflate your ego any more than it already is."

There was a pause in the chatter around the table, and Alice's face heated when she realized the rest of the group was looking at her and Chess. Her eyes dropped to the bread in her hand to avoid Indigo's scowl and Azalea's thoughtful gaze.

Chess, unbothered, pulled her close and dropped a kiss on her temple. "What would I do without you to keep me in check, love? My ego would be rampaging out of control by now without you to stomp it back to size."

A ripple of laughter went around the table, and everyone resumed their meal, including Chess. Alice watched him out of the corner of her eye. Did he mean he needed her? The way he was acting, it seemed almost as if... She pushed the idea away. They had to worry about the Queen now.

Besides, even if they were successful, she still needed to go home. She couldn't stay here, even if she wanted to.

That didn't mean she couldn't come back, though.

Thoughts of Hadley and her family chased each other through her mind as she nibbled on the bread. Somehow, the threat of her unwanted suitor didn't seem so scary after all she'd been through. She smirked. Hadley Beechwood wouldn't have lasted five minutes in Wonderland.

Azalea pushed back her bowl, and the scraping sound jerked Alice from her thoughts. She looked across at the other woman.

She had her fingers steepled in front of her. "Does anyone have any ideas on how we can capture the Queen?" Her sharp gaze went around the table and landed on Alice and Chess. "The two of you know her better than anyone else here."

Chess wiped his mouth and set his napkin on the table. "She's ruthless, and she's cunning. She has both the Flora Gift and the Drifter Gene, although we only learned about that recently."

Duir frowned. "How came she to have the knowledge to drain others' magic without an Alchemy Gift?"

Chess shrugged, his shoulder brushing Alice's. "We're not sure. The Prince and I thought for a while she might have hidden an Alchemy Gift, but that makes no sense. There's no reason to hide something like that. It's more likely she's using the magic she drains to increase and expand her own powers."

"I did not realize that was possible. How did she discover this?" The dryad's shaggy eyebrows lowered.

Chess's mouth pressed into a thin line, and he hesitated. When he spoke, Alice could tell he was picking his words carefully. "As you know, the flower maidens at the palace have their wings altered."

Duir nodded. "Yes, that has long been the custom to help the Wonderland residents not to fear us. Although flower maidens are quite harmless."

"Well, it seems the Queen has been using the clipped parts for a while now."

A murmur rose from the others, and Chess continued. "Nobody was aware she was abusing her power that way, of course. That isn't something the King would ever condone."

"I should hope not." Azalea's tone was curt. "It is shameful enough that our people have to submit to the indignity in the first place, but then to have their wings used in this way—it is intolerable."

Chess held up his hands. "We're all in agreement on that point, Azalea. I can't promise you that the practice of clipping will stop, but I can promise that the King will ensure nothing like this happens again."

"That is not comforting, since he let it happen in the first place." Azalea's chin jutted out, her expression dark.

Fia shifted in her chair, her face pinched at the tension at her table.

Alice spoke into the thick silence. "I'm not sure it matters how she came by her powers right now. The important thing is stopping her, and we still haven't figured out how to do that."

"Alice is right," said Duir, his deep voice echoing in the small room. "You have two problems here. She must not have a chance to flee, and you must keep her from shifting into her Jabberwock, as she will be very difficult to subdue in that form."

Chess pulled out the bottle his mother had given him and set it on the table. "I can help with that." He tapped the top of it. "This will bind her magic so she can't shift."

Duir nodded. "That is a good start, but there is still the problem of getting her to drink it."

Indigo pushed back his bowl and wiped his mouth. "I don't see what everyone is all worried about. I'll simply charm her." He beamed at them.

"Have you lost all your sense? Do you think this woman will just stand there and let you manipulate her into a drinking a potion that binds all her magic?" Azalea frowned at her brother.

Indigo shrugged. "Women like me."

Azalea slanted a look at Alice. "Obviously not all of them."

"She is unusually obstinate and doesn't realize the depths of her affection for me yet."

Alice resisted the urge to roll her eyes. "It's so deep, it will never see the light of day."

Indigo grinned. "I'd be happy to help you mine for it."

"I'd rather cuddle with a snark," Alice retorted.

"Excuse me," Fia's soft voice interrupted the back and forth. She shrank back in her seat when everyone looked at her.

"Did you have an idea for us?" Chess smiled at the Fae girl, who blushed in return.

"I only thought that this woman is looking for small Fae. Perhaps if you provided one, you might lure her into a trap."

"That's a brilliant idea," said Alice.

Fia twisted her fingers together and lowered her eyes. "It is only that I use bait to catch the grubs."

Alice swallowed, trying to steer her thoughts to other things. "But who would we use as bait?"

Surprisingly, Indigo spoke first. "My ferret form will be irresistible to her. If I allow my wings to show, I will be too big of a temptation to pass up."

Alice gave him a startled look. "You have wings when you aren't in your ferret form?"

"Of course. If our animal form has wings, then so does this form. They aren't like my sister's, though. My shirt covers them easily." Indigo smirked, and pulled his shirt over his head, exposing his muscled torso.

Alice blinked at him. He was so... blue. She almost forgot sometimes, but now, with so much of his skin on display, it reminded her, rather forcibly, how *other* he was. He twisted in his seat, and two gossamer wings fluttered between his shoulder blades, looking a bit incongruous on his large torso. Even stretched out, they barely reached his shoulders. No wonder he hadn't offered to fly them anywhere. She tentatively reached out a finger to touch the edge of a wing.

"I think we've all seen enough, cousin," Chess said, a bite in his tone.

"I find I'm rather warm." Indigo turned back around but didn't move to put his shirt back on. It wasn't until Chess nodded at Fia, who sat with her head down and her eyes trained on her lap, that Indigo finally pulled the material back over his head.

Alice touched the bottle. "Even if she takes the bait, how will you get the potion in her?"

"I'll sneak in after him," said Chess. "While he distracts her, I'll slip the potion into something she's sure to eat or drink."

Indigo scoffed. "And how will you get in unnoticed? You are only half Fae."

Chess's smile held a sharp edge. "Let me worry about that. You just do your part. Your charm is powerful, so you should have no trouble making sure she doesn't see me."

Indigo preened. "And don't forget subtle. My control is superb, and people don't even realize I'm charming them." He shot a glance at Alice. "Most of them, anyway."

Duir spoke up next. "I do not doubt your mother's work, but how will you be able to tell that the Queen's magic is bound? If she is using the Fae to boost her powers, will this be enough?"

Azalea met Duir's gaze. "Our trust must be in Aunt Larkspur, my brother's charm, and my cousin's ability to not be seen." She set her palms on the table and pushed to her feet. "We have a plan, so I suggest we get some sleep. Tomorrow will be taxing."

Chapter 55

Chairs scraped as the group got up from the table. Fia hopped off her chair and scurried off to gather blankets for them.

"What's bothering you?" Chess's voice startled Alice from her thoughts.

"Why do you think something is bothering me?"

He touched the space between her eyebrows. "You always get this crease here when you're worried about something, love."

"I didn't realize you were watching me so closely," she teased.

"You're my favorite subject."

Alice's face heated, and she couldn't decide if she was relieved or disappointed when Fai's small voice interrupted them. "You will need to share a room with the Princess, Miss Alice."

Alice couldn't help smiling at the coinin faery. "Thank you, Fia."

The Fae girl handed a small stack of blankets to Chess, her small face scrunching into worry. "And you will need to share a room with the prince. I hope you will not mind."

Chess winked at her. "As long as he doesn't snore."

Fia giggled and scampered off to find more blankets for Duir.

Chess turned back to her. "Now, tell me what's bothering you before we're interrupted again."

Alice worried the edge of the blanket with one hand. "It's only... doesn't it seem too easy to you?"

"Sometimes, the answers are straightforward."

"But what if Indigo's charm doesn't work, or the Queen sees you? What if the potion isn't strong enough?"

He shrugged. "That's not something you need to worry about, love."

"What do you mean?"

He clasped her hand and tugged her out of the kitchen and into the hallway.

"What's with all the secrecy? Where are we going?" Alice asked, her heart speeding up.

Chess glanced back at her. "Somewhere where nobody will interrupt us."

Alice followed him down the hallway until they reached the entrance. A small alcove off to the side offered some privacy, and he pulled her into the nook.

The light was dimmer here, and shadows hid his face when she looked up at him. She licked her lips, her stomach jumping.

"There's something I need to talk to you about—without the others hearing."

Alice tried to cover her nervousness. "I gathered that."

He didn't respond to her teasing, and his expression remained serious. "I don't want you to go with us tomorrow. There's no need for you to put yourself in danger this time."

"But you're..." He put a finger against her lips, and her skin sparked where he touched it.

"Hear me out." He kept her gaze until she nodded. His shoulders loosened. "I want you to stay here with Fia. I know I can't make you, but the Queen is dangerous. We have no idea what's going to happen or, as you said, if that potion will work fully. I promised you I'd get you back home, and I can't do that if something happens to you."

"What about you? Am I supposed to wait around here and hope you don't die?"

A half smile tipped his mouth. "Don't worry, love. You'll get home whether or not I make it."

Alice stared at him, anger prickling her skin. Then she poked him in the chest. "Take that back!"

"I'm just trying to—"

Alice stepped closer and jutted out her chin. "If you think the only reason I'd care if you died is that I couldn't get back home, you really are a git."

His mouth stretched into a smile. "Tell me, Alice, what other reason could there possibly be?"

She scowled at him. "That is a horrible thing to imply, as if I didn't lo—" She stopped, her face flaming, and looked away.

He put a finger under her chin and tipped her face up so his burning gaze met hers. "Tell me, as if you didn't... what?"

Alice's stomach did a slow swoop, and goosebumps pebbled her arms, even as the inevitability of this moment pressed in on her. She wanted him to know, but the idea of laying her heart bare, especially if he didn't feel the same... She sighed. "You're really going to make me say it first, aren't you?"

His eyes danced. "What kind of gentleman would that make me?"

Her lips quirked into a smile, her dimple peeking out. "I thought you said you weren't a gentleman."

A velvety chuckled rumbled out of him. "Maybe not, but I have a surprising desire to try when you're around."

Alice's heart was beating so hard, it echoed in her ears, but she didn't think she misunderstood the look in his eyes. If he wanted her to say it first, she would. She opened her mouth, but he stopped her, pressing his lips to hers in the barest whisper of a kiss.

He pulled away just enough to speak, their faces so close she could see the tiny flecks of silver in his blue eyes. "I love you, Alice."

He pressed a kiss to the corner of her mouth. "I love that you're strong but have a soft heart." He trailed another kiss along her jaw. "I love that you say what you think." His lips touched the skin by her ear and then spoke into it, his breath sending a shiver through her. "I love that you have a wonderful right hook and aren't afraid to use it."

A laugh escaped her mouth, and he caught it with his lips, the kiss lasting long enough to make her breathless. He smirked, obviously pleased with himself, but he wasn't done. Staring into her eyes, he said, "I love you,

Alice Cavendish, and I can't imagine ever entrusting my heart to anyone else."

Words crowded into Alice's throat, but she couldn't speak past the lump there. Her eyes prickled, and the smile she gave him trembled.

After several beats of silence, his mouth quirked. "I saved you from going first, love, but it's only fair you take your turn."

Alice's face heated, but the words were easy to say. "I love you, Chess Felinas, even if sometimes I'm not sure if I want to smack you or kiss you."

"Then let me persuade you towards the latter."

They were both smiling when his mouth claimed hers.

Alice wasn't sure how long they stayed twined together before the sound of voices filtered through her blissful fog. When Chess pulled away from her, she made a sound of protest, the absence of his warmth chilling her. He rested his forehead against hers, his arms still loose around her waist. "We should get back to the others before someone comes looking for us."

At the possibility, Alice's cheeks flushed hotter. "I suppose you're right."

Her obvious reluctance made him grin, and then his expression sobered. "But before we go back to the others, will you stay with Fia?"

His words—and, to be honest, his kisses—had driven all thought of their earlier conversation out of her head. Now she considered his request. While she didn't like the idea of having to wait around for his return, she also saw his point. After all, there would be little she could do if the Queen shifted into her Jabberwock, but she'd go crazy not knowing what was happening.

Finally, she looked up at him. "What about a compromise?"

His eyes twinkled with amusement. "I'm almost afraid to ask."

Chapter 56

CHESS PUSHED HIS BACK against the rough bark of the tree where he and Alice perched. Off to his left, Indigo and Azalea had found their own tree. The forest tiptoed right up to the sides of the little cottage that was partially visible if he craned his head a bit to the left.

Alice shifted on her branch. "I hope she shows herself soon."

"She will," he said with more confidence than he felt. Fia had shown them the cottage about an hour past dawn, but it had, unsurprisingly, been quiet and still. As the hours passed, though, with no signs of anyone stirring inside, it became more and more obvious that the Queen was not at home.

"What will we do if she doesn't come back?"

Alice's voice pulled Chess from his thoughts. It was a question he didn't want to think about, so he shrugged. "I guess we keep looking for her, then."

"But what about Zander? Does he have that kind of time?"

Chess rubbed the back of his neck. "The truth?"

She nodded.

"Probably not." He sighed. "Lord Beecher is hell-bent against anyone with the Drifter Gene, and the only thing that might keep him from running Zander out is this artifact."

"But who would rule? From what you've said, the King isn't any shape to do it."

Chess's gut twisted. He stared at the outline of branches and leaves. "The Commander is next in line."

Alice's mouth dropped open. "The Commander? Would he even want to do that?"

Chess lifted one shoulder. "As the King's brother, he'd see it as his duty, and the Commander is nothing if not dutiful." Chess snapped off a leaf and twirled it in his fingers. "It's not even that he'd do a terrible job of it, but after everything Zander's been through, he deserves that throne. He's done the right thing by the Kingdom all of his life, and it kills me to see them turn on him just because of something he can't help."

Alice reached out and took his hand. "People can be complete idiots sometimes, can't they?"

Chess bit back a bark of laughter. "You aren't wrong, love."

The birds nearby suddenly fell silent, and the forest held its breath as a long shadow passed overhead, a flash of ruby scales visible through the leafy canopy.

The Queen was back.

Instead of landing at the cottage, though, she flew past.

"Where's she going?" Alice asked in a whisper.

"There probably isn't enough room to land. Those trees practically go up the steps to the front door." Chess pointed. "I'd lay odds she's circling behind to find a clearer spot."

He shifted on the branch to get a clearer view, and sure enough, a few minutes later, the Queen sauntered around the side of the cottage. She trotted up the three steps to the front door and disappeared inside.

The leaves rustled on the neighboring tree as Indigo rose to his feet, but Azalea held up a hand and motioned for him to sit back down.

He gestured impatiently towards the cottage, but Azalea shook her head, mouthing the word "wait."

A few more minutes passed, and the squat chimney sent out puffs of smoke. Still, they waited. The sun climbed even higher. It had to be close to noon.

By the time the Queen finally emerged, Chess's backside had gone numb. He leaned forward to get a better view of her and swallowed his surprise.

She still looked like the Queen with her carefully braided hair and pastel dress. She carried a pretty woven basket over her arm, but Chess could see the dark circles under the woman's eyes from here, and her face was gaunt.

"What's wrong with her?" Alice whispered.

"Perhaps Lyssandra is not a fan of living rough," he murmured.

"She looks... unwell."

Chess shrugged. "She's living in the middle of a forest, love, doing unwholesome magic."

"I suppose that must come with a cost. I wonder if she realized that."

Alice shivered, and Chess took her hand, twining their fingers together. "It does, but she's made her choices. Whatever it's doing to her, I don't feel sorry for her."

A blur of blue and silver flashed in the corner of his eye, and Indigo leapt from the trunk of the tree in his ferret form before trundling off into some undergrowth that lay in the Queen's path.

It didn't take her long to find him.

Alice squeezed his fingers, almost cutting off his circulation as she leaned forward. He tugged her back. "Easy there, love. You're going to topple out of this tree if you're not careful, and you promised you'd stay hidden."

She nodded absently, but her attention was riveted on the scene playing out below her.

Indigo nosed around in the vegetation, letting out occasional chirrups and chitters while the Queen approached slowly from behind. Even though he knew Indigo was aware of the Queen, Chess couldn't help tensing as Lyssandra got closer.

Finally, Indigo looked back over his furry shoulder and then froze. The Queen stopped about a yard away and cooed something at him that Chess couldn't quite hear. Indigo stood up on his hind legs and spread his wings behind him.

"Well, he's certainly making sure she doesn't miss him, isn't he?" Chess smirked.

Azalea glared at him. "Shhh."

The Queen crouched down and reached into her basket for a tiny morsel of some kind. She held it out. The ferret's lean body swayed forward as he sniffed at the food.

Indigo lowered his front half to the ground and moved forward a few steps at time, as if hesitant. The Queen continued to croon nonsense words until he had gotten close enough for her to run a hand over his head.

Indigo leapt into her arms, and the Queen gave a delighted laugh as he snuggled the top of his head under her chin.

"That's a mite obvious," Alice muttered.

It must not have been, though, because the Queen cuddled the ferret in her arms and meandered back towards the cottage.

Chess pressed a kiss on the back of Alice's hand. "Well, that's my cue, love. Remember, you promised to stay hidden if you came with us."

"I will, but you be careful."

He winked. "That goes without saying."

He pulled his invisibility around him like a cloak and shinnied down the tree before he carefully trailed behind the Queen with Indigo in her arms. He glanced back, needing to know Alice was tucked away safely.

His foot came down on a branch, the crack sounding overly loud to his ears. The Queen paused and turned, her eyes searching the woods behind her. Chess froze, not even daring to breathe as her gaze passed over his form.

And then returned.

Suddenly, the Queen gave a loud squawk.

Chapter 57

"THAT WAS NOT WHAT we planned," Azalea hissed.

Indigo shimmered into his human form, and the Queen gaped up at the blue Fae man now towering over her.

He leaned down and cupped her cheek in his hand, whispering something in her ear. She swayed towards him, her eyes fixed on his face.

For a brief moment, Alice thought Indigo had done it. She could hardly believe it had been that easy.

Then the Queen's back bowed, and she threw her head back.

"Watch out! She's going to shift!" Alice shouted, scrambling to her feet and almost toppling out of the tree. Indigo's head swiveled at the sound of Alice's voice. In his arms, the Queen's body stretched and elongated.

He bounded backwards, barely missing the Queen's claws as she swiped at him. Her roar shook the trees, and terror pooled in Alice's stomach as Indigo shrunk down to ferret form and darted into the foliage. The Queen sent a gout of flame after him; the fire skittered over leaves and flushed Indigo out of his hiding spot. He shimmered back into human form and leapt towards a tree trunk, using his momentum to push off it towards another tree. The way he bounced from trunk to trunk reminded Alice of how easily he'd moved around the beams in the prison tower.

The Queen's massive jaws snapped, tearing a chunk from his tunic as he twisted through the air, and he flickered and then disappeared from view. Her tail lashed, and a cry of pain rang out. Alice's frantic gaze found Chess lying at the base of a tree, shimmering in and out of view.

The Queen heard the cry, too, and her head twisted around, spotting him. Her jaws opened, but a dagger whistled towards the Jabberwock and clinked against her side. Her scales were too thick for it to stick, but it provided a needed distraction. The Queen whipped around as Indigo flew by, having hurled the missile in mid-leap, before he disappeared again.

The Queen whirled, her body smashing trees as her tail hit something with a slap. Alice stared in horror as Indigo, visible again, slammed into a tree and plummeted down, hitting the ground with a sickening thud. The Queen rushed towards him, her large, scaled body slithering through the trees like a snake, but before she reached the downed Fae, a loud cry rent the air.

Azalea dove towards the Queen, a hawk hunting a rabbit. She landed at the base of the Queen's neck, both swords in her hands. The Queen bucked and writhed, trying to throw the Fae woman off, but Azalea clung to her back like a burr.

Alice tore her gaze off the drama unfolding and found Chess again. He was now fully visible and hadn't moved. She scrambled down the trunk of the tree and picked her way towards him. She was halfway there when the Queen slammed into a tree, and a large cracking noise ripped through the air.

Azalea grunted at the impact and slid sideways, disappearing behind the Queen's massive bulk. Alice didn't wait to see what happened. She ran to Chess and dropped to her knees.

"Can you get up?" she asked even as she tugged at him.

He grimaced and tried to stand, but he couldn't quite manage it. He sank back down. The ground under her shook, and Alice shot a hurried glance over her shoulder.

Azalea had both swords drawn and was diving again and again, her feathery wings a blur, striking at the Queen. While her sword tip didn't penetrate the scales, the constant attacks kept the Queen's attention. She snapped her jaws, trying to catch Azalea, but the Fae woman was too agile.

Sweat snaked down Alice's back and her heart raced as she tugged at Chess again, but she couldn't get him to his feet. "What's wrong?" She dropped back to her knees, her hands frantic as she ran them over his chest and sides. "Where are you hurt?"

He blinked at her, his eyes unable to focus on her face. "It's my head. I must have hit it."

Alice ran trembling fingers through his hair, but he grabbed her hand and pushed something into her palm. "Take it," he said.

Her fingers closed automatically around the cool glass. "What am I supposed to do with this?" she demanded, staring down at the vial in her hand.

A loud crash shook the forest and leaves showered down onto their heads. She crouched over Chess, trying to shield him, her shoulder mashing into his face.

"Can't... breathe, love."

She jerked back and then slid her arm behind his shoulder. "You have to move."

He gripped her wrist and his eyes slid shut, his face creasing with pain. "Just... get it down her gullet."

A whoosh of sound followed by a scream made Alice whirl around. One of Azalea's wings smoked as she spiraled towards the ground. The Jabberwock opened her mouth, and Alice didn't think. She grabbed a broken branch at her feet and hurled it. It smacked into the back of the Queen's head, and her jaws clicked shut.

"Uh-oh." Alice shifted to block Chess from view as the Queen slowly turned her head. Her gaze made Alice's knees go liquid. The Queen's jaws spread in a horrible rictus of a smile as her head darted forward on its long serpentine neck.

It seems every time I run into problems, there you are. It's time to get rid of you once and for all.

The Queen's voice echoed in Alice's head, and Alice shuffled back a step, her heel hitting Chess's leg. There was nowhere to go. Her hand tightened around the vial. She tore her gaze from the Queen and glanced down at it as an idea formed. It was a risk, but she was out of options. Using her thumb, she worked the cork out of the top of the vial and tightened her grip.

Alice looked back up at the Queen. "Well, you can certainly try."

Oh, I'll do more than try, my dear.

The Queen reared up and opened her mouth. Alice cocked back her arm and threw the vial. It sailed through the air and clinked against one large fang, and for one horrible moment, Alice thought it was going to bounce out, but then it rolled back into the Queen's mouth. The Jabberwock jerked her head back and reflexively swallowed.

Alice held her breath. The Queen shook her head and made a choking noise.

You... you... But that's all she got out.

Her eyes rolled wildly, and she twisted and bucked as her body shrank down into her human form. The Queen swayed on her feet, her gaze landing on Alice. Her nostrils flared and, chest heaving, she let out an inhuman screech and staggered towards Alice.

Before she had taken more than a few steps, Azalea closed the distance between them and grabbed her from behind, her dagger pointed just below the Queen's ear. Lyssandra tried to twist away, but Azalea touched her dagger to the Queen's skin. Alice wasn't sure how the other woman was standing, never mind restraining someone. Wisps of smoke still rose from one of her wings, and several gashes dripped blood, but her voice was steady when she spoke. "Do not try it. My Father wants you alive, but I am not above telling him you died along the way."

The Queen's posture slumped, and it was clear she knew she was beaten.

Alice's knees suddenly gave, and she dropped onto the ground next to Chess. He grasped her hand and tugged her back against his chest, pressing a kiss against her temple. "Did I mention I also love you for your throwing arm?"

Alice's laugh turned into a sob. "I... I can't believe that worked."

Chess gave a tired smile. "And to think I wanted you to stay behind."

Alice pushed away the what-ifs that clamored at her, threatening to break her apart. What she really wanted to do was have a good cry, but they still had to get the Queen back to Underhill, and Chess needed her.

She pulled away from him and twisted around, running her hands through his hair. He tried to straighten and groaned. She gave him a stern look. "Sit still. I need to fix you before you can go anywhere."

"So bossy," he murmured.

She ran her fingers through his silky curls until she found the lump at the back of his head, and he winced. Closing her eyes, she let her mind visualize the bruised and swollen area. Concentrating, she pictured the swelling going down and the bruising smoothing out until the area glowed in her mind's eye. A sigh left his mouth, and when she opened her eyes, his expression was clear and his gaze was once again focused.

"Thank you, love." Chess took her hand and pressed a kiss against her palm.

Then, Azalea's voice called her name. "Alice, you must help my brother. He is badly injured."

The Queen grunted, and when Alice turned towards them, she spotted a trickle of blood dripping down the woman's neck. A snarl twisted Azalea's face, and Alice hoped she wouldn't kill the Queen before they got her back to Underhill.

Alice clambered to her feet and offered her hand to help Chess up before searching for Indigo. In all the chaos, she hadn't realized he was still lying at the base of the tree he'd hit earlier.

His motionless blue body stood out against the green of the leaves, and she hurried over to him. He lay on his back. His long limbs spread at awkward angles, blood trickling from the corner of his mouth. His labored breath wheezed in and out.

Alice dropped next to him. "What have you done to yourself?" she asked, keeping her tone light.

His eyelids fluttered open, and his lips formed a weak smile. "I knew you cared." He coughed and more blood trickled from his mouth. "I am... the hero here. I saved my... cousin for you."

Alice swallowed the lump in her throat. "You need to be quiet and let me heal you."

Without waiting for his response, she placed her hands on Indigo's chest and let her eyes close. She tried not to flinch at the damage. Healing Indigo took much longer than Chess, but she repaired the hole in his lung and the two broken ribs. She also had to seal the crack in the back of his skull.

When she finally sat back on her heels, exhaustion smothered her like a blanket, and sweat beaded her forehead. "There, I think that's everything. Do you hurt anywhere else?"

Indigo brow furrowed as he drew in an experimental breath and patted his chest. After a moment, his face brightened. He sat up and pulled Alice into his arms, engulfing her in a hug. "Thank you, my... Alice."

It was the first time he'd called her by her name instead of some stupid nickname. She gave him a tired smile. "You're welcome, Indigo. As irritating as you are, I didn't want you to die."

His chuckle reverberated under her cheek. Alice knew she needed to pull away, that they had to get back to Underhill, but weariness sapped her limbs of strength. She was so tired. She let her eyes shut. Just for a minute.

"If you don't let go of her, I'm going to undo all of her work." The low growl of Chess's voice jolted her, and she realized she must have dozed off.

Indigo released her slowly, his silvery gaze watchful, as if she might keel over at any minute. Which, come to think of it, was a distinct possibility. He rose to his feet and pulled Alice up with him. She swayed, and he reached out to steady her, but Chess bumped his cousin out of the way and slipped his arm around her waist. "I checked the cottage while Alice was healing you, but there was only one creature inside." His mouth thinned. "And it was dead. It's probably why she was so keen on you."

Indigo frowned and opened his mouth, but then shut it. Something was different, but her brain was too fuzzy to think about anything right now.

"I don't suppose I can take a nap," Alice said and looked at the soft plants longingly.

Chess chuckled. "I'm afraid not, love. We have a prisoner to take back to my uncle, but I've always wanted to stride around with a beautiful woman in my arms."

Before she could tell him she could walk just fine, he swung her up into his arms. Alice wanted to protest, but her head felt too heavy. She let it fall against his shoulder, and her eyes drifted shut. She'd tell him to put her down soon. She'd only rest for a few minutes.

The world drifted away into blackness.

Chapter 58

ZANDER STARED INTO THE small cell. The King lay on his side, his back soaked in sweat. He struggled more and more to control himself during the daylight hours.

Lapin tugged Zander back from the bars on the door. "He's resting now. There's nothing else we can do for him at the moment."

Zander heard Lapin's words as if they were muffled. Everything had been muted since Citrine had died—like someone had wrapped him in cotton wool.

The small memorial service they'd held seemed both too much and not enough. Under the circumstances, they'd had to keep the service closed to only a handful of people. Her steward Bliss's stoic face and his wife's wailing still echoed in his brain. If only he'd...

"Sire?" Lapin tapped his arm and Zander realized the rabbit had been talking to him, but he'd missed it.

"I'm sorry. What did you say?"

The rabbit frowned at him. "I only asked how you were doing."

"I'm fine." The words were automatic, what he'd been saying to everyone.

Even though it was a lie. But this was his new reality. Citrine was gone.

At the reminder, a panicky feeling rose in his chest, threatening to choke him. His lungs refused to pull in air, and black spots danced in front of his eyes.

A hard shake broke the fogginess, and he blinked to find Lapin in front of him, his hands on Zander's shoulders. "Breathe, Sire. You need to breathe or you're going to pass out."

Zander sucked in a lungful of air, and then another. His vision gradually returned. "I'm sorry. I didn't mean to—"

"Don't apologize to me." The rabbit stepped back, his face creased in concern. "And at the risk of stating the obvious, you are NOT fine."

Zander shrugged. "You're right. I'm not, but it doesn't matter."

"Of course it matters."

Zander shook his head. "No, it doesn't. She's gone, and she's..." He swallowed. "She's not coming back." He gave a humorless laugh. "Maybe I could dose myself with Love's Bane. Then I'd..." His voice broke off as Lapin gripped his shoulders, his eyes wide and his mouth open.

"Lapin?"

The rabbit shook his head, ears quivering. "That might just be the answer."

Zander stared at Lapin. "I'm sorry... what?"

"The potion—for your father."

Leaving Zander with his mouth hanging open, Lapin trotted towards the stairs. Zander hurried to catch up, still not sure what Lapin was so excited about.

"It's brilliant, really. The suppression aspect of the plant might be capable of keeping your father lucid." Lapin threw the words over his shoulder as he jogged up the steps.

They reached the dungeon door, and Zander fell into step with the large rabbit. "I'm afraid you've lost me."

"Love's Bane."

Zander squinted at Lapin. "You think Love's Bane will help my father?"

The rabbit nodded. "I'm sure it's the missing ingredient Citrine and I were looking for, before... Well, I've discovered what it is now, and you suggested it."

Lapin continued to talk about the plant's properties, but Zander's attention wandered. Any help he'd given was a happy accident. A new worry bobbed to the surface. He didn't have good luck, after all. "What if it doesn't work?" he blurted, interrupting Lapin mid-word.

The rabbit blinked and then cleared his throat. "Yes, well, as to that, there is no guarantee with anything, but I'm quite optimistic." He tilted his head. "Even if it doesn't work, we'll keep trying until the others return. I haven't given up hope, and you mustn't either."

It was too late for that, Zander reflected bleakly. They arrived at his study, but Lapin stopped outside the doorway. He opened his mouth, but Anders materialized behind them.

He bowed quickly and then spoke. "Your Majesty, the Commander has returned, and he is looking for the King." His eyes darted to his feet and then back up to meet Zander's gaze. "I told him the King wasn't available, but you were."

Thankful for Anders' quick thinking, Zander blew out a breath. "You did well. Bring him here."

Zander walked into the study, gesturing for Lapin to follow. "It would help if you stayed, too. I know you'd probably rather work on that potion, but under the circumstances..."

Lapin waved a paw and dropped into a chair opposite, crossing one leg over the other. "Of course, I'll stay. I can't pick the Love's Bane until dark anyway."

"I can talk to the Commander myself if you feel you should—"

Lapin shook his head. "No, offering my support to you is more helpful right now."

Sadly, Zander knew the rabbit was right, but before he was able to follow that bleak train of thought, footsteps sounded out in the hallway.

The Commander strode into the room, his armor clanking and his blond hair dark with sweat. He obviously hadn't even stopped to get cleaned up. A small spurt of hope bloomed inside Zander. Maybe this would all be over.

Zander pushed to his feet. "Did you find her?" he blurted, and then flushed, aware he hadn't even greeted the man. "Sorry, it's good to see you, Commander." He found he meant the words even though he dreaded telling his uncle about everything that had happened since he'd left.

The Commander stopped a few feet from the desk. His gaze flicked to Lapin and then back to Zander before he gave a brief bow. "I'm afraid I wasn't able to find her, although I got close several times. The trail ended at the edge of Wonderland." He paused. "I found some evidence that she backtracked to this area. Have you heard of any sightings?"

The Queen standing on the balcony flashed through Zander's memory, making his tone sharp. "No, of course not."

The Commander regarded him with a hooded expression.

"I would have said something if I'd seen her!" Zander wished he could retrieve the words as soon as they left his mouth, sure his uncle would see right through him. Zander plowed ahead, hoping to distract the Commander from his blunder. "You said the trail ended at the edge of Wonderland?"

"Yes, and I found evidence she's been to the Faelands."

Zander leaned forward. "Did you track her over there?"

"Briefly. As it was best not to let King Thorne know I was there, it limited my movements somewhat."

Zander closed his eyes briefly. "That is not good news."

The Commander's gaze bounced between Zander and Lapin, his mouth thinning. "No, it's not. One of my sources told me that there has been a string of disappearances and strange killings—small Fae, wings shorn, magical essences drained. The timing is suspicious, especially after what you told me about the Queen and the flower maidens."

Zander couldn't hold back a groan, and the Commander's eyes narrowed. "Perhaps you'd best tell me what's going on here and where my brother really is."

Zander exchanged glances with Lapin before he spoke. "A lot has happened since you left."

The Commander raised an eyebrow, and Zander straightened, placing his palms on the desk as if that would keep him anchored. "I'm sure you noticed before you left that the King... well... that he wasn't quite himself."

The Commander nodded. "Go on."

"I was hoping you'd found the Queen." He paused, but the Commander remained silent, waiting for Zander to continue.

Zander opened his mouth to do just that, but the words lodged in his throat. Thankfully, Lapin stepped into the gap of silence. "I'm afraid the King's curse is not completely gone." He pulled out his pipe and tapped it on his knee. "Well, that's not completely accurate. It's gone, but we believe the Queen is manipulating him through the curse. I'm not sure what object she's using, but it's clear these Fae creatures are boosting her powers."

The Commander frowned and fiddled with a ring on his pinky finger. Something about it pricked at Zander, but the Commander's next question turned his attention back to their discussion. "Where is the King now?"

Zander looked up and met his uncle's gaze. "In the dungeons."

Shock flashed across his features before his expression shuttered. "I think you'd best start at the beginning."

So, Zander told him about the King's increasingly erratic behavior and what Chess had found in the King's bedchamber. He told him about the death of the gardener and a flower maiden, but he stumbled to a halt when he came to Citrine. Unfortunately, the Commander was too sharp.

"What else has he done?"

"My father... the King... he..." Zander swallowed and looked helplessly at Lapin.

Lapin took a long draw from his pipe and blew out a perfectly round ring before he answered. "I'm sorry to say, the Pearl Queen was also a victim of the beast."

The Commander stared at Zander, horror cracking his normally stoic expression. He slumped back in his chair and ran a shaky hand over his face. Finally, he straightened, his expression once again devoid of emotion. "Who knows about this?"

Zander blew out a breath. "The Council, and most, if not all, of the staff here at the palace, but so far I don't think anyone outside of that knows except Bliss and his wife. I had no choice but to tell them."

The Commander's mouth thinned. "Trust me, if the general public doesn't know already, they will. These things take on a life of their own. It's good you've put him in the dungeons."

"How can you say that?" The words tore from Zander almost against his will.

The Commander frowned. "Because, obviously, the King needs to be contained, both for the obvious reasons, and also because it shows the people that you are keeping them safe. If you're going to step into his shoes, you have to be able to do the hard things." He softened his tone. "And containing him might be the least of what you'll have to do."

"What do you mean?" Zander asked sharply.

"I mean, there are going to be repercussions. The Pearl Queen doesn't have any family left—at least none in Wonderland—to demand justice for her death, but the King killed a flower maiden. The Fae King could seek retribution—and be well within his rights to do so."

Zander gripped the edge of the desk, the weight of his uncle's words bearing down on him like boulders. His mind whirled at the horrible possibilities.

Lapin took another long draw on his pipe. The sound was the only one in the room besides the ticking of the clock. After several puffs, he spoke. "If the King's condition is on account of the Queen, I hardly think that King Thorne will lay the guilt at your father's doorstep, Zander." He turned to the Commander. "You're panicking him unnecessarily."

"And you're being overly optimistic, Sir Lapin. No offense intended."

Lapin lifted a furry shoulder. "Perhaps, but I don't view any benefits in spinning worst-case scenarios, either. I have a fair idea for a potion to help the King's issues, and I'm not ready to say all is lost. I hope you'll agree with me, Commander."

The rabbit gave the Commander a pointed look, and his words eased the vice around Zander's chest. He found he could take a deep breath again.

"I'd like to see him." The Commander's words startled Zander, and the band tightened again.

"My father?" Even as he said it, he felt stupid. Of course, the Commander meant the King. Who else could he possibly be referring to?

The Commander nodded, his expression sober.

Zander's gaze found Lapin's, and the rabbit gave a tiny shake of his head.

"We were just down there and he's resting. Perhaps after dinner," Zander said.

"No, I want to visit him now." The Commander stood up and, reluctantly, Zander pushed to his feet. As much as he wanted to put it off, it looked like he'd be visiting the dungeons again.

Chapter 59

AZALEA JERKED THE ROPE she'd tied around Lyssandra's hands, and the Queen stumbled and fell to her knees. Her bound hands barely caught her, but the tall Fae woman kept striding along, the rope going taut.

"Wait, you need to let her get up." Alice ran to help the tiny blonde woman, but Azalea waved her back.

"She can stand on her own." She jerked on the rope again, and the Queen's arms slid out from under her, her chin hitting the forest floor with a thud. When she pushed herself up, blood trickled from her lip. She wiped at it with the back of her hands and tried to get to her feet, but Azalea jerked the rope again.

"Stop it!" Alice grabbed the rope, but Azalea hung on, scowling at her.

"She does not deserve your pity."

"Maybe not, but she doesn't deserve to be treated like this, either. You're better than this."

Azalea glared at Alice, her eyes dilated and fixed, but Alice refused to back down or look away.

Finally, Azalea threw her end of the rope at Alice. "Fine, you bring her along, but if she gets away from you, it is your life that will be forfeit."

Chess stepped in between them. "That's uncalled for, Azalea, and Alice is right. I have no love for Lyssandra, but your treatment of her does not speak well of you or your court."

"That woman has killed an untold number of our people. She went after the smallest and weakest, using trickery and deceit to lure them to painful and prolonged deaths. I do not care what you think of me or my court."

Chess took a step closer until they were only inches apart. "And you imprisoned an innocent girl and allowed some madman to torture her to satisfy his curiosity. Don't push me, cousin, or you might not like what happens."

Azalea let out a low growl, and for the first time, fear's icy chill slid over Alice's skin. Chess's mouth curled into a snarl, his gaze not wavering.

Alice bit her lip, unsure if speaking would help or hurt the situation. Surprisingly, it was Indigo that stepped in between them. He took his sister's arm. "He's not our enemy, sister. Don't make him one."

Azalea's body lost some of its tension, and the crackle in the air dimmed. Indigo linked his arm with hers and began walking. "Besides, how can Father properly punish her if she doesn't make it to Underhill in one piece? Let them take charge of her for a while. It's only fair they take a turn."

Azalea allowed her brother to move her down the path, but her expression hadn't lost all of its tightness. In some ways, Alice couldn't blame Azalea. What the

Queen had done to the little bumble she'd found and to sweet Fia was truly terrible. She sighed.

The years of the Great War came back to her in a flood of ugly memories. The truth was, if you returned cruelty with cruelty, it didn't remove it from the world. It just made you both monsters.

She looked down at the rope she'd caught and then back at the Queen. Despite all she'd done, Alice couldn't help a pang of pity.

Lyssandra's tiny figure drooped, and dirt and blood clung to her cheek and above her lip from her close encounter with the forest floor a few minutes earlier. Alice couldn't help wondering what had driven the Queen to do such monstrous things.

Chess held out his hand, interrupting her thoughts. "I'll take the rope. You don't have to take charge of her."

"No, it's fine." She motioned for him to go ahead and then turned to the Queen. "Come on. I don't think Azalea will be too understanding if we fall behind."

The Queen trudged silently behind her. Periodically, her steps faltered and Alice paused, making sure the woman was still on her feet.

Chess walked a little ahead of her, but he kept looking back to check on her. It warmed Alice's heart. She wasn't sure how long it would take to get back to Underhill, but the longer they walked, the heavier her heart became. Once they turned the Queen over to King Thorne, there was no reason for her to stay.

She was finally ready to admit to herself she didn't want to leave Chess or this place. As much as she needed to see her family, she also needed the man walking in front of her just as much.

"Your luck is rather astounding."

The Queen's voice startled Alice out of her thoughts, and she was surprised and a little dismayed to realize the woman was walking almost right next to her. She needed to pay closer attention. No matter how much pity she might feel, Alice wouldn't forget what the Queen was capable of, even without her magic.

"I don't know that ending up in Wonderland or this situation could be considered lucky," Alice said drily.

The Queen rolled her big brown eyes. "You told me about your father yourself. Trust me, not all fathers want their children's happiness. And what about him?" She nodded at Chess's back.

Alice's cheeks heated. "What about him?"

"It's obvious he loves you." The Queen's mouth twisted into a bitter smirk. "And not only for your pretty face, either."

"Well, the feeling is mutual."

"Hmmm, but his looks don't hurt, do they?"

"The reason I love him has nothing to do with his face."

The Queen's smile turned wicked. "The rest of him is rather fetching, too."

Alice's face burned. It felt wrong to talk about Chess like he was a prized horse. Desperate to change the subject, Alice blurted, "You act as if nobody's loved you, but the King did, and you threw that away."

The smile fell, and the Queen's mouth tightened into a thin slash. "I forget how young you are sometimes."

Alice raised an eyebrow. "You can't be over three or four years older than I am."

A bitter laugh escaped the Queen. "Maybe in years."

Alice frowned at Lyssandra. "You seem to think I've led some charmed life. I may have a family now, but that wasn't always the case. I spent years of my childhood on the streets."

"And yet here you are. If that's not luck, I don't know what is."

When Alice frowned at her, the Queen continued. "Just how many other street children found their way into a loving home?"

Alice opened her mouth and then shut it again. Maybe the Queen had a point.

"Well, you were a queen. I still don't understand why you hurt the people who trusted you, who welcomed you into their lives—and for what—power? Riches? It seems you had luck, but it wasn't enough for you."

The Queen stumbled again, and Alice put out a hand to steady her. Lyssandra looked down at where Alice's fingers touched her arm. "There's nothing to gain in being nice to me. I can't do anything for you anymore." She held up her bound hands. "Obviously."

Alice drew her hand back as if burned. "I'm not helping you to get something." She blew out a breath. "You really have a twisted view of life."

Lyssandra drew herself up and lifted her chin. "No, I've merely learned my lessons thoroughly. You'd do well to learn a few yourself. Nobody's ever been kind to me unless they had a reason. Except for Leander, and he's dead." She shot a venomous look at Alice.

Alice held up her hands. "You can't lay his death at my door. You're the one who created the monster to begin with. I tried to stop Leander, to tell him the Minotaur wasn't the monster he thought, but he wouldn't listen to me. If anyone's to blame for his death, it's you."

The Queen's face froze and then crumpled. Her eyes brimmed. She looked away, and Alice felt like a heel. What she'd said was true, but the woman was already down. No need to kick her too.

"I'm... I'm sorry. I shouldn't have said that."

The Queen looked back at Alice, her smile sad. "Someday, someone's going to use your kindness against you. It wouldn't hurt you to be a bit more ruthless, my dear."

They walked in silence for a few paces. Finally, Alice's curiosity won out. "I still don't understand what you were trying to accomplish. Was the throne worth all this?"

The Queen's tiny hands clenched into fists. "For a smart girl, you can be incredibly stupid."

"If you don't want to tell me, just say so." Alice lifted her chin, ready to hand the rope off to Chess.

The Queen's eyes glinted as she turned to stare at Alice. "Do you truly want to know?"

Alice considered the question. Perhaps it would be best to end this conversation. The Queen's fate was sealed now, but her curiosity won out. She met the Queen's gaze and gave a slow nod. "Yes, I really would."

"For my entire life, others have used me for their own gain. The only way to change that was if I didn't have to answer to anyone. If I held the throne, everyone would answer to me for a change." The Queen's eyes glazed over and there was a world of pain in those words.

"Nobody is completely free to do what they want. We all have to bend our will to others at times, to adjust our choices to the people around us," said Alice.

The Queen snorted. "Obviously, the people in *your* life want what's best for you. Not everyone's family is like that." Her mouth twisted. "Mine certainly wasn't. My father..." She stopped, her throat working. When she continued, she stared off into the distance as if looking at something only visible to her. "I had a... a companion. She was a girl from our estates. Her name was Ana. Even though she was a servant, we were like sisters. But, my father..." Her voice choked off, her hands clenching..." Because of him, she died."

"Oh, Lyssandra, that must have been awful for you."

The Queen shook back her braid and wiped at her eyes with the backs of her hands, regaining control of her emotions. "Yes, well, he didn't care about my feelings. In fact, when I protested his plans for her, he beat me so badly I was in bed for a week. By the time I recovered..." She lifted her chin and blinked rapidly. "Ana was gone."

"I... I'm sorry." Even as she said the words, Alice felt their inadequacy.

The Queen grimaced. "It wasn't the only time he beat me. Thankfully, most of the time, I was beneath his notice. When I got older, of course, he realized he could use me to gain an advantageous marriage, but by then I had already learned how to protect myself."

"But once you married King Zane, weren't you safe? I mean, he didn't mistreat you... did he?"

The Queen turned her dark gaze on Alice. "He never beat me, if that's what you mean, but he was two years older than my father. And he wanted me as his wife."

She let that sink in, and Alice made a face. "I can see why that wouldn't be... ideal, but a lot of women marry older men and make the best of it. If he was kind to you..."

The Queen's face twisted into a scowl as she stepped over some fallen branches. "I was supposed to marry Zander. Did you know that?"

Shocked, Alice asked, "But, what about Citrine?"

The Queen's expression softened. "They had broken their engagement by then. My father expected to make a match between us, but Zander refused because he still loved Citrine. He told me he didn't think it was fair to marry me when he loved someone else. He's the only person who has never tried to use me." The Queen's face hardened again. "Since his son didn't want me, the King decided I'd make an ideal second wife."

"But you cursed Zander." Alice couldn't keep the accusation out of her voice.

"Only because he wouldn't take the chance I gave him." She sneered. "Do you think I wanted to be some old man's plaything for the rest of my life?"

Alice recoiled at the venom in the other woman's voice, her own words drying up in her throat. When Lyssandra put it like that, it was awful, but still.

"But there had to be another way than... all this."

The Queen's expression turned fierce. "After my honeymoon"—the word dripped with disgust—"I determined I would no longer be at the mercy of someone else's whims. That my husband thought me a delightful piece of fluff made it easy." She held up her hands. "Of course, things didn't work out quite the way I planned." Her dark eyes found Alice's, and a shiver slid down Alice's back at the coldness in them. "You were the snag that unravelled the entire thing."

Alice glanced at the others, who were now several yards ahead of them, and then back at the Queen.

The woman let out a bark of harsh laughter. "Oh, don't look so frightened. I'm not going to hurt you. Even if I wanted to, I'm rather tied up at the moment." A sigh slipped out. "I should have let that Fae woman cut my throat. It would be better than whatever punishment they have planned for me."

Alice frowned. "Surely, that's not true."

The Queen lifted an eyebrow. "I'm not sure if I should envy you or pity you for your belief in your fellow man. I'm afraid the Fae are not known for their mercy."

Alice didn't have any response to that. They picked up their pace to catch up with the others, and the Queen, having told her story, lapsed into silence.

Chapter 60

LESS THAN A QUARTER of an hour later, Zander found himself once again down in the dungeon with Sir Lapin, only this time, the Commander was with them too. They stood outside the heavy wooden door. Zander slid the panel back. Inside, his father lay on his side, his back to them, still asleep on the narrow cot.

Zander moved over so the Commander could see through the barred window into the cell. "How often is he lucid?" the Commander asked after a moment.

Lapin, who leaned against the wall behind them, answered. "I'd say about three-quarters of the time, but it's getting harder and harder for him to not lose himself to the beast."

The King rolled over on his cot, groaning. He slowly pushed himself to a sitting position and shook his head. When he looked up, his glazed eyes had a red cast to them. His face contorted, and sweat beaded across his forehead. He shook his head again, his hands gripping the edge of the cot.

A wisp of smoke rose from his nose, and he shot to his feet. This time, when his gaze landed on them, his eyes glowed a deep red. With a bellow, he rushed towards the door, his body hitting it with a dull thud. He shoved his arm partially out between the bars, a clawed hand scrabbling to make contact with the Commander's face, but he dodged back out of harm's way.

Zander turned his head away, a deep ache pulsing in his chest. He wanted to shield his father from view. The King would find his own behavior abhorrent if he was in his right mind. Self-loathing scraped across his soul. If he'd only gotten rid of the Queen while he had the chance. His hands clenched into fists, and he had to fight his own beast within.

A hand on his shoulder made him start, and his gaze flew up to meet his uncle's. The Commander's expression was full of sorrow. "That thing is not my brother."

The King backed away from the door, and Zander slid the window shut again, blocking his father from view even as thuds reverberated off the stone walls as his father threw himself at the door again and again.

"No, it's not." Zander's voice cracked, and he cleared his throat. "Thankfully, he's not always like that. It's only when he's sleeping that there's any genuine danger of the beast taking over. He can usually keep control when he's awake."

The Commander lifted an eyebrow. "Usually?"

Zander hesitated, but finally admitted the   "It's becoming harder for him, but we've been giving him a strong sleeping draught at night. It makes him groggy in the mornings, which is usually when he struggles more."

At the Commander's obvious skepticism, Zander gave Lapin a helpless look.

The rabbit straightened away from the wall. "It's a bit of a balancing act. The sleeping draught helps to keep these episodes to a minimum, but it also makes him more vulnerable for a short time when it wears off. It's the best we can do at the moment, I'm afraid."

The Commander gave a curt nod before he turned away and started back up the stairs, Lapin and Zander following him. Each step Zander took felt weighted with lead. He had little hope left. Even if Chess returned with this artifact, if they couldn't find the Queen soon, it might be too late. The longer this went on, the more chance there was that his father might never fully recover, and he knew the recent deaths had taken their toll.

It wasn't until they reached the top of the stairs and exited the dungeons that the Commander finally spoke. "It's much worse than I feared, Zander."

"I know. It's so hard to see him like this. He's the King, and he's in a cell like a common prisoner." Zander's head drooped and his shoulders slumped as the full ramifications hit him of what his father's life would be like if they didn't find a way to stop this.

"I'm sorry I wasn't able to find the Queen because it's only going to get worse the longer this goes on." A sigh gusted out of him. "I'm afraid of what we might be forced to do if he gets worse, if the beast fully takes over."

Zander's head snapped up, and he stared at his uncle, not sure he understood. "What are you saying?"

The Commander's expression was indecipherable when he answered. "I think you know the answer to that. He's a danger to everyone when he's like this. We're fortunate that those times are limited, but you said yourself he's getting worse." He put a hand on Zander's shoulder. "You need to brace yourself for the decisions that might come down the road."

Zander shook his head. "No, it won't come to that. I won't let it."

Something like pity flashed over the Commander's features. "These things are not always in our control. Something like this could throw the Kingdom into chaos and jeopardize your own rule—even fuel the fire of people's distrust of your Drifter Gene."

"I don't care. My father's a victim here, and he won't face further danger from me." Zander hadn't even realized he'd moved, but he found himself only inches from his uncle.

Lapin raised a furry hand. "Gentlemen, I think we are all getting ahead of ourselves. Although it may not feel like it, we have time. The King hasn't completely succumbed to the beast just yet."

The Commander's lips pressed together, and something dark flashed in his eyes before his expression smoothed back to neutral. "Of course, you're right, Sir Lapin." He turned back to Zander. "I suggest you call a Council meeting soon though. At the very least, I should update them about the Queen. Now, if you'll excuse me. I came right in to see you as soon as I returned, but I'd like to get cleaned up before dinner."

"Of course," Zander said, his mind still churning.

With a brief nod, the Commander turned on his heel and strode away from them.

As soon as he was out of sight, Zander turned to Lapin. "What am I going to do? I can't call a meeting right now. I don't even have that artifact yet, and what if the Council agrees with the Commander?"

Lapin took several puffs on his pipe before he answered. "I'm afraid the only thing you can do is try to delay. In the meantime, I'll work on that formula. Presenting the King calm and in control would go a long way towards ensuring nobody gets any unfortunate ideas."

Zander nodded. He'd thought he'd be relieved to have the Commander back, but now he wasn't so sure.

Chapter 61

By the time they got back to Underhill, the sun had almost set. Everyone was drooping from fatigue, and Indigo's face was paler than normal. Despite Alice's healing, it was clear he was still regaining his strength.

Chess had taken the rope from Alice several hours ago, and she'd let him, her expression troubled. After the Queen's long confession to Alice—of which he'd heard the majority—the woman had said very little to anyone. It made him wonder what she was up to because if there was one thing he had learned about Lyssandra, it was that she was always scheming.

The Queen might want to convince Alice she was an innocent victim, but he'd been there. He'd watched her turn her attentions on the King, and Chess still wasn't entirely sure if their marriage had been the King's idea or Lyssandra's.

Azalea drew the symbols in the air to open Underhill and then took the rope from him. She waved her hand in Chess and Alice's direction. "I will bring her to Father. You may go rest or eat or whatever you wish to do."

Indigo stretched his arms over his head. "I trust that directive also includes me, sister. I'm both exhausted and famished."

Azalea frowned at her brother, and then she relented. "I suppose it does not matter. I do not need your help to deliver the prisoner to Father."

Indigo's mouth curved into a smile, and he turned his gaze on Alice. "Thank you again... Alice. It would have been a terrible bother to travel with my injuries."

Alice smiled. "I'm happy I could keep you from being bothered, Indigo."

Chess stiffened when the Fae man cupped Alice's cheek. "Do not leave without wishing me farewell."

Faint pink tinged Alice's cheeks, but she nodded. "Chess and I will make sure we tell you goodbye before we leave."

Indigo leaned down and dropped a kiss on Alice's cheek, and with a jaunty wave at Chess, he slipped into an adjacent tunnel and disappeared.

"You can stop glaring at the man. He's undoubtedly handsome, but he isn't any real competition for you." Amusement laced the Queen's voice, and Chess turned to find her dark eyes watching him.

"Quiet!" Azalea barked. "You will be silent unless I give you leave to speak."

The Queen raised an eyebrow. "That seems excessive."

Azalea glared at her. "If you cannot follow my directions, I will have you gagged."

The Queen made a motion like turning a key at her mouth, but her eyes still held a mocking glint. Chess exchanged a glance with Alice, but before he could comment, Azalea spoke again.

"The small Fae will tend to your needs. I am sure you are both tired, too."

Chess was, but he shook his head. "Oh no, I'm coming with you. Your father made me a promise, and I'm not giving him any opportunity to squirm out of it." He turned to Alice. "You don't have to come. You probably want to rest."

Alice straightened her shoulders. "You remember what happened the last time you tried to get me to stay behind? I think I'd better come with you."

When he slid his hand into hers and brought it to his lips, she beamed up at him. A small sigh escaped him. Later, he reminded himself. They'd have time together later. With effort, he turned back to Azalea.

She wrinkled her nose. "Must you demonstrate your affection so openly?"

The Queen gave a low, throaty chuckle. "Don't be such a spoilsport, Princess. Just because you haven't found true love, don't begrudge it to others." She winked at Alice.

"I never thought I'd agree with you, Lyssandra, but"—he grinned at Azalea—"she has a valid point. True love is a marvelous thing. You should try it." Azalea's expression darkened to a thundercloud, so he gestured towards the tunnel. "Shall we? I am under a rather tight deadline."

Azalea pushed the Queen in front of her and marched her towards the throne room, the rest of them trailing in her wake. Chess glanced at Alice, but her head was down and she was biting her lip. Maybe she didn't appreciate his rather brash declaration. It was one thing to tell each other in private and another to share their love with everyone. He clasped her hand in his and she looked up.

"I'm sorry. Did I embarrass you, love?"

A fleeting smile curved her lips, and she shook her head. "No, why would you think that?"

He lifted a shoulder. "Well, you seem rather... preoccupied all of a sudden."

Her chin dipped down again. "It's only... never mind. We can talk about it later."

He shook her hand. "No, tell me now."

She sighed. "With the Queen captured, it reminded me about... home."

"Don't worry, love. Once I get the artifact from the King, I'll make sure you get home. If you want, I'll send you back before I head to the Red Palace. I know you've been waiting a long time to see your family."

Alice didn't answer for several moments, her gaze on the stone beneath their feet. When she finally looked up, her expression was almost shy. "That's the thing. I... I think I'd like to go back to the palace, if it's all the same to you."

Relief almost made Chess stumble. Not that he couldn't follow her later, but the idea of letting her go home without... deciding about their future had been lurking in the back of his mind since they captured the Queen. "Are you sure? I don't know what we'll be walking into when we go back. Things were rather grim when I left."

"I... I don't think I can go back to my family not knowing what will happen with the King and Zander, without telling Citrine goodbye. I never got to the last time, you know."

He rubbed his thumb on the back of her hand. "I'm glad you aren't leaving just yet. I'm not ready to say goodbye."

Alice's face bloomed into a smile even as her cheeks turned pink. "Me either."

They grinned foolishly at each other.

It was at this moment that the party drew to a halt at the entrance of the throne room. Chess had been so preoccupied with Alice that he hadn't realized where they were. He needed to get his head on straight. With a wink at Alice, he turned his focus to their party. Azalea stepped around the Queen to stand inside the room and announced herself to King Thorne.

The man turned from where he had been bending over a long table, a stack of paper in his hand. "Ah, you've succeeded." He smiled warmly at his daughter and motioned them forward.

The Queen stood as if rooted to the spot, and Azalea jerked the rope so hard she fell to her knees. When Azalea didn't move to help her, Chess sighed and reached down to pull the Queen to her feet. The woman gave him a dimpled smile, and it was all Chess could do not to roll his eyes. He wasn't sure if Lyssandra was trying to be coy, or if playing the males around her was such a habit, she did it without thinking.

Thankfully, he'd always been immune to her wiles.

Azalea took another step forward, her body rigid. "We have brought her back, Father. What would you like me to do with her while she awaits her sentencing?"

The King snapped his fingers, and one of the small Fae zipped to hover in front of him. He murmured, and she flew out of the room. He turned his dark eyes on the Queen, who visibly cringed under his gaze.

"So you are the one who has been killing my people. I did not expect a woman such as yourself." His tone was mild, but his eyes were hard.

The Queen straightened with effort, a cool smile on her face. "I am often underestimated, Your Majesty. As for why they brought me here, nobody deigned to tell me that information. They simply attacked me."

"That is untrue. You used your Jabberwock form and almost killed Indigo. If we did not have the Mirror World girl, he would have died." Azalea's words dropped like ice from her lips.

Dismay colored the Queen's face. "I was merely defending myself. When you ambushed me, I was frightened. As a woman alone..." She shuddered delicately. "Surely you understand."

Disgust colored Azalea's expression when she turned her gaze on the Queen. "What I understand is that you have hurt and killed those weaker than you are. I will watch with great joy when they strip you of your Gifts. If there is justice, there will be nothing left of your essence at all when it is done."

Alice's sharp inhalation coincided with the color draining from the Queen's face at these words, and Lyssandra fell once again to her knees, her hands reaching towards the King. "I beg of you, mercy. I have hurt no one. You must believe me."

The King frowned at the woman prostrate at his feet. "You will not be sentenced without cause."

Lyssandra sank back on her heels, and her head dropped into her hands, tears tracking down her cheeks. "I am grateful for your justness, Your Majesty. I am innocent. I swear it."

"We will find that out when one of my men tests your magical signature." If Chess hadn't been standing so close, he would have missed the way the Queen's body stiffened at these words. The King gestured to Azalea. "Help her up." He addressed Lyssandra as she clambered to her feet. "You'll await the testing in one of our cages. We have to assess the evidence of your involvement before we pass sentencing."

Two Fae guards appeared at the doorway. The King nodded at the warriors who strode in, and they took the Queen's arms, dragging her from the room.

Chess almost felt pity for the woman, but after what she'd done to Zander, he figured she deserved whatever she got. Which reminded him...

He turned back to the King, who was shuffling the papers in his hands. "Your Majesty..."

"I thought I told you to call me Uncle," the King said, not looking up from the words in front of him.

"My apologies, Uncle. We have delivered the Queen to you as promised. Now, I need you to keep your promise to me."

The King put down the papers and clasped his hands over his stomach. He gazed at Chess so long, Chess had to force himself not to shift or fidget. Alice's hand slipped into his, and she shifted so her shoulder touched his. Warmth flooded his chest, and he squeezed her hand.

Finally, the King rose and moved towards one of the shadowy corners of the room. When he turned around, he held a deep blue velvet bag in his hands. He walked to where Chess stood and carefully opened the bag. As soon as the tie at the top loosened, the power of what was inside flooded the room. Alice stumbled back a step, and Chess had to brace himself.

Inside was a glowing alabaster box, its sides and lid carved in intricate swirls of leaves and flowers. A golden clasp held it shut.

Chess reached for it, but the King pulled it back. "This is the Box of Augmentation. It is powerful and will amplify any spell a hundredfold if you place the ingredients inside. You must use it with great caution."

"I assure you, I will keep it safe and make sure it's returned to you." Chess held out his hands.

The King pulled the bag back up around the box and knotted the drawstring before he handed it to Chess. "You must return this. Promise me."

Chess nodded solemnly. "You have my word that I will return this box to you."

The words echoed and seemed to hang in the air, making the promise official.

The King nodded. "I will need to send someone with you, though, to see that nothing happens to this artifact."

"That isn't—"

"Azalea will go with you."

"That's really not necessary." Chess looked at the King. "I can assure Your... erm, Uncle, I will bring the artifact back safely."

"I trust you, nephew, but that is an artifact of the royal court. The clan leaders won't be happy with me for giving it to you in the first place. This is safer for everyone. Trust me."

Chess bowed his head. "Thank you, Uncle." He reached to take Alice's hand again.

The King stood and surprised Chess by embracing first him and then Alice. "Make sure you stop by to see your mother before you go."

Duty and desire warred inside Chess. Now that they had the artifact, he didn't want to delay, but he didn't know how soon he could come back to see his mother, either. His indecision must have been clearly visible on his face because Azalea spoke up.

"You will have plenty of time to see Aunt Larkspur. We will not leave until morning."

"But we need to—"

The King held up a hand, and his gaze rested on Alice although he addressed all of them. "A night of rest will do you all good."

As if to reinforce his words, Alice swayed on her feet. Resigned, Chess nodded. Alice needed to rest—they all did—but now that he had the artifact, his sense of urgency was back.

Chapter 62

A KNOCK ON THE open study door bought Zander's head up from the papers he'd been mindlessly shuffling on his desk. The Commander stood in the doorway. This was the first time Zander had seen his uncle since yesterday.

Zander leaned back in his chair. "Yes?"

His tone was barely polite, but he didn't care. After what the Commander had suggested, it was all Zander could muster.

"May I come in?"

Zander gestured at a chair. "Suit yourself."

The Commander walked into the room and sat down. "I realize you're upset with me, Zander, but I won't apologize for what I said." He paused, waiting for a response.

"You came in here to tell me that? Well, message delivered. You can go now."

The Commander let out a huff of breath. "I'm not the enemy here. I'm trying to help you."

"By suggesting I put my father down like a dog?"

The Commander ran a hand through his hair. "That's not what I said."

"It's what you meant," snapped Zander.

The Commander sighed. "The reality is, you need to be prepared for what the future might bring. If you ignore the possibilities, no matter how painful, you won't be ready when you need to be."

Zander straightened in his chair. "There is no future where I will ever kill my father."

"Not even if the beast takes over? Do you believe he'd want to live like that, knowing he could hurt others? I visited with him this morning. He's devastated by these latest deaths, and he agrees with me on this."

Zander stared at the Commander. How could this be the same man he'd known all his life, who had encouraged him and taught him to fight? Chess had complained for years about the Commander's adherence to duty, but he'd assumed Chess exaggerated, his opinion colored by his mother's absence.

Zander slapped his hands on the desk and leaned forward. "You did what?"

"I have every right to visit my brother." The Commander's tone was even as he held Zander's gaze. "And your father has a right to have a say in his future while he can still express his own wishes."

The anger leaked out of Zander, and he slumped back in his chair. "This can't be real."

The Commander's expression softened. "There's still time to find a solution to all of this. I only brought all this up because I care about you and this Kingdom's future."

Zander let out a sigh. "I know." He had no reason to doubt the Commander. He'd been nothing but loyal all of Zander's life.

Silence spread over the room for a long moment before the Commander spoke again. "You need to call a Council meeting. They need to be informed about what's going on, and as I said yesterday, I should share my findings with them."

Zander let his head fall back against the chair. "You're right, but it seems rather pointless. What is there to share except more bad news?"

The Commander leaned forward. "I can do it for you, if you'd like."

Zander nodded. The Commander tapped the edge of the desk and stood. "I'll schedule it for tomorrow then, if that works for you."

Zander pushed to his feet. "Before lunch, if everyone can make it."

The Commander nodded and walked to the door, where he paused. "This will all work out, one way or another. You'll see."

"Thanks."

The Commander left and almost knocked Lapin over on his way out. The rabbit skirted around him and came into the room, frowning. "Has something happened?" he asked.

Zander dropped into his chair, putting his head in his hands. "Not really, only more of the same." He looked up at Lapin. "Please tell me you're here to say the Love's Bane worked."

The rabbit eased himself into the chair opposite and leaned forward, his eyes alight, his nose twitching. "I believe I have the correct potion, Sire."

Zander's eyes closed as relief slid through him like cool water on a hot day. "Thank you, Lapin. I can't tell you how glad I am to hear that."

When he opened his eyes, the rabbit had relaxed back and crossed one foot over his knee. "It should achieve full potency by morning. Of course, I can't guarantee it will work. This is all theory until we test it."

"We don't have time for that. You need to give it to him as soon as it's ready."

Lapin pulled on one ear. "I'm not sure that's wise. It's always good to test..."

"We can't wait."

Lapin's eyes widened. "What's happened? Does this have something to do with the Commander's visit?"

"Sort of. I approved for him to call a Council meeting for tomorrow morning, and we need to have something positive to tell everyone."

The rabbit's face creased. "Ah, I see."

"So you'll do it?"

Lapin shook his head and Zander's stomach sank. "I'm afraid I can't do that, but I'll tell you what I will do. I'll get the potion to him as early as possible tomorrow. Certainly before that Council meeting of yours." Zander gave him a relieved smile, but he held up a paw. "As long as you realize it might not work even at full potency, in which case I'd need to adjust the properties."

Zander swallowed. "I'm willing to take that risk."

Lapin pushed to his feet. "All right then. I will go get a dose prepared for His Majesty and administer it first thing in the morning."

The rabbit walked towards the door. "Lapin?" The rabbit turned back. "I understand you can't guarantee anything, but do you think it will work?"

Lapin said nothing for a long moment and Zander's stomach sank, but then a smile spread across the rabbit's face. "There's a high likelihood that it will."

The words made Zander's knees weak. "Thank you."

"You are more than welcome, Your Highness."

Zander watched Lapin hurry out the door. He hoped the potion worked. It was about time his luck turned for the better.

Chapter 63

AFTER DINNER, CHESS FOUND himself once again outside his mother's cottage, Alice at his side. After a nap and Fariar's tonic, she seemed to be back to full strength. Wickle cheeped from her shoulder. He had been overjoyed to see Alice and was even twittering cheerfully at Chess.

Chess reached out a finger and stroked the tiny head. He never thought he'd be fond of a snark, but the little guy had grown on him. Even so, he said, "Maybe you should put Wickle in your pocket. I'm not sure how—"

The door opened to reveal a beaming Larkspur. She gazed at them for a long moment, as if drinking them both in, before she engulfed Chess in a hug. Then she turned to Alice but paused when the snark stood and stretched, his big eyes blinking up at her.

"That's a rather unusual pet," she said.

Alice covered the creature with her palm. "He's been a good friend to me. I hope you don't mind that I brought him along. He had to wait while we went looking for the

Queen, and he hasn't wanted to let me out of his sight since I got back."

Larkspur's face creased into a smile. "I can understand that feeling. I am so glad to see you both. I don't want to let you out of my sight, either."

Alice's shoulders loosened, and she leaned forward to embrace his mother, careful not to squish Wickle. "We're glad to be seen, let me tell you!" she said, her words muffled in Larkspur's shoulder.

The sight of the two of them together did strange things to Chess's heart, and he had to clear his throat before he spoke. "I'm afraid we won't be able to be seen too long, Meemee. We're going back to Wonderland in the morning."

Larkspur released Alice and stepped back from the doorway. "Come in, then. No use letting the sorrow of tomorrow rob us of the enjoyment of today."

Alice followed his mother in, and Chess shut the door behind him as they made their way to the now familiar wooden table. He sat down next to Alice, automatically taking her hand and twining their fingers together. His eyes roved around, taking in the plants that trailed or bloomed on most of the surfaces. He found his muscles relaxing in the cozy kitchen with its soothing smells of lemon and ginger and... something he couldn't define but which seemed quintessentially his mother.

Larkspur, in the meantime, poured cups of steaming tea and loaded up a tray with a plate of pastel biscuits. A teapot had already been steaming on the stove when they entered, making him wonder if she always had the kettle on or if she somehow had known they were coming.

She set the tray on the table and handed each of them a cup before settling herself on a chair. Chess blew on the hot liquid before taking a sip. One thing about his mother: She could certainly brew a good cup of tea.

Larkspur's gaze shifted from his face to Alice's and then down to their twined fingers, and she raised an eyebrow. "I am glad to see you spoke your hearts at last."

Next to him, Alice sputtered a bit, and his grip on her hand tightened. "Yes, I love Alice, and I hope you will too, Meemee."

Larkspur's eyes crinkled at the corners. "I already do, and as I told her the last time you were here, Alice is a perfect mate for you. She has a tender heart, but she's not soft. You need a few sharp edges to keep you in check, son."

Chess glanced between his mother and Alice. "On second thought, you two need to be kept apart or I might be in trouble."

"If you behave yourself, you won't have to worry, now will you?" Alice's eyes danced with amusement.

They all smiled at each other, and Wickle cheeped as if in agreement. Warmth filled Chess as contentment settled over him like a warm blanket. Sitting in his mother's kitchen with the two women he loved, he realized the feeling was new and novel.

The clink of Larkspur's cup on the table broke the spell. "What artifact did the King give you?"

"The Box of Augmentation." The artifact's presence weighed on him, and he had asked the King to keep it until they left.

Larkspur's eyes widened. "Thorne must trust you. That one is powerful. You must be very careful with it.

Once a potion is added, anyone who opens it will get the full force plus the added power of the box."

Chess shrugged. "One artifact is the same as another to me, I'm afraid. I'm just hoping we don't have to actually use it."

Alice nodded in agreement. "Larkspur, is there anything you can tell us that will help Zander? I'm really worried about him trying this."

Instead of answering, Larkspur stood and walked over to a cabinet. She pulled it opened and rummaged inside. When she turned, she held a glass vial similar to the one she'd given them for the Queen. When she held it up, a liquid foamed inside. It was impossible to tell the color, though, since the glass itself was tinted a dark green.

"While you were gone, I gave some thought to what you said about the Queen." She walked back over to the table and set the bottle in front of Chess. "I made this for Zane."

Chess picked it up and examined the liquid inside. "What does it do?"

Larkspur perched on the edge of her chair and leaned forward. "Since the King loses himself to the monster, this should help him resist and keep in his own mind." She shrugged. "I can't guarantee it will work. I am only going off theory, but Zane was always kind to me. I hate to hear how he's struggling so."

Alice looked at Chess, her excitement almost visible. "And if the King can control himself and not turn into the monster, then Zander won't have to give up his Gift, will he?"

Chess pocketed the potion and smiled. "Perhaps not. At least, it would give him more time to win over the

Council and the people, to show them he's the same as he's always been."

Alice threw her arms around his neck and squeezed, almost strangling him. Chess laughed and hugged her back. Over her head, he winked at his mother. "Do you have any other potions handy? I rather like this one's result."

Larkspur's laugh was infectious. "I don't think you need a potion, son."

When Alice sat back, her cheeks were pink. "Sorry, I got a little carried away."

Chess dropped a kiss on her rosy cheek. "Never apologize for being yourself, love."

A small sigh escaped his mother. "You'll leave in the morning, then." It wasn't a question.

He relaxed back into his chair, wishing they could stay longer. He lifted his cup and took another sip of the tea.

"I will expect an invitation to the wedding."

Chess choked on his tea. "I... we..." he spluttered.

Alice's face flamed, but she patted his hand. When she spoke, her voice was calm. "I'm afraid we haven't gotten nearly that far yet, Larkspur. Once things are settled at the Red Palace, I still need to go back home. My family doesn't know Chess exists, or even where I am, for that matter. There's a long way between here and any wedding bells." Her mouth slid into a smile. "Besides, Chess will have to meet Papa James, and there are no guarantees with him."

The vice that had clamped around his chest loosened. He winked at her. "Are you saying you doubt my ability to charm your father?"

Alice poked his shoulder. "Charm doesn't work on Papa James, and you don't want to get on his bad side."

Chess laughed. "You act like he's some kind of pirate."

Alice made a choking noise and murmured, "Something like that."

Larkspur watched the two of them and leaned back in her chair. "Regardless, when the time comes, I expect an invitation."

"Mother!" Chess said, exasperated and embarrassed.

Chapter 64

THE NEXT DAY, ZANDER stood at the head of the table in the meeting room. Sun glinted through the floor-to-ceiling windows, making stripes on the wooden table. He kept his gaze resolutely away from his father's empty chair. Five pairs of eyes stared at him even as his hope dwindled with each tick of the clock.

He straightened and gathered his unruly thoughts. He wanted to start with the potion, but he had heard nothing from Lapin yet. If it hadn't worked, it would only make things worse.

No, he'd stick to the facts. This was merely an update about the Commander's trip. Nothing had really changed. He cleared his throat. "Thank you for coming. I realize this whole situation weighs on everyone..."

Beecher thumped his cane on the floor, interrupting Zander. "What I want to know is what you're going to do about it? I don't see that anything's gotten any better. Only worse!"

"How can any of us learn what's going on, Wilfred, when you won't be quiet long enough to let him speak?"

The Duchess raised an eyebrow at the old man sitting to her right.

"In my day, women didn't even sit on the Council. Too soft."

The Duchess turned all the way around in her chair to look squarely at Lord Beecher. "Keep pushing me, Wilfred, and you'll find out just how soft I am." The quiet words held menace.

Beecher scowled, but kept his mouth shut.

"Yes, well, I'm afraid I don't have good news to share." Zander shifted his weight onto his other foot. "My Father, the King, has not improved, and we are still waiting to see if Sir Chess's trip to the Faelands will prove fruitful." He looked to where his uncle sat. "Unfortunately, the Commander was also unsuccessful, but I'll let him update you."

Zander dropped back into his chair, and the Commander straightened. "As you're aware, I was tasked with finding the Queen. While I did track her, the trail led into the Faelands. For obvious reasons, my search was hampered there, as I felt it best not to let King Thorne learn of my presence."

There was a collective gasp. "What if she assembles the Fae King?" Lord Dordo's face creased in concern. The Duchess let out a soft snort but didn't correct the man.

The Commander continued, "It's a possibility, but I'm more afraid she'll try to form an alliance with him. The Fae keep to themselves and may not even realize King Zane is alive or that the Prince has returned." He glanced at Zander. "It might be wise to make a diplomatic visit soon that doesn't include asking for favors."

Zander's gaze dropped to his hands. He knew his uncle was only trying to help, but the words were like a slap of criticism.

Lady Perma's expression brightened. "Maybe the Queen went there to hide, and we won't have to worry about her anymore."

The Commander twisted the ruby-stoned ring on his pinky absently. "While anything's possible, I don't think that's likely."

Lady Perma deflated in her seat, wringing her hands. "What will we do, then? Can't Sir Lapin help at all? It's too bad the Pearl Que..." She trailed off awkwardly, casting a furtive look in Zander's direction.

After a tick of thick silence, the Commander leaned forward. "We have to face the situation we are in—not what wish was true." He glanced at Zander again, an apology in his expression, before he turned back to the Council again. "The truth is, the King is not getting better. He's getting worse."

"But he's safely contained," Zander said.

"Yes, that's true, but it leaves us in a precarious situation. Right now, the citizens of Wonderland aren't privy to what's going on, but we can't keep this a secret for much longer." The Commander's gaze travelled around the table. "We must acknowledge the possibility that he'll continue to get worse, and we might never reverse his condition, that the beast might take over."

There was a stunned silence. Lady Perma started to cry, and even Lord Beecher had nothing to say. Lord Dordo's mouth opened and closed like a fish.

The Duchess was the only one who hadn't lost her composure. "You're right, Commander. While Lady Perma may harbor hope that the Queen is gone, I have no such illusions. There is no doubt in my mind, that wretched woman will be back, and when she returns, the last thing we need is a void in leadership. The Prince has been preparing for this role his entire life. It seems now would be a good time to put that training to use." Her words dropped into the shocked silence like pebbles in a pond, and Zander wanted to hug her.

Before he could say anything, though, Beecher regained his powers of speech. "Don't be daft, Leticia. The Felinas boy might not be successful, and nobody wants a Drifter as king."

Zander knew he should speak up, but he felt as if he were underwater, the voices muffled. He was so weary of trying to prove himself to people like Beecher.

Unfortunately, nobody else had that problem. The Commander turned to the Duchess. "That's definitely a possibility, but Beecher brings up a good point, too. We would need to counter any negative feelings about the Prince's unfortunate gene."

The Duchess raised an eyebrow and somehow looked down her nose at the Commander even though he was taller than she was. "It's only unfortunate to bigoted old fools, Commander. I hope that group doesn't include you."

"Well, no, but..."

"The Prince has made a hash of things, and he doesn't even have the crown yet." Beecher jutted out his chin.

"That's not fair, Wilfred. He's had a string of terrible luck to be sure, but it's hardly his fault," said Lady Perma, her voice wavering.

"Doesn't change the fact that all this happened on his watch. The Fae King will have a fit once he finds out King Zane killed a flower maiden, and what do you think will happen with all those critters now that the Pearl Queen is dead?" Beecher almost hit the Duchess as he shook his cane at Lady Perma.

The Duchess's lip curled as she pushed its tip away with one finger. "If you don't mind, Wilfred—" Her tone was frigid.

Beecher said something, but the Duchess spoke over him. They were both drowned out by Lady Perma wailing, her words indecipherable.

Zander watched it all as if hovering outside himself. He wished they'd all just shut up and leave him in peace. The noise grew like a mosquito buzzing around his head. Finally, he shot to his feet and slammed his hand against the wooden table. "Enough!"

Instant silence fell on the room as every pair of eyes swiveled in his direction.

Before Zander could say anything more, the door opened. Everyone turned at this new interruption.

In the doorway stood Sir Lapin with the King next to him, lucid and in his right mind.

Chapter 65

THE SMALL BOAT SPED along the surface of the water, bouncing on the waves, the sail on its mast flapping in the breeze. Alice leaned against the rail and took deep breaths, trying to calm the churning of her stomach.

Instead, she concentrated on the singing that came from the sides of the ferry. Indigo, seeing how urgent the need was to get to the palace, had proven himself useful for once by enlisting the help of the Sea Clan. A host of brothers and sisters were pushing the ferry at a blazing pace across the water.

The boat hit a wave, and another surge of nausea choked her. She gripped the railing tighter and patted the shirt pocket Wickle had tucked himself into. He gave a sleepy chitter.

Someone stepped up behind her. "It helps if you look at the horizon, where the sea meets the sky." Chess's voice spoke into her ear, his warm breath making her shiver.

Her eyes popped open. "Thanks."

Her eyes sought the line of the horizon as she continued to take deep breaths, surprised at how much it helped.

He slid his arms around her waist, and she leaned into his warmth. With her back pressed against his chest, she felt the tension in his muscles. "We'll get back in time."

"I hope so. I hadn't planned on a quest to capture the Queen." His hand curled into a fist where it rested on the railing.

Alice covered his fist with her hand. "We're going as fast as we can. We have to trust that's enough."

Chess sighed. "Are you sure you don't want me to take you to the Looking Glass first?"

"You just said how anxious you are to get there, but..." She hesitated, a kernel of doubt taking root in her heart. It wasn't the first time he'd asked her. Maybe he didn't want her with him.

"What? You may as well tell me. You know I'll get it out of you eventually." There was a teasing note in his voice as his lips found the hollow behind her ear.

She spun in his arms, needing to see his face when he answered, and his beauty struck her all over again.

"Keep looking at me like that and I'll have to kiss you." His nose brushed hers.

The ferry lurched under her feet, and the nausea that had abated somewhat surged up her throat. She clapped a hand over her mouth and sucked in a deep breath, afraid she was going to heave all over him.

Chess chuckled and turned her around so she was facing the sea again. "On second thought, kissing will have to wait. Eyes on the horizon, love."

After a minute, the immediate danger of getting sick eased, and Chess rested his chin on her shoulder, his arms once again around her. "Now, tell me what you were going to say before I got distracted."

She tried to turn towards him, but his arms tightened. "No, love. The horizon—remember?"

"It's only..." She sighed, suddenly glad she didn't have to look at him. "You don't seem very keen on me coming with you. Would you... rather I went home?" She wanted the question to come out casually, but her voice sounded small in her own ears.

He leaned forward, twisting so he could see her face. "Alice, you can't think I want to get rid of you. I love you. It's only... I don't know what we're going to find when we get there, and I'm afraid something will happen to you."

She searched his face and saw only honesty there. She let out a breath. "Well, that makes two of us. I don't want anything to happen to you, either."

Chess's mouth curved into a lazy smile. "I was actually hoping I could go with you when you go home. We wouldn't want you to get lost again."

Despite the smile, there was a hint of doubt in his eyes that tugged at her heart. "I would love for you to come home with me and meet my family, Chess Felinas." She arched an eyebrow. "You might even win over Papa James."

"He doesn't stand a chance, love." He straightened, his arms bracketing her on either side. She leaned against him, warmth spreading through her.

She wasn't sure what the future held, but she wanted Chess in it, whether she was in Wonderland or the Mirror World.

Her thoughts were interrupted when the ferry slowed. The Fae around the boat let go, paddling backward. As the boat drifted further, the air around them congealed.

"We are going through the gate," called Azalea.

Alice barely had time to tighten her fingers on the railing before a tremendous pressure constricted her entire body as if it were being shoved through a too-small space.

A loud sucking sound was followed by a pop, and the pressure abruptly disappeared. She shook her head to clear her ears of their ringing. Wickle popped his head out, his eyes wider than usual.

She patted his head with a finger and looked around. They were floating near the shore of a quiet lake, mountains rising on all sides of them. "Where are we?"

Azalea appeared next to them. "We have arrived at the Gilded Lake." At Alice's blank expression, she added. "It is in the Gilded Mountains on Wonderland's mainland."

"It's where the cave was where Zander and I holed up," said Chess. He winked. "I'm sure you remember that."

Alice elbowed him. "As if I would forget that!" To be honest, she still wasn't entirely sure where the Gilded Mountains were in relation to the Red Palace, but at least she had a general idea of where they were.

Azalea moved to the front of the boat and drew symbols in the air. Then she splayed her fingers out as if she were throwing something. The boat slowly drifted towards the shore until the bottom scraped onto the sand.

Azalea walked towards the other end of the boat. "I will get the gangplank so we can disembark."

Chess pushed off the rail. "I should probably help her."

It didn't take long. Soon, Chess took Alice's hand, and together they made their way off the boat and onto Wonderland's shore. Alice was glad, as they splashed through the shallow water, that the clothing Azalea had loaned her included this pair of trousers. Once her feet hit solid land, Alice's shoulders sagged. It was like she had been holding her breath all the way over here.

"I never thought I'd be so happy to be in Wonderland again," she said.

Chess put a hand on his chest and lifted his eyebrows. "I certainly hope so, love. After all, I'm here."

She pulled her hand away and gave him a shove. "Yes, you and your enormous ego."

Azalea frowned at them. "I believe you were in a hurry."

Chess and Alice exchanged smiles before she sobered. "We won't have to walk all the way to the palace, will we?"

Chess grimaced. "No, but we will have to get off this mountain. Once we do, it's not too far to Caterpillar's. I can get a horse there."

Alice wrinkled her nose, remembering the apothecary where Chess, stuck in his cat form, had taken her. That seemed like a lifetime ago. "That still sounds like a long walk."

Azalea interrupted. "Where is the Red Palace from here?"

Chess pointed. "If you go straight east, you'll practically run into it."

Azalea nodded. "Then we do not need this Caterpillar's horses. I can fly us to the Red Palace, but you will need to shift into your cat form so I can carry you both."

Chess grinned and handed the velvet bag to Alice. "That is not a problem." Then he frowned, his hand going to his shirt pocket. After a moment's hesitation, he fished out the vial his mother had given him and held it out to Alice.

She took it gingerly. "Why are you giving this to me? Won't it be safer with you?"

He lifted one shoulder. "I'd feel better if you looked after it." She frowned, and he winked. "Call it a cat's intution."

"All right. If that's what you want." After a moment's debate, she carefully tucked it deep into her shirt pocket next to Wickle.

She'd barely blinked before both Chess and Azalea stood in their animal forms. Awkwardly, Alice climbed onto Azalea's back. It wasn't easy with nothing to hold on to while also hanging on to the artifact. Once she settled herself, she held out an arm. Chess leapt up, snuggling against her.

I could get used to this, love.

"And I could drop you, so don't get any ideas."

Chess's purr rumbled against her as Azalea lifted into the air, her wings making smooth strokes. Alice dug her fingers into the ruff of feathers around Azalea's neck, her stomach swooping as the ground fell away from them.

As they lifted above the trees, the mountainside spread out beneath her feet, the forest canopy like a rumpled quilt along its flank. Alice tightened her arms around Chess. No matter what they found when they got to the Red Palace, at least they were together. She hoped it would be enough.

Chapter 66

THE KING AND LAPIN walked into the meeting room, their footsteps loud in the silence. Zander scrambled to give his father his seat, but the King waved a hand. Instead, he moved to the empty chair on Zander's left. When Zander opened his mouth to protest, the King gave an almost imperceptible shake of his head before he sat down.

The Councilmembers shifted in their seats, their gazes bouncing between him and the King. Zander knew he had only a few moments to take control of the meeting or it might dissolve back into chaos. He drew himself up and addressed his first words to the newcomers. "Your Majesty, Sir Lapin, am I to assume the potion has worked?"

Sir Lapin leaned back in his chair, his whiskers twitching with satisfaction. "I am happy to report that it worked a treat, Your Highness." He clapped a hand on the King's shoulder. "Isn't that right, Your Majesty?"

The corners of the King's mouth tipped up, but he kept his expression solemn. "That is indeed correct,

Sir Lapin. I am grateful to you." His gaze moved to the Council. "I am happy to say I have complete control over my mind and actions."

Zander wanted to collapse into his chair with relief, but everyone was watching him, so instead he nodded. "Sir Lapin has been working on a potion since—"

"What potion? Why weren't we told of this?" Beecher demanded.

"He's trying to tell you now, Wilfred, if you'd shut up." The Duchess rolled her eyes.

Beecher's face turned red. "You might be happy with whatever blather they want to tell you, but I want answers!" He banged his cane to emphasize his words. "How do we even know this potion works and the King isn't merely having a good day? I'm not sure I want to trust everyone's safety to a bunch of flowers mixed up in a bottle."

As much as Zander disliked the old man, it was a fair question, and he said as much. "I'll let Sir Lapin take over now. He's the one who made the formula."

Lapin folded his paws on the table and leaned forward. "I understand your fears, Lord Beecher," he started, but Beecher interrupted.

"I never said I was afraid, but you can't have some beast running around the palace, terrorizing the maids."

"Yes, well, if you'll allow me to continue?" The rabbit lifted an eyebrow and waited until the older man gave a reluctant nod.

"The formula contains elements that allow the King to assert his will over the beast, and the good news is that it is easy to replicate. I am confident if we dose the King at regular intervals, it will keep the beast at bay indefinitely.

The longer we can do that, the more control the King will have until, hopefully, he won't need the formula anymore. He said himself that his thoughts were much clearer than they've been in a while. Isn't that right, Your Majesty?"

The King nodded slowly. "That's true." He looked at Lord Beecher. "Wilfred, let me assure you, nobody is more eager than I am that the beast doesn't make another appearance. I will happily drink Sir Lapin's formula for as long as it takes to rid myself of this affliction."

Lord Beecher opened his mouth, but the Duchess coolly intercepted him. "That sounds reasonable to me. Sir Lapin, are you willing to stay in the palace to oversee this, at least for the immediate future?"

Lady Perma clasped her hands. "That's an excellent notion, Leticia. It would be so nice for an expert to be here, now that dear Citrine is no longer with us." She pulled a handkerchief from the sleeve of her gown and dabbed at her eyes.

The words reverberated in Zander's chest, but he pushed the grief away. His grief could wait. Now, he needed to prevent the King from being pushed off the throne. He'd examine later why the idea of replacing his father caused such dread.

"If that's settled, then we should..." Zander's voice trailed off when the Commander leaned forward.

"I'm afraid it's not settled, and we're getting ahead of ourselves." The Commander steepled his fingers, the ruby on his pinky winking in the light. He peered around the table, his gaze finally landing on the King. "I'm sorry to say this, but even with the formula, it's too risky for you to be on the throne now."

All the oxygen sucked out of the room. Lord Dordo's eyes bugged out, and his mouth gaped open. Lady Perma let out a whimper. The Duchess narrowed her eyes at the Commander. "And why do you say that?" she asked.

One side of the Commander's mouth lifted as he nodded at the Duchess. "That's a fair question, Madam." He straightened. "I have always supported my brother's reign, and if this unfortunate circumstance hadn't happened, I would continue to support him until his son stepped onto the throne, and then I would be loyal to him in turn. But it happened. Begging your pardon, Your Majesty, but you killed two women, and both deaths are going to have repercussions. Serious ones."

He looked at the other Councilmembers. "What will we tell the Fae King about his flower maiden, dead at the hands of the king? Do you believe it will make a difference if he was out of his mind from some wayward curse when he's still occupying the throne with no assurance that he won't turn back into a beast? And we haven't even addressed the death of the Pearl Queen, the last of her line—or she may as well be since that brother of hers disappeared into the Mirror World a decade ago. She performed an important function, caring for the creatures of this realm and keeping them from becoming a threat. Now she is gone with nobody to replace her."

Zander couldn't listen to anymore and shot to his feet. "That's not fair, Commander. My father is not at fault for this. He's as much of a victim as anyone."

The Commander held up a hand. "I'm not saying he's at fault, at least not for the curse, but if we can't guarantee the Fae King or the people of Wonderland that he's completely cured, he shouldn't be sitting on the throne."

The Commander sat down, and after a moment of stunned silence, voices erupted around the room. The Duchess started talking to the Commander in a furious whisper, while next to her, Lady Perma burst into tears again.

Lord Dordo kept repeating, "I say, this is a cannibal," over and over until the Duchess whirled towards him. "Either get a thesaurus or shut up, Dordo!" she snapped, and then whipped back around and continued whatever she'd been telling the Commander. By her expression, Zander didn't envy him.

Beecher thumped his cane on the ground, spluttering angrily, but nobody was paying him any attention.

"Quiet!" The King's voice drowned out the babbling, and silence fell like a heavy blanket over the room. He stood, shoulders back, chin up as every eye in the room zeroed in on him. Lady Perma dabbed at her eyes, an occasional whimper escaping.

"Now then, the Commander has some excellent points." When Zander protested, the King laid a hand on his arm. "No, son, I appreciate your support, but these are genuine concerns. This is not a time to let our feelings overcome our sense. I am grateful to Sir Lapin for the formula he devised and believe that it is the cause of my current clarity of mind. However, as the Commander said, we don't know how it will work long-term. I am hopeful it will be the answer I need, but to continue without actual proof isn't wise." He drew in a deep breath. "For that reason, it's my opinion that it is in the best interests of everyone for me to step aside as the ruler of Wonderland, and for my son, Prince Zander, to rule in my place."

The King sank back into his chair, his steely gaze daring anyone to naysay him. Zander wasn't sure what he should do. He felt stupid for not realizing he might end up asked to take charge, and at the same time, he wanted to protest his father's decision. It wasn't right.

Before he could say anything, though, Lord Beecher snorted. "Bah! Your son isn't fit, either, with that Gene of his." He pointed his cane at the King and shook it. "And if you think the residents of Wonderland will accept him any better than I do, you're not as clearheaded as you believe."

The Commander spoke up, interrupting as the others started arguing with Beecher. "We won't get anywhere if everyone simply shouts over each other." He waited until the voices died down again. "Now then, the Prince is a good man, but Beecher has a point. The residents are going to be wary of a prince who has the Drifter Gene, especially after recent events. They won't feel safe, and there is a reason for their worry."

The Commander's words hit Zander like a punch to the gut. "You believe I'd be a danger to my own people?"

The Commander blew out a breath. "Of course not, Your Highness, but we need to understand this from the people's perspective. All they know are the old stories of the last Jabberwock Prince. What makes you any different?"

"What about the artifact? If I get rid of my Drifter Gene, this won't even be an issue," Zander said.

The Commander sighed. "That's a possible answer, but the truth is, we don't know if that will even work. There's a good chance Chess won't be able to convince King Thorne to give him the artifact."

Lapin pulled the pipe out of his mouth. "And if the King can't rule and Zander isn't fit, who does that leave us with, Commander? You?"

He spoke his words in a mild tone, but everyone in the room heard the accusation in them.

"I still don't understand why you're here, Lapin. You aren't part of the Council, and your opinion doesn't count!" Beecher said, his face turning an alarming shade of purple.

"I'm merely asking a question that needs to be asked, Lord Beecher." The rabbit shrugged his furry shoulders. "I'm not sure why you're getting so upset."

"Upset? Upset? You haven't seen me upset, Rabbit!"

Lady Perma gasped. "Really, Lord Beecher. That's completely unnecessary."

"Quite ungainly, I say," chirped Lord Dordo.

"You haven't answered the question, Commander," said the Duchess, her cool voice cutting through the noise of the others.

The Commander looked down at her. "I am not an ambitious man, Duchess, and I didn't bring up these concerns to somehow connive my way onto the throne. I brought them up because I want to protect the throne and this Kingdom. That's my duty, after all."

Zander swallowed, a sense of defeat weighing on him. He knew what he needed to do. He couldn't deny part of him was relieved, but a bigger part of him felt like a failure. He refused to look at his father when he spoke, afraid to see the disappointment on his face. Instead, he lifted his chin and focused his gaze just above everyone's heads. "Although the Commander hasn't asked for the throne, it might be wise to give it to him."

There was a collective gasp, and Lapin leaned forward. "Are you sure that's what you want, Your Highness?"

Zander couldn't speak past the lump in his throat, but he nodded. He risked a glance at his father. The King's expression was sorrowful but resigned as he stared down at his clasped hands.

The Duchess spoke up before Beecher could say anything. "If this is what the Prince wants, I propose the Commander serve as ruler on the interim basis of a month, at which time we will revisit who should rule permanently. That should give young Felinas more than enough time to return with the artifact." She turned and narrowed her eyes at the Commander. "Are you willing to serve under those conditions?"

The Commander dipped his head. "I will serve in whatever capacity the Council sees fit to put me in."

"A month! What good will that do us?" interrupted Beecher. "I'm too old for all this nonsense!"

The Duchess's mouth turned into a wintry smile. "Then I suggest you quit, Wilfred, and someone with more vigor can take your spot." She ignored his spluttering and her smile turned warmer. "Who knows? Maybe the people of Wonderland will surprise us all."

It didn't take long for the Council to vote. In less than a minute, the power of the throne was transferred to the Commander with a unanimous vote. Zander felt numb.

After that, the meeting quickly adjourned. Chairs scraped as Councilmembers stood and began gathering their things, carefully avoiding both Zander and his father, but a commotion in the hall caught everyone's attention.

Zander looked up, and a smile spread over his face as his muscles loosened.

Chess and Alice stood in the doorway.

Zander ignored the eruption of voices and jumped to his feet. He ran over to his friends, grabbing Chess in a hug and then turning to Alice.

"What are you doing here?"

Alice laughed. "Well, hello to you too, Zander!"

"Whatever happened, I'm happy to see you—both of you," Zander said and pulled her into a hug too. When he released her, his gaze fell on the person still standing in the hallway. Although the tall Fae woman was beautiful in an alien sort of way, that wasn't what gave him pause. It was the fact she fairly bristled with weapons, and in her hand, she gripped a velvet bag. He had a sinking feeling that he knew what was in it. Her watchful stance and the way her gaze traveled around the room, obviously assessing it and the people in it, added to his suspicions.

"Who is that, and why does she look like she's ready to attack everyone?" he asked Chess, his eyebrows rising.

Chess grinned. "Oh, don't mind her. That's my cousin, Azalea. Between you and me, I think she cuddles her weapons when nobody's looking."

By this time, the Commander stood at Zander's elbow. His gaze flicked between Chess and Alice and then to the Fae woman. "Obviously, a lot happened on your trip, son. You'd best update everyone." He gave Chess's shoulder a brief squeeze before he turned and strode to the head of the table, motioning for Chess, Alice, and the Fae woman to join them.

As the three took their seats, the Council quieted, but Zander could see the speculation in everyone's eyes as some openly stared at the blue-skinned Fae woman and the bag she set on the table in front of her.

Chess shot him a glance, his brows rising when Zander sat on the Commander's left instead of at the head of the table. Zander sighed. Chess probably would not be happy about the news that the Commander was now the interim ruler. Come to think of it, should they still call him the Commander? He rubbed two fingers against the middle of his forehead where a dull headache had started.

"Now then," the Commander said once he had everyone's attention. "Why don't you update us, Chess, and perhaps introduce us to your guest."

Chess gave his father a cheeky smile. "This is Alice, whom you've all met before." He raised her hand and pressed a kiss to the back of it. Her face turned pink even as she frowned at him. "But I'm guessing you were more interested in her." He nodded at the Fae woman who straightened her already ramrod posture. "That is King Thorne's daughter, my cousin, and your niece, Princess Azalea."

If Chess's words bothered him at all, the Commander didn't show it. However, the others at the table had more reaction. Lady Perma's eyes gleamed as she glanced between the Commander and Azalea. Predictably, Beecher glowered, his knuckles white on the handle of his cane. Dordo gaped.

The Commander spoke, his tone mild. "It's good to meet you. Now then, Chess..."

But of course, Beecher couldn't keep silent. "I don't care who she's related to. She doesn't belong in our Council meeting, and for that matter, neither does that young chit of a girl." He jabbed a finger at Alice. "I thought we sent her home already, but she keeps turning up like a bad penny."

The Duchess rolled her eyes. "Honestly, Wilfred, this meeting has already dragged on for an interminable length. If you keep interrupting, we'll never get home for tea."

Lord Beecher snorted. "I think tea is the least of our worries, not when—"

"Yes, Lord Beecher, we do have weighty matters to discuss yet. Now, let's allow Chess to update us," the Commander interrupted, before turning towards his son. "I'm assuming you've been successful."

Chess nodded and held out his hand. Azalea passed him the velvet bag with obvious reluctance. "We were, but... I have to caution against using this."

"While I appreciate your thoughts, that's not your decision. It's the Prince's." The weight of every gaze fell onto Zander, and he suddenly found breathing difficult.

The Commander waved a hand. "Show us what King Thorne gave you."

Chess loosened the strings on the bag and pulled out the ivory box. He set it on the table. A plain cream color, its only ornamentation were the flowers and vines carved into it.

A long silence stretched as everyone waited for him to say something. He licked his lips. "I... I suppose..."

The door to the room swung open to reveal Anders, his wispy hair sticking up like a fuzzy halo. He drew himself up and bowed. "Your Majesty, Your Highness, there is someone who wishes to speak to you. Shall I tell him to wait in the—"

Anders staggered as a blue and silver streak darted between his legs. Before Zander could get a good look at the animal, it shimmered into a large blue-skinned Fae man. "We don't have time for this," the man rasped out, and various wounds on his face and torso dripped blood on the floor.

"Indigo?" Alice gasped and hopped to her feet.

He smirked at her as she hurried over to him, Chess right behind her. Whatever the Fae man had been about to say was interrupted by Azalea. She had already shot to her feet, her face pale. "Father?"

"He's fine." Indigo grimaced as Alice pushed a hand against a deep cut on his forearm. "I can't say the same for the rest of Underhill." He gestured towards the bag lying on the table. "If I were you, I'd hide that. She's not far behind me."

The Commander raised an eyebrow. "She?"

Indigo rolled his eyes. "The Queen, of course. She's escaped."

Chapter 67

THE WORDS WERE BARELY out of Indigo's mouth when a shadow fell over the large picture window on the far side of the meeting room.

Lady Perma shrieked as the ruby red Jabberwock arrowed towards the glass. Lord Dordo dove under the table, only his shaking ankles in view.

Indigo shoved Alice behind him, and she braced herself for the shattering of glass, but nothing happened.

Cautiously, she stepped around Indigo. The Queen had landed gracefully on the lawn just outside the window.

There was a moment of confused silence before Azalea reacted. Darting forward, she shoved the artifact back into its bag in one smooth movement and tossed it in Alice's direction. Azalea didn't even wait to see if Alice caught it before she drew both her swords, one for each hand, and faced the Queen.

Surprised, Alice barely got her hands up in time to catch the heavy bag before it smacked her in the face.

"Protect the artifact. The Queen must not get it." Azalea's gaze never wavered from the Jabberwock on the other side of the glass as she spoke.

Indigo tried to pull Alice towards the door, but Chess blocked him. "You help your sister. I'll protect Alice."

The Fae opened his mouth to argue, but a loud scraping sound made them all jump. When Alice looked at the window, ice skated down her spine and she hugged the artifact to her chest.

Using one long talon, the Queen was cutting a large square in the glass. Her reptilian mouth curved into a facsimile of a smile, as her dark gaze caught Alice's, pinning her to the spot. It was clear she was enjoying the dragged-out drama of her entrance. Chess's voice broke the spell. "We've got to get out of here. Now."

"But where will we go?" Alice asked as they hurried to the door.

Chess glanced over his shoulder. "We'll figure that out when we're out of here."

His hand closed over the doorknob but froze when a horribly familiar voice spoke. "I'm afraid I can't let you do that, son."

Chess's eyes closed briefly, as if bracing against a blow, and Alice felt his pain as if it were her own. She put her hand on his arm, and their gazes met briefly before they turned back.

The Commander stood at one end of the room, his drawn sword at Zander's throat. They were a bit removed from the rest of the group. Zander had probably been planning to shift before the Commander got to him.

Alice's gaze flew over the rest of the group, frozen in an odd tableau. The Duchess had a dagger in her hand, and Lord Beecher's cane was in the air. Sir Lapin stood by the King, who trained his anguished gaze on Zander. The Queen's talon scraping on the glass was the only sound in the room.

Beecher was the first one to break the silence. "What is the meaning of this, Commander? Have you lost your mind?"

A faint smile touched the Commander's lips. "You're the one that put me in charge, for which you have my thanks." His gaze swept over Alice. "Now put the artifact on the table or you'll force me to hurt the Prince." There was something about the Commander's emotionless, polite tone that was more menacing than if he'd been yelling at her.

Alice hugged the bag closer and glanced at the Queen. It wouldn't take her long before she was through, and then they'd all be done. Zander was their only chance against the Queen, and he couldn't shift with the Commander's sword at his throat. Alice's mind raced, and then Chess caught her eye, his gaze flicking from his father as he tipped his head the tiniest fraction towards the door.

Alice wasn't sure what he was trying to tell her, but then he turned back to his father. "I should have known nobody was that duty bound." Chess's voice was a snarl, and he took a step forward. The Commander's attention shifted from Alice to his son, and understanding hit Alice.

With the Commander's eyes on Chess, she slid closer to the door. She only had a few yards to go.

"I'm not the one who doesn't understand duty." The Commander's voice was even, but his hand spasmed on the hilt of his sword.

Chess gave a short bark of laughter and moved closer. "That's funny. I'm not the one holding the crown Prince at sword point. That would be you, the man who sacrificed his wife and son on the altar of duty, and now look where we are."

The Commander tightened his hold on Zander. "Hold your tongue. You have no idea what you're talking about." His eyes darted around the room and landed on Alice. She froze, now only a few feet from escape. The Commander frowned, but Chess continued to hammer at him.

"You should know by now I'm not very good at taking orders, Father. After all, you're always the one harping about that particular failing of mine." He sneered. "Tell me, when did love—or maybe it was lust—overpower your sense of duty?" Chess was now only a few yards from his father and Zander. Off to the side, the King's body was rigid.

A sheen of sweat broke out on the Commander's brow, and he jerked Zander tighter. A thin trickle of blood dripped down the Prince's neck. "Don't come any closer. I know what you're doing, and it won't work."

Chess halted and put his hands up. "You can't be stupid enough to think she'll be loyal to you. Look what she's done to the King and to Zander."

The Commander's hand shook, and the sword bit deeper into Zander's neck, who grunted with pain. "Please, son, back up. Do it now before you make me hurt him."

The sun sparkled off the ruby ring on his pinky. Alice reached the door as the square of glass in the window came loose. It fell in a shower of sparkling pieces, hitting the floor with an oddly harmonious tinkle of sounds.

Alice didn't wait to see what happened. She darted out the door as a loud roar shook the ground under her feet. Obeying instinct, she dove to the side and a moment later, a gout of flame rushed through the doorway after her. She scrambled up and ran blindly down the hallway.

Chapter 68

CHESS'S HEART STOPPED AS the gout of flame followed Alice out the door. When it died down, he was almost afraid to look, but the hall, while scorched, was empty. His heart picked up its rhythm again.

The Jabberwock pushed into the room through the window, her scaled sides scraping more glass onto the floor. The Queen didn't even glance at anyone in the room, but headed towards the hallway where Alice had disappeared.

Azalea vaulted into the Queen's path, both swords raised, and the Queen snarled at her. The Jabberwock drew back her head and flames erupted from her mouth, but Azalea leapt out of the way in a blur of speed, then darted back in and stabbed the Queen's front leg. The Queen blew another flash of fire, this time barely missing the Fae woman, but the flames caught on a cloth covering a side table.

Indigo shrank down to his ferret form and darted in and out of the Queen's legs, making himself a distraction so his sister could attack.

Chess hesitated, his gaze bouncing between the battle with the Queen and the Commander. His father had dragged Zander further away, his sword still pressed to the Prince's throat.

For now, the Fae siblings had the Queen's attention. There wasn't much Chess could do to help, but if he could get Zander away from the Commander, they might have a chance to survive this.

Lapin called his name from the other corner of the room where he was herding the Councilmembers towards a servant's entrance.

Another crash drowned out what the rabbit was trying to say, and Chess shook his head.

The rabbit held up his paw and wiggled his last digit. The only word Chess caught was "off" before the rabbit grasped Dordo by the collar and yanked him out of the path of the Queen's tail.

Chess ducked as a piece of furniture flew by his head, and behind him, Indigo let out a pained cry. The Queen roared, and Chess's ears rang.

He turned back to the Commander. The smoke tickled his throat, and the crackle of flames filled the air. If they didn't put them out, the fire would become more of a problem than the Queen. He edged closer to his father, but the Commander's blade dug into Zander's throat and blood flowed down his neck, staining the neckline of his shirt.

"Stay back, Chess. Neither of wants the Prince dead." The Commander's expression was strangely wooden.

A gust of wind from the window swept some of the smoke away, and as a beam of sunlight glanced off the pinky ring his father wore, the ruby winking at him, something niggled at Chess.

Another roar rang out, and the floor shook. Chess used the distraction to inch closer. Then the Commander glanced behind him and lifted his sword. Before Chess or Zander could react, he brought the sword pommel down hard on Zander's head, and his friend dropped like a stone to the ground.

Zander had barely touched the ground when the King lunged towards the Commander, who whirled to meet him. Chess launched himself towards the fray to help, but something hard slammed into him. His vision blurred, and he crumpled to his knees. By the time his eyesight cleared, the King was lying next to his son, and the Queen loomed over him, her jaws wide.

Chess slumped back onto his heels, his head still ringing from the blow. At least Alice had gotten away. It was small comfort, but he clung to it.

He stared defiantly up at the Queen. If she was going to kill him, she'd have to do it to his face.

Steam wafted up from her nostrils, and then her Jabberwock form shrank and twisted until the Queen stood there, a smudge of dirt on her otherwise pristine face. He staggered to his feet and with the last of his energy, he lunged at her, but his shirt collar brought him up short, digging into his neck. His father had grabbed him, and the sharp point of his sword poked into Chess's back.

The Queen held up a finger and wagged it at him. "Now, now, Chess, you, of all people, should know how to treat a lady."

Chess made a show of glancing around. "You'll have to pardon me. I didn't know one was present."

The Queen stepped closer and smiled at him. Then she slapped him, hard, across the face. Pain bloomed through his skull as his head rocked back, and his cheek throbbed. "That's your first warning to keep a civil tongue in your head." She turned to the Commander. "Have the guards lock the rest of them up."

"What about the Council and Sir Lapin?" The Commander asked.

The Queen gave a dainty shrug. "The Council doesn't matter. Once I have the artifact, they won't have any choice but to go along or they'll die. As for Lapin, if we act quickly enough, he won't be a threat."

The Commander tightened his grip on Chess's shirt, almost choking him. "What about him?"

The Queen looked him over. "As soon as you've taken care of the rest of them, bring him to my chambers. Don't dawdle. I don't want Sir Lapin to get any heroic ideas."

Ice formed in Chess's stomach, but he smirked at her. "I'm flattered, Lyssandra, but you really aren't my type."

She shook her head, amused. "Don't worry, you aren't mine, either." A smile spread over her face and her eyes glittered. "But you're Alice's, aren't you?"

Icy cold spread over Chess's skin. The Queen winked at him and then swept from the room, stepping over bodies and broken furniture on her way.

Chapter 69

ALICE HURTLED DOWN THE hallway, taking one turn and then another before she burst into the front foyer. Her feet skidded on the slick marble floor, and she almost crashed into a giant vase.

Her heart hammered in her throat as her gaze darted from the front doors to the grand staircase. Was it only a fortnight since she and Citrine had descended for Zander and Alice's engagement ball? So much had happened since then, and she still was running for her life. Alice shook her head, trying to get her careening thoughts under control

A muffled crash followed by a muted roar made her jump, and Wickle popped his head out of her pocket.

Alice hide. Not safe.

She absently patted his head. "Yes, but I'm not sure where..." She trailed off, her gaze going to the staircase. No, she shouldn't go up. She might get trapped. Another crash made Wickle cheep in alarm.

Alice not stay. Go.

She looked at the doors, tempted to leave the palace all together. Of course, then nobody would know where she was, and she wasn't sure how she'd let anyone know and... weren't there usually soldiers stationed by the front doors? She clutched the velvet bag to her chest and squeezed her eyes shut. If she could just catch her breath and think... but the band around her chest tightened.

A small paw patted her cheek.

Alice all right?

She looked down to find the snark partially out of her shirt pocket, staring up at her. His eyes narrowed in concern.

The band loosened, and Alice drew in a shaky breath. "I'm all right, Wickle. We just need to find somewhere to hole up until it's safe. Maybe the stables would be a good option."

Wickle chittered at her. She wasn't sure if he was agreeing or not, but she couldn't stay out in the open. She had no idea who was on the Commander's side in all of this. At the thought, her heart constricted for Chess. He sometimes clashed with his father, but this was a whole other level of hurt.

She gave herself a shake. Chess wouldn't thank her if she got herself caught. She needed to get moving.

"Miss Alice!"

Alice yelped in surprise and spun towards the voice.

"I didn't mean to startle you, Miss." Anders scurried out of a hallway on the other side of the foyer, his face pale and his hair standing out around his head like a fuzzy halo.

"Anders, what are you—"

A loud crash made them duck their heads and huddle towards each other. Wickle cheeped loudly in alarm. Anders eyed the snark before he glanced towards the noise. "You shouldn't be out here, Miss."

"I realize that, but I have to hide this." Alice held up the bag.

"Come with me, Miss." He led her back down the hallway from which he'd emerged.

By some silent agreement, neither of them spoke until Anders turned down another hallway, went through a door, and then down a short staircase. When they reached the bottom, his rigid posture relaxed a fraction. "We should be safe for the moment."

"Where are we going?" Alice asked. The simple stone floor and unadorned walls revealed this area was for the servants.

"This leads down to the kitchens and the servants' hall. You can access the stables easily from there in case you must leave."

Alice paused, and Anders looked back at her. "Miss, are you coming?"

"I appreciate this, Anders, I really do, but I don't want to put you or any of your staff in danger."

A faint smile ghosted across his face. "I'm fairly certain Her Majesty the Queen couldn't find her way down here without help." His mouth pressed into a line. "Help, none of my staff will give her, I can assure you."

They passed the doorway to the kitchens. Despite a Jabberwock attacking the royal family, the room bustled with activity, and steam billowed off of pots on a large stove. Apparently, luncheon was prepared whether the palace was falling on everyone's heads or not.

"You can rest in here." Anders pushed open a door to reveal someone's living quarters. The room held a neatly made bed in one corner. A plain dresser with a small basin and pitcher on top stood next to the bed. On the opposite side of the room, a deep club chair with a footstool sat next to a small pot-bellied stove. Behind the chair, books lined a set of shelves.

"Oh, I don't want to put anyone out of their own room," Alice protested.

Anders stood up straighter. "These are my quarters, Miss, and I don't mind. Sir Chess would want you safe. The Prince too."

Tears burned her eyes and Alice blinked rapidly, knowing she'd only embarrass them both if she started crying. "Thank you, Anders. You didn't have to do this for me."

Anders bowed his head. "Of course, I did, Miss. Would you like some tea or perhaps a snack?"

"A snack... now?" Alice raised an eyebrow.

Anders shrugged. "The kitchen is just a few steps away, so it isn't any bother at all."

"I... I guess so. Thank you?"

He bobbed his head again. "Now, if you'll excuse me, I need to check the servants' passages to make sure none of the staff are in harm's way. I'll inform the kitchen about your tea on my way out."

Anders turned and trotted back up the hall. Not sure what else to do, Alice dropped into the chair and hugged the velvet bag to her chest.

Wickle chittered at her and crawled out of her pocket to perch on her shoulder. *Safe now?*

She ruffled her fingers through his blue fur. "For now, but I don't know how long that will last."

Wickle wheeked softly in her ear. *Kill Queen?*

"You're a bloodthirsty little thing, aren't you?" She couldn't help the smile that curved her lips. "But I'll leave that up to the others. I don't want to be the one to make that kind of decision."

Queen bad.

"Yes, I suppose she is, but that doesn't mean I want to be the one to put an end to her."

Enemies must die. Wickle emphasized his words by stamping one of his small feet.

"Erm..."

The door cracked open and a young maid hustled into the room with a tray that held a teapot, a cup, and two plates, one of finger sandwiches and another with cookies glazed with some kind of jam. The girl set the tray on the side table next to Alice and then dipped a curtsey. "If you'uns need anything else, you only need to ask, Miss."

"Thank you, I will."

The girl hurried back out and pulled the door shut behind her. Alice poured some tea into the cup and lifted the steaming liquid to her lips. The only sound in the room was the tick of the fat clock that sat on the bookshelf. She set the cup back in its saucer and broke off a piece of a sandwich and gave it to Wickle. He hummed happily as he took it.

"It's freakishly odd that I'm sitting here in this cozy room having tea, and somewhere above us, everyone's fighting for their lives. It doesn't seem right, Wickle."

Wickle blinked at her. *Hungry. More food.*

Alice broke off another piece of sandwich and gave it to him. "Nothing bothers your appetite, does it?" Her own stomach grumbled loudly, and she snorted. "Or mine either, I guess." She picked up a sandwich. She supposed she may as well eat while she had the chance.

Chapter 70

ALICE FINISHED THE FOOD with Wickle's help, and the little snark curled up on her lap to sleep. Alice leaned her head back against the chair and let her mind turn the situation over and over. She still couldn't quite believe the Commander had betrayed them that way. It made little sense, from what she observed of the man. He'd always seemed dedicated and loyal.

She glanced up at the ceiling. Even if the fighting was still going on, she was on the opposite side of the palace. She wished there was a way to find out what was happening. If Zander hadn't gotten free, she didn't like their chances of beating the Queen in her Jabberwock form.

She wanted to get up and pace but didn't want to disturb the snark. She fingered the drawstring on the velvet bag. They had this powerful Fae artifact. Surely there was some way to use it to their advantage. Even in the bag, she could feel the object's faint buzz of magic.

A knock sounded on the door, and she jerked in surprise. Wickle sat up, yawning hugely.

She scooped the snark into her hand before she crossed the room to open the door.

Anders stood there, but he wasn't alone. Lapin, along with the Council, crowded behind him in the narrow hallway, all of them speaking at once.

A loud, shrill whistle cut them off, and silence descended on the group. The Duchess pulled her fingers from her mouth and smiled at Alice. "I see you've managed to survive."

Desperate for information, Alice didn't even bother with a greeting. "What's happened? Where are the others? Are they all right?"

Lapin reached around Anders and patted her hand. "Why don't we go to the servants' hall? We certainly can't all fit in here."

Alice felt her stomach clench, but he was right. She nodded at Anders, and he led the group to the servants' hall. When they got there, a few young men sat around the table. Anders shooed them out before he gestured towards the long table. "This room is at your disposal as long as you need it. Please inform me if you need anything at all."

Anders had barely moved away from the door before Alice turned to Lapin. "Was Chess all right when you left?"

Beecher harrumphed. "I would think the Prince and the King are more important than that Felinas boy."

"Not to me!" Alice said, a snarl in her voice. She turned back to Lapin. "Please tell me—I... I have to know if..."

In the brief pause, Lady Perma's soft sobs could be heard, and something in Alice broke. Chess couldn't be gone. He had to be all right. If he was... The words wouldn't form in her mind. Lapin covered her hands with his paw, and it was only then that Alice realized she was wringing them.

"He was alive the last time I looked, and so were the Prince and the King, for that matter..." He paused. "But I'm not sure about the Fae who accompanied you. I believe the woman was injured."

Alice slumped forward. Guilt and relief warred inside of her. Of course, she didn't want anything to happen to the others, either, but if it came down to Chess or them... A sob caught her throat and she swallowed it down.

The Duchess pushed a handkerchief into her hands. "I believe your young man will prove rather difficult to get rid of, my dear. Don't you worry."

Alice crumpled the handkerchief in her hand and straightened in her chair. "I hope you're right, but how did you all get away?"

"Servants' entrance. Every room has one in a place like this." Lapin leaned back in his chair.

"Glad someone was thinking clearly." Beecher's voice was gruff, but for once he wasn't scowling.

Lord Dordo had been silent until now, his eyes large and blinking as if he were in shock, so Alice was surprised when he spoke and it made sense, at least mostly. "I say, we're safe for the moment, but shouldn't we be doing something? There's a bastion going on upstairs, and it didn't look like our side was winning."

Everyone started talking again, and Alice let the voices ripple over her, her own mind once again turning over what she knew. Finally, she reached down and lifted the velvet bag and set it on the table. Carefully, she loosened the drawstring closure and pulled the alabaster box out.

As soon as she opened the bag, the magic of the item pulsed into the room.

Everyone fell silent for a long moment.

"What in tarnation do you think you're doing, girl? Do you even understand what it does?" Beecher scowled at the box and then Alice.

"Actually, I do. It's meant to amplify things, and if we put the right potion in it, we might be able to use it against the Queen."

Lapin folded his hands over his stomach. "Fae artifacts can be dangerous, but you're right. We…"

He trailed off when Anders appeared at the door again, his face devoid of all color. He lifted a shaking hand that held a piece of paper. "A message, for Miss Alice." He swallowed. "From Her Majesty, the Queen."

For a long moment, Alice felt paralyzed. She stared at the slip of paper in Anders' hand like a mouse stared at a snake, and the rest of the room disappeared from sight and sound.

Alice all right?

Wickle patted her face, and the sounds of the room rushed back in. She rose on shaking legs and walked over to Anders and took the paper. Still, she didn't open it.

"Don't just stand there like a nitwit. Read it!" Beecher's voice boomed out, making Alice flinch.

She unfolded the paper with trembling fingers. The words made her entire body go cold.

"Well? What does it say?" Beecher banged his cane on the floor.

Alice looked up at the group. She had to clear her throat twice before she could get the words out. "The

Queen wants the artifact... or she'll have the Commander kill Chess."

The Duchess's mouth twisted into a sneer. "It's so typical of that wretched woman to make this into a melodrama. She could at least strive not to be so tediously predictable."

Alice couldn't help but agree with the Duchess... but maybe they could use this weakness of the Queen's to their advantage somehow.

Lapin ignored the Duchess's comment and asked, "How much time do we have?"

"An hour." Even as Alice answered, the weight of trying to stop the Queen, to save Chess, almost crushed her into the floor.

Lapin got up and plucked the paper from Alice's nerveless fingers and examined it. The room seemed to hold its collective breath. When he looked up, his face creased in apology. "We can't let the Queen have that artifact."

Alice crossed her arms. "I'm not daft. I know that, but we can't let Chess die, either. Don't you have some kind of potion so we might use the artifact against the Queen?"

Lapin frowned, and Anders spoke up. "Begging your pardon, Miss, the palace is full of soldiers. Sir Lapin won't be able to get to any of his supplies without running into them. I don't think any of the staff can, either."

Alice's face scrunched up in confusion. "But why would they listen to the Queen? Surely, they can't all be turncoats?"

The Councilmembers exchanged glances, and Beecher cleared his throat awkwardly. Alice narrowed her eyes. "What aren't you telling me?"

The Duchess folded her hands on the table. "I'm afraid we made the Commander the interim king. They have no choice but to obey him."

"What? Why would you do that?" Alice wanted to punch something.

The Duchess shrugged. "It wasn't my idea, I can assure you, but the Prince was in favor of it. And it's only for a month."

"Well, that jolly well doesn't help us now, does it?" Alice turned back to the rest of the Council. "There has to be something we can do. I won't let Chess die, even if I have to kill the Queen myself."

Wickle purred loudly from her shoulder, and the Duchess frowned.

Help save mate. Kill Queen.

Lady Perma sniffled into her handkerchief. "He's such a handsome young man. Surely, there's something we can do." She looked around hopefully.

Beecher leaned on his cane. "Nobody wants to see the boy die, but surely even you realize we can't hand so much power over to that woman." He glanced up at Alice, and his voice was oddly gentle. "I'm sorry, girl. I can see you care for him, but there's not enough time, not with the Commander helping her too."

"And that's another thing—why aren't you all more surprised about the Commander? He's betrayed the entire Kingdom. Why would he do that?" Alice asked.

Lapin waved a hand. "Oh, that's not his fault."

Alice closed her eyes briefly. "Excuse me?"

Lord Dordo tapped his pinky finger. "The Queen's entailed him."

The Duchess heaved a sigh. "For heaven's sake, Dordo." She turned back to a confused Alice. "The Queen's enchanted him. I don't suppose you noticed the new ring he was wearing in all the commotion, but Sir Lapin is sure it's what's holding him under her spell."

Lapin nodded. "I'm afraid so. If we get that ring off of him, it would go a long way towards helping our cause."

"I don't see how we can do that, so as far as I'm concerned, he's still the enemy." Alice didn't want to sound unfeeling, but she was acutely aware that every minute that ticked by was one less Chess had to live. Tears pressed at the backs of her eyes, but she willed them away. She would break down later. Now she needed to act.

Her gaze swept over the group. "I'm going to save Chess whether you lot help me or not." She turned to Anders. "Do you know where the Queen is keeping him?"

Anders bobbed his head. "Yes, Miss. She has him with her and the Commander in the garden room."

"There's a servant's entrance into there, isn't there?" Alice asked.

Anders' eyes widened. "Yes, Miss, but—"

"Show me where it is."

Lapin put a hand on her arm. "What do you hope to accomplish by bearding the dragon in her den, my dear?"

Alice lifted her chin and put a hand over her snark's back. "I'm going to rescue Chess, and if I have to kill the Queen to do it, I will. Wickle will help me even if the rest of you won't."

"Wonder preserve me from young love," the Duchess said, rolling her eyes. "The only thing you'll accomplish by haring off is to get yourself killed. Do you really want to force Sir Chess to watch that witch kill you?"

Alice clenched her fists. "Well, none of you are going to help me, so what choice do I have?"

Lapin laid a paw on her shoulder, the one that didn't contain a snark. "We didn't say we wouldn't help you, only that it will be terribly difficult."

A tear slipped out and rolled down Alice's cheek. Impatiently, she wiped it away. "I won't lose him, not now."

Lapin smiled. "We'll try our hardest to make sure you don't, but…"

"You're giving the girl false hope," interjected Beecher. "There's nothing we can do. Even if you manage to pull a potion out of thin air, I'm not too sure we should mess around with that thing. We don't even know how it works." He gestured towards the ivory-colored box.

"That's not true," Alice protested. "Larkspur told us. You have to pour the potion inside the box, and then whoever opens it next, they'll be hit with a much stronger version of whatever's in there." Lapin pulled out a small bottle from his vest pocket, and hope soared in Alice's heart. He held it up and frowned. "This is what I used on the King, but there are only a few drops left." He pulled down one of his ears and worried its tip. "Perhaps I might find something in the kitchens to add to it…"

Suddenly, Wickle squeaked loudly and scrambled down Alice's shirt front into her pocket. After a moment of rummaging about, a dark green vial became visible and Wickle popped up next to it. Alice pulled it out, frowning, and then bolted upright as she realized what it was.

She patted the snark's head and he purred loudly. "I totally forgot this, Wickle." She turned to the others, the glass bottle lying in her palm. "Larkspur gave us this for the King. She said it might help him keep control."

Lapin held out his hand, and she passed it to him. He held it up to the light. "Do you have any idea what's in it?"

Alice shook her head. "No, but she said it would help the King resist the beast."

Lapin stroked his chin with one paw and examined the bottle. He pulled the cork out and took several whiffs, his nose twitching back and forth. "Hmm, this has Muddle Weed, and I also detect traces of Willwort. Both plants help to suppress magic. If the box amplifies it enough, this might work to keep the Queen from her Jabberwock form."

Beecher banged his cane on the floor, startling everyone. "What do you mean, it *might* work? We can't only hope. We have to be sure. If that woman gets her hands on this artifact, the Felinas boy won't be the only one dead. The entire Kingdom will be in jeopardy. Is one life worth that?"

The question hung in the air. Lady Perma whimpered, and Lord Dordo squirmed in his chair, looking everywhere but at Alice.

The Duchess raised an eyebrow. "Are you saying you're afraid, Wilfred?"

"Blast it, woman, that's not what I said and you know it." He creaked to a standing position. "I'm assuming you're planning on pouring the potion in the box there and, what, handing it over to the Queen?"

Lapin nodded. "Yes, that's about the sum of it, Lord Beecher."

"Have you all lost your minds? What if it doesn't work?" Beecher demanded.

There was a beat of silence and then Alice spoke. "But what if it does?" She glanced around the table. "Do you all plan on hiding down here forever? Once she kills Chess, do you think she'll stop with him?" Alice got up and paced back and forth. "No, she'll move on to Zander and the King. Then she'll hunt all of you down, one by one."

Dordo swallowed and hunched down in his seat, trying to make himself smaller. Lady Perma clasped her hands. "She's right, Wilfred. I say we let her try."

Beecher humphed. "You would. We should vote on it."

"Yes, since the last vote went so well," the Duchess said, a smirk on her face.

Beecher glared at her before turning to the rest of them. "All those in favor of going along with this cocka-mamie scheme, raise your hand."

Alice, Lapin, and Lady Perma immediately raised their hands. The Duchess was slower, and Dordo was the last one, but only after looking to see what everyone else had done.

Beecher scowled. "I don't care if all of you have lost your senses. I'm still going to cast my vote as no, if only on principle."

The Duchess turned to him, but he held up his hands. "No, Leticia, I realize when I've lost. Do what you want, but don't say I didn't warn you when all this comes crashing down on your heads."

Alice's shoulders inched down from her ears, and she turned to Sir Lapin. "So, how do we do this?"

Chapter 71

A BELL RANG IN the servants' hall, making Alice jump. Anders disappeared to answer the summons, and Alice exchanged a look with Sir Lapin.

"It looks like it's time," he said. "Are you ready, my dear?"

Alice nodded, but her body jangled with nerves. "How will I know if it works?"

Lapin frowned. "That's a good question, but I suppose... if she doesn't shift?" His gaze landed on Wickle, who sat on Alice's shoulder. "Your little friend there is a good backup plan if things go sideways."

Wickle hissed and puffed up to twice his size, and Lapin chuckled. "I don't mean any offense."

Alice put her hand over the snark's back. "We talked about this, Wickle. I don't want you to end up a roasted marshmallow, and we don't want to kill anyone, not unless there's no other option." She patted her shirt pocket. "You'd better get in here. They won't let me near the Queen if anyone sees you."

Wickle blew his fringe upward, but he crawled down into Alice's pocket. The door opened, and Anders reappeared. "The Queen is asking for you, Miss." He swallowed. "She says your time is up."

The Duchess reached over and patted Alice's hand. "Good luck, my dear."

Lady Perma sniffled into her handkerchief, and Beecher refused to look at her at all.

Alice rose on shaky legs and picked up the alabaster box. "This is going to work." She didn't know if she actually believed that, but somehow it helped to say it out loud.

Lapin smiled. "I have every hope that it will."

With a last look at the Council, Alice followed Anders out of the servants' hall.

"Are we going to the garden room?" Alice asked. There would be something satisfying in defeating the Queen where they first met.

But Anders shook his head. "She's out on the back lawn."

Alice wondered uneasily why the Queen wanted her to bring the artifact out there. Her insides jittered with nerves, and she clutched the box to her chest, wishing it were all over. Time stretched like taffy, making the walk to the back of the palace both slow down and go too quickly.

Before Alice was ready, they stopped in front of the large glass doors that led out to the back terrace. Through them, the Queen was visible in the middle of the back lawn, the Commander next to her. A long line of soldiers stood at attention behind the pair, and Alice realized why the Queen chose this spot. There would be no running or hiding out there.

When she finally looked at Chess, her heart lodged in her throat. He was on his knees in front of the Commander, a sword at his throat.

A searing flame of anger burned away any hesitation Alice harbored about what the artifact might do to the Queen. If that woman thought she could threaten the man Alice loved, she bloody well could think again. She reached for the door handle, but Anders spoke.

"The staff are all cheering you on, Miss. Sir Chess is a favorite with everyone downstairs."

Alice smiled at the steward. "Thank you, Anders. Chess would be glad to hear that."

He nodded and then took hold of the other door handle. "Allow me, Miss."

Alice stepped back and let Anders open the door for her. She took a deep breath and squared her shoulders. Then she stepped outside.

The sun shone, and the sky was a deep vibrant blue with wisps of cotton-candy clouds floating in the gentle breeze. The faint but heady perfume from the rose garden wafted in the air. Alice kept her steps slow and measured as she approached the group, her boots clicking across the stones on the terrace. Despite her outward calm, her heart thumped in her ears as she walked down the shallow steps.

Alice's gaze flitted over the tableau posed on the lawn. The Queen's smile reminded Alice of a cat who had gotten into the cream, and the Commander's expression showed no emotion at all. Finally, her gaze landed on Chess. Their eyes met across the lawn, and her footsteps faltered before she caught herself. She worked to keep her own expression blank as she took in the bruise on his cheek and his swollen-shut eye.

One side of Chess's mouth kicked up, and he winked his good eye at her. "Hello, love."

Alice allowed a tiny smile to curve her mouth before snapping her attention back to the Queen. She couldn't afford to get distracted.

The Queen, watching the interaction, clapped her hands. "I knew true love would win out." She turned to the Commander. "I told you, darling, didn't I?"

The Commander's nod was curt. "You did, my love." The affectionate term seemed almost dragged from his mouth.

A frown flitted across the Queen's features, but a beaming smile quickly replaced it. Alice stopped a few yards away and glanced between the Queen and the Commander.

"After what you told me, I'm surprised to see you with another older man." The words popped out of Alice's mouth before she could stop them.

Thankfully, the Queen was amused and let out a husky laugh. "He's much more fit than Zane, and I think you'll agree that he's very handsome." Her gaze slid to Chess, and her smile turned wicked. "Or is that too awkward to say in front of his son?"

Alice shrugged. "I doubt Chess's ego is that delicate."

The Queen's eyes gleamed with amusement. "You are always such a delight, my dear, but as much as I'm enjoying this conversation, I believe you've brought me something." The Queen's gaze fell to the box in Alice's hands and she licked her lips, her expression turning hungry. Alice was surprised the woman didn't grab it out of her hands.

Alice glanced at the Commander and the row of soldiers behind him and then back at the Queen. "Are you sure you want to do this? King Thorne said this artifact is dangerous." Even now, its magic buzzed almost painfully against her palms.

Laughter gurgled out of the Queen. "Oh my dear, of course he said that. Do you think he wants his precious artifact to fall into someone else's possession? Oh no, I've been waiting for this all my life. Now, no more stalling." She reached out her hands.

Alice backed away. "No, let Chess go first."

The Queen frowned, her hands falling back to her sides. "You're in no position to negotiate with me."

Alice tapped the top of the box. "I think this says differently, don't you?"

The Queen flicked a finger at the Commander, who moved his blade, and a bead of blood welled up on Chess's neck. Heat flared in Alice's chest, but she tamped it down. Never had keeping her cool mattered more.

"Do you truly want the Commander to slit his throat while you argue with me?"

Alice gripped the box tighter. "Do you want me to smash this on the ground so you can never use it?"

"You'll ensure his death if you do that."

"And you'll never get the power you want."

The Queen reached under her skirts and pulled out a wickedly sharp knife. In one move, she grabbed Chess's hair and yanked his head back, holding the point of the dagger under the eye that wasn't swollen. "I'd hate to ruin these lovely blue eyes, but if you don't give that artifact to me right now, I will start with his eyes and end with that silver tongue of his."

Alice purposely kept her gaze on the Queen's face and tried to keep her breathing steady. If she blinked, they were all dead. "Hurt him in any way, and I'll smash this box, consequences be hanged."

The tip of the knife bit into Chess's cheek, and he swallowed as a drop of blood traced down his face. The Queen stared at her for a long, hard moment, and Alice refused to blink. Finally, the Queen's lips thinned and her gaze faltered.

Alice pressed her slight advantage. "There's no real risk in untying him. Even if I wanted to run, there's a dozen soldiers not three yards away. Where would I go? Where would he go?"

The Queen's eyes narrowed. "You might still break the artifact."

"I could, but I won't. You have my word."

"Why should I trust you? You've been a thorn in my side since you arrived here. Maybe I should kill you both and be done with it."

Alice raised the box. "You could, but I'm pretty sure I can break this before that happens, and then where will you be?" The Queen's face twisted into a snarl, and Alice rushed on. "The only thing I want to do is go home with the man I love. I don't care what happens to this wretched world after that." Alice kept her eyes trained on the Queen, afraid if she even glanced at Chess she'd give herself away.

The Queen hesitated, and then a smile stretched across her face. "Why, my dear, that statement's almost worthy of me." She snapped her fingers without looking away from Alice. "Untie your son, Commander."

"My love, are you sure..."

"Don't question me. Just do as I say," she said.

The Commander bowed his head. "Of course." Two slashes of color appeared on his cheekbones as he sliced the ropes that bound Chess's hands and hauled him to his feet.

Chess shook out his arms, grimacing, and stepped away from his father. Alice barely resisted the urge to run over and hug him, but his freedom was only the first step.

The Queen turned back to Alice, her hands outstretched. "Now, it's your turn, my dear."

Alice moved closer and held out the intricately carved box. The Queen snatched it. Her expression took on a dreamy quality, and she ran a caressing hand over the alabaster lid like it was a beloved pet.

Alice edged towards Chess, but the Queen suddenly jerked her head up, her dark eyes narrowed on Alice's face. "Not so fast, my dear. No reunion until I make sure there's no trick."

Alice did her best to appear innocent as the Queen unlatched the box and opened it. Alice held her breath, but nothing happened. Her heart hammered in her chest as doubt curled in her belly. Had she just handed the Queen the means to take over Wonderland?

The faint buzzing in Alice's ears muffled any sound as the Queen's smile turned radiant, her eyes shining. "Finally." The soft word had barely left her mouth when the box began to glow.

The glow spread over the Queen until a vivid ball of light filled Alice's vision. The Queen laughed as the power of the box pulsed outward, pushing Alice back.

Then the laughter turned to screams.

Chapter 72

THE POWER SURGED UP and out of the box. It lifted Alice off her feet and flung her onto her back, the breath knocked from her body. She shielded her face from the blinding blaze of light.

The screams turned shrill and piercing.

Then abruptly cut off.

The glow around the Queen slowly dissipated, and she crumpled to the ground.

The box clattered from her hands and bounced across the grass before it snapped shut.

Alice pushed herself up to sitting, dazed and aching, and Wickle popped out of her pocket.

Bad woman dead?

Her gaze found the Queen, who lay unmoving in a circle of scorched grass. Behind the Queen, the Commander blinked and shook his head as if waking up. The soldiers broke their formation and stood in awkward clumps. "I... don't know, Wickle."

Then Chess dropped next to her and hugged her tightly against him, making the snark squirm out of her pocket and scamper up to her shoulder. "Are you all right, love?"

Alice pressed her face into his shirt, her eyes suddenly burning with unshed tears. "I'm fine, but what about you?"

His lips brushed against her hair. "Don't worry about me. I've got nine lives, remember?"

Alice pulled back and touched the fresh cut on his cheek. "But you're hurt. You should let me heal that for you."

"It looks worse than it is." He took her hand and kissed the palm. "I..."

A low groan made them both turn towards the Queen. Her eyes opened, and her hand twitched on the grass. "I can't..." Her voice was barely audible, and a shudder ran over her body.

Alice and Chess exchanged glances as black lines ran from the corners of the Queen's mouth and eyes.

Her hand twitched again, and her eyes widened as her body jerked and went rigid, her back bowing off the ground. A strangled scream tore from the woman's throat as the black lines spread down over her jaw.

Alice frowned. "What's happening to her?"

Chess shook his head. "I don't know. What did you put in the box?"

"The potion your mother gave us, but I didn't think it would do this."

Alice crawled over to the Queen, kneeling next to her. Wickle chittered loudly from her shoulder, and the Queen's eyes rolled towards the sound, a low moan escaping from her lips.

Alice put a hand on the woman's shoulder and then almost yanked it away as the pain flowed into her mind. Much like the bumble faery, there was a deep, gaping hollow at the Queen's center, but instead of being empty, many of the strands lay in charred, ashy lumps and most of the remaining ones were burning and slowly turning to ash. The entire space was charred, and the Queen's life force flickered in fits and starts.

Alice looked up at Chess and shook her head. "I can't fix this. She's too far gone."

Chess squeezed her shoulder, and a shadow fell over them. It was the Commander, his face haggard and haunted.

"Move." His voice was raspy.

Alice stared up at him dumbly and the Commander pulled out his sword. "Move." He kept his eyes fixed on the Queen.

Alice looked at Chess. "But..."

"Come away, love." Chess reached down and helped her to her feet. He slid an arm around her waist and tried to pull her away, but Alice stood rooted to the spot, unable to look away from the scene playing out in front of her.

The Queen moaned, her body jerking in a futile effort to get away when the Commander stepped next to her. He didn't say a word—only lifted his sword.

The Queen's voice came out garbled with panic. "No... please... I..."

The Commander's arm came down, and Alice turned her face into Chess's shoulder.

The voice cut off abruptly.

Silence descended, the only sound the Commander's harsh breathing.

Then Wickle purred loudly. *Queen dead.*

Alice shuddered and pressed her face more deeply into Chess's shoulder. He tightened his arms around her. "It's over, love."

The tears she had held back for so long streaked down her cheeks, and her legs suddenly felt rubbery. If Chess hadn't been holding onto her, Alice was pretty sure she'd be on the ground.

"I... I thought she was going to... kill..." A sob choked off Alice's words.

"But she didn't. I'm right here."

She didn't know how long she stood in Chess's arms crying while he rubbed her back and Wickle snuggled against her neck before someone cleared his throat. Alice lifted her wet face from Chess's shoulder. A large handkerchief appeared, and Alice realized the Commander stood next to them. Her gaze drifted past his shoulder where the Queen lay, her head separated from her shoulders. Alice jerked her eyes back to the Commander, her stomach lurching.

"I'm grateful to you, Miss Alice. You saved my son's life." He paused as Alice took the handkerchief and blotted her face. "You've done all of Wonderland a service, and we won't forget it."

Alice's face heated. "I'm just glad it's over now."

The Commander's expression clouded. "I don't understand how all this happened."

"Do you remember anything at all, Commander?" Alice asked.

He shook his head. "I was tracking the Queen to the Faelands and then…" He spread his hands wide. "Everything's a fog."

Chess raised an eyebrow. "I think it's safe to say you found her—or rather, she found you."

The Commander frowned and twisted the ring on his pinky. "I don't understand how she could do this."

Chess nodded towards the piece of jewelry. "Lapin thinks the ring is how the Queen got control over you."

The Commander stared down at his hand in horror before jerking the jewelry from his finger and holding it away from him like it was a venomous snake. "I still don't understand how…" His gaze drifted to the bruises on Chess's face and he closed his eyes briefly. "Regardless of how it happened, I'm so very sorry, son. We've had our differences, but I would have never hurt you on purpose."

"I know you wouldn't, at least not like this." Chess's tone was cool.

Confusion flashed over the Commander's face before understanding dawned on his face. "Of course, you visited the Faelands. You talked to Larkspur." It wasn't a question.

Chess crossed his arms. "Yes, I did."

The Commander's expression fell, and he pinched the bridge of his nose. "I need to explain—"

"Now isn't the time." Chess cut him off curtly.

"But—"

The glass doors from the palace burst open and Zander, along with the King, Azalea, and Indigo, spilled out onto the terrace, weapons in their hands.

Chapter 73

ZANDER SKIDDED TO A halt on the terrace steps and took in the scene in front of him. The Queen sprawled in the grass, a large red stain covering the front of her dress. The box lay a few feet away from her outstretched arm. Behind her, clumps of soldiers stood in wary groups. Chess had his arm around Alice, the Commander nearby, his shoulders slumped in defeat. Apparently, he was no longer a threat because nobody seemed concerned about his proximity, although Zander wasn't sure how that had happened.

Azalea sheathed her sword. She nodded towards Chess and Alice. "I am glad to see you have some allies here that appreciate you."

A smile tugged at Zander's mouth at the sour expression on her face. "They aren't the only ones."

She raised an eyebrow, and he gestured towards her and Indigo, who limped behind her. "You and your brother helped me a great deal, and you didn't have to. Neither of you owes me anything."

Indigo slung an arm around his sister, a smirk on his face. "Oh, but we *did* have to help, didn't we, Sister?"

Azalea shrugged off his arm. "Enough, Indigo." She nodded towards the group on the lawn. "The Prince must deal with the situation, not waste time on your nonsense."

"You're right," Zander said, and started towards the group with the King and Azalea on his heels. Indigo skirted around him to reach Alice and Chess first. He bent down and peered into Alice's face. "Are you well, my flower?"

Alice's mouth twitched. "I'm not your flower, Indigo, but I'm fine."

Then he turned to Chess and slapped him on the back. "I'm glad you survived too, cousin, even if it would be more expedient for me if you didn't." He winked at Alice, who rolled her eyes.

Chess ignored the Fae man and instead turned to Zander, his expression sober. "As you can see, the Queen is dead. Alice used the Fae artifact, and then the Commander finished her off."

"But, he—"

Chess gestured towards the ring that lay in the grass. "The Queen enchanted him with that."

Zander blinked at him and wished he had time to sit down and absorb the news. After everything the woman had put all of them through, he couldn't quite wrap his mind around the fact that she was truly gone. His legs moved without conscious thought until he was standing next to her body. In death, she didn't even seem human—more like a broken doll than a person.

Around him, there was the murmur of voices and the sound of people moving around. In some dim recess of his mind, he realized Alice was healing the large gash in his father's side, and the Commander hovered somewhere in the background.

Zander drew in a shaky breath and had the overwhelming urge to sink down and weep. He didn't mourn the Queen's death, not after everything she'd done, but everything he'd lost over the past year washed over him in a suffocating wave. Someone's shoulder brushed his, and he jerked in surprise.

"It is such a waste of life." Azalea's gaze was thoughtful as she stared down at the Queen. Indigo stood silently next to her.

"You believe it was wrong to kill her?" Zander asked.

She frowned. "No, she brought this on herself, and she caused so much destruction. She might have chosen differently, but she did not."

He nodded and then gestured towards the body. "Will you still need to take her back to King Thorne?"

Azalea shook her head. "No, there is no reason now."

Zander took a step back and turned towards his father. This had been his wife, after all. He had to be upset.

Azalea put a hand on his arm and held something out towards him. He realized, with a start, it was the artifact. He'd almost forgotten about it. Automatically, he took it from her and stared down at the flowers and vines carved into the top of the box.

When he looked up, he found everyone watching him. His gaze went around the small circle and landed at last on his father. The King smiled at him, his expression sad and broken.

A shout came from the door and the Council, along with Sir Lapin, poured out of the palace and onto the terrace.

Zander's gaze stayed on the artifact as they crowded around. Voices rose and fell, and he heard Chess informing them the Queen was dead. There were more voices, but all Zander saw was the artifact and a future without his Jabberwock.

A loud thump startled him out of his thoughts. "Well, you have the artifact. Get on with it!" Beecher bellowed at him.

"Are you insane?" Chess waved an arm at the Queen. "Look what happened to her."

Beecher scowled. "It's not the same, boy. That was an unknown potion from some Fae woman."

Chess glared at the man. "Watch yourself, old man. That *Fae woman* is my mother."

The Commander put a hand on Chess's shoulder. "Enough, the both of you. It's Zander's decision."

Chess shrugged him off and turned his gaze to Zander.

Zander looked at all the faces surrounding him, their expectations pressing down on him like a thick, smothering blanket.

The truth was, he loved his Jabberwock. He loved soaring through the sky with the wind in his face. He loved hunting and diving and being free. And it wasn't just selfishness either. His Jabberwock had saved not only his own life, but that of his father, Alice, Chess. Citrine's words reverberated in his mind—he couldn't tear out a piece of himself and ever expect to be whole. He owed his Jabberwock, and he suddenly knew that no matter what the consequences, he wasn't willing to give up such a big part of himself—not for the Council, not for duty, not for the throne. If the people of Wonderland didn't want him as he was, then so be it.

He lifted his chin and met each gaze. "No, I'm not. I've already proven over and over again that my duty lies with the Kingdom. I gave up the woman I loved for Wonderland. That should be enough, and if it isn't, then I'm sorry, but I don't want the throne."

He handed the artifact to Azalea. She smiled and nodded at him.

His gaze slid over to his father. Even though he had meant every word, he dreaded seeing the disappointment on his father's face. Instead, the King's eyes shone with pride, love, and something that looked a lot like relief.

A weight lifted from Zander's shoulders as everyone around him all started talking at once.

He smiled. Trinny would be proud of him.

Chapter 74

LORD BEECHER HARRUMPHED LOUDLY. "The King isn't fit to rule, and his son won't give up his Drifter Gene. I propose the Commander be the permanent ruler. Now can we vote on it so I can go home already?"

"Aren't you forgetting the last hour or so, Wilfred?" The Duchess's tone was tart. "The Queen has managed to either enchant or curse all three men. I don't see why the Commander gets your vote."

Beecher scowled. "Well, at least the Commander didn't turn into some rampaging beast. I suppose that's something in his favor."

"The King doesn't seem to be any kind of creature now—or the Prince either, for that matter," pointed out Alice, and Chess could have kissed her.

"You don't know anything, missy, and I'll thank you to be quiet."

Chess narrowed his eyes at the old man. "Watch yourself, Beecher. Besides, she knows more than you do. The Queen is the one who caused all this trouble, and as you can see, she's no longer a threat."

At this reminder, a tense silence fell over the group as everyone's glances skittered to where the Queen's body lay.

The Commander cleared his throat. "After what happened, I feel I must remove myself from ruling, even for the set upon month." He drew himself up. "I have proven myself unworthy of the responsibility."

"Oh, for Wonder's sake," Beecher bellowed. "You're the only one left, Commander. Besides, we'd have to vote you out. Ask those Fae friends of your son's if they want the King ruling after he turned one of their flower maidens into a corpse. That'll have some ramifications."

The words landed like rocks in a still pool. "Ramifications?" Chess echoed, and then wanted to suck the word back into his mouth. Of course, the flower maiden. He slanted a glance at Indigo and Azalea and then at Alice. She was biting her lip, her eyes darting in the Fae's direction, too.

Beecher's face tightened. "Yes, ramifications." He looked at the Fae brother and sister. "I'm sure nobody bothered to tell you that the King killed one of the flower maidens in the palace."

Chess had to exert all his willpower not to punch the man in the face. He didn't know what he was playing at, but dropping that tidbit right now was a terrible idea.

Azalea's face creased and Indigo frowned as they looked from the Commander to the King. The King straightened and met their gazes squarely. "You have my deepest apologies, and I know that isn't nearly enough to make up for a life lost, a life I took. Whatever payment or penalty you wish to exact, I will pay it." When he finished speaking, he bowed his head, waiting.

Zander stepped in front of his father. "No, I'll pay it. I should have been guarding him more closely. It's not his fault. It's mine."

Silence stretched like taffy, the only sounds the twitter of birds, the drone of insects. Finally Azalea spoke. "King Thorne would not hold you responsible for this tragedy, King Zane, or you either, Prince Zander, although it is noble of you to take your father's place. It is yet another life put to the Queen's account."

Everyone glanced at the scorched circle of earth around the Queen and then away. Azalea looked at the Councilmembers and her frown deepened. "I am sorry, but I do not understand this." She waved a hand. "Your King and your Prince are honorable men. Your Prince has the Jabberwock form, I am told. Why would you not want someone so strong and fierce to protect you?"

The duchess smirked. "I've been asking them the same thing for weeks now."

"I think the Prince would make a fine ruler," said Lady Perma. Her gaze darted to Lord Beecher, but she lifted her chin.

"He's still greener than grass," Beecher said, a scowl on his face as he glared at Zander.

Finally, Alice cleared her throat. "Maybe after this month is over, the King and Prince Zander could rule together? It seems the King needs time to heal fully from his ordeal, and the Prince still has things to learn from the King. The month would allow them to organize themselves and recover." She glanced over her shoulder. "I don't think anybody here wants what happened to the Queen to happen to the Prince, do you?"

Beecher looked down at the grass under his feet, and the others shook their heads. The Commander's mouth turned up into the smallest of smiles. "I will do whatever is required, but that seems like a fine idea to me."

"I propose we should take a vote, don't you, Lord Beecher?" said the Duchess. "That is what you wanted, right?"

"Is it even official if we're standing on the lawn?" he grumbled.

"I don't think there's any rule that we have to be in the meeting room to take a vote." When nobody disagreed with her, the Duchess looked around at the other Councilmembers with a satisfied smile. "All those in favor of the Prince ruling, with the King serving in an advisory capacity once the Commander's month is out, need to say *aye*." She winked at Zander. "I'll cast the first vote. Aye."

Chess held his breath as the vote went around the group. Beecher was the only one who hesitated, but seeing he was outnumbered, he finally nodded. "Oh, all right."

The vote was unanimous.

Zander let out a breath, and his shoulders relaxed.

"Now that we're finally finished, I'm going home." Without another word, Beecher stalked back into the palace and disappeared.

The other Councilmembers left rather quickly. Chess understood he had things to settle with his father, but that could wait. Besides, the man still looked shell-shocked from the afternoon's events.

Zander's voice interrupted Chess's thoughts. He was turning to the King. "You should get some rest."

The King nodded. "I'd tell you the same, but I think some time with your friends will do you more good, especially now." He clapped a hand on Zander's shoulder and nodded to Azalea and Indigo before he turned towards the Commander. "Would you have a few of the soldiers move her body into the cold cellar? We'll deal with her later." The Commander nodded his agreement, and the King gave the Queen one last sad look before he and the Commander both turned towards the palace and plodded up the steps. Both of them looked like they'd aged ten years in the past hour.

Zander gestured towards the door. "Why don't we all go to the east parlor? I don't know about you, but I'm exhausted, and it's quite comfortable in there. I'll have Anders send up some dinner. I'm sure everyone is hungry."

Alice's stomach growled loudly as if in response and everyone laughed, breaking some of the tension in the air. Chess slid his hand into hers, and she smiled up at him, making his breath catch again. They could have lost each other so easily today.

Azalea pointed to the Queen. "Will you send her body back to her home?"

Zander shook his head. "There's nobody left to bury her. I'm not sure where Father will decide to have her buried, though. It seems wrong to put her in the family crypt."

"Well, we don't need to worry about that right now. It's not as if she's going anywhere," Chess said.

One side of Zander's mouth lifted. "No, I guess you're right, although I might not have put it quite that way."

Grasping Alice's hand, Chess led everyone back into the palace towards the parlor while Zander left in search of Anders. By the time Zander joined them, a maid had delivered sandwiches, lemonade, and two plates of cookies and tiny cakes. Everyone tucked into the fare quickly, even Azalea and Indigo, who had studied the sandwiches with interest before biting into them.

It wasn't until Zander settled himself in a chair close to the fire that Chess realized someone was missing. "Hey, Zan, did Citrine go back home?"

The innocent question made Zander freeze in the act of lifting his sandwich. Slowly, he lowered it back onto the plate. Agony twisted his features and alarm sprang up in Chess even as Alice breathed out, "Oh no, not Citrine."

Zander blinked rapidly and cleared his throat twice before he finally spoke. "She... My father..."

Alice got out of her chair and knelt by Zander, taking both his hands in hers. "Oh, Zander, I'm so sorry." She pressed her cheek against the backs of his hands as tears tracked down her face. Zander bowed his head.

Chess drew in a shaky breath, his own food forgotten.

Just when he thought the horrors of this day were over, now this. His mind refused to wrap around the idea. It wasn't possible Citrine was... He shook his head. "You can't mean she's... dead?"

He choked on the word, his throat closing with grief.

Zander nodded, his head still bowed, and tears dripped off of his chin.

Indigo and Azalea exchanged glances before quietly putting their plates of food on the side tables and silently exiting the room. Chess didn't know where they went, and at the moment he didn't care. He crossed over to his friend and knelt next to Alice, pulling Zander into a hug.

The Prince wrapped his free arm around Chess and gripped him tightly, even as he clung to Alice's hands. Together, they mourned for a loss that left a gaping hole in all of their lives.

Chapter 75

CHESS PULLED ANOTHER SHIRT from the drawer and tossed it in his rucksack. Nerves danced in his stomach. He had no question about going with Alice. No, it was her Papa James that had him worried. Well, not worried—more *concerned*.

A knock on the door interrupted this train of thought. "Come in," he called, scooping up his coat, but when he turned, it wasn't Zander.

Instead, the Commander stood awkwardly in the doorway. "May I come in?"

Chess hesitated and then gave a wave of his arm. "Sure."

The Commander stepped inside the door and glanced at the bed where Chess's bag sat opened. "Looks like you're almost packed. How long are you planning to be gone?"

Chess folded his jacket and tucked it into his bag. "I'm not sure. It rather depends."

The Commander raised an eyebrow. "On what, if you don't mind me asking?"

Chess lifted one shoulder. "A lot of things."

A slight smile tipped his father's mouth. "That's specific."

Irritation made Chess's tone curt. "I'm going to meet Alice's family for the first time, and we're going to have to explain where she's been."

Both the Commander's eyebrows rose to his hairline. "You're going to tell them about Wonderland?"

Chess pulled the bag's flap shut and secured it. "Yep."

"Aren't you worried they'll wonder if you're crazy?"

Chess sat on the edge of the bed. "Alice assures me they'll understand, but I guess I'll find out when I get there."

The Commander edged further into the room. "You are coming back, aren't you? I mean, you aren't planning on staying in the Mirror World with Alice, are you?"

"Would you care?" Chess wanted to suck the words back into his mouth, but they were out there now. He refused to look away from his father.

The Commander sighed. "I didn't come here to fight with you."

"Why did you come then? I've lost count of the times I've left here on one trip or another, and I don't remember you ever making a special trip to tell me goodbye before."

"This isn't just a trip. You're going to the Mirror World."

Chess raised an eyebrow.

The Commander walked over to a chair by the fireplace and dropped into it. "I'm not any good at these kinds of conversations." He leaned forward and clasped his hands between his knees. "I know you talked to your mother. You must have questions."

The force of his own anger surprised Chess. He jumped to his feet and began pacing, afraid if he didn't move, he'd start shouting. "You could say that."

The Commander spread his hands out. "I'll answer anything you want to ask me."

Chess whirled on his heel to face his father. "Why?"

The Commander frowned. "Why what? I'm afraid you'll need to be more specific."

Chess blew out a breath. "Why did you send Mother away, and why did you lie about it?" His hands curled into fists. "I thought..." he shook his head. "You lied to me for years, and for the life of me, I don't understand why."

The Commander leaned back in the chair and met Chess's gaze squarely. "I loved your mother." His voice softened. "I still do, but she wasn't happy here. The court required she clip her wings, and after a while, she refused to do it anymore. That meant she couldn't leave the grounds of our home." He dropped his eyes to his hands. "I watched her wilting little by little with every year that passed, so when you reached an age where I thought you could do without her, I sent her away. I knew she'd never leave you on her own."

A band tightened around Chess's chest, and he stared at his father. "Did it ever occur to you that you might have asked her what she wanted rather than assume you knew?"

The Commander shoved to his feet. "It was for her own good. She's Fae, and they don't fare well in isolation. She was already apart from her people."

"Surely there was another solution than sending her away like she was unwanted baggage." Chess's voice rose, and he stopped, drawing in a breath. "That still doesn't explain why you told me she left us and why you kept all of her letters and gifts from me."

The Commander's lips pressed together, and he bowed his head. "I was afraid for you," he said finally.

The answer startled Chess. "Afraid? Of what?"

The Commander clenched his hands together. "You're half Fae, and it was obvious you took after your mother's side more than mine—both in your Gifts and your temperament. I knew that would work against you at court."

"So, you what? Decided to keep my mother from me because you thought I was too Fae for your liking?" Chess couldn't keep the venom from his voice.

The Commander flinched. "I also thought a clean break would be less painful—for both of you."

Chess shook his head. "So, let me get this straight. You decided—without talking to either me or my mother—that it would be in our best interests for her to go back to the Faelands and never have contact with me again, and for me to believe my mother left me and wanted nothing to do with me. Did I get that about right?"

The Commander gave a jerky nod.

"You're unbelievable. What gave you the right to decide that for me and for Mother?"

"I realize you're angry, and you have every right to be. I acted in the way I thought best at the time, but I can see I might have been... that is... I was wrong." When the Commander looked at him, the sheen in his eyes surprised Chess. "I hope you can forgive me."

Chess picked up his bag and then put it back down again before slumping onto the edge of the bed. "I don't want to be angry with you, but I can't act like this is nothing, either."

The Commander nodded. "I don't expect you to. I only... that is, I hope we'll get past this, eventually."

Chess rubbed a hand on the back of his neck. He could almost hear Alice telling him to give his father a chance. Finally, he sighed. "Yeah, I want that too, but it won't happen today, or probably for a while."

His father's shoulders slumped, and they stared at each other for a long moment. Finally, the Commander stood up. Chess got to his feet, too. His father clapped him on the shoulder and his mouth curved into a faint smile. "I hope your trip goes well, son."

"Thanks. I do too."

The Commander turned and walked to the door and then stopped. "Let me know when you get back. I'd like to hear how things went."

Chess nodded. "I'll do that."

The Commander turned to go and Chess spoke again. "Wait."

His father turned back.

"Larkspur still cares about you, you know."

Surprise flickered across the Commander's face.

Chess shrugged. "You should go visit her once that month is up. I think she'd be happy to see you."

"You do?"

Chess nodded and then grinned. "Yeah, I do."

The Commander's mouth tipped into a smile. "Maybe I will, then."

Chess watched his father walk out the door. For his mother's sake, he hoped the Commander actually visited.

Chapter 76

Two days later, Alice stood with Chess and Zander in front of the Looking Glass. Next to them were Indigo and Azalea, who held the velvet bag with the artifact. Alice supposed the simple alabaster box had been worth all the trouble since it had helped them defeat the Queen for good.

Zander gestured towards the Looking Glass. "I'm sure you understand how this works. Hold where you want to go in your mind as you go through."

Azalea held out her hand to Zander, her face solemn. "Thank you for your hospitality. We are grateful for your kindness."

Zander looked at her hand before he clasped it in his own, and smiled. "It was my pleasure, Azalea. I was happy to meet Chess's other cousins."

Indigo clapped Zander on the back, almost knocking him over. "You'll have to come visit when Chess does. I'll show you around. You need some fun in your life."

Azalea rolled her eyes at her brother's enthusiasm. "You will be more than welcome, but I would advise you to avoid letting my brother show you around if you do not wish trouble."

They all chuckled, and then Indigo punched Chess in the shoulder. "Don't take too long to come visit us."

Chess rubbed his shoulder and grinned. "I won't. Tell my mother I'll see her soon."

Indigo turned to Alice, and his smile changed. Alice shifted closer to Chess, but it didn't keep Indigo from engulfing her in a hug and pressing a kiss on her cheek. "And you must come too, pet, while I still have time to show you how much more delightful I am than my cousin."

Alice couldn't help laughing even as she shoved him away. "I doubt I can take that much delight, Indigo, but since I want to see Larkspur and Azalea again, I guess I'll have to put up with your company, too."

Indigo gave a dramatic groan and grabbed his chest. "You wound me. How will I ever survive?" Throwing the back of his hand to his forehead, he winked and flung himself backwards through the Looking Glass.

"It would serve him right if he lands somewhere strange," said Azalea. Her gaze flicked to Zander and away again, a faint blush turning her cheeks a deeper blue. With a wave, she ducked through the mirror next.

That left just the three of them. Alice couldn't believe she was really going home—for real—or that Chess was coming with her.

As happy as she was to leave, she was going to miss this place. She knew she'd be back, and that helped. Zander had told her about Citrine's wish, and serving as the new Pearl Queen would solve a lot of problems. She still had to talk to her family, though.

"Take care, Alice." He grinned at Chess. "Both of you, don't be gone too long, all right?"

Chess put his arm around Alice's waist and pulled her close. "That, my friend, you can count on."

For the tiniest moment, Zander's eyes clouded, and his mouth drooped. She guessed he was thinking of Citrine, and her heart ached for him. She reached out and touched his arm, and their eyes met in perfect understanding. "Someday you won't feel like this, Zander."

He nodded and put his hands in his pockets. When he looked up, he had a smile on his face, but Alice wondered what it had cost him.

She looked at Chess. "Are you ready?"

In answer, he took her hand, and together they stepped through the Looking Glass.

There was the familiar sensation of walking through gelatin, and then Alice and Chess popped through into a forest that she recognized—even in the dark with the trees casting strange shadows on the ground.

Chess looked around. "I think we ended up in the right place this time."

Excitement fizzed in Alice's chest. Ahead, she could make out the shape of the stables.

"Come on!" She grabbed Chess's hand and started to run.

She didn't let go as their feet skidded through the leaf litter on the ground and they skirted a tree stump.

They burst through the edge of the forest, and there were the familiar outbuildings. She pulled to a stop. A long moment passed as she just breathed and drank in the sight.

She was home. She was really home.

Alice flung her arms around Chess and hugged him for the sheer joy coursing through her. Suddenly, she couldn't wait, not one minute longer to see her sister, Papa James, Mother.

She practically danced with impatience as she tugged him up the path to the house.

As she got closer, doubts raced through her mind. What would she say? She didn't even know where to begin. She glanced at Chess as they approached the front door.

"What am I going to tell them?" She bit her lip, a sudden vision of Mother fainting on the doorstep flashing through her mind. What if Papa James did something... regrettable?

Chess took both her hands in his. "Look at me, love." She peeked up at him, and his blue eyes gleamed in the dusky light, anchoring her runaway thoughts. Her shoulders inched away from her ears, and he smiled. "Better?"

She nodded, even though her heart was still lodged somewhere in her throat.

He squeezed her fingers. "They're going to be overjoyed to see you. You know that, right?"

Tears welled in her eyes, and she slid her arms around his waist as he hugged her close, his cheek resting on her hair. "I... I don't even know how long I've been gone."

His chuckle rumbled against her chest. "It's probably not nearly as long as you think." He pulled away from her and framed her face in his hands, his thumbs wiping the tears from her cheeks. He nodded his head at the house.

"Go on, then. Go spend time with your family. I'll wait here—close enough if you need me, love."

She drew in a shaky breath and bounced up on her toes, pressing a kiss to his cheek. At the last minute, he turned his head and caught her mouth with his. The heat seared through her, and then it was gone. She made a sound of protest, and he smiled.

"Later. You don't want your father to catch us snogging on the front stoop, do you? From what you told me, even my charm wouldn't overcome that first impression."

She laughed, suddenly nervous about what Papa James would say when she introduced him to Chess. She pushed the doubt away. Papa James would be fine, and if he wasn't—she lifted her chin—then too bad for him.

Alice stopped at the bottom of the steps next to one of the thick porch columns. "You'll wait here? Just until I say hello." She suddenly felt ridiculous.

He cupped her cheek. "Take a breath, love. It'll be fine."

"You're right."

With a last glance, she turned back towards the house. She rubbed her hands down the sides of her dress and climbed up the steps.

She stopped again at the door. It seemed peculiar to knock, but it felt equally odd to open the door and walk in after being gone for so long.

Taking a deep breath, she lifted her hand and knocked. A moment later, the door swung open.

Rommy stood on the other side. At the sight of Alice, her eyes went huge, and then she swooped in and grabbed Alice up in a bone-crushing hug.

"Alice! Alice, darling, where have you been all day? Mother's been worried sick, and Papa was ready to call in his old crew to find you!"

Alice squeezed her eyes shut, breathing in the scent of her sister: lavender, ink, and paper, with a faint hint of something wilder.

"Is that my girl?" Papa James' booming voice echoed from the back of the house, probably the kitchen. It only took a moment before he loomed up in the doorway. His face was stern, but his blue eyes twinkled. Behind his shoulder, Mother peered, her face creased with worry. She hurried forward, pushing Rommy aside to examine Alice.

"Alice, dear, where have you been all day? Hadley came up here with some tale of a giant cat he fought off, saying you ran away. He was all scratched up and bleeding. We had no idea where you had run off to."

Alice snorted. "That's not quite what happened."

Papa James' chest puffed out. "Ha! I've always said that Hadley was a wet blanket. Didn't I tell you it was our Alice that fought off the cat and not the other way round?" When Mother didn't let go of her, Papa James sighed. "Goodness, Elizabeth, let the poor girl breathe."

Mother tsked, but her mouth twitched. "Don't be ridiculous, dear. If that was the case, where has Alice been all day?"

Alice blinked. A day? She'd only been gone a day. The thought made her dizzy, and she shook her head to clear it.

Rommy was watching her with narrowed eyes. When she leaned in to hug her again, she whispered in her ear. "Whatever you tell Mother and Papa, I want the truth. Don't think I didn't notice you're not wearing the same thing as when you left."

Alice pulled away from her sister and took a step back. "No, Rommy, you're right. Leave it to you to notice, too, but I didn't get these clothes from around here."

Papa James frowned. "What do you mean, my dear?"

Alice took a deep breath and looked at her family. "Actually, that's a rather long story, but first, there's someone I want you to meet." She held out her hand, and Chess stepped out from behind the column. He sauntered up to the porch, taking the steps two at a time. When he reached her, he reached for her hand and twined their fingers together.

Turning to her sister and parents, he gave them that charming smile. "Hello, my name is Chess Felinas. I've heard so much about all of you."

Epilogue

Six months later

ALICE STOOD BY THE small pond in front of Citrine's home, Zander next to her. Water dripped in a small puddle by her feet. Grenmar, the water dragon, towered over them.

Several yards away, Chess, her family, plus Bliss and his wife observed the interaction. Even Wickle was here, sitting on Papa James' shoulder. The little snark had surprised everyone when he'd taken a shine to Alice's father. The only ones missing were Rommy and Finn, but they had left for the States after their wedding. She wished they could be here, but they deserved to follow their dreams too. Besides, with the Looking Glass, visiting would be much easier now.

Everyone was ready to rush to the rescue in case things didn't go well. It had taken a bit to persuade her family that Wonderland, more specifically, becoming the new Pearl Queen, was really what she wanted. In the end, they wanted her happiness more than social standing—even Mother.

While Chess's charm failed to win over Papa James, the pair had bonded over their equal loathing of Hadley Beechworth. It turned out he'd exaggerated her father's debt, and the senior Beechworth had been furious with him about his lie.

Another drop of water landed on Alice's shoe, and she turned her attention back to the task in front of her.

She'd already passed inspection from the flying wolves. Bliss had been invaluable there. Now she had to convince Grenmar. Before Alice had unwittingly awakened him in her quest with Zander and Chess to break the Jabberwock's Curse, the water dragon hadn't shown himself in generations. Since then, however, he'd taken to popping up at regular intervals, so she had no choice but to get his blessing to stay here.

You are not the Pearl Queen. He squinted down at her. *You are the thief.*

Alice drew in a deep breath, trying to stop the knocking of her knees. "The Pearl Queen has died without heirs." She held up the lock of Citrine's hair Zander had cut off before she'd been put in the crypt.

The water dragon lowered his head and sniffed at the hair. Alice tried to keep her arm steady, but her entire body trembled. If this didn't work...

Grenmar drew back, his head drooping. *I smell her death.* He turned his fathomless eyes on Alice, and it seemed as if he were staring into her soul. *What has that to do with you?*

Alice nodded at Zander. He bowed to the water dragon and repeated the words he'd practiced. "I was with the Pearl Queen when she passed. She wishes Alice to take her place." He produced the note Citrine had written right before she died. He held it up so the water dragon could see it.

Grenmar's face wrinkled. *You do not have the right blood... or name, but this is the Pearl Queen's symbol.*

Alice clasped her hands in front of her. "I know I'm not part of the family, but there is no one else. The creatures here need a voice, and I'm willing to be that."

The silence stretched. More water plunked onto the ground. The water dragon bent his head again, this time snuffling her hair and shoulders. Alice held herself motionless as dampness seeped into her clothing. She wasn't sure what they'd do if Grenmar proved uncooperative.

Finally, he lifted his head. *The creatures here do need someone, but I cannot call you Alice.*

"Does that mean..."

He tilted his head. *Amethyst. You will be the stand-in Pearl Queen, Amethyst.*

Alice let out a big breath, her shoulders loosening.

Zander's gaze went from her to the water dragon, and she nodded. Sadness tinged the smile that spread across his face.

Grenmar sank down. When his head was level with hers. *Do not forget. You are Amethyst now, and the creatures depend on you.*

Alice nodded solemnly. "I will guard them well, Grenmar. You have my word."

See that you do. I will be watching you, Amethyst. With a last long look, the water dragon sank below the surface.

Zander raised his eyebrows. "Well? Did he agree or not?"

Happily, she nodded. "He did, but you might have to call me *Amethyst* when he's around. He was rather insistent on that point."

Zander patted her shoulder. "I'm glad that worked out. This would make Trinny so happy." A cloud briefly darkened his expression, and Alice touched his arm.

"How are you, Zander? Truly?"

He shrugged, kicking at the rocky soil with the toe of his boot. "I'm all right."

Alice raised an eyebrow, and a smile tugged at the corner of his mouth. "Well, most of the time. I still have to deal with Lord Beecher, after all." Then the smile faded and he sighed. "I miss her. Every day. It's like I've lost a limb or something, but I have work to do, a purpose. That helps."

Alice's heart ached at her friend's loss. She wished she could take away his pain, but there were some things only time could mend. She squeezed his arm. "Citrine would be so proud of you, Zander."

They exchanged a smile before Zander nodded and then walked back towards the group. Chess broke away and jogged down the slope to where she stood. He grabbed her around the waist and swung her in a circle before setting her back on her feet and planting a kiss on her mouth. "You did it, love! You're official now."

Alice grinned, her heart swelling with happiness. "I am, aren't I?"

He glanced back at her family and then to her. "Well, almost."

Alice rolled her eyes. "Please don't tell me there's another creature I need permission from. I'm not sure my nerves can handle it."

She started towards the rest of her family, but they were all moving away from her towards the Pearl Palace.

She frowned. "Where's everyone going?" In truth, she felt a bit hurt as they drifted away from her. This was a big moment in her life, and she wanted her family around her.

"I think they wanted to give us a little privacy, love."

"What..."

Chess dropped to one knee and looked up at her, his eyes gleaming. "So I could ask you a very important question, Alice Cavendish."

Alice swallowed; her knees suddenly weak. "And what question would that be, Chess Felinas?"

The sunlight glinted off the gold ring and its purple stone Chess held in fingers that weren't quite steady. "I love you, Alice, and I never want to be without you. Say you'll marry me."

Overcome, Alice could only whisper, "Yes."

With great tenderness, he slipped the ring onto her finger and stood, drawing her into his arms.

"*Now* you're official, love."

He leaned down, his eyes holding hers until their lips pressed together. Alice melted into him with a sigh. She was finally where she belonged.

Wondering how Prince Zander ended up cursed? Find out in Jabberwock Prince, your free gift for signing up to my newsletter. Just scan the code below.

One secret may cost him everything.

Prince Zander thought he had years before he would ascend the Kingdom of Wonderland's throne.

But then he is summoned back to the palace and finds his father dead. Before he even has time to mourn, he's informed that the Queen will be the interim ruler until his 21st birthday. Which is news to him.

Suddenly, he is thrust into a cat and mouse game with his stepmother. And she knows more than she's saying.

If he doesn't thwart the Red Queen's schemes, he won't survive long enough to blow out his candles or claim his crown.

Acknowledgments

Writing can be a solitary endeavor, but once you move into the publishing part of things, that's not something you can do by yourself, not by a long shot. There was a small, but mighty team that helped me get this book out into the world. First, I'd like to thank my beta readers who were the first eyes to see this story. Emily Bontrager, Amanda Sutton, Marrin Skinner, and Steph Hesseling who gave me invaluable feedback. Thanks, ladies – without you, this story would not exist in its current form. Another invaluable set of eyes was my editor Jody Skinner, of Skinner Book Services. She did a stellar job. Not only was she easy to work with, but her eagle eye caught a lot of important things I would have completely missed, including historically appropriate language. Finally, what's a book without its cover? Elona Bezooshko from Psycat Studio created my gorgeous cover and put up with all my requests.

I also want to give a special shoutout to my students who helped me with some of the names in this book. Carter Johns gets another nod because he came up with the name Wickle which could not have been more perfect for everyone's favorite snark. Na'Talya Wilson named Arthur Tweed, and Hewitt Wright came up with the name for Chess's mum, Larkspur.

Of course, I also want to thank my family. My husband and kids had to deal with me wandering around muttering to myself about plot points and character arcs, not to mention all the leftovers when I needed to make my deadlines. Writing the first draft is the easy part, but the revising, editing, and getting the entire thing ready for my readers takes a lot of time and attention, and the people who allowed me that time and focus were my family. I also want to thank my mom, Mary Ann McColm, who had to listen to me explaining different plot points and wrestling with a few of my characters when I'm sure she would have rather talked about other things. Thanks, Mom! You're the best!

Finally, I want to thank you, my reader. Without you, there would be no point in writing because a story is just words on a page until readers brings it to life. I'll never get over the magic of how my ideas and your imagination meld so that characters, worlds, and events spark into existence. I am thankful every day for you because you enable me to do what I love!

R. V. Bowman

About the Author

R.V. Bowman spends her days sharing her love of writing and literature with her high school students. By night, she hits her keyboard to write fantastical tales full of magic and heart. She is also the author of the middle grade fantasy trilogy, *The Pirate Princess Chronicles—Hook's Daughter, Pan's Secret,* and *Neverland's Key.*

She currently lives in Northwest Ohio with her husband, The Coach, two sons, and a nosey dog named Sherlock. You can find out more about her and her books at www.rvbowman.com or follow her on Instagram under the handle @r.v.bowmanfantasyauthor.